Praise for S

"Steven James writes pulse-pounding n
shocking twists that always leave me w
actually thrill, you'll love Steven James."

D.R. WALKER, US Department of Homeland Security/FLETC Senior Instructor/Firearms Division (retired)

Fatal Domain

"No one ratchets up the tension better than Steven James, and *Fatal Domain* is a thriller tour de force. High stakes only work when the reader is invested in the characters, and James is deft at creating realistic, flawed, deeply human characters through whom we all see ourselves. *Fatal Domain* is proof that James is a master storyteller at the top of his game."

CARTER WILSON, *USA Today* bestselling author of *Mister Tender's Girl*

Broker of Lies

"A taut, page-turning thriller exploring good and evil. Tense, twisty, and an edge-of-your-seat ending. James is a master of suspense."

ROBERT DUGONI, *New York Times* bestselling author of *Her Deadly Game*

"Master storyteller Steven James delivers with *Broker of Lies*. You're going to love Travis Brock!"

DON BENTLEY, *New York Times* bestselling author of *Forgotten War*

"*Broker of Lies* offers all of these James trademarks, while carving out a slightly different niche. This is a cerebral thriller, mixing politics, espionage, and technology. It feels like a fresh new direction—and with a major final surprise."

ERIC WILSON, *New York Times* bestselling author of *American Leftovers*

"*Broker of Lies* rockets out of the gate like a flame and never cools."

THE THRILLER ZONE

"The true successor to Vince Flynn."

BOOKANON

Synapse

"This is a remarkable novel, perceptive and thoughtful. *Synapse* challenges the reader in the same way as Isaac Asimov's *I Robot* or Frank Herbert's *Destination Void*. We don't use the comparison lightly. Steven James' provocative and landmark book reeks of becoming a classic. Simply outstanding."

W. MICHAEL GEAR and **KATHLEEN O'NEAL GEAR**, *New York Times* bestselling authors of *Lightning Shell*

"*Synapse* is a thoroughly audacious thriller that weaves both science and religion into its suspenseful plot. Steven James explores one of the most fascinating questions of our technological age—can a robot have a soul?—and answers it brilliantly."

MARK ALPERT, internationally bestselling author of *Doomsday Show*

"A tense thriller . . . unique and thought-provoking."

ASSOCIATED PRESS

Singularity

"The story is well researched, a hallmark of Steven James' novels, and by the time it reaches its climax, one may wonder if *Singularity* is fact or fiction."

NEW YORK JOURNAL OF BOOKS

"Steven James knows how to tell a story that gets under your skin and challenges the way you think as only the most talented writers can. If you're looking for a mind-bending tale, strap in and take the ride with *Singularity*. I can't recommend it highly enough."

TED DEKKER, *New York Times* bestselling author

"Readers are introduced to a spider web of thrills."

SUSPENSE MAGAZINE

Placebo

"The characters are utterly alive, the story memorable, gripping and intense, it will keep you on the edge of your seat until the last page."

GAYLE LYNDS, *New York Times* bestselling author of *The Hunt for Dimitri*

"The writing, pacing and plot lines are impeccable."

PUBLISHERS WEEKLY

"Fascinating, gripping, and thrilling—love this book. The Master Storyteller has woven another spell in *Placebo*, where the lines of science, reality, and fiction blur into one compelling tale. Intelligent and absolutely unputdownable, you will lose sleep over this one."

TOSCA LEE, *New York Times* bestselling author of *The Long March Home*

The Queen

"James is a master storyteller and doesn't disappoint in his latest installment in the Bowers Files."

RT BOOK REVIEWS

"This fifth book in James's Bowers Files exhibits all of the page-turning, tightly woven plotting and whiplash pacing of the others in the series."

LIBRARY JOURNAL

The Bishop

"Heart-pounding. As thrilling and unexpected as any five-star action movie."

JOHN TINKER, Emmy Award–winning screenwriter

"Steven James sets the new standard in suspense writing."

JOHN RAAB, editor of *Suspense Magazine*

"A fine thriller, featuring a strong compassionate protagonist, and a couple of pretty scary villains (imagine if Bonnie and Clyde were serial killers and if they were completely mad). James . . . clearly knows how to spin a yarn."

BOOKLIST

The Knight

"Exquisite."

FICTION FANATICS ONLY

"You won't find a thriller with more thrills, a novel with more action, a crime story with more twists and turns."

WINDOW TO MY WORLD REVIEWS

"I'm a retired homicide detective and love diving into Steven James' novels. The stories are very engrossing, suspenseful, and not predictable. It's always hard to find books that combine creativity and realism in a way that is believable to me, but Steven James writes just such books."

MICHAEL PUSATERE, 11-year veteran homicide detective (retired)

The Rook

"Steven James has mastered the thriller."

THE SUSPENSE ZONE

"James' ability to use modern, up-to-date investigative techniques to solve his criminal mysteries places him at the forefront of current mystery writers."

SPECIAL AGENT E. CLEON GLAZE, FBI (retired)

The Pawn

"Steven James combines 21st-century high-tech law enforcement techniques with 18th-century Sherlockian deduction to craft an exciting, suspense-filled story."

DR. KIM ROSSMO, internationally known geographic profiler

"A killer plot—complex and riveting, it had me guessing, reeling, sweating, and hanging on for dear life at the end of every single chapter. There is nothing not to like."

THE SUSPENSE ZONE

FATAL DOMAIN

Also by Steven James

~w~

A TRAVIS BROCK THRILLER

FATAL DOMAIN

STEVEN JAMES

Tyndale House Publishers
Carol Stream, Illinois

Visit Steven James online at stevenjames.net.

Tyndale and Tyndale's quill logo are registered trademarks of Tyndale House Ministries.

Fatal Domain

Copyright © 2024 by Steven James. All rights reserved.

Unless otherwise noted, cover images are the property of their respective copyright holders on Depositphotos.com, and all rights are reserved. Underwater bubbles © vitaliy_sokol; city skyline copyright © Jktu_21; metal © kokoroyuki; grunge brush strokes © Olga_C; redaction background © Sergey Nivens/Shutterstock.

Author photo by Mallory Zynda, copyright © 2021. All rights reserved.

Designed by Ron C. Kaufmann

Published in association with the John Talbot Agency, Inc., a member of The Talbot Fortune Agency, LLC, 180 E. Prospect Ave. #188, Mamaroneck, NY 10543.

Scripture quotations are taken from the Holy Bible, *New International Version,*® *NIV.*® Copyright © 1973, 1978, 1984, 2011 by Biblica, Inc.® Used by permission. All rights reserved worldwide.

Fatal Domain is a work of fiction. Where real people, events, establishments, organizations, or locales appear, they are used fictitiously. All other elements of the novel are drawn from the author's imagination.

For information about special discounts for bulk purchases, please contact Tyndale House Publishers at csresponse@tyndale.com, or call 1-855-277-9400.

Library of Congress Cataloging-in-Publication Data

A catalog record for this book is available from the Library of Congress.

ISBN 978-1-4964-7335-6 (HC)
ISBN 978-1-4964-7336-3 (SC)

Printed in the United States of America

30	29	28	27	26	25	24
7	6	5	4	3	2	1

To John Talbot, who believed in me

The shadows skitter around me,
unattached to the day
unconcerned about the light,
which is only a foreigner here,
here where I live.

They will do as they please.
This I have learned, living in this cell
that I've constructed around myself—
a prison called unforgiveness.
I will never let more light in.
It is not welcome here.
No, it cannot come in,
and because of that,
I cannot go out.

—ALEXI MARËNCHIVEK, POET

—〰—

The soul lives by avoiding what it dies by desiring.

—ST. AUGUSTINE

IJAW⌐OPJBAW⌐OPJBAWER
WFPOWEIRRONTHRTRVRDEST
WWPOFII
JAWPOEI
WIJERPF
WWEOPFI
⌐POIIAJW
⌐JV⌐LKMERO
⌐⌐AOMW⌐GFP
WHVV⌐NAVPO
WRFPIGUHER
WNEVG⌐GANNE
V⌐OANRV⌐OOAN
⌐DAIVPOAEWIJVGG
⌐JERV⌐AKJERVPO
⌐POIREJBEO
⌐POAIJ
WIVF

⌐HEP
⌐IJAW⌐O
WFPOWEIRPO
WWPOFIIJAS⌐OOJ
JAWPOEIFJAPWOI
DIJERPFJR⌐POIAP
WWEOPFIJAWEPEOO
⌐POIIAJWEPEOFIJA
⌐JV⌐LKMEROFIFI
⌐⌐AOMW⌐GFPOOAWG
WHVV⌐NAVPOAWEEHFA
WRFPIGUHERE⌐ENRE
⌐KBOOKBJPO
⌐IOIOAUERHR
⌐AHC⌐OAJVPOJ
WHUNFDEIOJOIJA
WVAIIUUHVHNAOIU
WVUHERVUNEV⌐OZ
⌐AWJVPOOEARJHV
WJVPOOEARJWO
⌐HEPORI⌐O
DIJAW⌐OFIJAW⌐O
WFPOWEIRPOWIUR
WWPOFIIJAS⌐OOJ
WWPOEIFJAPWOIE
DIJERPFJR⌐POIAP
WWEOPFIJAWEPEOO
⌐POIIAJWEPEOFI
⌐JV⌐LKMERO
⌐⌐AOMW⌐GF
WHVV⌐NAVPOAWEEHFA
WRFPIGUHERF⌐FNSE
⌐KBOOKBJPOKBJAR
⌐IOIOAUERHRFG
⌐AHC⌐OAJVPOJJHS
WHUNFDEIOJOIJARI
WVAIIUUHVHNAOIUSH
WVUHERVUNEV⌐OZIISH
⌐AWJVPOOEAR
⌐JERV⌐AKJERVPOAIJE
⌐POIREJBEOIJVPO
⌐POAIJERGBOOAIJE
⌐IJERVBEOAWIEJGE
WJVPOOEARJHVVOAE
⌐HEPORIIHQWPOIFFH
DIJAW⌐OFIJAW⌐OFIJAWAB
WFPOWEIRRONTHRTRVRDEST
WWPOFI
WWPOB
DIJER
WWEOP
⌐POII
WWEOPFIJAWEPEOOIUO
⌐POII⌐WEREOEIJAWE

PART I

By a Thread

Dust in the wind.
Barbie feet.
Star Girl's second envelope.
A door left open in the night.

CHAPTER 1

THURSDAY, MAY 19
HIGHWAY 17
FIFTEEN MILES NORTHEAST OF CHARLESTON, SOUTH CAROLINA
12:17 A.M.

Søren Beck told himself that it was a dog, or maybe a deer. The thud.

He stopped the car and got out.

Darkness, apart from the narrow beams of his headlights slicing through the fog-enshrouded night.

For some reason, he found himself speaking, his words sounding hollow along the edge of the woods, here on this lonely road: "Hello? Anyone here?"

No reply.

Of course there was no reply.

Because there was no one else around.

This is what he told himself.

He clicked his phone's flashlight function on.

Kneeling close to the front of the car, he found blood on the bumper and a wretched dent crunching up the left headlight. Light still streamed out of it, but it was splintery and skewered because of the shattered plastic. A mangled beam of light. Part of it lanced off to the side.

A dog.

It must've been a dog.

But there was no fur in the grille on the front of the car.

He'd been texting an associate at the architectural firm where he worked when it happened, when the impact occurred, and now he swallowed a dry gulp of guilt.

You should've known better. You do *know better.*

He searched for an injured animal along the edge of the road and in the ditch just beyond the shoulder, but saw nothing. Crickets chirred loudly. Somewhere in the distance, an owl made its presence known in the night.

The other side of the road. Search over there.

Scrambling out of the ditch, he made his way across the road to the other shoulder and swept the phone's light before him. A thick clutch of bushes and undergrowth lined the road, clinging tenaciously to the edge of a steep ravine.

There was no sign of an animal.

Of course, with the force of impact, its body might've been hurled deep into the underbrush.

Søren was nearly forty years old but kept in shape. He knew he could make it down the incline and back up, but would it be worth it? He told himself that there was no need to investigate.

Blood on the bumper, though.

There was blood on the bumper.

It was probably dead.

Probably.

In truth, he didn't really want to go down there. Not now. Not at night. Not like this.

For a long moment he stood there beside the shoulder, studying the leaves but finding no sign of blood.

At last, he returned to the driver's seat of his car, turned off the phone's light, and tried to figure out what to do.

To calm himself, he pressed his shaking palms against his thighs.

He would go home. Yes. He had another car he could drive for the time being until he sorted all this out.

At least no one was present. No one had seen what had happened. At least there was that.

Just in case it had not been a dog or a deer.

CHAPTER 2

ONE WEEK LATER
THURSDAY, MAY 26
TWENTY MILES WEST OF MADISON, WISCONSIN

The night had long since settled in around us, deep and still and draped in a thick, hesitant silence, as if it were holding its breath and listening in on us, waiting to hear a secret. The waning moon brought just enough light for us to see our way around the rooftop without having to use flashlights. Cool air. A touch of a breeze. Almost enough to make you shiver.

Five abandoned stories below us, the sandstone bluff that the deserted hotel overlooked dropped off another thirty feet or so to the lake, which rippled faintly in the moonlight. A hundred yards away from the base of the hotel, a bone-white Tesla sedan quietly approached the bridge to the compound on the other side of the bay, a quarter mile across the water.

Other than the occasional muffled sound of a truck on the county highway on the far side of the island, the night was hushed and laced with frayed anticipation.

The car crossed the bridge, passed the security gate, and then disappeared into the dark mouth of the complex's parking garage, leaving the night to itself.

I knelt on the flat rooftop behind the three-foot-tall parapet rimming the building and brought the night vision binoculars up to my eyes. Some NVB models allow you to wear glasses while using them; these, unfortunately, did not. Without my glasses, everything was a little blurry, but it was just too awkward to use the binoculars with them on, so I'd zippered them up inside my jacket's chest pocket so I wouldn't lose track of them.

I adjusted the magnification, and it was almost as good as it would've been with my actual glasses on.

My friend Gunnar Bane had gotten the NVB while serving as an Army Ranger, before retiring nearly fifteen years ago right around his fortieth birthday. Because of my job, I was aware of some extraordinary advances in night vision technology over the last few years, but these were still legit and plenty adequate for what I was using them for tonight.

Gunnar crouched beside me as I peered through the binoculars at the building across the lake. The room we were interested in lay on the third floor of TalynTek's headquarters. The expansive, sweeping windows would've likely provided employees with an unimpeded view of the lake and the nearby nature preserve, but also served us well in what we were here for tonight. In fact, it was one of the reasons we'd chosen that particular room.

That, and one of the technicians' affinity for classic seventies rock bands. Kansas in particular.

The album: *Point of Know Return*

The song: "Dust in the Wind."

When the CEO of the company first acquired TalynTek from a Silicon Valley entrepreneur a few years ago, she'd moved the headquarters from California to this 182-acre island campus in southwestern Wisconsin. The lake that surrounded it and the nearby nature preserve offered seclusion and privacy. From all indications, she'd chosen this location partly for its beauty, partly for its isolation, and partly for the generous tax incentives from the state. Besides, this much land in rural Wisconsin cost only a fraction of what it would've cost near a major city or established tech hub.

The computer servers in the room we were targeting were all air gapped and so, presumably, TalynTek's computer technicians wouldn't be particularly worried about them being compromised.

Which would make sense, since air-gapped computers aren't connected to any network or to the Internet.

Most people, even those in cybersecurity, consider air gapping to be a decisive mitigating factor in forestalling cyberintrusion.

And they were right. After all, how do you hack into a computer that isn't communicating with any other computers, that isn't connected to them in any way?

That was the question Project Symphony, a Pentagon-funded cyber-security initiative, was meant to solve.

And, in this case, the music of Kansas helped.

I saw no movement in the room and nothing unusual in the bright lobby on the ground floor, no guards on the series of uniformly lit pathways criss-crossing TalynTek's sprawling campus. Nothing. Just a calm, peaceful night cradling the island.

"We should be good to go," I told Gunnar, who held the drone's controller in his left hand so he could control it with his right. He was being gentle with that left arm. A bullet had fragmented into his shoulder last month during a shootout and he was still recovering. He hadn't been complaining about it—never brought it up, in fact—but the surgeon had needed to dig pretty deep to get all the shrapnel out, so I knew it was still an issue, still hampering Gunnar's movement and keeping him from his beloved push-ups. It wasn't clear if he would ever fully recover the strength in that arm.

"Do it," he said.

Cupping the camera-equipped, hummingbird-sized drone in my hand, I tossed it off the building. It caught air immediately and hovered quietly before us in the night, buzzing only slightly louder than a nearby mosquito might have. Gunnar directed it forward, and it zoomed across the lake toward that third-story room overlooking the water.

According to our intel, we still had eight minutes before the guard would come through on his rounds again on this side of TalynTek's headquarters—but of course you need to be careful about assumptions. People don't always follow their routines and schedules, and security personnel who do their job well actually make it a point *not* to be predictable or stick to specific routes or timeframes.

Tonight, we were doing our best not to take anything for granted.

Something I wasn't exactly an expert at.

After all, I was one of those pattern-keepers by nature, and was only now, at thirty-seven, learning to pivot from a plan and respond on the fly.

I was learning experientially that, as important as it is to plan, adapting to changing circumstances is just as vital. Spending the last fifteen years working in the deepest recesses of the Pentagon redacting Department of Defense documents hadn't exactly prepared me to work in the field like this, but, honestly, even after just a few short weeks, I found that I had an affinity for it and I didn't miss the sub-basement as much as I'd thought I would.

"That close enough?" Gunnar asked as he maneuvered the drone around the side of the building to get the line-of-sight angle we needed.

Lowering the binoculars, I studied the live video feed on the tablet resting between us on the roof's layer of fine cinder. "Just a little further to the left."

He carefully adjusted the drone's camera directed at the window to center the computer server in the tablet's screen.

I tapped the screen twice to zoom in on one of the server's red, blinking LED operational lights—the third light from the top and second to the left. Those LEDs fluctuate as the computer searches and indexes data. This one was blinking in a slightly and almost imperceptibly different sequence from the rest of the lights, sending us data with the length of each blink.

"That's it," I said.

"Check again for guards," Gunnar replied quietly.

I took a moment to do so.

"All clear," I told him. "Seven minutes and we should have everything we need."

"Roger that." He set the drone in hover mode to keep it stationary in the night so we could record the repeating series of shorter and longer flickers of light that the server was emitting. Then, he settled back onto the rooftop to relax a bit and monitor the live feed being recorded on the tablet.

Seven minutes and we would be good.

If all went as planned.

CHAPTER 3

Earlier this afternoon, while a technician named Darrell Strider was listening to Kansas's 1977 album *Point of Know Return*, the air-conditioning on that floor had gone out—something we could thank a zero-day vulnerability for.

Zero day simply means that zero days have passed since the vendor realized that they had the bug or the vulnerability. In other words, they know nothing about it yet.

In this case, the DOD had identified a zero-day bug with a component in TalynTek's network hardware that we were able to capitalize on, and in order to cool things off, Darrell and his team had needed to resort to fans and open windows.

The lake was known for panfish and bass and even, in the deeper water on the north side near the flowage leading into it, walleye. So, it wasn't unusual for people to fish in jon boats throughout the lake, and the fourteen-footer we'd trolled around in this afternoon wouldn't have appeared to anyone to be at all out of place.

Adira Halprin, the third and final member of our team, had used the boat's motor to guide us into position while I tilted a handheld "fishing net" toward the window we were targeting.

The "net" was really a signal booster, enhancing what we were using, an idea she'd come up with and the DOD was on board with.

Adira had spent several years with the Secret Service, then worked for Homeland on their Red Team, testing the security of TSA checkpoints, seeing if she could sneak weapons and bomb-making materials past them using ingenious devices like hair dryer guns, blades hidden in curling irons, and plastic explosives in lipstick tubes.

She'd been successful on nearly a hundred consecutive attempts, until her last one in April when someone had betrayed her and given her up to be caught.

That's what ended up causing our paths to cross, and honestly, in retrospect, I wasn't upset about that at all. We'd both noticed the chemistry between us right from that first day together and had subsequently started seeing each other, trying to navigate through the unfamiliar territory of being coworkers who were becoming romantically involved.

She was thirty-four, extremely fit, and could handle herself in a fight against just about anyone. She wore her blonde hair short, in a pixie cut, to make it easier to wear a wig if the situation called for it. Her entrancing blue eyes flashed with a deep intelligence and also a flirty playfulness, and when I looked into them it was hard to look away.

The Project Symphony prototype was small enough to fit in a fishing tackle box. In all honesty, it simply looked like an overly thick tablet computer with an external electronic receiver and a small sonic emitter array. It'd been developed through a collaboration between DARPA, or the Defense Advanced Research Projects Agency—the Pentagon's research arm—and a private-sector defense contractor, Paraden Defense Systems, which had supplied some of the components.

Unlike a fishing pole, which was Paraden's suggestion and would've provided us with an omnidirectional transmitter, with the shape of the net, we were able to create a unidirectional one, which was what we needed in this case.

A clever adaptation from Adira.

The Project Symphony research was focused on surreptitious ways of exfiltrating data from air-gapped computers to obtain administration privileges, record keystrokes, detect or hash passwords, upload files, discover log-in credentials, or obtain access to closely guarded root system files—the golden ticket to everything else. Typically, only system administrators have access to those files, but if you can get in, then you can have complete control of the machine.

The capability to hack into air-gapped systems is the future of cybersecurity—a future that has already begun.

In fact, there were two branches of research that the Pentagon had going on at the same time—one that was trying to figure out how to infiltrate air-gapped computers, the other that was trying to stop anyone from exfiltrating data from them. The goal of each of them was to find a way to better protect our secrets.

A little friendly competition.

In this case we were actually doing both—tonight we would be obtaining data, but first we'd needed to get the virus into the system.

Often, compromising a computer was possible by simply getting someone to click on a link or download a "software patch" or "system update" or insert a USB drive to set the virus free on the system. Over 95% of compromised systems are accessed in one of those ways.

Project Symphony approached this from a unique angle, creating an asymmetrical threat to our adversaries.

The device was designed to both send data through sound waves and use ultrasound technology to hack into computers that were air gapped and even stored in Faraday cages, which are specifically designed to block radio signals.

To be honest, I wasn't exactly sure how it all worked, but data can be carried along through sound waves—that's how music gets from a speaker to your ear, for instance, when you listen to a stereo. So, if you could travel in the *other* direction, moving through the sound waves back to the source, back into the computer, could you convey information to it? In the simplest of explanations, that's what the device was doing while we were in the jon boat—transmitting a virus that would help us to exfiltrate the data later.

Which brought us to tonight.

Now, the server was communicating with us, not through sound waves, but through a pattern of optical blinks. We had the Israelis to thank for this idea, specifically the teams at their Defense Force Unit 8200 and the researchers at the Ben-Gurion University of the Negev's Cybersecurity Research Center. The drone tactic was a move right out of their playbook. The Israelis had made more advancements in researching ways to hack into air-gapped computers than all the nations in NATO, combined. All of that paved the way for the innovations that led to the Project Symphony prototype.

I scrutinized the labyrinthine paths of TalynTek's campus again through the binoculars.

Still no guards.

Taking advantage of the moment, I repositioned myself to get more comfortable as I sat next to Gunnar. "So," I said to him, "I've gotta ask you: How's that novel of yours coming along?"

"Pretty good. I'll read you some of it later."

I'd only met Gunnar a month ago but had found out on the very first day that he was writing a romance novel, which he was hoping to sell to a publisher to earn some money to help pay for his niece, Skye, to go to college. Apparently, ever since he'd left the military, for whatever reason, things hadn't been quite where he wanted them to be between him and his sister. I didn't know what'd happened and he wasn't forthcoming about it, but I knew he believed that if he could help her out financially with Skye's tuition, it might be a step in the right direction, a way to start mending their relationship.

I didn't know about any of that, but his heart was certainly in the right place.

"Have you decided on a title yet?" I asked him.

"Still toying with ideas, but I think I've narrowed it down."

"To?"

"*Huntress of Desire, Huntress of Passion,* or *Huntress of the Night.* I might actually do a trilogy. Not sure which one to start with, though. The huntress bit is a way to help readers identify the series," he explained. "All part of my brand."

"Your brand?"

"It's a big thing in publishing. Helps your SEO and discoverability."

"I see." I scanned again for any sign of guards.

Nothing.

I checked the tablet.

It was continuing to record the seemingly random progression of the computer's operational light's blinks, which were happening every second or two.

Short. Long. Short. Short. Long.

But of course, the length of each blink wasn't random at all.

The computer was communicating with us in a modified version of International Morse Code that allowed for capital letters and keyboard symbols and was sharing usernames, log-in credentials, and root system file passwords.

Later, I would translate the series of longer and shorter blinks to figure out what letters, numbers, and symbols were being transmitted.

If there weren't any hiccups, we would be out of here within the next few minutes with information that, if we were right, would lead us closer to finding a domestic terrorist we were tracking.

Though I had a law degree, I didn't want to dwell too long on the legality of what we were doing. The op was sanctioned by the Pentagon, so at least there was that. Colonel Clarke had given us broad operational latitude, and capturing the passwords tonight was certainly within it. Because of the nature of this op, we had warrants for wiretaps. What we were doing was *slightly* beyond that, and that's where things became a little murky around the edges. Consequently, we wouldn't have wanted to try to explain our intentions to the local authorities, which was why we hadn't notified them beforehand about what we were doing here tonight.

Adira's voice came through my earpiece. "Hey, boys. How's it going up there in the nest?"

"I was wondering if you were still with us," Gunnar said lightly.

"Just chillin'." She was stationed down below, to the east of the building that Gunnar and I were on top of, keeping an eye on the road leading up to the entrance, monitoring it for any sign of movement or possible incursion. "You good?"

"Golden," Gunnar told her. "Should have what we need in the next five minutes or so. You see anyone?"

"No movement down here. Nothing but a little splashing around down by the water. I'm thinking a beaver or maybe an otter. I checked it out. Didn't see anything."

The Department of Defense had learned a few things over the last decade from studying the manner in which the most effective terrorist cells and the most innovative corporate teams operate, and there was more in common between their approaches than you might expect. The DOD had found that the management strategies weren't all that different, and, in our case, had put that intel to work in developing the covert unit that the three of us now served on.

Small. Independent. Self-reliant. Free to adapt and respond to situations as necessary to facilitate optimal outcomes. Taking risks was rewarded rather than punished, and a creative, out-of-the-box approach was valued more than merely following protocol or SOPs. Focusing not so much on how things *had* been done, but how they *might* be done. It was a different paradigm than I was used to, but one that seemed to produce results.

We reported directly to Colonel Clarke. With my experience redacting Defense Department files, Gunnar's military service and private security consulting expertise, and Adira's background with the Secret Service and her subsequent work in executive protection and at Homeland, we'd been given an extraordinary amount of freedom from bureaucratic entanglements to do our work.

The three of us were part of the effort to track down and take down the Pruninghooks Collective, a group that had attempted to detonate a dirty bomb in Knoxville, Tennessee, last month. Ostensibly, they were a pacifist antinuke group that took their name from a verse in the biblical book of Isaiah that talks about a time when nation will not rise up against nation, people will beat their swords into pruninghooks, and no one will study war anymore. However, the group had gone off the rails, so to speak, when one of their leaders, a billionaire named Janice Daniels, steered them in a whole new, much more radical direction.

She'd become convinced that by precipitating a limited-scale radiological dispersion event, she could sway public opinion away from the use of nuclear weapons and nuclear energy of all types—something she thought would be beneficial for the human race. And she very nearly pulled it off. We'd barely been able to stop the attack, and, in all truth, public opinion had pendulumed away from supporting the use of nuclear energy over the last month, just as she'd hoped it would. So, even though lives had been saved, her plan had, to a certain degree, succeeded.

Now she was on the run and we were after her. Before she'd disappeared, she'd told Adira the dirty bomb was "just the beginning." But unfortunately, we had no idea what else she and her associates were planning.

Janice was also the one who'd bought TalynTek from its founder, Cliff Richardson, a few years ago. TalynTek's board of directors had obviously tried to distance themselves from her, but we suspected she still had ties to the organization, which we were hoping to identify tonight.

We had no idea how many other teams like us were out there. The colonel had been tight-lipped about that, but I'd seen enough intel come through to suspect that there were at least two other teams, similar to us, tracking different domestic terrorist groups: a far-left Antifa offshoot that was firebombing crisis pregnancy centers, and a white nationalist militia that was trying to form its own state out on a massive ranch in New Mexico that was nearly thirty times the size of Manhattan. Two eye-popping examples of what the Far Left and the Far Right had to offer. Go far enough in either direction and you'll find people who believe that violence really is the answer.

We had no official information about the other units; only Colonel

Clarke did. This way, we could retain plausible deniability regarding their operations, if it ever came to that.

In most cases, sharing intel was profitable, even vital. However, in this instance we weren't sure who—besides Clarke—we could trust. Janice Daniels had proven that she had a long reach and over the last year had even managed to bribe Adira's boss, infiltrating the highest echelons of the Department of Homeland Security.

I was learning that, often, working off the books you can avoid having to cut through a mountain of red tape and get more done. As long as you have people you can trust.

So, in our investigation, we were playing things pretty close to the vest.

Our job: gather the intel, pass it along to Clarke, and trust him to take things from there.

"Be careful out there," he'd advised us solemnly at our last meeting. "And remember: Don't trust anyone."

I examined the campus that slept before us in the night.

Three minutes left.

"Hey, Gunnar," Adira said.

"Yeah?"

"I heard you earlier. The title ideas for your book. You know I'm a sucker for a good romance novel."

"What do you think? Which one do you like best?"

"Tough call. I'd probably go with *Huntress of Desire*."

"Cool. Yeah. Good to know. Oh, I have another idea too that I've been kicking around: *Huntress of the Hunted*."

"Um . . . that might be a little too on the nose."

"Yeah," he acknowledged. "True."

"Too bad you're not writing a young adult fantasy novel," she said. "Then the titling process would be a lot easier. Just plug and play."

"What do you mean?"

"Well, basically, you just use twelve words and pretty much randomly stick them together to name the next book in your series, on the spot. *Voilà!*"

She'd definitely sparked my curiosity. "What twelve words are those?" I asked her.

"First, choose one of these: *sky, forest, dreams*, or *night*."

"I'll go with *forest*," Gunnar said.

"Then add the word *of* and choose one of these four: *glass, bone, ash,* and *fire*."

"*Bone,*" he said.

"Right. And finally, just add the word *and* and then either *ice, frost, blood,* or *stone*."

"Let's say *frost*."

"So," she said, "your YA novel would be *The Forest of Bone and Frost*."

"Huh. I like it."

"Your turn, Travis," Adira said. "Do you need me to repeat the twelve . . . but I suppose you don't, do you?"

"I should be good. I'll go with *A Sky of Glass and Stone*. Wait . . . that doesn't even make sense."

"It's not supposed to make sense," she reminded me helpfully. "It's supposed to sell books."

"We could also do *Dreams of Ash and Ice*," Gunnar noted. "Or *The Night of Fire and Blood*. Who'd have ever thought it was this easy?"

"I know, right?" she said.

"Hmm . . ." He reflected on that. "Maybe I *should* be writing YA fantasy. I mean I could maybe do something with angsty teenage vampires or wizards or demigods. I'm not sure if there are enough of those books out there."

I honestly couldn't tell if he was being serious or not.

"You know," Adira said, "come to think of it, you might want to stick to adult romance. It'll give you a lot more freedom to . . . well, to be anatomically correct in your descriptions of physical intimacy."

"Aha," he said. "Good call."

Over the last few weeks, Gunnar had read us some of his drafts for the love scenes in his book, and . . . well . . . they were memorable—I could say that much with all honesty. *Cringeworthy* was the word that came to mind. It made for an interesting conundrum since I was now both enormously curious to hear his latest revisions and also dreading it quite sincerely. Both. At the same time.

"Hang on, guys," Adira said, her voice tightening. "We've got company."

CHAPTER 4

I studied TalynTek's dark campus through the binocs but noticed nothing unusual.

"What do you see?" Gunnar asked her.

"Two people walking along a trail skirting this side of the lake. Hand in hand."

"Suspicious?" Gunnar said.

"You mean, apart from the fact that it's basically one thirty in the morning and they suddenly showed up out of nowhere, here in the middle of nowhere?"

"Right. Were you made?"

"I don't think so—wait. One of them, the guy, he's looking at his phone. Now he's typing on it."

Across the lake, through the binoculars, I saw the guard at the front desk pick up a phone of his own.

"They're onto us," I told Adira and Gunnar, perhaps assuming too much.

But probably not.

Gunnar turned to me. "How much time do we have left before you've got what you need with the blinking light?"

I consulted the tablet. "At least another two minutes."

He shook his head. "That's not gonna happen. We need to move."

Using the drone's controller and being cautious not to jar his left arm too much, he carefully repositioned the drone, easing it back from the TalynTek building.

"Wait," I said. "Give it a little time."

Through the binoculars, I scanned the building and saw the gate in front of the nearby parking garage lift and two dark SUVs appear, heading for the bridge.

Nope, not assuming too much.

"That's it. We move," he said.

"The couple," Adira said, "they're taking off into the nature preserve. I still don't think they saw me, but somehow they knew what's up. Pursue and detain, or let 'em go?"

"Let 'em go," Gunnar said, making the call. He toggled the drone's controllers and then grunted. "I think we've got someone trying to hack into our drone, take it over."

I turned my attention to the tablet and saw the feed flicker as whoever it was tried to disrupt the signal, or perhaps track it back to us.

Technology wasn't exactly my primary responsibility, but over the last fifteen years I'd redacted thousands of pages of Defense Department documents detailing cyberintrusion techniques and ways to counter them, and it *was* my responsibility to remember the key aspects of what I read. And now I needed to lean into that knowledge.

MIJI is an old military intelligence term that stands for *meaconing, intrusion, jamming,* and *interference.* It's about all the ways to block, confuse, or mislead enemy sensors and navigational signals. And right now, that's what we were dealing with.

I scrolled to a terminal window to view the coding and check the stability of the firewalls. Tracing the origin of the hack, all I got was a signal bounce through somewhere in Venezuela and then through Kazakhstan, which didn't make a lot of sense if it was just these guys across the lake. Why go to all that trouble?

Unless it isn't them.

As I quickly worked at the tablet, the screen flickered and a dense map of code appeared for a few seconds before flashing back to the splintered, pixelated footage from the drone's camera. This time it was corrupted, blinking into and out of focus. The feed was deteriorating, and our firewalls weren't going to hold—I could tell that much. I could also tell that I was out of my league here.

"How long can you keep 'em out?" Gunnar asked me.

"Not long."

A shot rang out from across the lake, startling me so much that I almost dropped the tablet.

"Okay, brother, you're up," Gunnar said. "Let's see how good that memory of yours really is. How many random digits can you memorize in a row?"

"I don't know . . ." I was anticipating what he had in mind and, honestly, I wasn't sure I could pull it off. "I mean, a few thousand, given enough time to study them, but . . ."

"Well, time's the one thing we don't have. I'd say you have a minute, maybe ninety seconds, to memorize those blinks—however many you can get."

It didn't take long to calculate that, based on the rate at which the server was emitting the blinks, it would likely be a series of several hundred dots and dashes.

Not impossible, but certainly not a cakewalk.

Savants have been known to memorize pi up to 150 digits on the first glance. That wasn't me. I could memorize two shuffled decks of cards on the first pass, but since you can form meaningful clumps of numbers and combinations with card decks, that was much easier than this progression of visual dots and dashes appearing in no easily discernible order.

Another shot rang out. This time, the round clipped the drone, sending it circling sideways, spinning uncontrollably through the night. The footage tilted and twirled crazily as the irretrievably damaged drone careened downward, out of control, angling toward the water.

Gunnar fought to keep it in the air, but it plummeted toward the lake and finally splashed in. The feed went dark.

"That was not a bad shot," he said with clear admiration. "Probably AI targeting, but still . . . Looks like we're dealing with someone here who knows what they're doing."

He tapped the controller to self-destruct the drone so the tech wouldn't fall into TalynTek's hands, but I wasn't sure if that would work anymore, not with the disrupted and corrupted signal, especially now that the drone was in the lake.

Our options at this point were limited and shrinking by the second.

To avoid being hacked, we hadn't been transmitting the drone's feed directly to the Pentagon's servers, and I didn't want to start doing so because TalynTek would likely be able to pinpoint our location if we did. The tablet was dying, and I wasn't going to be able to save it. Not out here. Not a chance.

Gunnar was right; if we were going to save the data, there really was only one option.

Memorize it.

CHAPTER 5

I swiped the video back to the beginning of the recording.

A klaxon cut through the night, screaming out from across the water as a series of searchlights from the complex on the other side of the bay cut on, panned the lake, and came to rest on our building, illuminating it. As the lights swept toward us, Gunnar and I ducked down beneath the waist-high parapet surrounding the rooftop.

"Those SUVs are on the way," Adira announced. "We've gotta go, gentlemen."

"You're up," Gunnar said to me. "Time to earn your pay." He unholstered his handgun, which he'd affectionately named Maureen, after an ex-girlfriend, and peered past me toward the bridge.

Even with all of my experience committing esoteric facts, random alphanumeric sequences, twenty-digit routing numbers, and disparate dates and data points to memory, I wasn't sure I'd be able to do this.

It only took a moment to calculate that I'd need to play the video back at twice the recording speed to even have a chance of getting through to the end before the tablet died or TalynTek's security forces found us—all while keeping track of the blinks.

I tapped the screen, enhanced the playback speed, then studied it carefully as the progression of longer and shorter pulses of light flashed.

As I concentrated on the length of each blink, memorizing the order, I waited futilely for a pattern to emerge.

No one's memory is perfect. The idea of having a photographic memory is a myth—research in the fields of neuroscience and cognition just doesn't support its existence. Mine was sharp, but I wasn't certain it was sharp enough to do what needed to be done right now.

People who compete in memory events use a variety of techniques to achieve their impressive feats—from memory palaces to mnemonic image methods to peg systems to group compression, and more. Even though I didn't compete, I'd studied the techniques to help me at work and I'd come up with my own hybrid system of picturing myself walking through a garden and remembering words, digits, and images hanging at different heights from different types of plants. Since the method was three-dimensional and I could arrange the pathway itself into meaningful shapes or letters, if necessary, the system was flexible and, by varying the size and type of the plants, it gave me pretty much limitless options.

Now, I adapted it to remember larger and smaller hedges corresponding to the lengths of the blinks. I pictured myself on that path, passing my hand across a hedgerow on my right side. Tall. Short. Short. Short. Tall.

Dozens of them at this point, trailing behind me, as I walked forward.

"Now would be a good time to leave," Adira said. "I have two SUVs on their way across the bridge toward your building."

"We need to move, bro," Gunnar emphasized.

"Thirty seconds. Give me thirty seconds."

"I'm not sure we—"

"I've got this."

Focus. Focus. Focus.

I sped up the playback even more and dialed in, trying to keep track of the series of flashes.

As I did, I was generally aware of the searchlights and the sound of the SUVs arriving, but, mentally, I'd traveled to the garden path beside the hedges.

But it was becoming too much, too fast. If I didn't slow down, I was going to lose sight of the hedges, lose hold of the order. To regroup, I hit pause, closed my eyes, and carefully studied the hedges trailing back behind me beside the path, reviewing their height, trying unsuccessfully to identify any patterns while also attempting to lock the image in my memory.

I wasn't counting the blinks, but based on how far along the path I was, I suspected that we were closing in on two hundred of them.

Five stories below us, car doors slammed.

"I've got five—wait, six—party crashers on their way in," Adira announced. "You need to get down that stairwell. Now."

Maybe they'd tracked the tablet. Maybe the drone signal or the earpieces. Really, right now none of that mattered. What mattered was memorizing this code and then getting—

The tablet went dark.

I tapped the screen, trying to wake it up, but there was no bringing it back. The device was dead. Flatlined.

I scanned the hedgerow paralleling the path behind me. As long as I didn't get too distracted, I could do this. I could remember the sequence.

"Okay," I said. "Let's get out of here."

CHAPTER 6

I f this had been a spy movie, we might've had some sort of clever rappel system set up that would've allowed us to simply leap off the roof and glide effortlessly to the ground to escape, but unfortunately this wasn't Hollywood. We needed to use the stairs.

Snatching up the drone's controller and the tablet, I followed Gunnar as he darted across the roof and threw open the door to the stairwell, his gun at chest level, angled downward. Position Sul.

I was close enough on his heels to see the swarm of flashlights already ascending the stairwell. He leapt back, almost knocking into me, slammed the door shut, and latched it.

Though the door was metal, by the hollow sound it made when it closed, I doubted that it was solid enough to stall our party crashers—as Adira had referred to them—for long.

Scanning the roof, I came up with a four-foot-long piece of rebar, which I tossed to Gunnar. He caught it deftly, jammed one end beneath the door handle and angled the other against the roof beside his foot, then kicked it hard to auger it into place.

It looked pretty secure, but it was also blocking our only way off the roof.

Well, our only *preferred* way.

"Okay, plan B," Gunnar said, eyeing the other end of the building, near where we'd been just moments ago when the drone was shot down. "I was hoping it wouldn't come to this."

"Yeah," I said, "me too," already aware of what plan B was.

There really weren't any other options before us.

He started quickly across the roof with me at his side.

"You told me earlier you knew how to swim," he reminded me helpfully. "How good are you?"

"Gunnar, just to remind you, we're five stories up," I said unnecessarily. "That, plus the roofing, and that bluff drops down probably another thirty feet to the water. We're talking about at least an eighty-foot drop."

"Yeah. I should've asked how good you are at falling first."

Behind us, the security detail members were either kicking at the door or throwing their bodies against it; I couldn't tell from here. The hinges groaned as they strained valiantly to withstand the impact.

"With your shoulder," I said. "Can you even swim?"

"Well . . ." He paused and I sensed that he was seriously debating things. "There is that."

Even as we spoke, I tried to keep the pattern of flashes in mind.

There are three fundamental steps to enhanced recall, easily remembered with the acronym CAR: *concentrate, associate, review.* Concentrate on the data or idea, make memorable associations, and review regularly to lock the information in.

I pictured that pathway lined by bushes, spreading backward, some bushes shorter, some taller, each corresponding to the length of each progressive blink, and tried to picture it all closely, but adrenaline pulsed through me, making it tough to concentrate. From past research, I knew that adrenaline was meant to prepare us for fight or flight, and not necessarily designed to benefit recall—in fact, studies had shown that it will often actually create gaps in your memory, something I tried not to dwell on at the moment.

A bullet tore through the metal door and ricocheted off the roof nearby, kicking an angry flurry of roof cinders up against my leg.

Gunnar turned to me. "That door's not gonna hold."

I knew he was right. We hustled to the parapet overlooking the lake. In the moonlight, the water looked much farther away than seventy-five or eighty feet.

"When you were a Ranger," I asked him, "what's the highest you ever jumped from?"

"Don't overthink it, bro." He slugged my shoulder. "This is survivable."

Not exactly the most comforting choice of words.

"Uh-huh."

If I was right—that our fall would be at least eighty feet—that meant we'd be traveling at over fifty miles per hour when we hit the water. That's not nothing.

The problem with physics is that it's not very forgiving. Force equals mass times acceleration. My mass and velocity were beyond my control, so that meant that, in this case, *decreasing* the force of impact would require *increasing* the time it would take to decelerate.

It's not so much about the distance you fall as it is about slowing the rate of the final descent so that the stop isn't so sudden—which is why bungee jumpers can safely fall hundreds of feet and not get injured: the elasticity in the cord they're attached to slows their descent enough so that, in some cases, they hardly feel the impact. But without a bungee cord tonight, there was nothing here to slow my descent except water that might, for all we knew, be only a few feet deep.

Gunnar seemed to read my mind. "I used the depth finder this afternoon when we were in the boat. That cliff drops off sharply into the water. I'm pretty sure we'll be alright," he assured me.

"Pretty sure."

"Fifty-one percent."

"Right."

He held up Maureen. "I'll hold 'em off. You go first. I'll see you on the other side."

"Okay." I didn't love the way he put that either, but I followed suit. "See you on the other side."

Adira's voice came through my earpiece. "Quit jabbering, guys, and jump."

"Keep your legs together," Gunnar told me. "Toes pointed down like a Barbie doll."

"A Barbie doll?"

"Stiff and pointy. If you don't, at this height, that water's going to feel as hard as concrete, could break both your legs."

"Barbie feet. Gotcha."

I took off the binoculars, which were hanging from a lanyard around my neck, and tossed them aside so they wouldn't bang into my face when I hit the water.

"Hands and legs crossed," Gunnar said. "Head up. Hold your arms x-ed across your chest like this and squeeze your nose shut." Without thinking, he crossed his arms but then winced in pain as he stressed his left shoulder.

A high-pitched screech startled me as the door gave way and banged open, sending the rebar skittering across the roof.

I stepped onto the parapet while Gunnar swiveled toward the door, gun in hand.

"Go!" he called.

I didn't have much room for a running start, but I was able to manage two hurried steps and then, drawing in a quick, ragged breath, I leapt as far from the building as I could, launching myself into the night.

CHAPTER 7

I was aware of the sound of gunshots above me—
Of my stomach lurching upward—
Of space and time sailing by—
Of falling—
A dizzying, dizzying drop—
Plummeting. Accelerating. And then—
The shock of impact.
Under the water.
Aware.
Aware.
The plunge.

I couldn't tell how deep I went, but I didn't hit the bottom. I stroked upward, straining for breath, and burst through the surface, snagged some air, and scanned the lake for Gunnar, but didn't see him.

Treading water, I turned in a slow circle. "Gunnar?"

No reply. No splashes. Nothing.

Adrenaline racing.

I looked up toward the top of the building that I'd just jumped from.

In the stark light cast from the complex's towers across the bay, I could see a figure high above me, leaning over the roof's edge. The person directed some sort of tactical rifle toward me.

Okay, that was definitely not Gunnar.

I didn't wait around to see how good their aim was, but instead drew in a quick breath and surface-dove into the water, heading in the direction of the nature preserve where we'd agreed earlier to meet up with Adira.

Bullets whirred into the lake all around me, making tight *pishing* sounds that I'd never heard before and wasn't too excited about hearing right now.

Although, to a certain degree, the water would slow the bullets' velocity, I imagined that they would still cause significant damage, so I kicked deeper.

That guy was shooting at you from the spot you jumped from, right where Gunnar was standing. Which means he wasn't there. Which means either he did jump, he's been captured, or he's . . .

I didn't even want to consider that final possibility.

Somewhere along the line, I'd lost track of the drone's controller and tablet. Now, I just tried not to lose track of the order of shorter and longer blinks that I'd memorized.

As I swam through the pitch-black water, I tried to review the sequence, but found that the adrenaline was making me jittery and causing it to become tougher and tougher to retain the mental image of the hedgerow. The more I tried to concentrate on it, the fuzzier it became and the more I began to doubt that I had the sequence right.

Focus. When you get to the car you can write it down. Just make it until then. Don't forget it. Hold on.

I surfaced for air, then dove again, hoping to get under before the shooter could locate me.

From here, it was maybe another two hundred yards to the inlet where Adira would be waiting. Not an unwieldy swim, but made trickier because I couldn't stay on the surface for long.

Every time I came up for air, I kept an eye out for Gunnar, but saw no sign of him.

I assured myself that he was doing the same thing I was—surfacing for air and then diving back down again to get out of sight of the shooter perched on the roof. Gunnar must have just been surfacing at different times than I was, or maybe swimming in the opposite direction.

That was it. He was okay. He'd made it. I would see him in just a few minutes.

CHAPTER 8

Adira Halprin studied the building that was now illuminated in the blazing searchlights across the bay. A cable of anxiety tightened inside her heart.

From her position here on the ground near the lakefront, she couldn't make out what was happening on the top of the building, but she'd seen six security force members enter it earlier. And she hadn't seen Gunnar or Travis leave it.

Less than a minute ago, through her earpiece, she'd told the two men to jump and almost immediately afterward had picked up the sound of rapid gunfire and then two splashes—or maybe the sound came from someone stomping on the earpieces. She couldn't be certain one way or the other.

When she'd called their names into her earpiece, she hadn't gotten any response, so she didn't know if they were dead, caught, or if they'd managed to get into the lake.

Or if they had, if they'd survived the fall.

Although she was obviously concerned about Gunnar, she knew that, with his background, a jump from that height wouldn't be a huge deal. But that wasn't necessarily the case with Travis.

He worked a desk job. Had for years. Yes, he was a runner. Yes, he stayed in shape to compete in half marathons every month or so, but she didn't know how good of a swimmer he was.

And besides, five stories plus thirty feet was a long drop any way you cut it, Barbie feet or not.

In addition, she'd developed feelings for him. She didn't tend to do things halfway, so when she fell for someone, she fell for them big-time.

Travis wasn't just some egghead Pentagon redactor; he'd also shown remarkable courage and had a generous nature that attracted her. He was resilient, resourceful, and wholeheartedly dedicated to whatever he was doing—almost to a fault. She didn't normally have the best luck with guys, but she was hoping that this time, it would be different—that was, if he was okay.

She wasn't necessarily a religious person, but she also wasn't someone to eschew prayer when the circumstances called for it—or when bullets were flying at people she cared about. And right now, prayer didn't seem like that bad of an idea.

She kept her prayer brief and to the point: *Help 'em make it, God. Seriously—but also respectfully. I mean . . . well, you know what I mean. Protect 'em if you can—I mean, I know you can, I just . . . Anyway, you get it. Amen.*

Yeah, not a great prayer by any means, but at least it was an honest one.

The intermittent gunfire from the roof hadn't subsided.

In her experience, it wasn't usually the case that sustained gunfire was a good sign, but it seemed that tonight it just might be: it meant that the guards were still shooting at someone—which meant that they thought someone was still alive. After all, there was no reason to think that they would find it necessary to riddle a corpse with bullets.

Avoiding the complex's searchlights, she hurried to the shoreline, making sure she was shielded from view by the nature preserve's grove of weeping willow trees that drooped wearily over the water.

If someone would have asked her a month ago if she'd ever thought she might be serving on a task force with a redactor who had an eidetic memory and a wannabe romance novelist former Ranger, she would have laughed it off.

But hey, life does have its twists and turns.

Travis's job: when a Freedom of Information Act request came in to the DOD, he would evaluate it, taking into account all of the Top Secret and classified initiatives and programs that might be impacted by the release of the information, and then decide what could, and what could not, be released to the public.

The job required an ability to keep the operational details of dozens of, even hundreds of, projects in mind at the same time. He needed to consider how they interacted with and impacted each other, and then make the most informed choice possible regarding the rights of the public to know about—or the necessity for them to remain in the dark about—those projects and initiatives.

In truth, no one knew more about the DOD's Top Secret programs than Travis did.

No one. Not even the president.

Because of that, a few weeks ago the Russians had sent two men to capture him, and it'd nearly cost him his life—nearly cost her hers as well. Thankfully, the pair of Russians were no longer a threat. She'd taken one of them out; Gunnar had neutralized the other.

Adira heard rustling in the forest nearby. She couldn't make out what it was—an animal? A person?

She unholstered her Springfield XD. She wasn't about to aim it at a person without good reason, but she also wasn't about to be taken off guard if this wasn't one of her team members. "Travis?" she stage-whispered. "Is that you? Gunnar?"

More rustling. The snap of a twig. Footsteps.

Yes. Definitely someone walking her way.

"Travis?"

As she peered into the darkness, she readied her weapon. "Who's there?"

"It's me," a shadowy figure replied as he emerged, dripping wet, from the tree line.

"Gunnar," she said, with a mixture of relief and apprehension. "And Travis?"

"Haven't seen him since he jumped. He's not here yet?"

"No."

Gunnar stepped into view in the moonlight, soaking wet. He was cradling his left arm with his right hand and grimacing, despite what appeared to be a valiant effort not to.

"You okay?" Adira asked him.

A nod.

"Your shoulder?"

"It's felt better."

"How'd you even swim with it?"

"I babied it."

She peered past him toward the water. "And you didn't see Travis in the lake?"

"I did not."

"Well, I'm sure he's alright." She said the words a little too quickly. "I'm sure he'll be here in a minute." But she immediately chastised herself for stating something that she did *not* know for sure, not at all, something that might very well be completely untrue.

Gunnar said nothing. "How well can he swim?" he asked her at last.

"I honestly don't know."

For a long moment neither of them spoke as they studied the black water rippling indifferently before them in the moonlight.

"I swam directly to shore," Gunnar said. "He might've gone toward the car. What do you think, stay here or head back?"

"We were going to reconvene here, so let's give it a couple more minutes," she said. "I heard a lot of gunshots up there. Are you sure you're alright? Were you hit?"

"I'm good."

"Can you track Travis somehow?" Adira asked. "Through his earpiece? Or maybe through the tablet? Or do those tracking nanobots in his system still work?"

"The nanobots have run their course. The tablet died, and I doubt he'd still have it with him anyway. Tracking the earpiece is a possibility, though." Gunnar nodded thoughtfully. "Let me call Clarke."

Earlier, he and Travis had left their phones in the car, so Adira unlocked her cell and handed it to him.

As he stepped aside to make the call, she found herself biting her lower lip. A stupid, annoying, nervous habit. Not helpful at all.

Chewing bubble gum sometimes helped calm her down when she was tense, so she unwrapped a chunk of it and popped it into her mouth.

Flavor: cotton candy. Not her favorite, and this piece tasted pretty old, but it'd have to do. Better than nothing.

She hated feeling helpless to solve a problem.

Not her bailiwick.

After college, during her ignominious stint at the Secret Service, while she was at a leadership training seminar, the presenter had handed out puzzle pieces to all of the hundred or so participants in the auditorium—some yellow, some purple, some green, some blue. Then, he called out through the microphone, "Alright! When I count to three, I want everyone to form into groups with the other people holding your color! Let's see who can do it first. Then we'll talk through the strategies that each group used!"

Brilliant teamwork exercise.

Or not.

While he counted to three, Adira stared down at her purple puzzle piece. As soon as he finished and said, "Go!" it was pandemonium while everyone started gesturing and shouting, holding up their pieces trying to find the other people with their color.

No strategy at all.

She ignored the cacophony, walked up to the mic, blew into it, and said, "Excuse me. If I could have your attention, please. Everyone, please quiet down for a moment. I'd like all of the purple puzzle piece people to meet with me here onstage. Thank you."

Then, taking the microphone with her so no one else could use her technique, she crossed the stage and waited for her team to join her.

It wasn't the approach the speaker was looking for, at least that was her impression, because she was called in later to explain herself. "There was a goal," she'd said, "to be the first group to form, right? Using the microphone wasn't cheating. It was utilizing the assets that were available at the time to solve the problem as quickly as possible."

"Do you think you're special?"

"No. I think that exercise was stupid and way too easy."

Not exactly the right thing to say, as it turned out.

State the problem, define the parameters you have to work within, and then solve things as efficaciously as you can: identify, clarify, resolve. It was how she'd worked then and still did in order to get the job done.

However, the whole incident hadn't exactly put her in the good graces of her supervisors, a situation that had only deteriorated over the next three years until her less-than-illustrious departure from the Secret Service. And that's when her life had spun off the rails.

Pretty far off them, as a matter of fact.

Oxy is the most common gateway drug to heroin. Yeah, she knew that all too well. One open surgery on her left heel bone after a fracture, one innocent prescription, and suddenly you're plummeting into yourself, wanting more than Oxy can provide. And the only way to climb up to the surface again is to lean on something that you know is going to knock you down into a much deeper hole.

But you can't bear the thought of not having more, so you take it anyway.

A problem, yes.

A problem she'd only managed to conquer with a lot of help, a lot of support, and a lot of self-control. But there were still days when it didn't seem managed at all.

Identify, clarify, resolve.

Not quite. More like identify, clarify, and flounder.

And now, in this moment, she felt a similar helplessness—unable to take any steps toward solving the issue at hand, toward finding Travis and making sure he was okay.

As she jawed her gum and scrutinized the water, she could hear Gunnar nearby in the night, speaking in hushed tones with Colonel Clarke. She couldn't make out what he was saying.

The searchlights on the far side of the bay cut off.

It struck her that the gunshots on the rooftop had quieted as well, and it didn't take long for the night to settle back to normal—just the susurrous lapping of water on the shore, the chitter of crickets in the underbrush nearby, and the soft rustling of leaves overhead in the breeze.

In truth, however, the tranquility of the night actually made her more uneasy. It was too silent. Too still. She wanted to hear splashing, to see someone swimming her way.

Gunnar strode toward her and handed her phone back.

"Anything?" she asked him.

"Clarke's put some people on it. The earpiece was a good idea. Should know in a few minutes where he's at."

As she pocketed the phone, she noticed someone in the moonlight glistening across the water—maybe thirty yards out—swimming toward them.

"Travis?" she called, relieved, but not yet certain that it was him. She readied her Springfield, just in case it wasn't him. Finger off the trigger but lined up along the side of the gun. "That you?"

The swimmer stopped and looked her way.

CHAPTER 9

I stopped and looked her way.

"It's me," I said to Adira, treading water. "I'll be right there."

A few moments later, I was climbing out of the lake and scrambling up the bank to where she and Gunnar waited at the edge of the forest. I'd kicked off my shoes in the water so I could swim more easily, and now I did my best to avoid stepping on the rocks.

The moonlight was just bright enough for me to make out the look of relief on Adira's face.

"Good to see you," she said.

"You too."

I took my glasses out of my zippered pocket. Obviously, they were too wet to be of any use at the moment and I couldn't use my clothes to dry them off, so I handed them to Adira, who was wearing a cotton shirt that would absorb the moisture. "Do you mind?"

Using the bottom of her shirt, she dried the glasses off and handed them back to me.

After putting them on, I could see that she was chewing gum, which wasn't all that unusual, but it was something she often did when she was anxious, so I figured I'd reassure her without making her ask. "I'm okay," I said. "I'm good. Barbie feet came in handy."

"You just survived an eighty-foot drop, plus getting shot at while swimming through an unfamiliar lake in the dark." Gunnar sounded proud on my behalf. "I do believe you're well on your way to becoming an action hero, Travis Brock."

"I'm not so sure about that."

"You never know," Adira said. "Hang around us long enough, and before you know it, you'll be kicking butt against the bad guys—I said *butt* there, but that's not the word I was actually thinking of."

"Aha," I said, mentally reviewing the hedgerow.

"I'm trying to clean up my language. That was from the family-friendly side of my brain."

"Right. Listen, do you have a piece of paper? A notebook? Anything like that? I need to write down this sequence before I forget it."

Gunnar held out Adira's phone to me. "Record it? Audio?"

I shook my head. "I need to write it out. That way I can more easily correct myself as I go if I make a mistake."

"Old school," he said. "Pen and paper."

"You know me." I was having a tough time splitting my attention between him and recalling the sequence.

We quickly made our way to our car. Adira dug through the glove box and came up with a mileage log, which she handed to me, along with a pen from her purse.

Gunnar slid into the backseat while she positioned herself behind the wheel and I took a seat beside her.

When you use a car for undercover work, you disable the dome lights so they won't come on and reveal your whereabouts or your identity when you open the door. Another team had done that for us before we picked up this car, after we'd flown in from DC to Madison, so even if I'd wanted to click them on, that wasn't an option at the moment.

However, my phone's flashlight app gave me plenty of light to work with.

I wiped off my hands on the cloth seats and spread a discarded Culver's ButterBurger wrapper on my damp lap to protect the mileage log as much as possible from getting soaked, then started recording the progression of dots and dashes by visualizing the hedges' heights and writing down what I saw.

Both Adira and Gunnar knew enough not to interrupt me.

I alternated between closing my eyes and picturing the bushes along the garden path, then opening them again and adding to the growing list of dots and dashes.

As I did, Adira guided us along Highway 12 toward the house we were staying at about twenty miles away, near Baraboo, not far from Devil's Lake State Park.

I walked that garden trail in my mind, mentally running my hand along the top of the hedgerow, with the height of each bush corresponding to the length of the blinks: longer blink, higher bush; shorter blink, shorter bush.

Quickly, in a kind of thrall, I scribbled down the sequence.

I didn't know how long it took me, but I finally finished and then spent a few minutes reviewing the marks. I changed four dots in the middle of the sequence to dashes and then, after a short debate, drew a question mark beside them. I honestly couldn't be positive about those either way. Maybe my memory would become clearer when we analyzed them in context later.

At last, I let out a breath that I didn't even realize I'd been holding in.

"Get it?" Gunnar asked.

"I think so. I can start translating the dots and dashes into English here in a minute. I need a sec to regroup."

"The house is close. Relax. It can wait 'til we get there."

Adira glanced at the gas gauge. "This'll only take a minute, but it looks like I need to grab some gas. If I remember right, there's a station about a half mile up on the left. Maybe we can score on some cereal for the morning as well."

—ɷ—

CHARLESTON, SOUTH CAROLINA

Søren Beck's phone rang, waking him up.

The screen told him that it was from an unknown number. He wouldn't normally have been inclined to answer it, especially at this time of night, but a couple weeks ago, before the Incident, he'd had to get a new phone when his old one bricked and his contacts hadn't been backed up. So, it was possible this was someone from work or from the gym. Really, since he was a widower and lived alone, those were the only people who called him anyway. But still? Why call now, in the middle of the night?

Curious, he tapped the screen. "Hello?"

"Søren. It's a pleasure to meet you, albeit only by phone." It was a woman's voice. A neutral, Midwestern accent. "Or do you prefer 'Mr. Beck'?"

Immediately, he recognized that this wasn't a spam call. After all, the person knew his first and last name, noted that it was nice to meet him, and asked which name he preferred. Not exactly how most robocalls or tele-marketers worked.

"Who is this?" he said.

"I have a proposition for you. One that I think you'll be interested in."

She sounded older than he was—late fifties? Could be early sixties. Hard to tell.

"Listen, I don't even—"

"I know why you have a broken headlight."

"What are you talking about?"

"I'd like to speak with you in person, Søren. I'm sure we'd both appreciate the privacy that such an opportunity would afford us for a conversation regarding what happened last week on Highway 17."

A pause. "What do you want?"

"A face-to-face meeting," she went on. "After all, you never know who might be listening in on your phone calls these days."

"Yes." Søren glanced at the Glock 19 he kept beside his bed. "I think meeting in person would be a good idea."

"In the morning, then. Let's go with seven o'clock. Maggie Ellen's Diner."

The line went dead.

"Hello?" he said. "Are you there?"

When the call ended, there was no number on the screen and when he scrolled to the log of his recent calls, nothing appeared. It was as if the call had never happened. How could someone pull that off? How was that even possible? The capability to erase the record of a call from someone else's phone? Really? He was no expert, but he'd never even heard of technology like that.

Unless it didn't happen? Unless it was all in your imagination?

No, it'd happened. He was sure of that. He wasn't losing his mind.

You can find out what all of this means in the morning.

Yes. Alright. He would drive to the diner and see what was going on. He would meet with this woman and learn what she knew—or did not know— about what happened out on the highway when he hit that animal that he couldn't find.

And then, he would respond accordingly, with whatever action the situation required.

CHAPTER 10

G unnar and I entered the gas station's convenience store.
Since the cabin we were staying in wasn't very well stocked, we'd been addressing the food situation day by day. So now, as Adira fueled up, Gunnar headed to the Beer Cave while I went in search of cereal for the morning and chips for tonight.

Near the candy aisle, I passed a girl who looked maybe four or five and a woman whom I assumed to be her mother. The girl sleepily rubbed her eyes and wore pajamas, which made sense if they were driving through the night.

They both gazed my way in a friendly enough manner, but their looks turned into wide-eyed stares when they saw the scars that covered the left side of my face and trailed ruthlessly down my neck. Thankfully, apart from what was visible there and on my arms, my clothes covered the rest of my scars.

Dealing with the stares was always a bit awkward, but I was used to it—or at least as used to it as I could be. Ever since the fire a year and a half ago, I'd been contending with the uneasy, uncertain looks of strangers.

It goes with the territory when you have scars covering nearly a third of your body, but it doesn't mean you have to enjoy what happens next, as the person gulps, then looks away a little too quickly—or a little too slowly. Eye contact can speak volumes. In this case, the woman tucked her daughter behind her leg—to shield her? To keep her safe from this terribly scarred man in soaking-wet clothes walking past them? It was such a quick and instinctive movement that I doubted she even noticed. Just being protective.

I overlooked all of that and nodded cordially at them as I walked past, hoping I wasn't frightening the girl too much.

I located a bag of crunchy cheese curls, some tortilla chips, and a jar of bean dip, then snagged a box of Tooty Fruity Curlydoos—Adira's favorite— and headed to the front counter as Gunnar emerged from the Beer Cave with a six-pack of Spotted Cow beer. "Can't get these anywhere but Wisconsin," he told me, grinning. "Good ol' Spotted Cow."

He'd also grabbed some oat milk for the cereal, and since I had the cash, he handed me the drinks and I found my place in line behind the girl and her mom, who'd made their way to the checkout counter ahead of me. Then, Gunnar exited the store, leaving me alone with the two of them and the cashier.

The woman was eyeing me suspiciously while the girl leaned out from behind her leg to get a better look at me. "What happened to you?" she asked with a mixture of the innocent curiosity and genuine concern of a small child.

"I was burned," I said. "In a big fire."

"But you're all wet!"

"Oh." I smiled. "The fire was a long time ago."

Her mother tried shushing her, but the girl asked a follow-up question anyway. "Does it hurt?"

"Don't mind her," the woman said quickly.

"Oh, it's okay," I assured her. Then I smiled again at the girl, that lopsided grin that I have now, and will always have. The skin grafts weren't as success- ful as the doctors had hoped and the scar tissue tugged down the left corner of my mouth slightly, making it look a bit like I was scowling or grimacing, even when I was doing my best not to. "It doesn't hurt anymore," I told the girl. "All better."

"Is it raining?"

"It's not raining. I took a little swim."

"That why you don't have any shoes?"

"That's right."

She processed that, then asked a question I hadn't expected: "Are you a stranger? I'm not a'pposed to talk to strangers."

"It's not polite to ask that," her mom scolded her.

The girl looked up with big, questioning eyes. "But I—"

"Hush, now."

"It's all good," I said. "Not a problem."

I wanted to assure the little girl that I wasn't a threat, but I didn't want to undermine her mother's important lesson about not talking to strangers, so in the end, I said nothing more.

Her mom hustled to pay the guy behind the counter for the energy drink she'd picked up and the candy her daughter had found.

Then they were on their way out the door and, though I couldn't make out anything else that the woman was saying, I could tell she was sternly admonishing her daughter.

I didn't love being the person that a little girl was being warned against, but I could understand where the mother was coming from. You do have to be careful talking to strangers when you're an innocent little girl. A sad reality of the world we live in.

The cashier rang up my purchase. "I guess you get that a lot, huh?" he asked me, even though it wasn't really any of his business. I assumed he was referring to the scars and not the fact that the girl had asked if I was a stranger.

"Goes with the territory." I gave him the cash, showed him my ID for the beer—a picture taken before the fire, before the scars. He stared at it for a long moment, then after a quick flick of a glance my way, he slid the change across the counter to me.

"Thanks," I said.

"You betcha," he replied, busying himself with needlessly studying the cash drawer in front of him rather than making eye contact with me.

It's so much easier that way.

So much can be communicated by the way you look at someone.

Or don't.

Back at the car, I stowed the food and drinks beside my feet while Adira keyed the ignition.

As we drove away, despite the distorted reflections on their car's backseat window, I saw the little girl wave to me. I waved back.

"Looks like you made a friend," Adira said.

"Yeah." I found myself placing my hand against the scars on my face, tracing the divots and ridges of skin that I'd traced so many times since the night of the fire. "Looks like I did."

That fateful night I'd awakened to the smell of smoke in my bedroom and the crackling sound of flames outside the door. I still felt a chill when I remembered the frantic search for my wife. Then, there—a scorched figure on the stairs reaching out to me. Rushing toward her through the living room. Then tripping and falling headfirst into the flames. Failing to get to her. A firefighter hurried to save me as I strained to pull free.

But I could not.

And I did not save her.

We'd found evidence that accelerants were used, and for seventeen months I'd searched for the arsonist, locating him at last, only a few weeks ago. I'd felt the nearly irresistible urge to kill him in return for what he'd done to her—to make him pay—but he took his own life before I could take it from him. I'd wanted justice, thinking that his life for Sienna's would somehow balance some sort of cosmic scale.

But, of course, it doesn't work like that. A life for a life doesn't balance out anything; it just leaves more people dead. I'd finally had to acknowledge that vengeance is a tricky business best left in the hands of God and not the hands of Travis Brock.

Still, I'd come to believe that striving for justice, as elusive as it might be, was worth it. Either that or nothing was. However, what justice looked like in the end wasn't always easy to discern beforehand.

I ripped open the bag of cheese curls and tried some, but found that I'd lost my appetite.

I set it aside.

I'd told the girl in the gas station that the scars didn't hurt anymore, and that was true. But other parts of me still did ache—my soul, my heart, my memories. Sienna was gone. While it was true that I was developing feelings for Adira, I didn't want to weigh down our relationship with unrealistic expectations. She wasn't here to fill in for Sienna, or to take her place in my heart. They both had their place there and always would. Maybe recognizing that was the best way to begin healing, to begin moving on. I wasn't sure.

Right now, I just needed to take things one day at a time. That meant no promises I couldn't keep. And no pressure Adira didn't deserve.

"Almost home, guys," she announced, interrupting my thoughts. "Just a few minutes out."

I glanced at the mileage book on my lap and thought of tonight's agenda: decode the dots and dashes, send the results to NSA for them to analyze, then grab a few hours of sleep before our ten o'clock flight out of Madison to DC tomorrow morning.

I found that I'd lowered my hand, but now felt my scars again, the uneven furrows of skin that had changed so much of who I was. The nerves had been damaged, so I didn't really feel the touch of my finger against my face.

Adira had told me one time that she liked my scars, that they make me unique. When I'd mentioned that they were just the shape of my skin, she'd told me they were the shape of my life, of my story. I guess she was right. My life was reshaped that night of the fire. A new tale being written. And now, with her, a night of loss being retold.

But still, I wished the nerves hadn't been damaged so badly. It would've made it so much easier to feel when I smiled. To feel like I did before.

Yes. It would be nice to feel.

Like I did before.

CHAPTER 11

FIVE YEARS AGO

PHILADELPHIA, PENNSYLVANIA

Rain had been Dr. Maia Odongo's companion all the way home from work. She'd left the institute half an hour ago and it still hadn't let up when she stopped by her mailbox and then wound her way up the winding dirt driveway that led to her house just south of Philly.

Despite not being born in the States, she had not faced much discrimination at work, but today she'd run into a visiting researcher who'd spoken to her condescendingly, perhaps because of the dark color of her skin, or her accent, or her gender.

It didn't matter and it shouldn't have bothered her, but she had a lot on her mind today as she anticipated the upcoming conversation with her dad, tonight.

She was Ugandan and, like so many people in her country, had learned English from the time she could speak. It felt just as natural to her to use as Luganda. She'd come to use her name Maia first, rather than Odongo, because it caused less confusion in her work in the United States. And the man had joked about that, about her name, if she was "really supposed to be Ugandan."

Only as she arrived at the house did the rain lighten up and the clouds begin to part.

There were no other cars in the driveway, which meant the home nurse had already left. Reginald was supposed to wait until she got home but didn't always do so. Which, honestly, was one of the reasons she'd made the decision that she had earlier today—the one she was going to tell her father about tonight.

She parked in the driveway as close to the house as possible to avoid walking through too much mud. Still, she had to slog through some of it to get to the porch, where she wiped the soles of her shoes on the shaggy welcome mat outside the front door, slid the key into the lock, and eased the door open.

"Dad?" She kept her voice low and calm.

She'd learned not to knock. Most of the time the sound of knocking or a doorbell ringing would startle him and upset him, and it could take hours to calm him down again. Instead, she'd found that it was less disruptive if she simply came in quietly and announced herself as she did.

"It's me. Maia." She set the mail and takeout on the table near the door and tried to prepare herself for tonight's conversation.

It was painful to watch someone who'd been so sharp, who had two doctorates and was at the top of his field, decline so rapidly. You watch him deteriorate before your very eyes. And you can't help but remember who he had been, the person who was now disappearing.

Growing up, she'd always idolized him and admired his groundbreaking work as an ethologist, studying animals in their natural setting in the jungles and highlands of Uganda's famous Bwindi Impenetrable National Park. She'd enjoyed paging through his many books on primates in his office at Harvard while she waited for him to finish up his lectures.

Her dad was her hero. His love of the natural world was what had gotten her interested in primate cognition in the first place. It was amazing what our closest relatives in the animal kingdom were capable of: from tool use, to planning for the future, to what could only be described as morally informed behavior, making choices that would benefit others in the community above the individual making the sacrifice.

Early on in her studies, some of her professors had warned her not to anthropomorphize too much when striving to understand the primates she studied, but she'd always found that to be the wrong way of looking at things. If evolution was true, attributing human traits to the animal kingdom wasn't a misguided approach; in fact it would have been foolish to assume that our traits would *not* be reflected in the biology or behavior of our relatives in the animal kingdom.

So, yes. The question was less whether we should attribute human traits to animals, but why we *wouldn't* do so. Certainly, we should marvel instead at the traits we *don't* share with animals—where did those come from? Worship? Prayer? Guilt? Culture? Art? Did we invent religion to find a sense of reassurance and hope, or was our desire to worship instilled in us in another way, by an almighty Creator?

These were, of course, important questions, but ones she didn't feel at all qualified to answer. She believed in God, but her specialty was cognition, not religion.

She'd eventually moved on from the primates to get her PhD in neuroscience, with her postdoc work focused on emerging trends in cognition research in humans.

So, now here she was, a neuroscientist studying human memory while her father suffered from the very condition she'd dedicated her life to combating: dementia. There was a poignant irony to it all, that someone in her field, someone with her expertise, had to watch a loved one in cognitive decline, helpless to stop it. But it wasn't the kind of irony that might make you laugh; it was the kind that just might make you cry.

"Shaula?" The voice that came from the other room was cracked and weak with age. "Is that you?"

It made sense that a man of science would name his two daughters after stars. "If anyone ever asks you what your name means," he'd said to them, with a conspiratorial smile, "I want you to point up to the sky and say, 'I was named after a star!'" And Maia had done exactly that, so many times, feeling pride and a sense of greater purpose every time she did. All that, just from a name. It was an amazing gift to give to a little girl, to name her after a star. The other kids had taken to calling her Star Girl, a nickname that she didn't mind at all.

"It's Maia, Dad." She found him seated in a grim pool of jaundiced light that was leaking in beneath the heavy, drawn curtains.

She sighed. Reginald knew better than to close up the shades like that.

"It's dark in here, Dad." The smell of feces met her as she walked past him, went to the curtains, and gently parted them, letting in a wash of post-storm sunlight.

He blinked at the sudden brightness, shielded his eyes, then looked up at her from the overstuffed recliner that seemed to be in the process of devouring him whole.

At first his expression was blank, lacking any recognition, but then—a spark. "You're here," he said. "Maia. *Oli otya?*"

"*Gyendi.* I brought some *matooke* for dinner. Your favorite." In

Philadelphia, Ugandan food wasn't easy to find, but there was one place you could get it, and she was hoping that perhaps tonight the staple food of the Buganda tribe would take some of the edge off what she was going to say.

He blinked again, as if the light were still the problem, or perhaps as if he were uncertain if that dish really was his favorite. She wasn't sure. "Did you bring any stamps?" he asked.

He hadn't worked on his stamp collection in nearly half a century. In fact, he'd given it to her when she was nine and neither of them had really done anything with it ever since. She was fifty-three now, and the box of stamps was still up in the attic somewhere, unsorted, abandoned, and languishing, no doubt, under a thick layer of dust.

"No, Dad. I don't have any stamps." Over the last few months, it'd been a struggle to get him to wear the adult diapers, but she was glad now that it was one battle she'd won. "Come on. Let's get you cleaned up."

"Oh." After a curious look, he sniffed the air and finally noticed the smell himself. "How did that happen?"

"It's okay."

His lips trembled and a tear leaked out of his left eye, emerging from a place of understanding about what was going on. A tear of shame.

He hastily wiped it away.

As hard as all of this was for her, it had to be infinitely harder for him. Because he was still aware enough to know how things used to be.

"Don't worry," she told him. "Let me help you up."

When she was done cleaning him up and they were back in the living room, Maia said, "Dad, can we talk for a second?"

"Yes."

He was slumped back in his recliner again, this time positioned in a warm pool of fading evening light.

She sat nearby, on the edge of the couch she'd grown up jumping off from into his strong arms, and leaned forward, taking his frail, elderly hand. This was the hand she'd held as a little girl when they walked along the beach and he told her of the ocean's marvels, and the one she'd taken on the safaris and treks into the bush as a child to observe gorillas in their natural habitat. She'd been twelve at the time. Maybe too old to still be holding her dad's hand, but love between a daughter and her father wasn't concerned about those sorts of things, so she'd done it anyway. And he had led her on many incredible adventures, his eyes twinkling with childlike charm.

Anyone who has watched a loved one suffer from a form of dementia knows how difficult it is, but for those who've never seen someone they care deeply about decline in that way, it's tough to imagine and nearly impossible to explain.

Alzheimer's doesn't just eat away at your cognition, but at your personality as well. The person that you know so well starts to disappear beneath the disease. Swallowing them up just like that chair was threatening to do to him now.

And sometimes he just wasn't the man she'd grown up knowing and loving. The outbursts of anger, the tears, the cursing. She knew it wasn't really what he was like, not really what was in his heart—which made it all the tougher when those things happened. There were fleeting moments of lucidity, but they were unpredictable and becoming more scarce, and Reginald couldn't stay the whole time and her dad simply couldn't be left on his own at home anymore. And so, tonight's conversation.

"Dad, I found a new place, a better place for you to stay."

He looked at her curiously. "Where?"

"It's called Pine Meadows," she said. "Doesn't that sound nice?" Her voice had taken on a saccharine cheeriness that she hated to hear herself use.

"Pine Meadows?"

"That's right. There are people there who can help you, who can watch you while I'm at work. But I'll still come to see you. I'll stop by every night on my way home. Do you understand? It's going to be best for both of us. It'll make things easier."

His curiosity turned to a look of deep confusion. "It's called Pine Meadows?"

"Yes."

"But meadows don't have trees, Maia. Shouldn't it be a forest? Maybe Pine Forest or Pine Glen? Wouldn't that make more sense?" He looked at the sunlight landing on his free hand and studied his fingers as if he were noticing them for the first time. "Or Spring Meadows? Or Fair Meadows?"

"Well, yes. That would make sense." She pivoted the conversation away from the facility's name. "It's a beautiful place, Dad. There's a river that runs past it, just on the other side of this field of flowers. And there are lots of activities to do—bingo and cards and . . . social hour." She struggled to think of other group activities that might appeal to him. Coming up short, she said at last, "And they'll read to you. You can choose the book. Any book you want." *Even the two you wrote*, she thought, but wondered if that would really be a good thing to say since he might not remember them at all.

He stared at his hand for a long time, moving his fingers gently and rhythmically as if he were finding chords on an invisible keyboard, as if he were playing a Bach concerto on the piano, like he used to.

After a few moments he stilled his hand, laid it on his leg, and looked at her with sudden, stark understanding. "It'll be easier for you?"

"It'll be easier—better—for both of us."

"I want you to be happy. I don't want to be a burden."

"You're not a burden, Dad. Not ever. I love you."

"I love you too." A long moment. "I'm sorry."

"Don't be sorry. There's nothing to be sorry about."

He nodded and then the clarity in his eyes faded and he looked at her from that other place, the place that the dementia took him to, behind the jail bars of lost memory, lost personality. Lost self. The cruelest kind of confinement.

"Maia?"

"Yes?"

"Did you bring any stamps?"

"Not this time, Dad." She gulped almost imperceptibly. "Next time. I promise."

"Have you seen Shaula? Can you tell her to come visit? I'd like to see her."

Shaula had been dead nearly thirty years, killed in a car accident when a drunk driver swerved into her lane and hit her head-on one night when she was on her way to her second-grade son's school play.

Maia had been the one to raise Madangu, the one to help him with his math homework, to teach him to drive—all those afternoons in that empty parking lot south of town where the Walmart used to be. She'd been the one to take his picture on prom night, the one to watch him walk across the stage at his graduation, the one to see him off to college. And she'd been the one to ID his body after the overdose two days later. Cocaine. A fraternity party the week of freshman orientation. He hadn't even had the chance to unpack all of his things. She'd ended up carting the boxes back home, unopened. Remnants of the dead. Of the past. Of a life lost far too soon.

But her dad didn't remember any of that. To him, Shaula was still alive, and Madangu was still a little boy who wanted to have bedtime stories read to him at night by *jjajjaawe*—his grandpa.

All of her dad's tears, all the mourning, all the grief—all of it—gone. Lost to the dementia that ate away at his memories.

But maybe there were some things better left forgotten. Maybe there was a hidden blessing to his condition after all. When you remember, you're forced to grieve again. When you forget, it sets you free. Right now he needed the memories of Madangu as a little boy and Shaula as that boy's young, loving mother.

"Sure, Dad," Maia said, telling herself that in this instance a lie was the best way to show her love to him. "I'll talk to Shaula. I'll tell her to come by."

"And to bring some stamps."

"Yes. Stamps. I'll tell her."

An hour later, after they'd eaten and she'd helped him to bed, she sighed wearily and, to distract herself from thinking about next steps, went to sort through the mail she'd brought in earlier.

The conversation about the nursing home had gone about as well as she could've hoped, but still, it'd been tough and, in that moment when he apologized to her, stingingly painful.

But the time had come. It was for the best. For everyone.

This is what she told herself. This is what she needed to believe.

However, she still found herself wondering if there was more she could do for him—or should have done for him over the years as she watched his cognitive decline continue to accelerate.

Distracted by her thoughts, she sorted through the mail, tossing flyers and junk mail into the recycling bin and laying the bills aside to tackle later. Toward the bottom of the surprisingly thick stack, she found two envelopes: an official-looking one from the Grainger Institute, the firm that granted the funding for her work, and an envelope with no return address. Her name had been printed on it with a light calligraphic flourish. That was all.

Someone must have personally placed it in her mailbox.

Hmm.

Her paycheck was automatically deposited into her bank account and any other correspondence would most naturally be done through email, so she wasn't sure what this letter from the institute might be concerning. It might possibly be a notice about a change in staff or an update on the upcoming donor banquet, but she doubted that. So, although she was curious about that personalized envelope, she decided to open the one from the institute first.

With a touch of trepidation, she used her letter opener to slit the envelope open.

Inside: a single sheet of paper. She unfolded it somewhat hesitantly.

And read.

And shuddered, finding herself needing to sit down.

The words in the two succinct paragraphs all blurred together with only a few phrases jumping out at her: *We're sorry to inform you* and *Your grant has not been renewed* and *We appreciate your hard work and diligence over the last eight years* and none of the other words really mattered.

Those three phrases told her all that she needed to know.

Maia let go of the paper and it drifted down onto the table, where it stared defiantly up at her, and where the faintest breath of air would've sent it feathering off to the side and onto the floor.

Without the grant, there was no research, no job, no income. She didn't have enough saved up to retire, especially not with the burden of paying for her father's care.

No, he's not a burden. Remember that. He's never a burden.

Sure, she could look for another job, but to find something nearby? That would be unlikely. A teaching position? She had her PhD, and most universities would be thrilled to have someone with her credentials and publishing history on their faculty, but at her age she would never get tenure. Maybe she could land a job at a pharmaceutical firm somewhere, but what about her dad? She already had everything set up at Pine Meadows.

The transition there would be difficult enough, let alone moving to somewhere else in the country first. And what about her research? All that she'd done—who would take it over?

It had the potential to help millions of people who were experiencing cognitive decline. It could greatly increase their quality of life. People just like her father.

Or was it all for naught? All her years of study? All her thousands of hours of research?

Now it was her turn to cry.

With tears clouding her eyes, she remembered that other envelope, the one that was handwritten to her. Upset, uncertain, and hoping for some sort of good news, she slit it open.

A business card with only a phone number printed on it fell out.

On the back of the card was a note written in the same precise hand as the outside of the envelope: *Call me after you receive the package tomorrow morning.* It was signed *Janice.*

What on earth?

Maia looked inside the envelope again, but there was nothing more there.

Who was Janice? As far as Maia was aware, she didn't know anyone named Janice.

But, obviously, this Janice knew her.

She wiped away her tears with the back of her hand.

Could it be a coincidence that this business card arrived on the same day that the notice from the Grainger Institute came in?

She sincerely doubted it.

Okay, so if they were related—how? And what did it mean?

Could this person be involved with the institute? Maybe contacting her would open up some sort of door. Maybe there was just a managerial misunderstanding that could get straightened out with a simple phone call.

And what sort of package might this mystery woman be sending her?

Tomorrow was a Saturday, and Maia hadn't planned on going in to work anyway. She would get up early, wait for the package, and then see if this Janice woman could help her get her job back.

CHAPTER 12

At the cabin, Gunnar and I changed into some dry clothes, then I positioned myself on the brushed-leather couch facing the inlaid-stone fireplace to translate the Morse Code, while he went to the kitchen to crack open some beers. Adira found a few bowls for the chips and dip and joined me in the living room.

I set the slightly soggy mileage log on the rough-hewn pine footstool in front of me and dove in, translating the sequence of dots and dashes into letters and numbers. Although there were certainly apps and websites that could do this for us, I felt like I needed to do it by hand so I could review it as I worked, and continue to verify that I had all the dashes and dots in the right place.

It was a chore, especially since I was dealing with passwords that included random sequences of letters, numbers, and even keyboard symbols. It was similar to Morse Code, but more robust—a cipher the intelligence community had been using for the last three years.

Despite its name, Morse Code is technically a cipher since it substitutes symbols—dots and dashes—for letters. Knowing the syntax, or algorithm, is the key to deciphering it. A code, on the other hand, shares meaning—often through abbreviation—and requires a codebook to decode it.

Codes and ciphers.

So close, yet not quite the same thing at all.

Fraternal twins. Not identical ones.

Gunnar popped the caps off three bottles of Spotted Cow, gave one bottle to me, handed one to Adira, and then set up shop on the dining room table with his laptop and began to type. I wasn't sure if he was filing an incident report to Clarke about us getting shot at or working on his novel and I didn't ask.

Taking the chips and dip with her, Adira found a chair on the other side of the living room beneath the head of a taxidermy-stuffed ten-point buck that was staring across the room from its perch on the wall, then began to munch on the chips while flipping to her bookmarked page in the romance novel she was halfway through—an unabashed bodice-ripper with a sweaty, barely clad woman on the cover, swooning in the arms of a shirtless hunk, Adira's favorite genre of story.

The cabin must have only been constructed recently, because the fresh scent of the cedar logs was still present all throughout it, and it made me think of us sitting inside a giant cedar hope chest.

As I worked, it didn't take long to realize that—as I'd expected—I was translating a soup of alphanumeric characters and symbols that contained very few complete English words or discernible sequences.

One sequence, however, caught my attention: 4SF18O<3f22UzT!

In Department of Defense work, we have very specific parameters for creating our passwords: They must be at least fifteen characters long and include numeric as well as special characters and upper- and lowercase letters. Also, the characters can't appear in repeating sequences, contain easily identified patterns or sets of numbers, or include English words.

So, in order to remember them, many people used a combination of zip codes, street addresses, birthdays, and initials of friends.

But Sienna did not.

"Huh." I didn't realize that I'd said it aloud until I noticed Adira looking my way.

"What's up? Everything good?" she asked.

"Yeah . . . I mean . . ." I paused to stare at the pattern again and caught myself scratching my head. "This doesn't really make sense."

"What is it?"

"Most of what we have here is a random alphanumeric sequence, but there's a series in here that I actually recognize."

"What do you mean? Buried in the passcode?"

"Yes."

She closed up her novel. "Go on."

"Sienna had this little quirk where she would text me the word *Be* and then, a moment later, text me, *Loved*. In the end, I'd decided it was the most appropriate word to leave behind, engraved on her gravestone, a legacy of who she was and what she meant to me. Anyway, on a trip to NSA's National Cryptologic Museum one time, we came across an actual Enigma machine from World War II. They allowed us to use it. I chose the numbers on the three rotors and typed in the word *BELOVED*."

Adira looked confused. "And?"

"And when you choose the numbers four, eighteen, and twenty-two for the rotors, the cipher comes up as *SFOFUZT*."

"So, to decode it, if you set those rotors correctly and typed in those seven letters, the word *BELOVED* would come up? Is that how it works?"

"That's right. There are no numbers or lowercase letters on an Enigma machine's keyboard, so she inserted the rotors' numbers, a heart emoticon in the middle, and made some of the letters lowercase, then used that for her password one week: 4SF18O<3f22UzT! And now it's here, in the passcode to TalynTek's root system files."

That got Gunnar's attention. "What are you saying?" He looked up from his work and peered at me with keen interest from across the room.

"Two and a half years ago, Sienna used that same exact alphanumeric sequence as her Federal Digital Database password. She changed it the week before Christmas."

"You remember that?" A hint of skepticism had crept into his words. "Seriously? I mean, no offense, and I don't know how many of her passwords she told you, but we have to change those weekly . . . That's like a hundred and fifty passwords ago. Even for you . . ."

"Trust him," Adira said. "She was his beloved. He remembers it."

"Hmm." Gunnar contemplated that. "Alright. So, this means someone got a look at her passwords. They were probably leaked onto the dark web."

"Yeah," I said distractedly. "That's probably what it was."

"What are you thinking?"

"Nothing . . . I mean, when a password gets out there, it's fair game, right?"

"Sure." Gunnar shrugged. "You might be reading more into this than you need to and maybe both Sienna and TalynTek got the *beloved* idea from someone else—a common ancestor, so to speak. The NSA cryptanalysts and codebreakers can take a deep dive into it. If you've got it translated, for now, I think you've done all you can. Let's call it a day. Or maybe I should say 'a night.'"

"Right." I sighed.

But you were the one who chose the numbers on the Enigma's rotors, I thought. No, a common ancestor didn't make sense.

I snapped photos of the pages and sent them to Colonel Clarke through the end-to-end encrypted phone that he'd provided me with.

"There's just one more thing we need to do tonight," Adira said to Gunnar.

"What's that?"

"When we were at the lake, you promised to read Travis some of your novel."

"What? Now?"

"No time like the present."

As they spoke, I found myself distracted by my thoughts of Sienna and the TalynTek password, trying to puzzle out what the connection between them might be. Maybe it was nothing, but I couldn't quite get myself to believe that.

Adira managed to convince Gunnar to read a scene, and he pulled up his work in progress, or his WIP as he'd taken to calling it. "Alright. So, here I'm writing about the protagonist, trying to really climb into her psyche and encapsulate the reticence she has to allow anyone into her life or to form any meaningful intimate relationships."

"Because she was hurt in the past?" Adira ventured. "Maybe jilted at the altar? Suffering from unrequited love? Betrayed by her best friend stealing her boyfriend?"

He was quiet for a moment. "Something like that. There's a flashback where I introduce her Defining Wound and her Fatal Flaw—that's something we novelists do to clarify the Story Question."

"I see."

"Anyway, here's the part I'm working on right now, how it starts out: 'She had constructed an impenetrable fortress that no one could get through around her heart. It was a gloomy wall, looming, tall, and dooming. The only way in was to burrow, like a hungry groundhog, beneath the ramparts of her pain and pop up on the other side looking for a slice of lettuce.'" He looked up at us expectantly. "Well?"

"I think you've done a good job of . . . staying in your narrative voice," I offered.

"Thanks. That's a huge deal to agents and editors—voice is. They always want to see that from an author, especially if he's not established in the marketplace yet."

"What comes next?" Adira asked. "After the lettuce?"

"'But then he appeared before her out of nowhere like a six-foot-tall person lumbering toward her on legs like tree trunks. Heavy and oaken, but covered with skin instead of bark.'"

"I see what you did there," she said, "with *lumbering* and *tree trunks.* Imagery, right?"

"Yeah. Subtle, huh?"

"Um. Right."

"Then," Gunnar went on, "'She warmed at the thought of his hands around her waist, of his lips against hers. The soft pleasing pleasure of pleasant pressure of lip on lip on lip on lip. Heat flushed through her. She awaited his embrace, her mouth puckered and ready, as she longed to feel his arms wrap around her like two strong appendages jutting from a man's torso might do.'"

"Wow," I said to Gunnar, unsure what else to say.

"It's hard to put into words how your writing is affecting me," Adira told him judiciously.

"Thanks. That means a lot. I'm pretty proud of that graph—*graph* is how writers refer to a paragraph."

"Gotcha."

I said, "And with that line about the pleasing pleasure of pleasant pressure—alliteration, right?"

"You got it. And a subtle little rhyme there too. You can thank Mrs. Stonewall for that line. She was my high school English teacher. Taught me all about alliteration, onomatopoeia, symbolism, all the good stuff."

"If I ever meet her, I'll have a chat with her."

He finished off his beer. "Maybe I'll work on this scene in the other room for a bit, now that you've got me thinking about the story again. Then I'm gonna hit the hay." A wink. "Don't stay up too late, you two. And behave."

"Thanks, Dad," Adira said, playing along. "We'll be good little campers."

"If you come up with anything fun for me to use in my book, let me know."

"Uh-huh."

"Experience is the best teacher, after all, and—"

"Go to bed, Gunnar."

I was still thinking about that password.

Be loved.

Beloved.

It really makes no sense that TalynTek would use that. How did they come upon it? She would've had to give it to them. It had to have come from her.

Gunnar disappeared down the hallway, leaving Adira and me alone in the living room.

"I should probably get changed for bed," I said.

"Hmm." She slow-sipped her beer, eyeing me demurely. "Need any help with that?"

"Um . . ."

While it was true that we'd been seeing each other for a couple of weeks, we'd been taking things slowly—slower, I think, than both of us might have wanted. But I was still getting used to the idea of being with someone after losing Sienna, and right now slow was what I needed.

I'd been taught at the Presbyterian church I grew up attending with my mom—after my dad left us when I was nine—that sex is a gift meant to only be shared between married couples; that people are more than simply animals driven solely by the biological drive to procreate; that we are born free instead of constrained by instinct, and honoring the marriage bed was important to God and a way to express that freedom. Very traditional. But also, very respectful and honoring of your spouse. However, admittedly, it was also tough to put into practice in today's world.

Very tough, actually.

Clarke knew about our relationship and had no problems with it as long as it didn't affect our job performance. So it wasn't that. It was more on the practical level: I didn't want to end up making a mistake with Adira that would hurt either of us or undermine our work.

Because of that, we were staying in separate rooms tonight, and had been since we'd started dating. Old-fashioned, maybe, but if it was meant to be, it would be—when the time was right. However, tonight when I looked at the sly, coquettish look on her face I began to doubt my resolve to wait until then.

Before I could formulate an answer to her question, she read volumes in my hesitation, sighed slightly, and rose. "Good night, Travis."

"I just . . . It's—"

"No explanation necessary." She cut me off with a wave of her hand. "I'm just glad you're okay and that I didn't have to fish you out of that lake."

"That makes two of us."

"Good night, Mr. Barbie Feet."

"Night."

The kiss she gave me was quick and perfunctory, and then she was strid-ing down the hall toward her room, then she was inside of it, closing the door, with a click, behind her.

After dealing with the dishes and beer bottles, I changed into shorts and the Boston College T-shirt that I'd kept from my law school days. As I got ready to shut off the light, I thought of that alphanumeric combination that Sienna had used.

Gunnar was right: the chance that a federal employee's password from two years ago might find its way onto the dark web wasn't at all out of the realm of possibility. We changed them weekly for a reason: they get leaked and hashed all the time.

Still, how this one in particular might've gotten from there onto TalynTek's server was another question altogether. Why would they use an alphanumeric sequence that'd been compromised, one that other people might be using as well?

None of it really made sense, given the fact that Sienna had made up the password *after* I'd chosen the numbers for the rotors.

If TalynTek's IT department didn't know the password was compromised, that meant they weren't nearly as careful as we'd been led to believe.

But if they didn't assign it, who did?

I had no idea what any of this might mean, except that at one point someone might have had access to Sienna's Federal Digital Database account and leaked the sequence. The solution was probably just as simple as that.

Still, it all seemed awfully coincidental—that they would have chosen it and I would have then discovered it in this cipher tonight while searching for clues to the Pruninghooks Collective. Too coincidental.

I needed to find out if Sienna ever had any ties to this organization—stocks, consulting work, investment, anything.

I decided to look into that in the morning.

With the beer catching up with me, I slipped down the hallway to use the bathroom and, on my way back to my bedroom, found that Adira's door, which had been closed a minute earlier, was slightly ajar.

An invitation.

I paused beside it, my thoughts racing. We were consenting adults. Neither of us was married or in another serious relationship. In truth, it was what we both wanted, and this was a clear indication of that fact. We could stop at any point. We didn't need to go one kiss further, one step further, than we were comfortable with.

But what about free will? What about the marriage bed?

Yes, but what about our feelings for each other?

I placed my hand on the doorknob.

As I was about to press the door open, I thought of the implications of entering her bedroom, of joining her for the night. It would be a decision that could not be undone. A promise that I honestly wasn't sure I was ready to make. It would certainly cause us to turn a corner that could not be unturned, and I wasn't ready for that to happen. Not tonight.

The scriptural admonitions from my childhood weren't the only reason, but they were there too.

And so, rather than open her door, I let go of the doorknob, stepped back quietly, and found my way to my room once again, hoping that she hadn't heard me pause there beside hers.

A few moments later, I heard her door close. Softly, not angrily. Just a click once again.

I tried not to read too much into either the invitation of the open door, or the finality of it being closed.

Then I sank beneath the covers and closed my eyes to try for some sleep, but the questions about that password pestered me and kept prodding me awake again and again all throughout the night.

POWEIR
POFII
UPOEII
JERPFJ
EOPFIJ
OIIAJUE
V;LKMERO
AOMW'GFP
VV;NAVPO
FPIGUHER
EVG;GANNE
OANRV;OOAN
IVPOAEWIJVGG
ERV'AKJERVPO
OIREJBEOI
AIJE
JE
EP
JAW
POWEIRPOW
POFIIJAS;OOJ
UPOEIFJAPUOIE
JERPFJR3POIAP
EOPFIJAWEPEOO
OIIAJWEPEOFIJA
V;LKMEROFIFIJ
AOMW'GFPOOAWG
VV;NAVPOAWEEHFA
FPIGUHER
BOOKB]PO
OIOAUERH
HC;OAJVPOJ
UNFDEIOJÖIJ
AIUUHVHNAOIUS
UHERVUNEV;OZI
WJVPOOEARJHV
VPOOEARJWW
EPORI
JAW;OFIJAW;OI
POWEIRPOWIURT
POFIIJAS;OOJR
UPOEIFJAPUOIE
JERPFJR3POIAPO
EOPFIJAWEPEOOI
OIIAJWEPEOFI
V;LKMERO
AOMW'GF
VV;NAVPOAWEEHFA
FPIGUHERF;FNSI
BOOKB]POKBIA
OIOAUERHRFG
HC;OAJVPOJJHSZ
UNFDEIOJOI
AIUUHVHNAOIUSH
UHERVUNEV;OZI
WJVPOOEAR
ERV'AKJERVPOAIJ
OIREJBEOIJVPO
AIJERGBOOAIJEE
JERVBEOAWIEJGE
VPOOEARJHVVOAE
EPORIIHQWPOIFFH
JAW;OFIJAW;OFIJAWAE
POWEIRPOWTHRTRUDOE
POFI
UPOE
JER
EOPF
OIIA
EOPFIJAWEPEOIUFH
OTIAJWEPEOEIJAWE

PART II

Secrets to Keep

The scent of sweat and blood.
Rusty nails.
To dig and to love.
Two corpses by the fence. ⸺

CHAPTER 13

The familiar scents of sizzling bacon and percolating coffee permeated the air as Søren Beck waited in his local diner's corner booth for the person who'd called him in the middle of the night. She'd been cryptic on the phone, and he wasn't sure what to expect.

He had a clear view of the front door. An unobstructed sight line.

With so many people present, he didn't want to use his gun, but he also knew that he needed to be prepared for whatever situation might arise. Because of that, he had his unholstered Glock resting on his lap under the table, Han Solo style. He was ready for her, whoever she was.

Half a dozen other patrons sat scattered throughout the restaurant at various stages of finishing their breakfasts. The clank of utensils and plates along with soft snippets of laughter and murmured discourse drifted through the twenty-four-hour diner.

After receiving the phone call last night and getting the odd and rather blackmailish "invitation" to meet, he hadn't been able to sleep. Yet, now, even though he was tired, he somehow also felt surprisingly alert. Jacked up. Ready to resolve things.

What did this woman want from him?

What did she actually know about the Incident last week? What *could* she know?

As he waited for her, he finished off the side of hash browns and the hefty stack of buttermilk pancakes he'd ordered earlier. At least his appetite wasn't gone.

At precisely seven o'clock, the diner's front door swung open, the entry bell jingled, and a burly, bearded man entered. It took him only a moment to get eyes on Søren. As soon as he did, he strode directly toward him through the restaurant.

Søren observed him carefully: Mid to late thirties. His eyes were set back in his head further than they should have been, giving the impression that he was staring at you from another place altogether. Stout—close to six-two and pushing two hundred twenty pounds, but he carried it well. He wore a suit that was just a shade too small, and it strained against his barrel chest and bulging biceps, making it look almost like he'd been stuffed into it. The suit didn't offer him much freedom of movement, but rather appeared to constrain it instead.

It would hinder him in a fight.

Søren took note of this.

He knew street fighting from when he was a teen fending for himself in East St. Louis when neither of his parents showed him much attention and even less concern. In his early twenties, he'd attended the police academy there and, although he'd never served in law enforcement, he still shot competitively. Additionally, he'd studied mixed martial arts for years. He would do what he needed to do in order to keep the reason for the blood on the front of his car a secret.

When the man reached Søren's booth, he didn't take a seat. "Mr. Beck?" His voice was a growling murmur and he kept it low.

"Yes."

"I'll need you to come with me." There was a touch of a European accent there, but Søren couldn't quite place where it might've been from.

Søren didn't move from his seat. "Before I do that, I'll need you to sit down and tell me what this is all about."

The bearded man didn't move. Didn't sit. Didn't even blink.

Instead, they stared at each other as if they were each waiting for the other man to show some sign of weakness. A game of chicken that was only interrupted when an overly enthusiastic twentysomething server appeared, flashed the stranger a toothy smile, and launched into her pitch.

"Morning!" she chirped. "Welcome to Maggie Ellen's Diner, where customers come first! My name's Tiara and I'll be taking care of you today. I'd *love* to tell you about today's special: our yummy toasted bagel and bacon breakfast sandwich. Comes with bacon—obviously—or you can substitute sausage if you like—that's the way *I* like it. Cheese is all melty. Egg on there too, plus our special secret-ingredient sauce. It's totally killer! Whaddya say? Can I get you one?" She seemed oblivious to the fact that he was still standing and had not indicated in any way that he was planning to sit, to stay, to eat.

"I'm not here for—" he began.

"He'll have one," Søren told her. "With sausage." He gestured toward his empty coffee cup and said to the man, "Coffee?"

"No."

"Breakfast's on me," Søren said, holding his hands out, palms up, in a nonthreatening way. He indicated the other side of the booth. "Take a load off."

The server, who was still beaming, stepped aside so the man could have a seat.

Finally, he sighed and crammed himself into the other side of the booth, grunting a bit as he did.

"Can I get you anything else, hon?" Tiara asked Søren.

"An orange juice. Bring us two, actually. One for me, and one for my friend here."

"Okay! Couple a OJs and one totally yummy *sausage* bagel sandwich coming right up!" Then she flitted off, tossing her free-spirited ponytail to the side behind her as she did.

When she was gone, the man leaned forward. "It's time to go, Søren."

"Where's the woman I spoke with last night?" Søren replied. "Why isn't she here?"

"It wouldn't be prudent for her to be seen in public."

"And why is that?"

"You ask a lot of questions."

"What can I say? I'm a curious guy."

Wait him out. You can do this.

The man said nothing, but just stared at him with those cold, dead, inset eyes.

"What's your name?" Søren asked him.

A head cock and a smirk. "Why don't you just call me Bill."

"Okay, then. Bill it is."

The man, who Søren sincerely doubted was actually named Bill, folded his arms and leaned back. "I'm guessing you have a gun aimed at me under the table. Is that the deal?" He kept his voice soft enough for only Søren to hear. "That why you didn't stand up to greet me a moment ago? Show me some of that famous Southern hospitality? I need to inform you that if you do anything to me, there's information that my employer is in possession of that will be released. If that were to happen, it would not be profitable for you. You get to choose how we proceed from here."

Søren eyed him. "What information?"

"About the dent. About the broken headlight." Bill unfolded his arms and placed his elbows on the table, looming in toward Søren, swallowing up half of the space between them. "It would be best for us to leave now. There's only a limited window of time during which my employer will be available to speak with you. If we miss that, it would be unfortunate. For both of us."

Tiara appeared, agilely maneuvering through the diner toward them, carrying two sweating glasses of orange juice on a silver tray, supported expertly on one flattened hand.

"That breakfast bagel will be right up!" she told them brightly, as she swept up to their booth.

"It looks like we won't be needing it after all." Søren laid three twenties on the table. "Keep the change."

"For real?" Her eyes were plate-sized and focused on the cash.

"Yes." He rose, surreptitiously sliding the gun into his concealed carry holster as he did. "Thanks."

Bill gestured toward the front door. "After you."

Søren didn't argue, but left the diner with Bill at his heels. Once they were outside, Bill pointed to a tan Lexus SUV with darkly tinted windows and Søren wondered if the woman was perhaps waiting for them in the car. However, when Bill opened the backseat door, Søren saw that the car was empty, apart from a black hood lying on the plush leather seat.

"You're kidding me," he said.

"A precaution."

"Mm-hmm."

Søren debated what to do, and finally decided that if Bill and his employer wanted to harm him, they could've easily done so by now, either by releasing the damaging information or by targeting him at home. After all, they had the tech to remotely erase call records from his phone, and had somehow located information about the Incident. They were tech savvy and resourceful, that much was obvious. Clearly, the mystery woman didn't want him out of the picture. She needed him alive for something and he wanted to know what that was.

Bill held out his hand. "Phone, please."

Søren handed his cell over. Bill dropped it unceremoniously into a crinkly metallic bag that would no doubt conceal or cancel out its signal, sealed the bag, and then tossed it somewhat remissly into the front of the car, onto the passenger's seat.

Søren sat in the back. Bill closed the door for him and then slid behind the wheel. He redirected the rearview mirror to observe Søren and waited to see what he would do with the hood.

"Your move," he said.

Yes, it is.

It's your move, Søren.

What are you going to do next?

As Søren unfolded the hood, he hesitated, but in the end, he realized he needed some answers and the only way to get those was to comply, so he tugged it on, over his head. With the dark windows shielding out most of the morning light and the hood taking care of the rest, Søren found himself in a thick and stifling darkness. He caught the distinct scent of blood and the reek of sweat, probably from whoever had worn the hood last.

Bill keyed the ignition. "I suggest you leave your gun behind in the car when we get there." Then he added, "You wouldn't want to have it on you when you meet her."

"And why is that?" Søren's voice sounded strangely muffled and thick, there inside the hood.

"Trust me here. I'm telling you this for your own good."

Søren felt the car rolling forward, turning left out of the parking lot, and then accelerating down the street in the opposite direction from the highway.

He considered Bill's advice about leaving his Glock behind. He didn't like the idea of meeting with whoever was behind all of this unarmed, but he had other skills that could come in handy if necessary.

He had never needed to use them before, but he was open to the possibility of doing so today. He might never have served as a cop, might never have needed to kill anyone before, but he was ready to take decisive action if necessary to keep the Incident secret.

And, honestly, a part of him that he'd never been aware of before hoped it would be necessary.

What has gotten into you? Why are you thinking these things?

Self-preservation. It's okay. It's only natural. You're just trying to take care of yourself. That's all.

Søren found all of this very interesting. Maybe he'd never known before who he truly was. Maybe he was on the way to finally finding out.

That's what he thought of in the dark as Bill drove him toward his future.

CHAPTER 14

I didn't hear any indication that Gunnar and Adira were up and about yet, so I got dressed quietly and padded down the hall barefoot to the kitchen for breakfast.

We didn't have many culinary options other than the Tooty Fruity Curlydoos and oat milk from the gas station last night, so it wasn't tough figuring out what was going to be on the menu.

After I poured my cereal and was about to add the milk that wasn't actually milk in any way that made sense whatsoever, I logged in to my account to check on the status of NSA's analysis of the password's origin to see if it truly had been floating around on the dark web as we'd been speculating, but they hadn't posted anything yet.

While I was on the computer, I decided to check in for our ten o'clock flight but saw that it'd been delayed until noon.

Hmm.

I'd been planning to research Sienna's possible connection to TalynTek, but since we wouldn't need to leave for the Madison airport for a couple of hours and I hadn't been able to exercise in the last few days, I decided to slip in a little run first. If nothing else, it'd give me a chance to stretch my legs and collect my thoughts before our flight.

I figured that I had time to run for about thirty minutes before I'd need to turn around and come back. Maybe by then NSA would have filed its report.

Leaving the uneaten cereal there for later, I found my Hokas, laced up, and slipped outside into the brisk morning air.

It was cooler than I would've expected for a May morning in Wisconsin: low sixties. But it felt just right. Perfect for a run.

Whenever possible, I prefer trail running to road running, but there were no nearby trails that I knew of, so after starting my watch, I headed toward the county road that ran along the edge of the cornfields paralleling the quarter-mile driveway to the cabin.

After about ten minutes, I rounded the bend in the road around a nearby kettle, one of the rock-strewn valleys scattered throughout southern Wisconsin, created during the last ice age—a unique feature of the state's topography.

Pushing myself, I fell into a familiar rhythm of pulsed breathing in sync with the swing of my legs, feeling the welcome impact of my feet landing stride by stride on the road, my muscles loosening up and my pace quickening as the cool air brushed across me, keeping me from sweating too much.

As I did, I considered once again the height of the imaginary hedges, the cipher, and the enigmatic password, wondering what it all meant.

I'd flipped through a variety of possibilities last night about how Sienna's password might have ended up on TalynTek's server and now one more idea occurred to me: in my urgency to memorize the sequence, I might have superimposed my memory of Sienna's password onto the series of dots and dashes, subconsciously altering what I thought was there.

Memory can do things like that, and stress can contribute to it.

But then you wouldn't have just been misremembering, right? You would've also been subconsciously translating her password into that cipher. Is that really believable?

Actually, it probably wasn't, and the more I thought about it, the less likely that scenario seemed.

My memory wasn't by any means perfect. It wasn't infallible. No one's is. But even as a young boy, it'd become clear to me that my memory was different from that of my friends.

At the time, I didn't really think anything of my ability to remember what I was told, what I saw, or the stories I heard. I expected that other kids would remember things just as I did, and when they didn't, I was genuinely surprised, and, at times, even a little annoyed.

Why wouldn't they remember things? What made it so hard for them, yet so easy for me? In class, our teachers told us they wanted us to remember what we went through and then we were expected to write down the answers later. So, that's what I did. Isn't that the point of going to school in the first place? To learn things and then remember them when you're asked to?

I was in the second grade when the school counselor and my teacher began to pay more attention to the answers and responses that I gave. In that grade we didn't do too much testing or have much homework, so that year and the next went by quickly, easily, as I read voraciously and aced nearly all of my assignments.

Third grade came and went.

The school administrators made me skip fourth grade even though that wasn't what I wanted. Skipping the grade meant I couldn't be with my friends, and I guessed that the new kids I'd be spending every school day with wouldn't like the fact that I was younger and smarter than they were. And, as it turned out, I was right.

By then, my dad had left us, so my mom was raising me alone. She was a middle school English teacher and knew how the school system worked and I trusted her when she said, "It'll be better this way, Travis, if you move up a grade. All I want is what's best for you."

I knew that last part was true, so I didn't argue. I wanted to be a good kid. I didn't want to go against what my mom was telling me to do.

So, I skipped a grade, leaving my friends behind, and I felt out of place every day when I went to school. The boys and girls in my new class left me out of their games, their gossip, their birthday parties and sleepovers.

I didn't want to be a freak or get made fun of, so I started purposely writing down the wrong answers on tests and assignments to attract less attention to myself and to avoid standing out.

But it didn't take long for my teacher to become wise to what I was doing. She contacted a friend of hers, a cognitive researcher from MIT. He and his associates were working on AI technology and wanted to better understand how humans formed and retained memories so they could design and program machines to "think" the way humans do.

They paid my mom for the opportunity to study me and, without a spouse around to contribute to paying the bills and meeting the rent, I knew that Mom really did need the money.

So, I dutifully answered the researchers' questions. I dutifully took their tests. I dutifully laid in the functional magnetic resonance imaging machine and let them scan my brain. As the fMRI scanner made all those troubling groaning and popping sounds, I imagined that the machine was choking on a throat full of its own electronics. Yet, as frightened as I was, I obeyed. I didn't complain. I didn't tell anyone that I was scared.

It was all for a good reason.

It was for my mom.

In the end, although the researchers were able to map different parts of my brain and find which areas lit up when I was remembering different combinations of letters, numbers, images, and words, they were left with just as many questions as they'd started with. They still didn't understand how I could do it, what made my memory so unique, so acute. So noteworthy.

"You've been given a special gift," one of the researchers told me on the last day that I saw her. Dr. Farling had always been kind and thoughtful to my mother and to me, and I liked her. And when she said that, she smiled warmly and I'm sure she meant well, but still.

A gift?

Well, I remember thinking, *that's one word for it.*

That wasn't quite how I viewed things.

Because, in addition to information, I remembered the emotions associated with that information—which included the times I'd been made fun of, grade by grade, month by month, day by day. I remembered arguments I'd had, insults others had hurled at me, vindictive looks, betrayals—all of it—all more keenly than most people do. More keenly than most people could even imagine. For all that can be said about the innocence and naiveté of children, they can also be remarkably cruel and coldhearted.

And I remembered the wrongs I'd done to others too. I recalled the times I'd hurt the feelings of those I cared about, the times I'd spoken too soon—or too late—broken another person's heart, been the one to put others down. Shame is a hard thing to shake when the past crawls in that deeply. It can take up permanent residence in your heart. Eventually, by the time I entered college, my mind was a graveyard of jagged, painful memories.

If only I could forget more easily, I told myself, then things would be better, would be easier.

My *gift.*

Yes, that was the word she chose.

The sharper your memory, the more isolated you'll be from other people who *can* easily forget, who *do* easily forget, who move on with life without the chains of the past still shackled around them.

And the older I grew, the more I realized that.

My memory wasn't a gift.

It was a prison.

I wasn't wearing a smartwatch this morning, so I didn't know the exact mileage I was clocking, but I felt pretty good and I figured I was on a sub-eight-minute pace. It wouldn't have been my best time, but it wouldn't have been my worst either. When I hit thirty minutes, I turned back toward the house.

As I picked up the pace, I processed what we'd found out last night but didn't come to any conclusions other than that I needed more information about Sienna and any ties she might've had to TalynTek.

I made it to the front yard right at fifty-nine minutes and thirty-one seconds, out of breath and feeling the good sort of tired.

After a couple minutes of stretching—which I was always tempted to skip or skimp on—I entered the cabin and found Gunnar seated at the kitchen table working his way through a heaping bowl of oat milk–drenched Tooty Fruity Curlydoos next to the bowl I'd poured earlier.

"How was the run?" he asked, swallowing a mouthful of Curlydoos.

"Good." I went for a glass of water. "Any word from NSA?"

"Yes, actually." He dug in for another bite. "That password was on the dark web after all, just like we were thinking it might be."

"Could they identify when it first appeared?"

"That's the thing. It was only just recently—less than three weeks ago. They dug around for a while. They're pretty sure. No evidence of it before that. Seems like it might've been leaked by a Russian hacking collective."

"Huh. Interesting."

How does that make any sense?

He munched away while I downed some water.

What did the timing of the leak mean, considering what we knew?

I glanced out the window and saw Adira in the backyard, doing yoga near the edge of the cornfield. I'm not too familiar with all the different yoga poses, but I did know that this one was sometimes called the dancer pose. And she was making it look effortless. If it were me, I probably would've ended up falling over onto my face.

No, I wasn't exactly the most coordinated yoga-er.

Not like her.

In the golden sunlight, Adira might have been posing for a commercial for a healthy lifestyle. She wore a navy blue sports bra and black leggings that fit her lean, athletic body just like they were supposed to. It took a bit of effort to guide my eyes away from her and direct my focus back onto the conversation with Gunnar.

"Um." I turned from the window. "What were you saying?"

"Just that the cipher was leaked onto the dark web only recently, not two and a half years ago when Sienna changed her Federal Digital Database password. We don't know how it got there, but there's some indication it might've come from the Russians." Then he added, with a glint of a smile, "Getting distracted there?"

I flagged a hand up, palm toward him. "Guilty as charged."

He nodded toward the window. "How's it going between you two, anyway?"

"I'd say pretty good, but it's unfamiliar territory."

"How's that?"

"It's been a while since I've been in a relationship. Ever since . . . Well, you know. The fire. And plus, trying to navigate through letting things get personal and also remain professional at the same time—it's not easy. Balancing all that out."

"Tell me about it."

I sensed a story coming, but he just turned to his cereal and offered nothing more and, curious though I was, I didn't ask him to elaborate.

In the shower, I thought of one more option about the password.

It was a possibility that seemed outlandish, almost incomprehensible, but I didn't want to prematurely discount anything from consideration, no matter how ludicrous or unbelievable it might seem.

A chill ran through me.

I'd heard an FBI agent named Patrick Bowers mention one time at a meeting at the Pentagon that to get answers in an investigation, you need to brush off the facts until only the truth remains. Right now, a little fact-brushing was in order.

I shut off the water.

Sienna's *beloved* password appeared on the dark web just a few weeks ago, perhaps posted by a member of a Russian hacking collective.

Sienna had first used it over two years ago.

Now TalynTek was using it.

The fire was eighteen months ago.

I'd set the numbers on the Enigma machine, then she came up with the password *afterward*.

The more I considered the implications, the more it seemed like the rug had been pulled out from beneath me.

Beloved.

Be.

Loved.

After the fire there was no autopsy.

Means, motive, opportunity . . .

Was that even possible? What would it mean?

No, it couldn't be.

Or could it?

While I toweled off, my hand shook slightly as I considered the possibility and the ramifications it would carry. A swarm of emotions buzzed around inside me: a mixture of hope and possibility, stalked by darker feelings crawling along the bottom of my heart: shock, dismay, betrayal.

Once I'd gotten dressed and returned to the kitchen, I found that Gunnar was still mulling over our conversation from a few minutes ago because he said, "I've been wondering about the timing of the password's appearance on the dark web."

"Me too." I was anxious to tell him what I'd been thinking, but at the same time hesitant to do so because of what it might mean. "What are your thoughts?"

"Well, somehow, her password leaked after she came up with it—but if it wasn't in use for almost two years, why would it suddenly resurface?"

"Unless it never went under the surface at all."

He looked at me curiously. "What does that mean?"

"We know that she used it for her Federal Digital Database account, but we don't know *precisely* when TalynTek started using it, just that its dark web appearance was a couple of weeks ago. It's unlikely they would use a password that they knew was compromised or was floating out there in the dark web. Right?"

"Right."

"And it'd be unusual to use a two-and-a-half-year-old password without changing it."

"Okay," he said. "But what did you mean when you said it might not've gone under the surface at all? How'd they get it?"

"From her."

"How?"

"I'm wondering if Sienna might still be alive."

CHAPTER 15

There. I'd said it. And once I'd spoken the words aloud, the possibility seemed to somehow become more plausible, more credible.

Gunnar slid his cereal bowl aside. "You're going to have to talk me through that. She died in the fire, right? You saw her reach for you. She was surrounded by flames. The firefighters found her body right where you said it'd be."

"Maybe it wasn't her. Track with me here." I was thrilled by the possibility that she might be alive, however, there were also troubling implications that I tried not to think about. "I had no reason to think that it might have been anyone other than Sienna there on the stairs. Because of that, and the nature of her death, they didn't do an autopsy—it wasn't required by law, and I didn't see any reason to request one. Also, before the arsonist took his own life, he told me that I knew the person who'd hired him."

"And you're saying that was Sienna?"

"Maybe. Yes. He also said that things were not what they appeared to be. And he mentioned someone by the name of Lena."

"Hmm . . . I don't know."

It'd taken some digging, but a few weeks ago I'd found out about a State Department employee named Lena Rhodes who'd worked with Adira just prior to the fire.

"Lena disappeared the week of the arson," I said, "after filing a report questioning some of Sienna's work. I'd thought the arsonist was talking about

Lena being the one who'd hired him, but maybe he meant that she was the one who was killed."

"Because you didn't know her beforehand?"

"Yes."

Logic and emotion were warring inside of me. The evidence was pointing toward Sienna being alive, but that didn't simplify things; it only made them more complex—especially if she was involved, was responsible for the fire.

"There's gotta be more or you wouldn't even be considering this," Gunnar said.

I was slow to reply as I found myself sifting through moments with her that I'd never paid much attention to before—the phone calls from the "office" at such inopportune times, the trips to Russia, the texts in the night, the canceled dinner plans and late-night meetings. All innocent enough. All easily explained away. But now, I saw them in a different light.

It reminded me of instances when, in the wake of a suicide, family members look back and realize the warning signs were there all along. But that was only apparent in retrospect. Only after the fact.

I took a deep breath. "We know Lena was with the State Department's Office of the Legal Advisor and that Sienna had worked with them on a translation project. A Russian treaty. And also, that a DC detective wrote Lena's initials and the words *Were you there?* in his case files."

"Before he was brutally tortured and killed."

"Right."

"Which might or might not point to Lena again," Gunnar noted. Doubt traced through his words. "I still think that's thin."

"Since Lena had alerted her superiors about her concerns, that could give Sienna a motive to get her out of the way and then disappear. The inquiry went away after the fire. You said a Russian hacking group might be involved—"

"And Sienna was a Russian translator for the intelligence community," he acknowledged, completing my thought for me. "Do you really think Lena Rhodes was the woman on the stairs?"

"I think we need to eliminate that possibility."

A touch of silence. "And Sienna might what—still be alive and working with TalynTek? Connected with Janice Daniels? Part of her terrorist network? Is that believable? You knew her better than anyone—was she really capable of that?"

I was quiet. Any way you cut it, it was a lot to process. *We need to brush off the facts,* I thought, *until only the truth remains.*

"Hmm . . ." Gunnar evaluated my lack of a reply. "All of this," he said at last, "because of a password?"

I recalled the charred body I'd seen in the morgue, stiff with the rictus of death, curled in a fetal position as so often happens when people burn to death, their muscles contracting in the flames. I shook the macabre thought. "There's only one way to know for sure who that was in the house the night of the fire."

"Exhume the body," he said, anticipating what I was about to say.

"We have to find out the truth."

"Are you okay with that? With digging her up?"

I'm okay with finding out the truth. I'm just not sure I'm okay with what the truth might mean to me, to all of us.

"If it is Sienna," I said, "then no harm done. We search for other possibilities regarding the password. If it *isn't* Sienna in that grave, if it is Lena Rhodes—or someone else—their family deserves to know the truth, and that woman deserves a grave of her own. It's not so much about what I want; it's about what's right."

And about the truth, I thought.

"How would that work? To get permission for something like that?"

From a DOD redaction I'd done a couple of years ago, I knew that, surprisingly, there weren't really that many boxes that needed to be checked off for a disinterment to happen—just the permission of the owner of the plot, which was typically the next of kin, and the permission of the owner or operator of the cemetery, which was usually just a rubber-stamped approval if the family member had a valid reason for the disinterment.

"I'm the next of kin," I told Gunnar. "As far as I know, we just need to contact the cemetery's management to request the disinterment. I can't imagine there'll be any trouble getting the permission if we tell them it has to do with a homicide investigation. I'm not sure who owns the graveyard, though." I was thinking aloud now. "Also, we'll need to arrange for a DNA test."

"Fire degrades DNA," he said delicately. "So that means any burned soft tissue would be worthless . . ."

"Yeah," I said, the grim impact of his words settling in. "Bones and teeth can still be tested—but even then, it's hit or miss."

"Do you have a sample of Sienna's DNA that we could match it to?"

"She had an ancestral DNA test done after we were married; we both did.

We'd talked about having kids. We wanted to . . . well . . . you know, find out if there were any disorders we would've been passing along to them."

"Gotcha." He nodded. "So, I gotta say this: you do realize some of the repercussions here, don't you? I mean, if she is alive, if she is the one who hired the arsonist . . ."

"Yeah." I swallowed. "It's sinking in."

"Alright, finish your breakfast. I'll make a few calls. It's Saint Andrew's Cemetery, right? Up in DC?"

"Yes."

He stepped away to get his cell.

On autopilot, I went for some oat milk and doused my cereal with it, but as I processed everything and tried to work my way through my bowl of Tooty Fruity Curlydoos, I found myself distracted.

I was staring at my cereal, deep in thought, when the back door opened and Adira breezed into the kitchen, her skin shimmering with a sheen of sweat, a turquoise sports towel draped casually around her neck.

"Morning," she said as she dabbed sweat off her face.

"Good morning," I said. "Listen, there's something I need to tell you. It has to do with Sienna. You might want to sit down."

CHAPTER 16

FRANCIS MARION NATIONAL FOREST
THIRTY-EIGHT MILES OUTSIDE OF CHARLESTON, SOUTH CAROLINA

The stocky driver who'd told Søren to call him Bill pulled the Lexus to a stop and clicked off the ignition.

"Okay," he said in that throaty voice of his. "You can take off the hood."

Although Søren had been trying to keep track of how long they'd been driving, in the dark beneath the hood he'd honestly lost any clear sense of time. He guessed it'd been just over an hour, but that's all it was—a guess.

They'd turned onto a dirt road maybe ten minutes ago; that much he did know, based on the sound of the ground crunching beneath the tires, the abruptly bumpy ride, and the reduced speed.

Søren removed the hood, hoping that maybe he could identify a local landmark, road sign, or trail marker—anything.

However, when he peered out the window, all he could see was that they were parked near the end of a road that terminated at a forest. Clumps of scraggly Spanish moss hung drearily from the grove of trees spread across the swampy ground.

No landmarks. No signs. No houses or buildings in sight. Nothing to indicate to Søren where they were.

He placed the hood on the seat beside him as Bill exited the SUV, opened Søren's door for him, and gestured for him to join him outside.

No one else was around. No sign of the woman who'd called him last night.

Søren paused to give his Glock one final consideration, then unholstered it, laid it on the seat next to the hood, and climbed out of the Lexus.

"That's a good boy," Bill told him.

Søren let the condescending remark pass without comment, but simply took in his surroundings, with one eye on the sky.

The position of the sun overhead indicated that they'd probably been driving for closer to two hours than one, which—taking the region's winding roads into account—could get them maybe eighty miles from the diner at tops.

Of course, Bill might've just driven around in circles to confuse him and they might be much closer.

A narrow path led into the woods just to the left of the car's front left bumper, but it was faint and looked more like a game trail than a hiking path.

"It's a fifteen-minute walk from here." Bill pointed to the trail. "You first. You're the guest of honor. I'll bring up the rear. Just follow the path."

—⚬⚬⚬—

MADISON, WISCONSIN

We arrived at the Dane County Regional Airport and dropped the car off with the two federal agents that Colonel Clarke had sent to meet us. The Project Symphony prototype hadn't been cleared to go through civilian airport security yet, so this team would deliver it to the Marine Corps Base Quantico, which was located about thirty-five miles south of DC and was where the device was currently being tested and stored.

On the drive here from the cabin, I'd gotten permission from the cemetery owner for the disinterment. In fact, one of their gravedigging crews was going to be at St. Andrew's later this afternoon for a funeral and he told me that they could disinter Sienna's body at four o'clock if I wanted to do it today. I couldn't think of any good reason to wait, so, even though it might be tight getting there in time through DC traffic after we landed at Dulles, we'd set the wheels in motion.

The owner of the cemetery told me that normally they would pull the whole vault out and transfer the casket to the medical examiner's office, where they'd open it up to do an autopsy, but I informed him that I was just going to get a small DNA sample, no autopsy. "I don't want to disturb the body any more than is absolutely necessary. It doesn't need to be much. I can take care of that right there at the cemetery."

"You sure?" he pressed me. "That's pretty . . . unusual."

"I don't want to explain to someone else's family member why we disinterred their loved one and then transferred them to the ME's office without their permission. No. We'll get what we need at the cemetery and leave the rest of the remains there, at rest. If it turns out that this isn't my wife, then it'll be up to the next of kin, whoever it is, whether or not they want to do an autopsy."

The FBI Lab at Quantico had the resources to do the DNA test both promptly and accurately, a rare combination when it came to government work, and since this was a possible murder investigation involving ties to a domestic terrorist group, they were willing to prioritize it so we could get some answers ASAP.

Right now, I knew that law enforcement nationwide was swamped with testing DNA, with a backlog of more than 150,000 tests waiting to be done—some of which had been in the queue for years. Triage of the worst kind while Lady Justice waited, as Colonel Clarke had put it to me one time, "with her arms crossed, and a tear in her eye."

However, maybe we *could* get justice in this case. If the Lab was willing to bump this to the top of the docket, I wasn't about to argue with them. It was one of the only places in the country that could get us the results in twenty-four hours.

They offered to send a tech to acquire the sample, but I felt like it was something I needed to do myself, perhaps with him there to direct me. We made the arrangements for a member of their team to meet me at the grave.

So, it looked like we would have some answers by tomorrow afternoon, one way or the other.

If Sienna was alive, there were some deeply troubling implications: she might have been kidnapped, held all this time, and forced to give up the password. Yes, that was possible.

On the other hand, it *could* mean that my wife of four years was involved with the Pruninghooks Collective and had perhaps even hired the arsonist who burned another woman alive and nearly ended up killing me. Which would also mean that I hadn't really known her at all—and that would be shattering, considering she was the person I thought I'd known better than anyone else.

As we entered the airport terminal, I said softly and only half-jokingly to Adira, "Now, no sneaking weapons past security."

"I wouldn't dream of it."

"Mm-hmm."

"But then again," she added with a wink, "old habits do die hard."

Last month, Colonel Clarke had sent Gunnar to locate me and had found me at the mercy of an assassin who was trying to recruit me. Gunnar had needed a way to track me and had convinced me to inject some nanobot trackers into my leg. As far as I knew, they weren't currently active, but nanobots don't die and these did set off most metal detectors.

Because of that, as I approached the TSA agent, I forewarned him about what was likely to happen. "Your metal detector is probably going to go off when I walk through. I'm just letting you know so it doesn't surprise you. I have a . . . medical implant."

"Pacemaker?" he said tediously, as if he'd heard it all a thousand times before.

"Not quite. It's—"

"Lemme guess: knee replacement."

"Um . . ."

"Hip."

"Not quite. It's a long story."

He gave me an ungracious look and waved me toward the metal detector. Surprisingly, it did not go off.

Hmm. Interesting.

Didn't expect that.

After we'd made our way to the gate and the boarding process began, I checked my phone one last time and noticed that a text had just come through from my mom, asking me to call her as soon as possible.

She'd retired a few years ago. Since I was an only child, I had no siblings to help look in on her, so she'd moved from Cincinnati, where she'd raised me, to DC to be closer to me. These days, I typically dropped by to see her every week or so.

At sixty-four, she was quite independent, surprisingly tech savvy, and not a person to get easily rattled or given to sending urgent messages like the one staring at me now. Because of that, the text concerned me and, with her heart condition, all I could think of was that there was some type of health emergency. I wasn't about to wait until we landed to call her.

I told Adira and Gunnar to go on ahead and board the plane. "I'll be there in a minute." Then, so I could speak with my mom privately in case this was a sensitive matter, I slipped off to a nearby corner of the terminal and tapped the phone's screen to check in on her.

She picked up after just one ring.

"Hey, Mom." I tried not to sound too worried. "I saw your text. What's up? You okay?"

She cut right to the chase. "He's back, Travis. Your dad. And he wants to see me."

CHAPTER 17

Wenn hat?" A chill. "What do you mean? What are you talking about?"
"He found me," she said. "He messaged me through Krazle. He wants to meet."

Krazle was her go-to social media site. As far as I knew, they had a pretty stringent friend request policy and messaging protocols, and also did a commendable job of weeding out fake accounts and bots. So, whoever might have contacted her claiming to be Dad would've needed to jump through quite a number of hoops to set up a fake account.

But maybe it isn't fake.

Neither of us had seen my dad in nearly thirty years. However, considering how many times he'd hit her, left her with contusions or black eyes—and even broken bones—we didn't miss him at all and weren't bothered by his absence from our lives. In fact, honestly, I think we were both thankful he'd never returned.

However, I knew that even now, all these years later, as courageous as my mom was, she still got nervous when she saw men his size coming toward her in stores or on the street. And she still had sturdy locks installed on the doors to every room in her townhouse. Fear's tentacles can have a long reach, even through years. Through decades.

But, admittedly, I found it tough to believe that he was back.

"Mom, I don't think that's him. It couldn't be. Maybe it's someone claiming to be him. A scam of some kind."

"I think it's for real," she replied. "Do you want me to send you a screenshot of the message?"

"Yes."

It can't be him, can it?

But if not him, then who?

It took only a moment for her to share the screenshot with me.

The man's profile picture showed someone with a matted salt-and-pepper goatee. His gray hair was pulled back into a loose ponytail that lay slanted across his left shoulder, making me think of a rodent peering at me from its perch.

I zoomed in to study the eyes and the shape of his face, and even though I didn't want to leap to unfounded conclusions, I had to admit that it certainly did look like my dad, aged another thirty years or so from the last time I saw him.

Quickly, I scanned the message he'd sent her:

Isa, it's me, Terry. Can you believe it, after all these years, that I found you again? I wanted to reach out to you. There are so many things I need to tell you, but most of all that I'm sorry. I spent eighteen years incarcerated for something I never should have done, something I'm ashamed of and will always regret. But I'm a changed man. I paid my debt to society and now I'm trying to reconcile with the people I've hurt in the past. I would like to see you to ask for your forgiveness and to tell you about my personal Lord and Savior, Jesus Christ. Please message me back.

"It looks like him, doesn't it, Travis?" Mom said. "The picture, I mean."

"You can do amazing things with deepfakes and computer imaging these days."

"I was going to click on his profile picture," Mom informed me, "but I thought I should talk with you first."

"That was smart. Don't click on it. Don't respond to it. And I want you to change your password just to be safe."

"Do you think it's really him?"

"Hard to say, but whoever this is, you're not going to want anything to do with them." The gate agent gave me an unfriendly look and pointed authoritatively at the boarding door, directing me to hurry. "Listen," I said to my mom, "I'm flying back to DC here in a minute and I have a few things to take care of this afternoon, but I can swing by and see you tonight. Will that work?"

Mom had been close to Sienna, had liked her right from the start, and I didn't want her to needlessly worry—or get her hopes up—so I decided not to tell her about the disinterment.

"Oh, you don't need to bother coming over," she said. "I'll be alright."

"It's not a bother. Trust me. I'll look into all of this and we can talk about it tonight. What time is good?"

A small pause. "Well, seven. If that works for you. I'll make spaghetti." Another pause, but not quite as long. "Why don't you bring Adira? Tell her we'll have those spicy meatballs she likes so much." My mom, if nothing else, was persistent in trying to help me find love again.

"Sure. I'll ask her. In the meantime, like I said, don't reply to that message, delete it, and change your password. Oh, and block this user—whoever it is—from your account."

"Do you really think all of that is necessary?"

"Mom."

"Okay. I understand. I will."

The disgruntled gate agent rolled her eyes, let out an exaggerated sigh, and started to close the boarding door.

I signaled that I was coming and started toward her. "I need to go," I told my mom, "but I'll see what I can find out about this person. I'll get you some answers. And I'll see you tonight."

"With Adira."

"Goodbye, Mom."

"I love you, Travis."

"Love you too."

I hustled aboard the flight and found my seat beside Adira in the seventh row. Gunnar was seated in the back of the plane so no one could sneak up on him from behind and so he could keep an eye on everyone during the flight. There was no reason to think that any of our fellow passengers would do anything suspicious here today, but it was a habit he'd established over the years in his line of work, and once something like that gets ingrained in you, I imagined it was something that would be tough to shake.

As I buckled my seatbelt, Adira gave me a concerned look. "Is everything okay?"

I filled her in on what was going on with my mom and the Krazle message.

"That's crazy," she said. "You think it's him? That your dad is really back?"

"Could go either way." I showed her the screenshot.

"Huh," she said. "And you think this looks like him?"

"Actually, yes, it does."

"Did you do an image search online for this picture?"

"I'm about to. But . . . I just don't know."

"You don't know?"

"About the religion part in the message," I said. "It doesn't jibe at all with what he's like. I think it's probably some sort of scam."

"You don't buy it? The stuff about Jesus?"

"No." I shook my head. "If you knew my dad, you'd realize he would use anything to his advantage, to get his way. If he thought that claiming to be a born-again Christian would help him, he'd do it. If he thought that claiming to be a Buddhist monk or a Hare Krishna would do the trick, he'd go with that. Nothing he says can be trusted."

"People change, Travis."

"Not that much."

A perky flight attendant welcomed us aboard with a smile, then informed us that the boarding door was now closed and that we needed to stow our laptops and make sure our seats were upright and in the locked position.

"I don't know," Adira said to me. "I mean, I can't say anything about your dad specifically, but I think people do change. They can. I mean, take something as simple as sports."

"Sports?"

"They build character. How could that be true if people don't change?"

"That makes me think of what Heywood Campbell Broun used to say—he was a sportswriter back in the day."

"And what did he say?"

"'Sports don't build character; they reveal it,'" I told her, quoting Broun's famous dictum. "What I think he means is that playing sports brings out the real you. And I think he's right. When a game is tough, when things don't go your way, that's when you act the most like who you truly are. You're not becoming someone different in those moments, you're just becoming more transparent."

She was quiet.

"Look," I said, backpedaling a bit, "I'm just saying, if it's my father, I don't trust that *he* has changed. And whoever this person is who messaged my mom, she needs to have nothing to do with them."

"Agreed." After a moment, she added, "Did you tell her what's going on when we get to DC? About the disinterment?"

"No. I figured she had enough on her mind. I didn't want to upset her any more."

Our flight attendant dutifully went through the preflight instructions about how to survive a water landing and the importance of adjusting your own oxygen mask before assisting others. The whole "white lights lead to red lights, and red lights lead to exits" spiel.

It made me think of a comedy routine I'd heard at a club that Adira and I had gone to last week: "So I'm on this flight," the comedian said, "and the flight attendant starts giving instructions on what to do in case of a 'water landing.' The last time I checked, a 747 is not equipped with pontoons. This is not an aquatic plane. A 747 does not *land* on the water. It explodes on impact, and your widely scattered body pieces are eaten by sharks, the denizens of the deep, and you're never heard from again. You're Shark Week fodder, bro. The proper way to prepare for this event is not to stick your head between your knees—as if there were room to do that anyway. It is to scream until your throat bleeds and pray for a miracle. Or a very big mimosa."

Water landings.

Shark Week fodder.

Huh.

Not exactly the most encouraging thing to think of right now. Even though there wouldn't be any oceans beneath us on this flight. Just Lake Michigan, perhaps.

As the flight attendant finished up, Adira said to me, "You told me last week that your mom liked Sienna."

"Right off the bat," I said. "She likes you too. Oh, by the way, what are you doing for dinner tonight? Seven o'clock?"

"I'm not sure."

"She invited us over for spaghetti and meatballs."

Her eyes lit up. "Her special-recipe spicy ones?"

"Yep."

"Hmm. I do like those . . . I need to get that recipe, by the way . . . But, yeah. Sure . . . I think I can clear my schedule, which basically consisted of me at home with a box of mac 'n' cheese and a bottle of Tabasco sauce."

We began to taxi down the runway.

"So, what now?" she asked. "I mean, regarding your dad."

"As soon as we're in the air and I can use the plane's Wi-Fi, I'm going to find out who this person is who messaged my mom."

CHAPTER 18

With Bill just a few steps behind him, Søren made his way along the trail toward the clearing up ahead. An old, dilapidated barn that was being reclaimed by the forest crouched at the far end of it.

"That's it." Bill gestured. "Over there. In the barn."

They crossed the meadow.

Half of the barn's weathered roof had caved in, leaving the entire south side in shambles. At least here on the north end, it remained mostly intact. The barn's doors were wedged permanently open, at an awkward, leaning angle against the bare earth.

"Go on," Bill told him. "She's inside."

Warily, Søren strode through the doors and into the slanting shadows inhabiting the barn. At first, the air smelled of hay and musty leather from a mildew-covered saddle left to rot on the ground, but as he went in further, the stale reek of a dead animal somewhere nearby soured the air, overwhelming the other scents.

A slender, small-framed figure stood vaguely visible in the shadows draped along the far wall. The filaments of sunlight that cut through the gaps in the barn's disintegrating roof weren't able to make it that far back into the corner, so Søren couldn't make out the person's face, but based on the height and narrow shoulders, he guessed it was a woman.

Søren waited, but she said nothing. As Bill joined him in the barn's entrance, he finally addressed the figure in the shadows. "Was all of that really necessary? The car? The hood? Hiking so far out here into the forest?"

"I need to be careful," she said.

Yes, it was definitely the same voice from the phone last night.

Søren gestured toward Bill, who had now moved a few yards to his left. "You never had your man here pat me down."

"Do you have any weapons with you?"

"No. I don't. Not anymore."

"I believe you." The woman stepped forward into the barn's mottled light. Caucasian. White-haired, yet her age was difficult to determine. Could be forty. Could be sixty. Though diminutive, she looked anything but frail. As she tilted her head to the side and studied him, she exuded an air of calm confidence and he got the impression that she was used to being in charge, used to calling the shots. He also had the sense that he'd seen her somewhere, but he wasn't sure when or where. Around town? Online? On the news? As hard as he tried, he couldn't place her. Maybe just a little more light. Just a little better view of her face . . .

"It seems that you know an awful lot about me," he said. "I don't know anything about you."

She clasped her hands behind her back. "Honestly, the less you know, the better. It's for your safety, I assure you. There are powerful people looking for me. If they found out you were speaking with me, they would stop at nothing to get information from you about this conversation we're having today. I'm afraid I'll have to leave it at that."

"What should I call you?"

"Jan will do."

"Alright, Jan." Søren gestured around him. "Here I am. What do you want from me?"

Now she stepped fully into view and he saw her face clearly. Her probing, perceptive eyes. Her resolute yet caring expression.

"Out on Highway 17," she said. "Was that the first time?"

"The first time for what?"

"That you killed someone."

"I don't know what you're talking about."

"The impact. The accident last week."

"It was a dog. Maybe a deer."

"No. It was a man named Jason McAllister. He had been homeless for nearly fourteen years and was on his way to see his granddaughter for the first time. He had been drinking, but that doesn't excuse leaving him there to die."

Søren stared at her, unsure what to say. "You're making this up." He scrutinized her face as best he could in the strangled light of the barn, trying to read her expression, to see if he could discern where she was going with all this, but she remained an enigma to him. "How could you know that?"

"Why didn't you go to the police or contact your insurance company? You knew you hit someone, didn't you? But you just didn't want to admit it. And you found a way to live with yourself."

"You don't have any proof of that," he said. "Of any of this."

"We've been watching you, monitoring you. The phone you have—well, let's just say that the camera and microphone aren't necessarily off when you think they are. You used your phone's flashlight function to search for what you hit. We simply went to the location afterward and found what you did not—Jason's body. In case you're curious, he bled out. It wasn't quick. Had you continued your search, you might have found him in time, might have saved him."

Søren gulped, unsure if he should believe her. "You hacked into my phone?" he said, trying not to think about the claim she'd just made about a man dying slowly and painfully, alone in the dark, all because he hadn't been attentive at the wheel. "Who are you people?"

"Who we are doesn't matter. What does matter is what you and I can do for each other."

"And what is that, exactly?" Søren's eyes were getting used to the barn's dim light. He noted a four-foot-long plank two strides away with a cruel clutch of rusty three-inch nails sticking out of one end. It would make a formidable weapon if he needed one. "Tell me why I'm here."

"As it turns out," she said, "we both have something the other person wants."

"Oh really? And what's that? What do I have that you want?"

"It has to do with a recent breakthrough at a drug company based in Atlanta. One that I believe you are familiar with."

"Valestra Pharmaceuticals. Victor's company."

His dead wife's father, Victor Dotson, was the firm's CFO. The marriage had been short-lived—less than a year before the breast cancer stole Sadie from him. That was nearly a decade ago, yet Victor still sent him Christmas cards. It'd been a few years since they'd seen each other, but the relationship was still there. Still intact.

"Yes," Jan said. "You're in a unique position to be able to speak with Mr. Dotson about a matter that affects us all."

"And what matter is that?"

"His team has been making some very promising progress in the field of memory research and reversing cognitive decline as we age. I established a company a number of years ago that researches similar compounds. If we combine Valestra's findings with our own, I believe we can provide a drug that will benefit millions of people worldwide. Here's what I want: access to all of Valestra's files containing the composition, formula, and manufacturing details for Nectyla."

Søren looked at her curiously. "What does this matter to you? What does this drug do?"

"It helps people become smarter. Ten to fifteen percent. It's a game-changer, Søren."

"If what you're saying is true, it could be worth billions."

"Try hundreds of billions," Bill interjected.

Ah. So this was all about money.

He should have known.

Søren shook his head. "There's no way he's going to release proprietary information worth that much."

"That's why I'm sending you," Jan replied. "To persuade him. To effectuate his cooperation."

"To effectuate his cooperation?"

"Yes. Whatever that might require."

"Ah. Let me get this straight. You needed someone with access to a C-suite professional at Valestra. And, as it turns out, I have experience in . . ."

"You were trained as a police officer. You're a sharpshooter. You've studied close-quarters combat. And you're able to do what most people cannot do."

"And what is that?"

"Live with yourself after killing someone."

A pause. "And it just so happens that you stumbled upon me?"

"I've been watching quite a number of people over the last few months. You're the only one who met a very specific set of criteria." She smiled reassuringly. "But let's hope you don't need to put any of your unique skills to the test. Victor will be in Atlanta tomorrow and then DC for the weekend in anticipation of an FDA approval meeting next week. We'll want this taken care of before then."

A pause. "And if I refuse?"

"There'll be an anonymous tip. The police will find out about the hit-and-run, about Jason. They'll get the footage that your phone recorded of you searching for the body, of you calling out in the night."

Bill spoke up, a smirk evident in his patronizing tone. "If we make any of that known, you'll go to prison. Reckless vehicular homicide in South Carolina—you're looking at a decade behind bars."

Søren was really beginning to dislike that man.

And so, he made his move.

He sprang forward, snatched up the nail-quilled board, and spun to face Jan, holding it high overhead, ready to bring it down—hard—in one fatal blow, driving the nails deep into her skull.

With a fierce enough impact, it would kill her instantly. And he would swing with merciful brutality. He would end her life quickly. Bill, however, he would take his time with.

Where are these thoughts coming from? What is wrong with you?

Would you really kill them? Are you really willing to live with yourself after killing these people?

While he'd gone for the board, out of the corner of his eye, he'd seen Bill whip out a handgun, which he was now aiming at Søren's chest.

At five yards away, even if he wasn't a good shot, it was unlikely that he would miss. And Søren suspected that someone working in this man's profession was probably quite an excellent shot.

"Easy now." Jan patted the air with two calming hands. "No one needs to get hurt."

"I can take him out." Bill was eyeing down the barrel. "Just give me the word."

"That would not be a favorable outcome for any of us. Lower your gun, Rollan."

"I'm—"

"Lower your weapon. Do it."

With a scowl, he complied.

"Now," Søren said. "Put it on the ground."

When he didn't obey, Jan said, "Go on. Then kick it toward our guest."

With an aggravated sigh, Bill—or Rollan, apparently—set down his handgun, then kicked it across the barn's dirt floor toward Søren. It came to a skittering stop about two yards from his feet.

Jan studied Søren's face. "I don't think you want to kill me."

He tightened his grip on the board, calculating if he would have enough time to kill her and then get to the gun before Rollan could. "Don't presume to know what I want. What's to stop me from killing you?" He gestured toward Rollan. "From killing you both, right now?"

"If that were to happen, the authorities would receive the information regarding the origin of your car's damage and your culpability in Jason McAllister's death. It'll be delivered unless I make a call here in the next—" she checked her watch—"three minutes and forty-two seconds. So, what do you say? Shall we work together and keep our secrets secret, benefit humanity, and reshape the future, or shall we all go down in flames?"

Søren sorted through his options.

He could always resolve things with Jan and Rollan at a later time, once he was certain that the evidence would not be delivered to the cops. For now, though, convincing Victor to hand over the Nectyla files seemed like an obtainable objective.

Søren tossed the board into the darkness, where it flopped inelegantly onto a pile of straw. He picked up the gun, unloaded it, threw the ammunition into the dark recesses of the barn, then lofted the empty gun back to Rollan, who caught it with his left hand, expertly, as if he did it all the time.

"Alright," Søren said. "I'll meet with Victor. What reassurance do I have that those files of yours will never reach the authorities?"

"You have my word," Jan vowed. "They will be destroyed. I swear it to you. Two days is all I ask of you. Give me forty-eight hours and then I'll be out of your life and you won't ever hear from me again. I'm going to have you meet up with a researcher who'll be able to interpret and verify Valestra's findings. She'll know what to do with them."

Even though Søren would have liked a little more solid of a guarantee, he believed that Jan was telling him the truth. He knew that, at this point, even though trusting her was a risk, the bigger risk lay in *not* doing so. Cooperating was the most prudent way to move forward. Really, the only way for them to all get what they wanted out of this arrangement.

"Rollan will provide you with everything you need," Jan said. Then, she stepped backward again, and the shadows enveloped her, and apart from the soft rustling of footsteps on hay, it was almost like she had vanished into thin air.

A nice trick.

"C'mon," Rollan said to Søren, impatiently. "There's a lot for me to cover on the way back to the car. And I have an engagement tonight that I need to get ready for."

"And what engagement is that?" Søren asked, though he doubted that

Rollan would give him an answer. But then again, he'd been the one to bring it up, so maybe . . .

"It has to do with a visit to a place where no one wants to go, and everyone wants to leave as soon as they can."

"A graveyard?" Søren ventured.

"No. A prison. Follow me."

CHAPTER 19

By the time we landed in DC I knew two things.

First, the message that'd been sent to my mom had indeed originated in a Krazle account set up by my father just a few days earlier. Whether or not he was actually the one who'd sent it, I couldn't confirm one way or the other. But at least some of the information in the message was correct: He really had served an eighteen-year sentence in a Louisiana prison for aggravated assault and manslaughter. This was also his actual picture, closely matching the one in his prison discharge records.

The business with Jesus and his conversion and supposed quest for reconciliation—I wasn't sure about any of that, but I *was* sure that I didn't trust him.

For his part, he'd attended chapel services in prison, had even gotten baptized. So, he'd certainly ticked off the boxes to make it look like religion had changed his life.

However, he definitely didn't deserve forgiveness and I could never forgive him for what he'd done to my mom. You don't send your wife to the hospital, beating her repeatedly and breaking her arm while you're in a drunken rage, and get to just move on from there, to simply pick up where you left off. No, that wasn't the way forgiveness worked, at least not the way I understood it. Choices have consequences and his choices precluded him from having a relationship of any kind with my mom, ever again.

His Krazle profile didn't list an address so I didn't know if he was in the DC area or not, but since he was hoping to meet with Mom and her address wouldn't have been difficult to locate online for anyone motivated to do so, I thought there was a good chance he was somewhere in the city.

I wasn't about to let him meet with my mother. I needed to make that crystal clear to him, and I needed to do so in person so there would be no misunderstanding or equivocation—which meant speaking with him myself, man to man. I decided that I would message him after the disinterment and set up something for later this week. The sooner the better, to put her mind at ease and to resolve this promptly.

I'd also spent time on the flight looking up any possible connections Sienna might have had to TalynTek. And so, the second thing I knew was that there was no evidence she'd ever invested with them, consulted with them, or traveled to their headquarters in Wisconsin.

So, if she ever did, she'd done so under the radar.

After deplaning in Dulles, Gunnar caught up with Adira and me just inside the terminal. "Alright," he said. "I've got a car coming to take us to the cemetery." Then he gave me a studied look when he saw the intense expression on my face. "What is it? What's up?"

"It's my dad," I said. "He's back."

"What does that mean? Back from where?"

Only then did I realize that I'd never told Gunnar my story of growing up or given him any background on my relationship with my father.

"He used to beat my mom," I said, "back when I was a kid. I was too young to stop him, but then, one day when I was nine, I tried to. He knocked me across the kitchen and then went on to break her arm in two places. She called the police, he got out on bail, took off—fled—and neither of us have heard from him since. Until today."

"How did he contact you?"

"Someone sent a message to my mom through Krazle, claiming to be him and saying that he was sorry, that he was trying to make amends. And that he wanted to see her."

"You just said 'claiming to be him,'" Gunnar noted, "but a moment earlier, you said he was back. Is it really him? Can you confirm it either way?"

"I should say, as far as I can tell, it's him," I clarified.

None of us had checked any bags, so we made our way through the crowded terminal and headed directly to the airport's exit, rolling our carry-on luggage behind us. As we did, Adira confirmed on her phone that the Project Symphony device was on its way to Quantico.

I explained to Gunnar that my dad had spent eighteen years in prison for assault and manslaughter. "A bar fight in New Orleans got out of hand. He was just released a few days ago."

"And the week he gets out, he contacts your mom."

"That's what it looks like, yes."

He muttered a string of expletives. "What are you going to do?"

"Block him from reaching out to her again on Krazle, or any other social media platform she might be on. Then meet with him and tell him to stay away from her, and to stay away from me as well. I'm going to tell him to get on with his life, but to do so without us." Then I added, "My mom is a very trusting person, always looking for the good in other people. I'm afraid she might be willing to give him another chance unless I put a stop to it."

"And you don't want that? For her to give him a second chance?"

"He had plenty of second chances when I was a kid. He's used 'em all up."

"Gotcha. Well, alright then, when you go to meet with him, I'm coming along."

"I'm not sure that's necessary, Gunnar, I just—"

"Brother, he just got out of eighteen years' worth of lessons on how to survive, how to manipulate people, and how to hurt them in ways they don't recover from. Prisons are training grounds for violence. You know that."

I was quiet.

"Let me put it this way," Gunnar said, "as a friend, I couldn't in good conscience let you go to see him alone. Set up a meeting in a public place and I'll be nearby. He doesn't even need to know I'm there. But I *will* be, just in case things go sideways."

I appreciated the offer and even though I didn't expect that I would need his assistance, I also didn't want to argue with him at the moment. "Alright," I said. "For now, though, let me get to the cemetery and find out if my wife is really buried in that plot with her name on it. I know you said that you sent for a car, but I think I'm going to want to be by myself at the disinterment."

"Oh, sure. No problem."

I turned to Adira. "See you at my mom's, then? At seven?"

"I'll be there."

Realizing that Gunnar might perhaps feel left out, I extended the offer to him as well. "Want to join us? I'm sure my mom can put a little extra spaghetti in the pot."

"Thanks, but I've already got plans."

Adira eyed him in a friendly way. "A hot date?"

"I wish. Actually, my sister will be in town. We're gonna grab dinner. Hopefully, it'll give us a chance to iron some things out. We've been . . . Well, let me just say, her daughter, Skye, is starting to apply for colleges, and I promised to send some money their way to help with tuition, but I gotta sell my novel first. So, a number of plates in the air. I'll let you know how it goes."

As far as I knew, Gunnar had never been married and had no kids of his own. I didn't know much about his family, but as far as I did know, his sister and Skye were his only close relatives and he'd recently been making a concerted effort to be there for the two of them.

"Good luck," I said. "I hope it goes well."

"Fingers crossed."

Outside the airport, I sent for a rideshare car to take me to the cemetery. While I waited for the driver to arrive, I called the lab tech and found out he wasn't going to be able to make it after all. However, he gave me instructions on what to do and said he'd send everything I would need over to the cemetery.

"Are you sure?" I asked him.

"All good." He seemed remarkably unconcerned. "You get the samples; we'll take it from there." A pause. "You do know what you're going to need to do though, don't you?"

"Soft tissue won't be viable," I said somewhat detachedly, trying to distance myself from what we were actually talking about here. "In order to get the DNA for the sample we're going to need a tooth or a bone fragment."

"Bring us both, just to make sure."

"A bone? Really?"

"That or two teeth," he said, matter-of-factly. "Either should work. We don't want to have to go through this again."

Yeah. No kidding.

"Okay. I hear you."

As we left the airport, it soon became apparent that DC's traffic today was going to be a nightmare—no huge surprise there—and my driver told me that it looked like it'd be at least an hour's drive, which would put us at St. Andrew's at about four fifteen. "That should be okay," I said. Then I made the call letting the cemetery owner know I was on my way but running a few minutes late.

As we drove toward the graveyard, I reviewed the information that we'd uncovered about Lena and how she'd known Sienna. Most of that was still unclear, apart from briefly working together on that translation project for the State Department. It felt like I was being drawn deeper and deeper into a riddle creased with shadows. Hopefully, the disinterment would be my chance to shine the light on a few of them and move that much closer to the truth.

CHAPTER 20

THREE HOURS EARLIER
CULPEPER UNITED STATES PENITENTIARY
CULPEPER, VIRGINIA

Turo Pärnänen stood a solid six and a half feet tall and even the most hardened criminals in the prison stepped aside to give him space as he crossed the rec yard. Moses parting the sea.

He'd only been incarcerated for a few weeks, after being charged with domestic terrorism and a slew of other crimes associated with his involvement as Janice Daniels's bodyguard in the attempted dirty bomb attack in Knoxville last month. Since he was considered such a high flight risk, he'd been denied bail and was currently awaiting trial.

However, he wasn't planning to be in here long enough for that day to roll around. He had no intention of waiting for his case to make its way to the top of the judge's docket.

He was going to get out this week.

Tomorrow night, to be precise.

The noonday sun was hotter than usual, and even though there were inmates exercising, the weight lifters weren't going at it as hard-core as usual, and the basketball players were lazily shooting around rather than running up and down the court.

Gangs rule most prisons from the inside, and most gangs are not exactly havens of equality or bastions of ethnic diversity. All too often, if your own ethnicity turns on you, you'll be left for the buzzards of other gangs to pick clean.

Turo, who was white, knew enough about prison life from speaking with his dad, who'd been incarcerated for nearly three decades before he was shanked two years ago, to know that.

Less than 1% of the prison population were members of the Aryan Brotherhood, but the group was responsible for close to 20% of murders in federal penitentiaries. However, today it wasn't the Aryan Brotherhood who sent someone over to speak to Turo; it was the newer white power gang Public Enemy Number One, which was vying to take that notorious distinction away from the Aryan Brotherhood.

As Turo sat in the yard reading a fishing magazine that his boss had mailed to him, a pale, muscle-bound guy with an unruly mustache and a swastika tattoo on his forehead strode toward him.

The tattoo was obviously a prison tat, probably done with soot mixed with body wash and then needled into the skin—prison ink, or black gold, as it's sometimes called. This one was a sloppy job, maybe even done by the guy himself using a mirror, but in either case, it certainly made a point about his allegiances and what he sought to be identified as. Though bald on top of his head, his disheveled hair stuck out in defiant tufts from the back.

Five pages in the magazine that Turo held had been soaked in fentanyl. Currently, that was the method of choice for smuggling drugs into prisons. Prison officials had debated the merits of scanning in and digitizing every book or magazine that came in to make sure there weren't any pages soaked in drugs, but that took time, effort, and energy, and—in all honesty—it was a lot easier to just confiscate the reading materials that *obviously* had drug-soaked pages and let the others through.

It was a Darwinian approach: eventually, things would sort themselves out as the prisoners either smoked the pages or ingested them. A few overdoses here and there would serve as warnings for the other inmates—or at least that was the theory. Didn't always quite work out like that, but, to those making the decisions, it justified the hands-off strategy.

Everything of value in a prison becomes currency or leverage, and a magazine page that's been soaked in fentanyl can buy you many things—including the use of a contraband cell phone, which was what Turo had in mind.

But first, he needed to prove himself worthy.

After exchanging glances with his gang members, Mr. Swastika Head approached Turo, who didn't look up from the magazine, but simply kept his attention on finishing the article before him.

Just the fact that this man had been the one sent to talk to him told Turo that he was a pawn. The real leader of the group wouldn't sully himself with a job like that. And, for a moment, Turo almost felt sorry for what was about to happen to this man.

Almost.

But that wasn't enough to stop him from proceeding with what he had planned.

The man stopped and stood beside Turo, towering over the bench where he sat, invading his personal space in a not-so-subtle attempt to intimidate him. "You look like you could use a friend," he said.

"I'm a private person," Turo replied, as he carefully ripped out the pages that he knew had been soaked in fentanyl.

The guy gave him a feral grin, revealing a mouth full of meth teeth. "If you join us, we'll protect you."

"I don't need protection."

"I'd suggest you rethink that. You're fresh meat. You're gonna want friends here on the inside."

"Like I said . . ." Turo carefully folded up the pages and slipped them into his pocket. He stood and then peered down at the man, who was four inches shorter than he was, but broad-shouldered. He didn't look like someone that it would be wise to underestimate. "I'm a private person. Not currently in the market for any friends. I'd suggest you rejoin your playmates over there."

The guy sidled up closer and licked the side of his lip. "And why would I do that?"

"So I don't make an example of you." Turo kept his voice low so that the man could save face if he decided to do the smart thing and walk away. "Right now, you're the one in need of protection. As I told you, I prefer being left alone."

He narrowed his eyes at Turo. "Well, we don't always get what we want, now do we?"

Okay then, time to make the statement.

"No." Turo sighed. "No, we don't." He cracked his neck to the side and took a moment to roll the magazine up into a cone shape, then tightened it until it was firm and solid in his hand.

The man who was about to die but didn't know it yet poked Turo aggressively in the chest. "I don't think you're hearing me."

"Alright then. An example it is."

Turo moved quickly, so quickly that his adversary had no time to respond or back out of the way.

Turo stabbed the tip of the cone-shaped magazine fiercely into the man's abdomen. He doubted that it would pierce his skin, but he didn't need it to. Instead, he trusted that the impact would be forceful enough to double him over and make him gasp. That's all he needed.

And that's what he got.

Turo grabbed the man's hair, yanked his head back to wrench open his jaw and straighten out his throat, then jammed the tip of the rolled-up magazine down as hard as he could into the man's mouth and deep into his throat. A sword swallower would have been proud.

Finally, with a flattened hand, he pounded the top of the magazine down hard enough to bury it so far into the neo-Nazi's throat that only the coroner would be able to remove it.

He bashed on it two more times just for good measure.

The man stumbled backward, head forced upright toward the callous sun, clutching frantically and futilely at his mouth. He tripped over a barbell that someone had left near the weight bench and fell onto his back, smacking into the hard, trampled ground with a heavy, inelegant thud.

He made a series of unfortunate, wet strangled sounds as he lay there dying. But soon enough, the sounds quieted as he convulsed one final time and then lay still, his open eyes staring unblinkingly at the yard where a dozen men stood by motionlessly, watching his life come to an end.

If the CCTV cameras had been working, they might have caught everything. If the correctional officers had been doing their job properly, they might have stopped the murder from occurring. But at this prison, neither of those was the case. Not today. Not at all.

Later, the other prisoners in the yard would be asked what had happened, and they would, to a man, swear that they hadn't seen anything. After all, there was a code in prison. You don't snitch. Not when you're locked up with murderers and rapists and there's nowhere to run. If you talk, people will come for you, so you do what you have to do to stay alive. And that meant keeping to yourself.

"Snitches end up in ditches," as they say.

Turo knew this.

His father had spent most of his adult life in one prison or another and often shared advice with his son, who'd managed to avoid getting into trouble with the law and found a career working as a bouncer and then as a bodyguard instead.

Well, until last month.

His dad had told him a number of helpful tips that were now coming in handy.

After the murder, the COs cleared the area of prisoners, removed the body, and sent everyone to their cells. Yes, they would do an investigation into the child molester's death, but failing to solve it wouldn't cause them to lose any sleep. It wasn't that they wouldn't look for answers; it was just that they didn't see any immediate urgency to doing so. The man was dead. None of the suspects were going anywhere and no one was talking.

Turo expected that by the time they'd narrowed the suspect pool down enough to pin the crime on him, he wouldn't be in prison anymore.

Over the next few hours, things began to get back to normal again. Though no one was being allowed in the rec yard, the inmates weren't confined to their cells, and Turo shouldered his way past the other white supremacists to the one they were surrounding, their bullet-headed, one-eyed gang leader.

The man had a skull tattoo sleeve on one arm, an American flag one on the other. Turo didn't know his real name. Prison nicknames were not unusual, and he went by the name Sidewinder.

Turo produced the five sheets of fentanyl-soaked paper and offered them to him.

"All I want is to send out a text message. You get me two minutes alone with a phone and I don't make any more of your men choke to death on their own blood. I'm giving you these as a gesture of goodwill."

"Fentanyl?"

"Yes."

Sidewinder said nothing, just studied Turo with that one probing eye of his.

At last, he accepted the five pages and signaled for one of his men to get Turo what he'd asked for.

Once he had the phone, Turo sent the text to Rollan, telling him which correctional officer's family to go after, when to send the video feed of the girls, and when exactly to release the rats into the prison yard tonight.

CHAPTER 21

My driver entered the sprawling grounds of St. Andrew's Cemetery, DC's largest graveyard.

"Where exactly do you need to go?" he asked. When he spoke, he kept his voice low, as if the reduced volume was a way of revering or honoring the dead, which was a nice gesture. He was studying the sea of gravestones spreading out around us in all directions. "I've never been here before."

"Just stay right up ahead where the road forks off," I said. "We'll take it around to the other side."

"Gotcha."

I tried to mentally prepare myself for removing the teeth.

I'd visited St. Andrew's more than a dozen times in the last year and a half to pay my respects at Sienna's grave. Now, I wondered if I might've been deluded all that time. Maybe she wasn't buried there. Maybe she was alive, and I was mourning, grieving, remembering an illusion.

"You got someone here?" the driver asked me.

I'm not sure, I thought.

"Yes," I said. "I do."

"Condolences."

"Thank you."

Then we were both silent as we drove through that rolling, sloping land of the dead. I couldn't help but reflect on how brief and fleeting life is, how so many people live their lives in the desultory denial of death. I've often wondered how different our priorities would be if we woke up each day and told ourselves, "Today I might draw in my last breath. How will I live differently in light of that fact?"

It seems to me that many of the things we worry so much about wouldn't end up seeming to be such big deals, and that we would stop putting off some of the things that the dying so often regret not having done more of, like telling people how much they love them, or taking the time to marvel at a rainbow, or embracing, really embracing, the moment without letting the future or the past sneak in and steal contentment from it.

I was no Bible scholar, but some verses had gotten locked in my mind over the years, and now the cemetery brought to mind Solomon's somewhat surprising words in Ecclesiastes 7:2: "It is better to go to a house of mourning than to go to a house of feasting, for death is the destiny of everyone; the living should take this to heart."

Was it true that going to a funeral is better than going to a party? I thought it was. Because it provided percipience. Clarity. Parties offer distraction. Funerals offer perspective.

Death is a certainty. It is our destiny. And we should take that to heart.

"That it, there?" My driver's words brought me back to the moment.

He'd made his way through the graveyard and was pointing to a compact, bright-red Kubota backhoe about a hundred feet away. It had a bucket on one end and a loader on the other, with a small cab for the operator positioned between them, and was pulled up to Sienna's grave. I hadn't really considered how the gravediggers would tackle this, but it appeared that they were set to do the disinterment in a quick and efficient manner.

I wondered if my driver thought I was here to bury someone.

"Yes," I said. "That's it. You can let me off here."

He brought the car to a stop.

I knew that, although in the past people were often buried six feet under, that was almost unheard of today. The top of the outer burial container—usually a concrete vault—will only be eighteen to twenty-four inches below the surface of the ground. With that backhoe, I didn't expect that it would take them long at all to clear off the vault once they got started.

"You want me to hang around?" My driver checked his phone, where a notification had just popped up. "Otherwise, I got another rider nearby."

"I'd appreciate it if you could wait, yes. I don't think I'll be too long. I'll pay you for your time. Then I need to get to Metro PD headquarters."

After delivering the sample to them, they would transport it to the Lab at Quantico. "That work for you?"

"Sure." He was fiddling with his phone. "No problem."

Stepping out of the sedan, I used one hand to shield my eyes from the obstinate afternoon sun glaring down at me. The piercingly bright sunlight didn't seem to belong in this place of death and regret, but the dreary shadows lurking out of its reach at the far side of the taller gravestones seemed right at home here.

I approached Sienna's grave.

There was her name, etched in stone. There were the dates marking the span of her life. There was that word, *Beloved*, the one that had initiated all of this and resulted in me being here today.

But was that legacy of devotion and affection even true? I had loved her, yes, but had she ever loved me?

A gangly man dressed in faded blue jeans and an unseasonably warm long-sleeve flannel shirt ambled toward me, one leg dragging awkwardly behind the other from some past injury or birth defect. A well-loved green and yellow John Deere cap sat perched on his head.

"I'm Leon." He extended his hand for me. "You Mr. Brock?"

"Yes." I shook his hand. "Travis is fine."

"Okay." Although I expected him to ask about the grave or maybe the reason for the disinterment, he didn't start with that. Instead, he softened his voice and said, "I'm sorry for your loss, sir."

"Thank you, Leon."

Two men stood nearby, leaning against the backhoe, studying me. Their Carhartt overalls were streaked with dirt. Their grimy hands and the soil crammed beneath their fingernails gave testament to the type of work they did.

Leon held a clipboard out toward me. "I just need you to sign off on this." He was missing several teeth and it was a little hard to understand his southern Appalachian accent at first. "For the lawyers."

"Sure." I accepted the clipboard and pen that he offered, quickly scanned the release form, and then signed and dated the bottom of it. When I handed it back, he gave it a brief, cursory look, nodded once, and then gestured for his team to go ahead and get started.

One of them climbed into the seat of the backhoe while the other stepped around the far side of the grave to direct him where to begin digging.

"This should only take a couple a minutes," Leon told me. "My men, they're good. They know what they're doin'."

"Okay."

While they got to work, he supervised them for a moment, giving them a few directions and warning them to watch themselves so they didn't disturb any nearby graves with the backhoe. Then, he turned to me. "Travis, I saw you got the same last name as there on the stone. Was she . . . ?"

"She was my wife," I said, because for all I knew that was the case.

"Then it's gonna be tough, what you're here to do."

A pause. "Yeah."

"You want me to do it for you?" His tone was gentle and kind. "The sample, I mean? I done it before. A paternity case, tryin' to figure out who the daddy was, if he was really the father of a girl who was suppos' to inherit his estate. A sad business, that one."

"I'll do it," I said. "But thanks."

A nod and then he produced an evidence bag, a pair of nitrile gloves, and a pliers and handed them to me. "A cop dropped these off for ya."

"Right."

When he handed me the pliers, it suddenly hit me—really hit me—what I was here to do, what it would require to get a DNA sample from my dead wife's corpse.

If it really is your wife. It might not be Sienna at all.

I would be tearing into her body, tugging it apart.

"My boss said she was burned," Leon said.

"Yes," I said. "That's how she died."

He was quiet for a long moment. "I'm so sorry."

"Thank you."

"What I'm getting at is, then she wasn't embalmed, I'm guessin'?"

"No. That's right. She wasn't."

"Well, for sure then you're gonna wanna wear a mask. A body sours when it's in the grave. Did ya bring one?"

"No." I hadn't even thought of that. "I didn't."

"'Course some people use Vicks VapoRub. Smear a bit of it under your nose. It'll help. I got some here, or I can get a mask from my car?" He held out a small jar of VapoRub.

I was about to decline the offer but realized that he probably knew what he was talking about. "This'll be fine. The Vicks."

After removing the lid, I dipped my finger into the greasy goo, dabbed a bit of it beneath my nose, and then turned toward the grave.

He'd been thoughtful and helpful, and I felt like I wanted to be polite. "Have you been doing this for long?" I asked him.

"I'm a vault man for life. Ever since I dropped outta school. I was sixteen, I guess. A long time."

I pegged him to be in his late fifties. That certainly was a long time to be digging graves and lowering bodies into them. I wondered how many people he'd buried. If he did it full-time, I anticipated that it could be upwards of several hundred people every year. For forty years. That would mean he'd likely buried more than ten thousand people. The population of a small Midwestern town.

He went on, "Grew up in Carter County, Tennessee. Right up there near Roan Mountain. Got started there."

I was no expert on funerals, but having redacted dozens of files involving military funerals of covert ops men and women who'd given their country the ultimate sacrifice, I probably knew more than most people did—and more than I particularly wanted to know—about cemeteries and the burying business.

After a visitation or funeral service, the casket is brought to a cemetery, where it's lowered into a vault. After the casket has been placed in there, a cover is attached to the vault, sealing the casket inside. In most cases, that outer burial container is concrete, although there are some instances where people go for a cheaper option—steel or even plastic.

To lift a concrete vault with the casket in it, you'd be talking about lifting close to three thousand pounds.

And so, the backhoe.

Then we were both quiet again, the only sound the motor's steady murmuring chug as the gravedigging crew worked nearby.

Talking seemed to help my nerves, so I said to Leon, "Does your team have to do this often? Disinterments, I mean?"

"Not a lot. No. But it happens. Sometimes if a family member forgot somethun in the casket. Family heirlooms, necklaces, even wallets. It's amazing what people will put into caskets and then regret later that they did." He shrugged. "But you can't blame 'em. They got a lot on their minds, you know?"

"Yes."

I heard the harsh scraping of the backhoe's curved blade as it met the cover of the concrete vault that encased the casket. Getting closer.

Vault covers are sealed in place with a type of thick adhesive called butyl, which will hold extremely well—except when it gets hot. In some cases, with some disinterments, the gravediggers use hair dryers along the edge of the vault's cover to get the butyl to melt more quickly and give way.

I saw a battery-operated hair dryer lying on the ground, waiting near the backhoe, but wasn't sure that today, with it being as hot as it was outside, it would be necessary. I pointed to it. "That for the butyl?"

Leon gave me a curious look. "Howdya know 'bout that?"

"I've read a bit about the process," I said simply, and then for some reason added, "I read a lot."

"Oh," he said. "I wouldn't know 'bout that."

"What do you mean?"

"I ain't educated. Don't read too good. I just know howta do two things: dig and love."

"Dig and love?"

"I dig the graves. I stay out of the way of them people who're mourning. I never let 'em see me smoke or nuthun. I respect 'em, you know? And I always say a proper prayer for 'em when I finish up the buryin'. Folks don't always respect people like me—gravediggers and vault men. But I figure, love 'em all and let God sort it out in the end. Dig and love."

"I'll bet it's tough being present, nearby, at all those funerals."

A nod. "The diggin' part. Not the lovin' part. It's hard to lose someone. The mourners, they ain't thinkin' straight half the time. I seen people cry at funerals and then just burst out laughin' in the same breath. I seen 'em drop teddy bears and wedding rings and even car keys into the grave. You never can tell. Can't get too bent outta shape if they act out. I just remember, someday that's gonna be me there by the grave, and then, one day soon enough, it's gonna be me down there inside it."

The gravediggers finished their work with the backhoe and brought out shovels and hand trowels to dig around the side of the vault so they could get the cover off and give me access to the casket.

"You a person of faith?" Leon asked me.

"Not as faithful as I should be. But yes, I'd say I am."

"And you believe in Jesus?"

A slight pause. "Yes."

"You ever wonder," Leon said, "'bout that verse in the Good Book that talks about God wipin' every tear away from our eyes up in heaven?"

"Revelation 21:4."

A head tilt. "You a preacher?"

"No." I shook my head. "I just have a . . . well, a reasonably good memory. I read it once and . . . What were you saying about it?"

"Whaddya think it means?"

"I suppose that in heaven there's an end to sadness and suffering, no more crying or pain or mourning. No more tears."

"Right. But think about it—you're in heaven and you're still cryin'? I mean, why would it say that? Why would you wake up from the dead and rise from the grave with tears still in your eyes? It seems to be sayin' that some people will be weepin' when they get there to heaven and meet the Lord. Why would you bring them tears with you into paradise? Shouldn't they be reserved for the place down below, with all the weepin' and grindin' of teeth?"

I'd never really thought about that before. "Maybe it's just a figure of speech."

"Sure. Yeah." He shrugged again, as I was noticing he was apt to do. "But what if it's not? What if it means what it says, right there in black and white? I think it might be sayin' that some people suffer so much in this life—from loss or grief or loneliness or sadness—that their tears well over into eternity. But not for long. Not for forever. They'll only cry them tears long enough for 'em to be wiped away by a loving hand."

I thought of the verse in Hebrews where it mentions that Jesus endured the cross for the joy set before him. Maybe that's what it was referring to: the joy of welcoming his beloved home, of wiping the tears from their eyes.

I looked at Leon, at his weathered, tender face. "Have *you* ever thought about becoming a preacher?"

He tapped his head. "Don't have the smarts for it. Told ya, I ain't educated. I just dig and love. That's plenty enough for me."

To dig and love. This man had found his calling and then embraced it, two things that all too many people are never able to do. His calling was both simple and profound. Maybe being around the dead all the time and being reminded so often of the brevity and fragility of life will do that to you—give you insight that the rest of us don't have.

"How's it comin'?" Leon asked the gravediggers, who were hard at work shoveling away the dirt from around the edge of the vault's cover.

"'Bout done," one of the men called through a mouthful of chewing tobacco. "Almost there."

I watched them finish edging the dirt away from the vault containing the remains of the woman who'd been buried beneath my wife's headstone. Watched them wrap a chain around it and use the backhoe to lift it up.

Watched them use that hair dryer along the vault's cover to melt the butyl, then, with the cover removed and slid aside, I watched them lower the vault back to the ground.

"You ready for this, Travis?" Leon asked me.

I don't know, I thought.

"Yes," I said.

Was this her?

Was this Sienna?

The casket lay there inside the vault, waiting.

Carrying the pliers and the evidence bag, I drew in a deep breath and approached the grave.

CHAPTER 22

I knelt in the upturned soil, the closed casket before me.

All I needed to do was open it, get the sample, and escape from this land of those who had perished, those who were gone.

This woman is dead and always will be. You're not hurting anyone; you're not desecrating anyone. You're just trying to uncover the truth.

Though I tried to prepare myself for what I was about to do. I found that I still wasn't ready for it. How is it even possible to get in the right frame of mind for a moment like this?

I placed my hand on the cold casket and thoughts of Sienna overwhelmed me—the way she'd smile in the morning and the sunlight would glance across her dimples, the way she'd get a glimmer in her eye when I messed up trying to say a word in a language she was trying to teach me, the way she'd rub her temples after a long day's work and then sigh and look my way and ask for a hug.

The DNA would tell us this woman's identity. It would give context to my memories and tell me if they were all rooted in the truth or infested with lies and disguises.

I found myself trying to sort through a storm of emotions: grief and a deep sense of loss, yes, of course, but also dread and the growing suspicion that things might not be at all what they seemed to be, that the woman here before me might very well not be my wife, and I thought of all of the implications that revelation would carry about Sienna's actions, motives, and whereabouts—not to mention her true identity, because if she was involved with TalynTek and the Pruninghooks Collective, she might be part of their terrorist network, in bed with the people I was now trying to take down and her whole life might've been a charade.

I reached for the casket's clasp but found that my hand was unsteady and shaky. I felt a bit dizzy and only then realized that I'd been holding my breath.

I let it out.

Took another deep breath.

In.

And out.

Breathe. Just breathe.

It was a half-couch casket, so once I unhooked the latch, I would be able to raise the top half of the lid and get what I came here for.

Finally, remembering the nitrile gloves, I slipped them on, undid the clasp holding the casket shut, and opened the lid.

Even with the VapoRub beneath my nose, I was aware of the sudden, acrid odor of death seeping out of the casket. It seemed to curl around me and clutch at me, trying to overwhelm me, as if to say, *"You do not belong here. You are not one of the dead. You have no business being in this place."*

I directed my attention away from the mephitic smell to the body.

There she was. A woman who had been alive, who had walked the earth, who had succumbed to the flames. Now, all that was left of her time on earth was a burned corpse.

The spray cloth inside of most caskets is white, but it's not going to remain that way. It fades, pales, turns yellowish. And even though Sienna had not been embalmed—or maybe because of that fact—that's what had happened here over the last eighteen months.

I guess I'd been hoping that I might somehow be able to discern her identity just by looking at her again, but that wasn't going to happen. There was, of course, no way to know yet if this was truly Sienna.

I clutched the pliers.

I wasn't sure if there was a specific way to do this, but I finally decided to just go for it. I carefully pried two teeth loose and tugged them free. I deposited them in the evidence bag.

A bone sample?

Maybe.

Gently, I took hold of her hand, thinking that I might retrieve a finger, but the tendons were still tough and stringy. It struck me that this was the hand I used to hold as we walked beside each other, hiking to waterfalls on the weekends.

Perhaps it was.

Or perhaps not.

Breathe. Breathe.

I let go of her hand.

The teeth would have to do.

When I'd finished, I sealed up the samples, closed the casket, and latched it shut.

And stood.

Breathe.

Leon and his men were all watching me.

"I guess that's it." I didn't know if there was anything I should be doing—pausing, reflecting, genuflecting, making the sign of the cross. I felt awkward and out of my element, uncertain what should come next.

"Can I tell you somethun?" Leon said.

"Sure." I stepped back from the grave.

"You know anything 'bout cremation?"

"A little," I said. "The body is placed in the retort, then, when it's been cremated, what's left is moved to a processor that, well, it grinds everything up, turns it to powder until all you have is the cremains."

He nodded as if he wasn't surprised that I knew that. "Mostly right. Yep. 'Cept not *everything* turns to powder. Everything that's metal remains. The knee and hip replacements, metal rods, tooth fillings, charred pacemakers and the melted batteries that go with 'em. All of that—that's what's left when the rest of you is gone. We gotta sort 'em out of the cremains."

I wasn't sure why he was telling me this. "Okay," I said, thinking of the nanobots in my system, wondering if that's what would be left of me one day when someone might sift through my cremains.

He went on. "I knew a good ol' boy down in Tennessee. He collected all them leftovers from the processor. Buried 'em all in his garden every weekend rather than just throw 'em away. There's no laws about it, about what you're suppos' to do with what's left. So instead of tossin' 'em in the trash, he took 'em to his yard and planted dotted blazing stars and black-eyed Susans over 'em and prayed over 'em. Believed that if them things was part of a person when they was alive, that they should be treated with respect after they were dead."

I could only imagine what the neighbors might think if they caught sight of that man burying those scorched implants and metal rods, saying a short prayer over them before tenderly planting flowers above them.

And what the cops might think if they ever came upon that garden.

"Instead a throwin' those pieces away," Leon said, "he wanted to give 'em a proper burial. You see?"

"I see," I said, though I wasn't quite sure I did.

"I buried that man myself, right before movin' up here," Leon said. "He was a good ol' boy for sure." I didn't know if Leon expected a reply and I still wasn't clear on why he'd told me his story, so I waited and finally he added, "All I'm sayin' is treat them parts of her with respect."

"I understand."

Then I thanked him for helping me today and I gestured to his crew. "Thank you. All of you."

Nods all around.

Taking the bagged teeth with me, I wiped the Vicks off my face and returned to the rideshare driver.

His eyes were on the evidence bag, and I had the impression that he wasn't too thrilled about the idea of me bringing it along in his car.

"It's okay," I said. "I'll call someone else if you need me to."

He debated that for a moment, then said, "Naw, go on. Get in. You said police headquarters?"

"Yes."

As we drove away, I looked back and saw Leon standing over the open grave, quietly, his hat in his hands and his head bowed. I had the sense that he was praying. Perhaps that this woman's tears had been—or would be— wiped away by a loving hand.

But maybe he wasn't praying for her.

Maybe he was praying for me.

CHAPTER 23

Turo Pärnänen's dad had been in and out of prison for decades and the last time they spoke, two years ago, he'd shared a few life lessons with his son. "I'm gonna tell you the three things that you need to know to survive in prison. Just in case you ever decide to follow in my footsteps."

"Okay."

They were in the prison's visiting room—that was a bit of a misnomer, since they were actually in two different rooms, seated in soundproof booths, separated by a reinforced, bulletproof glass barrier. They had to use phone receivers to hear each other.

"Go ahead," Turo said.

His dad held up one finger. "First, never trust an act of kindness. Favors are just another type of weapon that's going to eventually be wielded against you. Never become indebted to anyone. Remember: If someone's kind to you, they want something. And the day will come soon enough when they'll want to collect."

Turo nodded.

His dad added another finger. "Second, you're not gonna get out on your own. Almost never happens. And most of the time the help's gonna come from the inside, from a compromised CO. So, you need to remember that there are two ways to entice someone to do something they don't want to do. Two, and only two."

"And what are those?" Turo asked, curious about how to compromise a correctional officer.

"Bribe them or extort them."

"Talk me through that."

His father tapped the glass authoritatively. "You figure out what the person wants most and promise to give it to them, or you find out what they value most and threaten to take it away from them. So, the first thing you start looking for if you ever get locked up isn't a way out; it's a CO you can own."

"One who either wants to obtain something good or avoid something bad."

"In a nutshell, yes. What's he afraid to lose? What does he treasure more than anything else? Everybody covets something they don't have and desires to hold onto something that they do. What does he want to keep or what does he want to obtain? When you find out either of those two things, you're on your way to freedom. Bribe or extort. Every guard can be either bought off or threatened enough to get them to comply."

"What's number three?" Turo asked.

His dad's gaze went past Turo, to the wall behind him, and then beyond it, perhaps toward a future he was hoping for. "Always be looking for a way out. Never get used to being on the inside. Never accept things as they are. Sure, it'll make you crazy, but it'll also give you hope. And without hope no one makes it. The thought of getting out gives you something to live for."

So, putting his dad's words of advice into practice from the first day he arrived here at Culpeper, Turo had looked for a guard who valued something.

And he'd found one.

The wedding ring was a clue, enough to start with.

This is how it went down earlier in the day.

The correctional officer, a paunchy Hispanic man in his late thirties, was leading him toward the communal shower, not the most inviting place to visit when you're locked up.

"I see your ring," Turo said. "Married, huh?"

The guard, whose name was Pablo Serra, remained silent.

"I mean, you can't always tell these days," Turo went on. "Not everyone who's married wears a ring and some single people do. So it's just not the sure indicator that it once was."

More silence.

But Turo trusted that the next thing he had to say would elicit a response.

"Lemme guess," he said. "Yep. Married. And kids—yeah . . . I'll bet you have kids. So, let's see . . . daughters or sons . . . I'll say daughters, I think, maybe . . . Yes. Daughters. Two of 'em. How am I doing?"

Pablo paused there in the hallway and edged his hand toward the radio he wore. At a prison with this level of security, the COs who have direct access to the prisoners don't carry guns. That would just be asking for trouble. The firearms would be much more valuable to the inmates than the lives of the COs toting them around. Things wouldn't turn out too well for them if the prisoners became armed.

"What did you say?" Pablo asked.

Turo nodded. "Two girls. I knew it. Let me see . . . I'm just gonna take a shot in the dark here. Names . . . names . . . names . . . Angela and Gracie? Those are sweet names, Pablo. And you must be so proud of them—Angela with her violin lessons, and little Gracie with her kindergarten Little Lambs ballet class. From what I hear, she's been improving a lot recently. What do you think?"

"How did you—?"

"Something someone taught me years ago: everything is for sale, and it's for sale wherever you go, even in here. I'd hate for something bad to happen to either of those lovely girls of yours, especially with a little one on the way too. Do you think it's going to be a little baby brother or sister to Angela and Gracie?"

Pablo's eyes turned to coals. A slow burn. "You're threatening my family," he seethed through clenched teeth. "Doing that to a federal correctional officer can get a nickel added to your sentence."

"I haven't been sentenced yet. And it sounds like right now you're the one threatening me. Oh, and if anything were to happen to me, the person who gave me this information will act on it in a way that would not serve the best interests of your wife and children."

A long pause. "What do you want from me?"

"Put me on custodial duty in the morning. Seven o'clock. Send me out to clean the yard. And I'm going to need a set of civilian clothes."

A longer pause this time. "How am I supposed to get them in here?"

"Wear 'em under your clothes tomorrow when you come in to work. Just make sure they're big enough for me. You're not quite my size."

"That's it?"

"There might be something else. I'll let you know in the morning. Then, I'll be out of your hair for good."

Pablo's voice was strained. "And then, after all this is done, your people, they'll leave me and my family alone?"

"I swear it to you on my father's grave. What happens to them is entirely up to you from now on. You help me, you help them. You make trouble for me, we make trouble for them. You understand this, right?"

"Yes."

"I'm glad we've come to an understanding." Turo patted Pablo on the shoulder. "Now, can you find me a private place to shower? I'm feeling a bit modest and not really sure I want any company."

CHAPTER 24

B y the time I'd dropped off the DNA samples and then washed up, changed clothes, and unpacked at home, it was time to leave for my mom's townhouse for the spaghetti-and-meatballs dinner with her and Adira.

As I drove across town, I wondered what the DNA test would reveal.

Did I want it to be Sienna's body there in that grave? That wasn't a particularly easy question to answer. On the one hand, yes. I had buried her, grieved for her, met Adira . . . I was finally ready to find a center to my life again after all this time, to move past the fire and the loss and the scars. If Sienna were alive, it would devastate all of that and it would likely mean that she was not, and had never been, the woman I thought she was.

On the other hand, is it ever right to wish someone dead? And if she was alive, then I could find her again, discover what'd happened with the arsonist and the woman in the fire—the reasons behind it all.

I was caught between wanting closure and wanting answers. And somewhere in between those options was the desire to move forward with Adira. The desire to delve, without fear, without regret, as deeply into that relationship as this season in our lives would allow us to do.

Mom's place was on the first floor of a duplex in a nondescript red brick townhouse, the fifth in a row of eight other nondescript red brick townhouses.

I parked across the street and texted Adira that I was here.

She replied via her car's Bluetooth that she was on her way, had gotten caught in traffic, but was just a few minutes out.

Since she was so close, I figured I'd just wait for her and we could go into Mom's place together.

This would be the second time Adira had been over to see my mom. They'd seemed to genuinely like each other during the first visit last week. Adira had told me once, rather vaguely, that she wasn't close to her parents, hadn't been in a while, so it was nice to see that she was hitting it off with my mom, at least.

As I was thinking of that, she drove up in her breezy, cherry-red Mazda MX-5, the car of her dreams, which she'd finally allowed herself to buy, just this month. In the past, she'd always chosen cars that were inconspicuous, functional, and dutiful, but with the shift in her responsibilities from the Red Team to working with me and Gunnar for Colonel Clarke, she'd splurged. And I had to admit, that zippy little car sure was fun to drive.

She emerged and we walked together across the street toward Mom's townhouse.

"How'd it go at the cemetery?" she asked me.

"It wasn't easy," I admitted. "Getting the samples . . . But I managed. They should be at the Lab at Quantico by now. We should know tomorrow afternoon if it's Sienna."

"And if it isn't," Adira said, "potentially the woman's true identity."

"Yes."

As we made it to the sidewalk she asked, "You doing alright with all this?"

"I'm doing okay. Yeah . . . Oh, I met a vault man named Leon who had all of these insights about life, about death. Interesting guy. He—"

"Wait. A vault man?"

"That's what he called himself. Headed up a team of gravediggers. Anyway, he pointed out that if God wipes away our tears in heaven, it means some people will arrive there with tears still in their eyes, that maybe their lives were so full of pain that some of their tears spilled over into paradise."

She was quiet. "Interesting."

We approached the porch.

"What have you been up to all afternoon?" I asked her.

"Looking for past connections between TalynTek and other companies that Janice Daniels had her fingers in. I was hoping to uncover any connection to other Pruninghooks Collective members. I know it's ground we've been over already; I just wanted to see if I could dig up anything new."

"And?"

"There actually might be something. One of Janice's business ventures was a nonprofit NGO called the Davita Group. They offer humanitarian aid and medical care to displaced people groups and refugees around the world—particularly in war-torn areas of Africa. Their biggest presence is in Uganda with refugees from South Sudan. They're still operating."

I led her up the steps, onto Mom's porch. "What caught your eye about them?"

"Some of the same people are still in charge," Adira said, "even though Janice is on the run. I think the UN is hesitant to take action against them because of the humanitarian work they're doing."

"Huh. Interesting. Sounds like it's worth taking a closer look at them."

I had a key to my mom's place in case of emergencies, but tonight I knocked instead of using it, and almost immediately she answered the door.

She wore a silk lavender blouse and almost looked like she was dressed for a night out at an elegant restaurant rather than simply a night of spaghetti and meatballs here at her place.

"You look amazing," Adira said. "I love that blouse."

A tiny blush. "Thank you."

"Hey, Mom." I gave her a light hug and she welcomed us inside.

My mom had a fair complexion, silver-laced hair, and stood slightly hunched, as if the cares and concerns of all of the middle school students she'd taught English to over her thirty-year career had conspired together and were still weighing her down—their test stress and acne embarrassment and the broken hearts that she'd helped them navigate. Letdowns and highlights and that pendulum swing of emotions that preteens and young teens experience so often and so easily. Though all of that might've taken a toll on her, I couldn't recall her ever complaining about it.

She was the kind of teacher kids hope they'll get, and then, later, are thankful that they had.

Mom opted for a homey, country-esque vibe with the prerequisite hand-stitched quilt draped over the couch beneath a *Home is where the heart is* plaque. Nearby hung an embroidered poem she'd written and then stitched:

Dance as if all your chains were gone.
Laugh as if you were a child again.
Sing as if you were part of the song.
Dream as if your wings were real.
Live as if today really mattered
*   and you'll find that it does.*

She wasn't really a big fan of knickknacks, but she *was* a big fan of books and probably had at least two thousand of them crammed into her place on bookshelves or stacked on busy end tables and overturned orange crates. She was a voracious reader, and I sometimes wondered how many of them she'd made her way through. Probably a good chunk of them. Maybe all of them.

Tonight, the air in the townhouse was laced with the distinctive dusty smell of an old bookstore mixed with the freshly-baked-bread scent of an Italian eatery—an odd, and yet surprisingly inviting, combination.

I was hesitant to say anything about the disinterment, so I decided to put that off, at least until tomorrow when we would have an answer regarding the DNA test. However, I was anxious to tell her what I'd found out about Dad. "Mom, I really need to talk to you about the Krazle message. About Dad."

"We eat first," she said definitively, and I'd learned long ago that it would be useless to argue with her, so I didn't even try.

"Okay."

"Come on." She guided us past the dining room table, which was nestled up against—surprise, surprise—a packed bookshelf, to the kitchen. An overly large cooking island sat plopped in the middle of it with a jumble of unmatched pots and pans dangling somewhat precariously from ceiling hooks above it. The island swallowed up most of the space in the kitchen, actually.

We helped her shuttle the food to the table, which was set with her finest dinnerware.

After saying grace, she dished out the spaghetti. She'd outdone herself tonight, with warm French bread and a heaping garden salad gracing the table to complement the meatballs, sauce, and noodles.

My mom didn't drink—something I totally understood after being married to an alcoholic for nearly a decade—so tonight we had craft root beer instead of wine or beer.

As we made casual conversation, the message from my dad was still on my mind and I was distracted and caught up in my thoughts when she said brightly, "And how are you two doing?"

"How are we . . . ?" I said, trying to catch hold of what she and Adira might have been talking about.

"Doing. Yes." She smiled and looked from me to Adira and then back to me. "The two of you."

"Oh." Adira reached out and gently clasped my hand. "We're great," she said.

I smiled. "Yes. Things are great."

Mom offered us a warm smile. "Well, then. That's good news, isn't it?"

Adira let go of my hand. "The meatballs are amazing."

"Spicy enough for you?"

"Just right."

—⁓—

Adira kept an eye on Travis as the three of them worked their way through the homemade meal.

Obviously, she didn't know Isabella especially well, but she'd enjoyed her company and her quirkiness the first time she was here and thought it was sweet how concerned she was that Travis find a good match.

It was curious that Isabella was asking about how the two of them were doing because lately she'd been wondering the same thing herself. A few weeks ago, things had started out with promise, but had since stalled out. She didn't want to pressure Travis into taking their relationship where he didn't want to go, but she also wanted clarity so she could have realistic expectations. That wasn't too much to ask, was it?

He seemed to be hinting around the edges that he wasn't ready to take things any further. For instance, he'd walked past her open door at the cabin in Wisconsin. But it was also possible that he hadn't even noticed that it'd been left open for him.

That was *possible*, yes, but she thought she'd heard him pausing by the door, and doing so long enough to get her hopes up.

Then he went off to bed.

He needed space, she got that, but she wasn't used to a slow pace in a relationship. Usually, it was all fast and furious and breathless—most often all at the same time. And then, there'd be an inevitable, messy breakup and nothing to show for it.

Maybe that's why she was still single and had only a trail of broken hearts and carcassed dreams to show for thirty-four years of life.

Okay, that was too depressing to think about.

His wife might still be alive.

Another depressing thought.

Enough of that. "Isabella," she said, "I—"

"Isa, please."

"Isa—Travis tells me you're a bit of a conspiracy theorist."

A slight gleam in her eyes. "Does he now?"

"I wasn't . . . ," Travis said, obviously fumbling for how to reply. "I mean, in my defense, I don't think I ever . . . not in those exact words."

"Mm-hmm," Isa said. "Well, you never know what dark secrets the government is hiding that they don't want us to know about. I suppose . . . except for my son. He knows all the secrets we're not allowed in on . . . But still, we know the truth is out there."

The nod to the *X-Files* tagline wasn't lost on Adira. "For instance?" she said.

"UFOs. They're real, aren't they, Travis?"

"All I can tell you," he said somewhat evasively, "is that what the government actually knows about Unexplained Aerial Phenomena would shock you."

"What does that *mean*, though?" Isa asked. "That they have proof? Flying saucers? Grays? That Bob Lazar was telling the truth about Area 51? I mean, take all of the technological advancements we suddenly made after Roswell, for instance. How did we do that without relying on extraterrestrial technology?"

He shook his head. "There are some secrets I'm just not allowed to share."

"Okay, if aliens are off limits, what about secret organizations that control the world?"

"There are no secret organizations controlling the world," he said.

"Really? What about the Bilderberg Group or the Trilateral Commission? Or the Illuminati's connection with the NSA?"

"Mom, there's no connection whatsoever between the Illuminati and NSA."

"Uh-huh. Well, if that's true, then why, when you search online for *Illuminati* spelled backward, does it take you to the NSA site?"

"I think that's an urban legend."

Isa folded her arms. "Try it and see what happens."

Adira drew out her phone and did a quick search. A moment later she found her mouth gaping open. "Holy crap." She turned the phone to show Travis the website she'd pulled up. "Check it out."

It was the official NSA site.

"Told you," Isa said, sounding quite satisfied.

"That's . . ." he began. "That doesn't mean anything."

"The Illuminati." Adira shook her head. "Huh . . . Who knew? I never would have guessed. Maybe we never landed on the moon either. What do you think about that, Isa?"

"It *is* a long way away," she agreed. "And in the photo, the American flag is blowing in a breeze. I mean, a breeze on the moon? In an airless vacuum? Seriously, that's not even possible, that's—"

"Okay, okay." Travis held up his hands to stop this conversation, most likely worried that it was about to lead down a very long, very deep rabbit hole. "We actually did land on the moon. We don't have stealth fighters and Kevlar because of reverse-engineering alien technology from Roswell. Mesas are not the fossilized trunks of ancient trees the size of mountains. Energy drinks are not a gateway drug to Satanism. And dinosaur bones were not planted by the devil in order to turn everyone into atheists. Oh, and the earth is not flat."

Isa spoke up, "I'm not saying that I think the earth is *flat*, but I *do* think that NASA is withholding some key facts about all that they know and who they truly are."

"Who they truly are?"

"The word *nasa* in Hebrew means 'deceiver.' How do you explain *that*?"

"That is literally the easiest thing to check. Just google it, Mom. *Nasa* means 'to lift or carry,' *nasha* means 'to deceive.' Do you really think that choosing a word meaning 'to deceive' was President Eisenhower's goal in 1958 when NASA was founded? Or that they would decide 'to deceive' us into thinking the moon landing was real or the earth is round by choosing an acronym that means 'to help'?"

Isa folded her arms. "What better way to deceive people than to *almost* deceive them?"

"Mom, that doesn't even make sense."

Adira noticed Isa wink at her, and she winked back.

"So," Isa said definitively. "Anyone interested in dessert?"

CHAPTER 25

FIVE YEARS AGO

It was precisely 8:30 a.m. when the package arrived at Maia Odongo's house. She hadn't slept well the night before, not after reading the news right before going to bed about her grant funding being pulled. And not with that enigmatic business card with the phone number on it, urging her to call Janice, whoever Janice might be, after the package arrived.

Distracted and confused, she'd gotten only a few hours of agitated sleep. Now, as she was getting breakfast ready, the doorbell rang.

A bit unsure, she went to the door and saw a delivery van parked beside her car in the driveway.

She opened the door a sliver.

"Hello, ma'am," the delivery man said with an amiable smile. "I'm looking for Maia Odongo?"

He wasn't wearing an official-looking company shirt, and she was slightly suspicious, but she *was* expecting a package. "I'm Dr. Odongo," she said, but still didn't open the door all the way.

"Well then, it looks like this is for you." He held out a padded envelope mailer. "I was told to ask if you had a DVD player."

"A DVD player?" Maia shook her head. "No, I don't, actually."

"In that case, I'll be right back." He sauntered easily to his truck and returned a moment later with a box.

"What's this?" she asked.

"Looks like a DVD player," he said in his friendly manner, pointing to the labeling.

"I mean, what is going on? With all of this?"

"All I can tell you is that I was instructed to ask if you had a DVD player and then to deliver this to you if you didn't." She eased the door open, and he handed both the envelope and the box to her. "It seems like somebody really wants you to watch a DVD," he added. "I mean, if that's what's in the envelope. I'm just guessing."

She accepted them. "Right."

"I just need you to sign for those."

"Do you know who sent these things?"

"Nope." He shrugged. "Dunno. I'm just the delivery guy."

She scribbled her name across the electronic device he held out for her to sign, then he left the box and the envelope with her and, whistling, headed to his van, leaving her standing there with the two packages in her hands.

After he drove off, she closed and locked the door, then ripped open the envelope, and, sure enough, there was a DVD inside it with a sticky note that read simply, *Play me.*

It didn't take her long to get the DVD player set up and connected to her television. She opened the tray, carefully positioned the DVD on it, and then pressed Play.

The tray slid back into the unit and, a moment later, the TV screen lit up and a woman's face appeared. Maia recognized her immediately: Janice Daniels, one of the richest women and also most well-known philanthropists in the world.

She stood on a veranda overlooking a sweeping mountain vista. Maia wasn't sure, but she guessed it might be the southern Pyrenees.

"Hello, Dr. Odongo. My name is Janice Daniels and I have a proposition for you. By now I'm sure you've heard the news that your grant funding at the Grainger Institute was not renewed. I would like you to come and work for one of the companies that I've had the privilege of establishing—the Davita Group. We fund and perform humanitarian work and medical research around the world. I'm aware of your research on stopping neurofibrillary tangles from forming and I believe that you could be an invaluable member of my research team in Kampala. There's an excellent memory care facility nearby where your father would be very well provided for. And of course, you would pay nothing for his care. That would all be provided in the compensation package that I am pleased to be offering you. Take whatever a pharmaceutical firm or university might pay you for your annual salary and add a zero after it. That will be your salary for the first six months."

Maia paused the video. This was so bizarre. How had Janice Daniels—*the* Janice Daniels—found out about her? How did she know about her situation at work or anything at all concerning her dad's condition? It was a little creepy and unsettling.

And to return to Uganda? That was something she hadn't even considered in years.

Maybe Janice is on the board of the Grainger Institute? Or maybe . . . What if she was behind the grant not being renewed? No. That was ridiculous . . .

But it would explain a few things.

Maia pressed play again.

"However, I don't think it's just about the money for you. I believe it's about the results, about the impact, about helping others. I wanted to send you a video to show you some of what my team of biochemists and neuroscientists have discovered before we speak on the phone. Watch the video. Then call me."

The video shifted to a lab where researchers in white lab coats were working beside terrariums and mazes filled with curious, scurrying lab rats.

A male voice-over came on, as if this were a documentary:

"By injecting FGF17 found in cerebrospinal fluid from younger mice into older mice, our researchers have found that it can actually reverse memory loss. Certain cells, called oligodendrocytes, protect the 'wiring' in the brain by providing a protective myelin sheath. By increasing the FGF17, it might be possible to help restore oligodendrocyte function and assist memory in dementia patients. Extracting the CSF is quite time-consuming and it's very difficult to obtain sufficient amounts of it, but it does reduce cell quiescence, especially in the hippocampus."

Maia knew, of course, that the hippocampus was vital to memory and that the gene-encoded protein FGF17 found in spinal fluid decreases with age. The possibility that a drug could be developed that could increase FGF17 in patients experiencing cognitive decline was intriguing, and it appeared that Daniels's team was working on a synthetic drug that could do precisely that.

Huh.

Although Maia had read a little about this line of research in the existing literature, she'd never heard of the Davita Group—which would actually make sense if they were working in conjunction with a pharmaceutical firm. For financial reasons, propriety information in this field is closely guarded, and if these researchers were on the brink of any sort of breakthrough, they would certainly keep it as quiet as possible for as long as possible.

Neural pathways are much more resilient and adaptive than scientists used to think, even just a decade ago. Recent research has proven that the brain can—and does—form new neural pathways. Neuroplasticity. As it turns out, if you approach things in the right way, you really *can* teach an old dog new tricks.

That finding was one of the motivators for her research.

In the brains of Alzheimer's patients, you typically find neurofibrillary tangles and deposits of beta-amyloids. Some researchers were trying to stop the tangles from occurring, while others were trying to mitigate their effects or bypass them, so to speak. Still others were searching for ways of attacking the amyloids. If you could reverse the buildup of the enzyme HDAC-2, you could help with synaptic plasticity and improve memory function.

No one knew exactly why histone deacetylation impaired memory, but by increasing histone acetylation through HDAC inhibitors, it was possible to improve memory to a statistically significant degree.

Recent advances in Alzheimer's research had focused on giving intravenous treatments of monoclonal antibodies that target the buildup of those amyloids. Reducing the amyloids helps cognitive function and slows the rate of cognitive decline, but it also weakens blood vessels and can cause bleeding in the brain, especially if the patient is taking blood thinners.

The silver bullet would be finding a drug that could sort out the neurofibrillary tangles and reduce the buildup of amyloids, all without causing internal bleeding. That's what Maia had been trying to do, but the CSF injection idea added a whole new variable to the equation.

What if there was a drug, or a cocktail of drugs, that could increase FGF17, as well as reduce the neurofibrillary tangles while also attacking the buildup of beta-amyloids?

That could be revolutionary.

Her heart began to race as she considered the possibilities.

She finished the video and researched a little about the Davita Group and discovered that, though they were based in Kampala, they were also working at a refugee settlement located along the South Sudanese border.

When she finished, Maia called the number on the business card and waited anxiously while it rang.

"Bonjour?" A man's voice with a French accent. "May I help you?"

"The business card, it said to call this number. I'm Dr. Maia Odongo. I'm trying to reach Janice Daniels. Can you tell her that I watched the video?"

"Ah. She's been expecting your call," the man said. "Connecting you now . . ."

A short wait, and then, "Hello, Dr. Odongo. This is Janice."

"Ms. Daniels, I'm not really sure what's going on here, but before we talk about anything else, let me ask you a question."

"Please."

"I need to know—were you behind my grant funding being revoked at the Grainger Institute?"

"I won't lie to you. I did have something to do with that."

"But why?" Maia said with a mixture of anger and exasperation. "I don't understand."

"I thought it would be the best way to recruit you. Over the years I've found that people tend to remain in their jobs as long as there is security. Once that's removed, they're more apt to make decisions that result in a dramatic change in their lives. My team in Uganda has made some extraordinary gains in a country that has . . . well, broader research parameters and less red tape to cut through than the United States does."

"Less oversight."

"More freedom. Using our findings and your own research, I believe that we might be on the verge of a substantial breakthrough in reversing cognitive decline associated with dementia, one which would also benefit the general population in cognitive processing. I'm sure you have many questions. But let me assure you, I can provide the funding you need, and I believe you can provide the vision and expertise my team has been lacking. I'm confident that we can help each other here—and also benefit millions of people around the world."

"And my father?"

"Yes, I know it must be a challenge dealing with his condition. I realize that a move might be difficult for him at first, but what if you were to tell him that you were taking him back to Uganda, where he did his initial primate studies? The place where his two children were born?"

"How do you know about that? How do you know so much about us?"

"Research. I like to know all that I can about the people I'm working with. Dr. Odongo, I have a private jet fueled and ready to take the two of you to our facility in Kampala. We'll have caregivers onboard the whole time. He'll be safe, I assure you. And maybe, seeing the land he loved so much, he will be happy."

Maia looked at the chair where her father spent so many of his waking hours, the chair that had become his home, with that deep, sad indentation slumped into it, and she considered how best to provide for him in his final, faltering days.

You could potentially help millions of others just like him if you could bring the right drug to the marketplace.

On her own that would be impossible, but maybe with Janice Daniels's team, it was something she could actually accomplish.

"Send me the research you have," she said. "Let me look it over and I'll make a decision."

"Of course."

"When would you want me to start?"

"As soon as possible. Don't let finances be a concern. We'll pay for your move."

Within minutes of hanging up, the files were waiting in Maia's email inbox.

And all day, in between checking in on the home nurse and her father, Star Girl studied the research that Janice Daniels's team had been doing in regard to the cerebrospinal fluid extraction.

That evening, by the time she was done reading, she had made her decision.

After helping her father get ready for bed, she told him that she'd found a way for him to go back to the land he had always wanted to return to.

"Uganda," he said immediately, with a clarity and interest she rarely saw in his eyes. Despite the place his dementia had taken him to, it could not steal from him his first love. At least not completely.

"Yes. You're going to see the gorillas again."

Then, she called the number on the business card once again.

"I'm in," she told Janice. "Send the jet."

CHAPTER 26

After we'd had our fill of Mom's homemade apple pie dolloped with generous scoops of vanilla bean ice cream, Adira offered to do the dishes, but Mom scoffed at the offer. "I'll take care of them, sweetie. There's no need for you to—"

"No," Adira assured her. "It's okay. It'll give you two a chance to talk. Please. Let me help."

Then, before my mom could argue, Adira was gone, carrying the stack of dishes to the kitchen, and I was left alone in the dining room with Mom and her books.

The townhouse wasn't extraordinarily spacious, but the shelves and stacks of books everywhere created a bit of a sound baffling and, when we lowered our voices, I was confident that Adira wouldn't overhear what we were saying.

"Okay," I said to my mom. "Let me tell you what I know about Dad. The information in the Krazle message that was sent to you appears to be accurate. I think it's genuine, that it really is from him."

Then I told her about the manslaughter conviction.

"Oh." Her expression was difficult to read. "I see."

"Listen, Mom. You know what kind of person he is. You lived with him for a decade. He hasn't changed. He's the same man who sent you to the hospital, the same—"

"But how do you know he hasn't changed?" She gave me a careful look. "And besides, shouldn't we give people a second chance?"

Okay, that was weird. That was almost exactly the same question Gunnar had asked me earlier, when we were at the airport.

"You gave him second chance after second chance," I said. "I don't even know how many times. He used them all up. You can't meet up with him. It's not safe."

"I've decided to forgive him."

"What?"

"Travis, I've been thinking about it ever since I got the message. The Bible is very clear. How many times does it say we should forgive someone? Seventy times seven. And Jesus spoke of forgiving those who repent seven times *in a day*. He said if we don't forgive others that God won't forgive us."

"Sure, I know, but I don't think Jesus was talking about giving an abusive husband more opportunities to physically assault you. Besides, in some cases, doesn't it almost seem like forgiveness might actually perpetuate evil, might even encourage it?"

"What?" She eyed me quizzically. "How could it do that?"

"If you just freely offer forgiveness to everyone who wrongs you—no matter what—doesn't that sort of diminish the wrong? *'Oh, you stole my candy bar; I forgive you.' 'Oh, you physically assaulted my son and broke my arm; I forgive you.'*"

"It seems that by saying that"—her tone had become more stiff, more pointed—"you're making light of the importance of forgiveness."

"I'm not trying to make light of it. I'm just trying to understand it. After all, if you'll just be forgiven for a crime after the fact, what's holding you back from committing it—especially if you see a good reason to take that action beforehand? Wouldn't withholding forgiveness for certain crimes help to curtail them? Are there some things that would be better left unforgiven?"

From the kitchen, I heard the clink and clatter of dishes as Adira fed them into the dishwasher.

"I don't know," my mom told me. "I just . . ."

"Dad beat you, Mom. He demeaned you. I don't even know what other kind of abuse you might have suffered at his hands. Are you really saying that we should forgive people for things like that? I was only a kid, but I remember how he sent you to the hospital, and how he would bring you flowers afterward and tell you how much he loved you and that he was sorry and that he would never do it again. So contrite. So convincing. Until it happened again. And that's what's happening here, now."

She was quiet for a moment. "I think I should speak with him."

"No, Mom. I'll do it."

"What are you going to tell him?"

"That he needs to leave you alone," I said. "That he needs to leave us both alone. That his relationship with us is over." Then I added, "I could never forgive him for what he did to you."

"Travis, it's not your decision to make. It's mine. Your relationship with him is up to you; mine is up to me."

I opened my mouth to say something, but couldn't figure out exactly what that might be.

I certainly wanted what was best for her; of course I did. And I would do anything to protect her. But I couldn't be responsible for what went on in her heart.

"It's my choice," she said. "To see him. To forgive him."

"Yes, okay," I said. "Listen, we can talk about it more after I've met with him. Then we can—"

Adira poked her head in. "How are we doing in here? All good?"

Mom and I exchanged a look, then she said, "We're fine." She smiled. "Aren't we, Travis?"

"Yes," I said. "All good."

"Wonderful," Adira chimed. "I have to take off in a bit. I'll say goodbye in a minute, but I need to slip off to the washroom first."

She disappeared down the hallway and I said to my mom, "I should probably be heading out too. I'll let you know what Dad says when I meet with him. We can discuss this more then."

"When do you think you'll be speaking with him?"

"Not sure. As soon as possible. Hopefully in the next week. Get this resolved."

"Okay." I tried to read her tone, but it was flat and unaffected. I hoped I hadn't offended her, with my words about forgiveness, but I also hoped that maybe I'd given her something to think about.

When Adira returned, we said goodbye to my mom, and then the two of us stepped outside into the cool spring night, an enchanting twilit land of trilling crickets and blooming lilies by the curb and barbecue on the grill and laughing kids returning home for the night on their bikes. The sun was holding court low in the sky, throwing long, affable shadows down the street.

"How'd it go?" Adira asked. "Talking with your mom about your dad being back?"

"She wants to forgive him."

"Oh. Well then, I guess that's her choice. That's up to her."

"That's what she said. C'mon, I'll walk you to your car."

When we were about halfway there, she said, "I've got a riddle for you."

"What's that?"

"What's the one English word that starts with what we desire most and ends with what we want to avoid becoming?"

"*Soapscum*," I said.

"I think that's two words, actually."

"It should be one."

"And how is soap the thing we desire most?"

"True," I acknowledged. "*Soapscum* is just the first thing that came to mind. Let's see, you said it starts with what we desire most and ends with what we want to avoid becoming?"

"Yes."

"*Happydead*."

She raised an eyebrow at me. "Really?"

"Yep."

"I'm afraid *happydead* is not a word either."

"It should be."

"Oh, and why is that?"

"Because then I would've solved your riddle."

"Aha."

"Hmm," I said. "It's a good riddle, though. I'll need to think about it."

We arrived at her Mazda, and she pulled out her keys but didn't unlock it yet. "Wanna come over for a nightcap?" she said.

"I should probably cruise home and get some sleep."

"Just one drink, Duck Boy," she said, using the rather unfortunate spy name she'd given me last month, inspired by my middle name, Donald.

I returned the favor, using the only marginally better spy name based on her middle name of Chrysanthemum: "Flower Girl, I—"

"My place is close to your condo. It's not like you'd be going out of the way."

She was mostly right. Her apartment was *mostly* on the way.

"Just one drink," she said innocently.

"Yeah. Okay. Just one."

—ɷ—

Søren Beck had put everything in his life on hold for the next forty-eight hours.

For now, his priorities had shifted. He'd called Victor Dotson earlier in the day and told him that he was going to be in Atlanta tomorrow. "I thought that since it's been a while," he'd said, "maybe we could grab lunch."

Victor had said sure, that would be nice, that it'd been too long since they'd seen each other. "One o'clock?"

"Perfect."

"Meet me at my office."

So, tonight Søren was driving to Atlanta.

His plan for tomorrow: Meet up with Victor for lunch and obtain access to the Nectyla files that Jan was interested in. Then, in the evening, connect with the neuroscientist Jan had told him about so she could analyze the Valestra research.

Now, during the drive, Søren planned out what he would say to his dead wife's father tomorrow.

And what he would do if the man was not willing to comply with the demands of this woman who was blackmailing him, this woman who had the video footage of him searching for answers after the Incident, this woman calling herself Jan.

CHAPTER 27

Adira had a place in Charlotte, but Colonel Clarke's budget for our team was providing her with an apartment in Pentagon City until she could make a more permanent arrangement.

When I parked and got out of my car, she was standing outside her car door. Rather than inviting me in to her place, however, she said, "Let's walk to the park. It's not far. There's a swing."

"The nightcap?"

"That can wait. I want you to push me first. Just for a bit. I'm up for a little time travel."

"Time travel?"

"I'll explain when we get there."

Walking beside her toward the park felt comfortable and natural, as if being side-by-side with her was exactly where I was meant to be. I'm not a huge believer in fate or destiny—I fall much more on the free will side of things—but this night did feel like it was destined, in some way, to occur.

We crossed the soccer field toward the playground and swings.

"Travis," she said. "What about me do you find disgusting?"

"What kind of a question is that? I don't think there's anything disgusting about you."

"My ears aren't quite even."

"Didn't notice."

"I have a birthmark on my neck."

"It's cute."

"I sweat a lot."

"So do I."

"My pinky finger got broken when I was a little girl and it never healed right. See how it's kinda crooked?"

We paused and she held up her hand beneath the park's amber streetlight to show me her finger.

"How'd you break it?"

"I fell out of the tree house my dad made for me."

"And you broke your pinky finger? That was it?"

"I landed funny."

"I'd say so." I tapped the air introspectively. "That'll be your kidnap thing, then."

"My kidnap thing?"

"Yeah. If you ever get kidnapped and you're in danger and they're doing a proof-of-life photo, hold up that crooked pinky finger and it'll be a secret message for me to come find you."

"Otherwise you wouldn't?"

"No, I would, of course, but—"

"And just being kidnapped by itself doesn't count as being in danger?"

"I'm just saying."

"Okay, okay. Pinky promise?" She held up her crooked pinky finger, and I had to sort of twist mine to the side to make it work, but I didn't mind.

She smiled at me, then gave me a quick, flirty kiss and glided toward the swing set. Even though the rest of the park was designed with children in mind, these swings were more adult-sized, and she nested herself onto the seat of one of them, and then said in a gleeful, playful voice, "Push me!"

I positioned myself behind her and gently pushed her forward.

"Now," I said. "You told me that you were up for some time travel. What was that about? I don't see any time travel machines nearby."

"Oh, I'm on one."

I gave her another push. "How's that?"

"Time is not a constant. Gravity and speed affect it, right?"

"Relativity," I said. "Einstein. Sure."

She pumped her legs to gain more height. "So that means that someone on a roller coaster is aging at a different rate than those waiting in line."

"Hmm. I suppose it does."

I pushed her again.

"Are they aging faster or slower?" she asked.

"I'd need to check on that, but that's probably why it seems to take so long waiting in line and why the ride seems to go so fast."

"I'm not quite sure about that." She pumped her legs once more and ascended into the night. "But right now, I'm higher than you are and I'm traveling faster than you are. I'm aging at a different rate."

"I guess you are."

With each swing, she was reaching her legs higher and higher, until she was almost parallel to the ground at the vertex of her pendulum.

"But," she said, "gravity and speed aren't the only things that affect time."

"Really?" I had to step out of the way and then sneak in at just the right moment to give her another push to propel her forward, adding an extra little zip of velocity to her swing. "What else does?"

"Perception. When you're in love, a day away from your lover can seem like an eternity, and a day together can seem like an entire lifetime."

Another push. "I can't argue with that."

"So, that begs one question."

"What's that?"

She swung forward one last time and, when she was at the zenith of her flight path, she leaned backward, tucked her legs up, and did a smooth, effortless backflip off the swing, sticking the landing.

Okay, that was just plain impressive.

She held up her arms in a gymnast's pose, and I was reminded of the fact that she'd been serious about gymnastics all the way through high school.

"Nicely done." I gave her a couple of congratulatory claps. "I've never seen anyone exit a time machine so gracefully before."

"Thank you. So, now that we're together on the ground . . ."

"Yes?"

"We're traveling through the universe simultaneously, aging at the same rate."

"I guess so."

She walked toward me. "The closer we are, in space and time, the more in sync with each other we become."

"Is that how it works?"

"It's called *science*."

"Oh, I see. And what was the question you were referring to earlier? The one that was begging to be asked?"

There were only a few feet between us. "What does time feel like when you're with me?"

Her face was partially illuminated by a nearby streetlamp. I looked deeply into her eyes. "It feels like I'm traveling through a moment that I never want to leave."

"That," she said softly, "was a good answer." She took my hand and drew me toward her. "It's been a long time, hasn't it?"

"A long time?"

"Since you've been with a woman."

"Ever since I lost Sienna."

"And see now . . ." She kept her eyes locked on mine. "If this were a scene in Gunnar's novel, I would throw myself at you and tonight we would find solace in each other's arms."

"But then," I said, "the next day, to keep the story going, there'd be a new conflict introduced: a misunderstanding, a regret, a rift, maybe a rival."

"Or maybe one of us might get killed."

"Yes. True."

"I wouldn't want any of that," she said. "The misunderstanding, the regret, the rift, the rival, or especially not the getting killed part."

"Especially not that. Tends to ruin the entire day."

"But what comes before it might be interesting. The love scene."

And before I could reply, she leaned closer and we kissed there beside her time machine and we were in sync with each other and with gravity and with speed and, most importantly, with time, here inside the moment unfolding before us, holding us tenderly, oh so tenderly in its hands.

Just as things were getting interesting, my phone vibrated with an incoming text.

And so did hers.

I had notifications turned off, so there weren't too many people who'd be able to get through. I took a step back and we each looked at our cells.

When we compared them, we saw that we had identical texts from Colonel Clarke: **Meet at 8 tomorrow morning. My office. It has to do with Popovic.**

Ivan Popovic was a Russian oligarch who'd made his billions in the energy sector. He'd worked with Janice Daniels on a scheme to manipulate the US energy market by controlling our natural gas reserves, and they were well on their way to doing so before we discovered the plan last month and shut it down. Afterward, the federal government had seized his domestic assets and frozen his holdings and investments on the international front—at least the ones we were aware of. He was on the run and, from what we knew, hadn't been back in the States since his plan with Janice fell apart.

He had his fingers in illegal drugs and counterfeit drug smuggling, human trafficking, and providing arms shipments to radical jihadists. If something or someone wasn't supposed to cross a border, Ivan Popovic was probably helping to make it happen.

Finding him might be the ticket to finding Janice.

Adira and I put our phones away and tried to recapture the magic of the moment, but it was gone. The interruption had stolen the mood away.

I placed a tender hand against her cheek. "I think we need to say good night."

She took my hand in hers and I thought she might tell me no, or invite me back to her place for that nightcap, but she didn't. "Okay," she said instead. "Pick me up for work in the morning?"

"Sure."

Then, even though the thought of driving across DC just to sleep by myself in my own place, in my own lonely bed was not especially inviting, I did that very thing.

As I was leaving, I glanced back once in the rearview mirror to see if Adira was watching me.

And she was.

And so, I drove away from her and her time machine in the park before any of those things that so often happen to couples in love stories could happen to us: the misunderstanding, the regret, the rift, the rival, or one of us ending up dead.

CHAPTER 28

When I got home, swing sets and time travel and spending moments with those we care about were on my mind.

And the DNA test.

And Popovic.

And my dad.

Plenty to keep me occupied.

I realized that in the rush to get from the airport to the cemetery to home and then to my mom's, I'd neglected to send a message to my dad asking him to meet with me.

Gunnar had been pretty adamant about being present when we met, so I sent him a text first, asking if he had any free time tomorrow afternoon. Our team didn't really work on the clock, but more *around* the clock, so our hours and schedule were all over the map. Grabbing lunch or coffee off-site in the middle of the day wasn't anything unusual.

I wasn't sure how long the eight o'clock meeting with Clarke would last, but assuming that we would be tied up there for the morning and maybe even into the early afternoon, I figured the earliest I could sneak away to see my dad would be after one thirty.

Coffee at 2 tomorrow at Aurora's with my dad? I wrote to Gunnar. Aurora's Bakery and Coffeehouse was a popular restaurant just a ten-minute walk from the Pentagon and it would be convenient, even if we didn't have much time to sneak away.

I went to get ready for bed and by the time I had changed clothes, Gunnar had texted back: **Roger that. See you at 8 at Clarke's office.**

Okay, the time had officially come to reach out to my father, the convicted killer and felon.

Because of my job, I'm not on social media at all, so I didn't have a Krazle account. I didn't want to start a conversation with him using Mom's account, so that option was out. After kicking around some possibilities, I finally just went ahead and set up a ghost profile with a generic emoji picture and a fake job as a data analyst so I could access the function to send a message to his profile, figuring I could always delete the account later.

I left the notifications on so I would immediately see any Krazle messages he might send back to me. I typed up a first draft, but after reading through it and seeing how terse and aggressive it sounded, I deleted it.

Another draft failed—too familiar and collegial and not at all the tone I was shooting for.

At last, I opted for a blunt but honest note that would leave little room for misunderstanding: **Mom shared your Krazle message with me. I don't want you to contact her again. I'll meet with you, though. Are you in the DC area?**

With a touch of anxiety and a bite of anger that'd been festering for nearly three decades, I tapped enter, sent the message, and then went to wash up.

A few minutes later, while I was brushing my teeth, the phone vibrated on the counter.

A message from my dad: **I'm here in DC. When and where do you want to meet? I can't wait to see you!**

I typed: **2 tomorrow afternoon. At Aurora's Coffeehouse.**

Normally, I would've been more flexible, more understanding, given a number of options or meeting times, but I wasn't in the mood for that.

He wasn't my friend.

He wasn't my pal.

He was the man who'd physically assaulted my mother, mocked and ridiculed me when I was a boy, and then later killed a man in Louisiana. He wasn't a good man.

He was my dad.

—✳—

From across the street, the observer watched the lights in Travis Brock's bedroom flick off.

Things were not quite going according to plan, but that could all be resolved soon enough. Tomorrow night at this time, they would have the Project Symphony prototype and they would be able to use it to hack into the air-gapped computers of any of the United States' three-letter federal agencies they desired.

But before that, there was still one place to visit yet tonight.

The home of the enigmatic former Ranger, Gunnar Bane.

—◊◊—

FRIDAY, MAY 27
CULPEPER, VIRGINIA
2:05 A.M.

The sky above the forest glimmered with starlight. This far out in the country, there wasn't much light pollution and, to a trained eye, dozens of constellations would have been visible.

The man with the slingshot pulled off the road and parked his car along the gravel-strewn shoulder, about a half mile from the prison's two perimeter fences. He would walk from here.

He exited the car, went to the trunk, retrieved the burlap sack with the two dead animals inside it, and faced the prison.

A wooded plot of land with an old farmhouse on it lay between him and the prison's outer perimeter fence. The forest provided plenty of cover and the warden had wanted to clear-cut the land in case a prisoner escaped so that it would be easier to recapture him. However, the owner of the land made the case that if the prison did its job and kept the prisoners behind its walls, there shouldn't ever be anyone to recapture, so the argument was moot.

The man was refusing to sell his land to the government, and an eminent domain case was working its way through the courts, but until things were resolved, the woods remained intact and provided just enough cover for the man with the slingshot to ease away from his car and melt into the night.

Given the proximity to the prison, he suspected that the landowner wouldn't be too amenable to a stranger crossing his property at this time of night, so he kept to the shadows and edged, under cover of the night, closer to the prison.

The closer he came to the walls, the brighter the prison's harsh security lights appeared, glaring out against the night and stealing away the view of the stars overhead. A tower in each corner of the diamond-shaped facility housed a correctional officer with a high-powered rifle to stop any would-be escapees from getting over the fence.

The man knew this.

Yes, this, and more.

An intransigent coil of savagely barbed razor wire ran along the top of both the inner and outer fences that encircled the prison. There was maybe twenty feet between the two fences, enough room to trap someone trying to escape.

The man, whose actual name was Rollan but who'd told Søren Beck to call him Bill, came to the edge of the forest and positioned himself out of the guard's line of sight behind a towering oak tree.

From here, it was less than thirty yards to the fence, which rose nearly twenty feet into the air. He'd practiced this shot dozens of times earlier today with bags of sand the same weight as the dead rats, so he felt comfortable about his ability to launch them over the two fences and into the prison yard where Turo would be cleaning up, five hours from now.

As attentive as the guards might be, they would not be keeping an eye out for dark rodents flying over the fence from the nearby forest, but rather would be studying the fences for prisoners trying to ascend them from the other direction, hoping to find freedom in the night.

Rollan loosened the cord cinched around the top of the sack, tipped it upside down, and dumped out the two dead rats onto the dewy grass beside his feet.

The stitches on their white bellies were still fresh. He'd sewn the animals shut himself, after drowning them, gutting them, and hiding the items Turo would be needing inside.

He needed to get at least one of them over. He had two just in case one of them didn't make it.

These days, so many drones were flying over prison rec yards to drop in contraband, drugs, guns, and cell phones that some prisons now had mesh coverings over their outdoor yards. Others had installed signal jammers to disrupt the GPS and radio signals that guide drones and UAVs. Still others had resorted to hiring local duck hunters to shoot down the drones—that was not by any means common, but it had actually happened at a prison in Wisconsin.

No mesh here, so that was a plus. Rollan had considered using a drone to drop the items in, but this prison had recently implemented frequency-blocking technology.

Janice had also considered having him throw a football over the fence, but Turo informed them that the guards were wise to that technique and had taken to checking sports equipment for contraband.

But they wouldn't likely check dead rats. No. Instead, they would have an inmate dispose of the animals, which is why Turo had arranged to work on the custodial crew tomorrow morning.

And which is what led to the two healthy-sized Norway rats now lying on the grass.

Taking the slingshot in hand, Rollan positioned the first rodent's carcass in the leather strap, then raised it, carefully aimed it above the fence, and pulled back on the slingshot. Then he released it, launching the rat into the air.

However, he didn't correctly calculate the trajectory and the rat hit the top of the inner fence and dropped unceremoniously in between the two fences without making it all the way into the yard.

Rollan swore.

Okay. One more attempt.

He angled this rat higher into the air, drew the slingshot's band even further back, and let go, arcing the rat high into the night.

It sailed through the air and landed almost exactly where he'd hoped it would, near the weight benches and barbells just behind the basketball court.

No sirens. No alarms. No shouting. Just a sleepy prison with a couple of dead rats now inside it—one in the yard, and one between its two perimeter fences.

Taking the burlap sack and the slingshot with him, Rollan slipped back into the forest to return to his car. Keeping the cell phone's screen shielded with his body so the light wouldn't be visible to any guards or to the old farmer who owned the land, he texted his employer: **It's done. He'll have it in the morning. Is everything else in place?**

It took only a moment to receive the reply: **Yes. Be at Pablo Serra's home by 5 p.m. Take your gun and the zip ties but be prudent. Don't get carried away. We need the three of them alive.**

Understood, he typed, slightly reluctantly.

He would need more ammo, of course, since Søren had tossed his bullets earlier into the hay at the old barn in South Carolina. But yes, he would be there at the Serra household by five o'clock this evening and he would be armed.

And he would bring three sets of zip ties—one for Pablo's wife and one for each of his two young daughters.

And he would be ready in case there was any convincing that needed to occur when Pablo saw the footage of his family tied up there in the basement.

...TOP*IBAWAUPIJAWAWER
DWEIRBOAPRSTRMPOOT
DFII
POEI
ERPFJ
DPFI
IIAJUP
*LKMERO
DMU*GFP
V;NAVPO
PIGUHER
JG;GANNE;
ANRV;OOAN
VPOAEWIJVGG
RV*AKJERVPO
IREJBEO
CJE

AW
DWEIRPOW
DFIIJAS;OOJ
POEIFJAPWOIE
ERPFJR3POIAP
DPFIJAWEPEOO3
IIAJWEPEOFIJA
*LKMEROFIFIJ
DMW*GFPOOAWGP
V;NAVPOAWEEHFA
PIGUHERE;FNHR
DOKBJPO
COAUERHR
C;OAJVPOJ;
NFDEIOJOIJAE
*UUHVHNAOIU;
HERVUNEV;OZI
JVPOOEARJHVV
POOEARJHVV
PORI
AW;OFIJAW*O
WEIRPOWIURT
DFIIJAZ;OOJA
POEIFJAPWOIE
*RPFJR3POIAP
PFIJAWEPEOO3
IIAJWEPEOFI
LKMERO
DMW*GF
V;NAVPOAWEEHFA
PIGUHERF;FNSI
DOKBJPOKBIABO
COAUERHRFC
C;OAJVPOJJHSZ
FDEIOJOI;API
*UUHVHNAOIUSH
HERVUNEV;OZI;PD
VPOOEAR
V*AKJERVPOAIJE
CREJBEOIJVPO
JERGBOOAIJE
RVBEOAWIEJGE
DOEARJHVVOAE
DRIIHQWPOIFFH
W;OFIJAW;OFIJAWAE
WEIRBOWIURTBUROE
FI
*OB
*R
*PF
IA
PFIJAWEPEOOI*
TAIWEREOEIJAWE

PART III

In the Wind

Wound channels.
A lobster named Beth.
Esmé's empty stroller.
Two assailants instead of one. –

CHAPTER 29

My dreams chased me back through time to the surgeries following the fire.

The skin grafts. The searing pain from the nurses scrubbing my open burns to keep them clean and free from infection. All of it came back to me, except this time, in my dreams, the nurses were shaving the skin off me in great sweeping loops and snaking curls of moist flesh, like the skin of an apple being peeled. And there before me, the gruesome, sloping coil of tissue landed with a wet plop on the floor.

It didn't just happen once but cycled through at least three times.

Finally, I awakened with a start, the images from the dreams still vivid in my mind. Still troubling me. And from past experience, I feared that they might not soon go away. The truth was, I'd always been a vivid dreamer and I had an uncanny knack for being able to remember my dreams—or at least the most troubling parts of them—long after I'd awakened.

And today, that fact did not bring me much encouragement.

When you got right down to it, skin grafting was a bit of a horror show. And with recent advances in gene splicing and DNA manipulation, the island of Dr. Moreau might not lie as far offshore in the fantastical realms as it did when H. G. Wells visited it in his imagination and penned the tale, back in 1896.

When we play God, there are always unintended consequences that make it clear we're not up to the task.

He creates life in his own image.

We create monsters in ours.

Two messages waited for me on my phone.

First, Adira: she'd meet me at the Pentagon at eight and I didn't need to worry about picking her up.

Second, Colonel Clarke: he wanted us to hit the shooting range, so we should dress out for it.

Most people, even those who worked at the Pentagon, didn't know where the Pentagon Force Protection Agency's underground armory is. Recently, in order to provide a convenient way for the law enforcement and military members of our community to stay current in their marksmanship qualifications, the powers that be had shuffled some offices around, knocked out a few non-weight-bearing walls, and installed a twenty-five-yard indoor shooting range just down the hall from the armory.

Clarke was a bit of a gun nut and had even proposed to his wife at a shooting range.

Some people take coffee breaks.

He took breaks of a different kind.

I'd been down there once with Adira, but it ought to be interesting to visit with the colonel as well.

After my house burned down eighteen months ago, there were a number of tense and painfully unproductive meetings with my insurance company. They were suspicious of the circumstances regarding how the fire had started and they didn't want to get scammed, didn't want to give me a payout if I was the one responsible for it.

Navigating through those months was one of the most difficult challenges of my life. I was wracked with grief from losing Sienna, in constant crippling pain from the burns that covered more than a third of my body, and meeting with endless dead ends in the futile search for the identity of the arsonist. The implication from the insurance claims fraud investigator that I might be the one behind the fire hadn't helped anything.

In the end, however, the insurance company did settle, and I was able to purchase another place—a condo this time—with the money.

In truth, the smaller floor plan wasn't really a problem since it was just me living here and, at the time I moved in, I didn't have any prospects of or even the intention of finding someone else to share my life with.

Although I've never had as many books as my mother did, I admittedly did have my share of them. Then, I lost everything in the fire. Every page of every volume turned to ash.

I'd slowly been replacing my library with new volumes. Fewer, to be sure, but this way I could focus on acquiring some of my favorites.

Old-school reader that I am, I've never warmed up to using e-readers. I've tried them, given them a fair shot, but in the end, I always find myself gravitating back again to the printed page. Hardback, if possible. First editions when available.

Not that I was a literary snob.

Just a bit of a bibliophile.

That was all.

Honestly.

Although I had rather Spartan living quarters, I didn't mind. I'd never been much of a hoarder—more of a purger. And the fire did a world-class job of helping me with that.

So now, apart from a simple stand-up desk that a friend of mine had made for me, and a few pieces of used, functional furniture, I didn't own much in the furnishings department. I guess, in a way, the fire had helped me both purge and prioritize. And expensive furniture just didn't make the cut.

As I got ready to leave, I was distracted thinking about the case, the forthcoming DNA test results, and the prospect of speaking with my dad this afternoon.

Also, last night's little visit to Adira's time machine came to mind.

It sure was tough to shake thoughts of her.

Why fight it? You don't need to set those thoughts aside.

I wondered about her riddle—what word starts with what we desire most and ends with what we want to avoid becoming? Which one word encapsulates our desires in both directions? I wasn't sure. But I liked the riddle. It drew me into that place of delicious annoyance of being in the middle of a puzzle that you're trying to solve—the paradoxical desire to know the answer, but also of wanting to *not* know it, to figure it out yourself.

No workout or run this morning, just a quick shower.

If Sienna was still alive, that meant I was still married.

So, there was a thought.

Married to a woman who, by all indications, wanted me dead.

Usually, if I left my condo at six to drive to the Pentagon, with DC traffic it would take me about thirty minutes to get there. However, with the way morning traffic surged around that time, if I left at six thirty instead, it might very well take me an hour and a half to get there.

This morning, I planned to swing by and grab some coffee on my way to the briefing and made it out the door at ten after six, figuring that it ought to be early enough to get me there in time.

I chose clothes that I wouldn't mind getting gunpowder on, and took off for work.

CHAPTER 30

Turo Pärnänen walked dutifully in front of Pablo Serra, the CO he now had in his pocket, toward the prison's outdoor recreation yard. As he crossed through the hallway, Turo carried a push broom propped up jauntily against his shoulder.

For the most part, inmates are desperate to find anything that'll interrupt the monotony of their existence and help them pass the time. Because of that, they would bribe and bully and coerce their way into favorable work assignments any time and any way they could.

Cadillac Jobs, they called them: doing laundry, delivering mail, sorting library books, setting up chairs for chapel—anything, really, that wasn't too demeaning or difficult.

So now, a dozen prisoners watched Turo with a tinge of envy as he passed by their cells with that broom on his way to the yard.

Another guard, a man that Turo didn't know, stood sentry beside the yard. His face looked like it'd been molded out of old clay and had a permanent scowl scrawled across the bottom of it.

Pablo spoke up as they approached. "Cleaning duty. We need the dirt swept off the basketball court. They've got a three-on-three tourney coming up today. You know how the warden is about these things—always trying to give 'em a 'positive outlet' for their energy."

Turo deferentially held up the broom, and the correctional officer, who looked as disinterested in the broom as he had been in Pablo's explanation of why the outdoor court needed to be swept, slid his pass card through the electronic lock and let Turo out into the yard.

"Thanks, boss," Turo said.

Pablo stayed behind to make small talk just as Turo had instructed him to do earlier.

A distraction.

In order to avoid suspicion, Turo headed directly to the basketball court and started to sweep it, but, in reality, his attention was on the ground all around him as he scrutinized it for the two rats that were supposed to be somewhere in the yard.

It took him a few minutes, but at last, over in the deep shadows behind the weight benches, he saw one rat waiting for him.

He didn't see the other one at first, but finally located it between the two outer fences.

So, Rollan had failed to get them both over the fence and into the yard.

Well, one would have to do.

Anxious to get back to his cell with the contraband that was sewn up inside the rat, Turo made short work of the sweeping and then retrieved the dead, bloated rodent, and carried it dramatically by the tail toward the CO who'd provided him entry into the yard. "Found me a dead rat," Turo said.

He was careful to keep the stitched-up belly turned toward him rather than facing the guard.

The man gave him a look of disgust. "It's huge."

Turo held it high, then lowered it toward his mouth as if he were going to take a bite out of it. "Breakfast."

"Careful or I might make you eat that in front of me."

Turo shrugged. "It'd be an improvement to what's served here."

That brought a grunt of tacit agreement. "Get rid of that thing." He nodded toward the door. "There's a trash can in the corner down the hall."

Nearby, Pablo remained silent, waiting to escort Turo back to his cell.

Turo crossed down the hallway and found the garbage can. With his back to the guard, he tore open the rat's distended and mutilated body along the stitches that traced across its belly. Carefully, he removed the waterproof plastic bag that contained the cell phone and the thick layer of hundred-dollar bills encircling it. They had served their purpose well by providing padding for when the rat landed, and they would now come in handy to use as bribe money as needed with the guards—or even prisoners, if necessary—to entice them to cooperate.

A gun in the rat too might have been nice, but there was no sense in being greedy.

The phone was specially loaded with a sensor that could hack into passcodes and used a brute force attack to hash the password and unlock doors that used electronic locks. Very helpful at hotels and, as it turned out, prisons. Depending on the system and the level of security, it might take eight to ten seconds to hash it, but it would get the job done.

When he was in his cell, there were only four locks between him and freedom. Even with the ten seconds each, plus the time walking down the hallway, when you thought about it in those terms, it wasn't really that bad.

Less than three minutes to freedom.

There was also a wicked little blade included in the rat's carcass that was just the right size to be palmed inside your hand. It'd been included in case the CO gave him any trouble as he was disposing of the rat. It would also come in handy for removing the padding from the weight bench out in the yard.

Part of being prepared meant covering all your bases.

But Clay Face kept his distance and didn't bother him—and so he got to go on and live another day.

Turo slipped the contraband under the waistband of his prison-issue pants, dropped the rat's carcass unceremoniously into the trash can, and returned to the yard for the push broom.

Rollan would be paying Pablo's house a visit tonight to spend some quality time with his wife and daughters to make sure that Pablo complied with Turo's demands. Yes, Turo's dad had taught him to either bribe or extort, but he had come to believe that, sometimes, it was best to just go ahead and do both at the same time to make sure you received what you were trying to get from the person you were negotiating with.

Once Turo was alone in his cell he would make the call. After tonight, he didn't care what happened to Pablo, but he did have some ideas about what *ought* to happen to him in order to tie up loose ends.

Something Turo had learned while serving as a bodyguard for the billionaire Janice Daniels was that correctional officers and law enforcement personnel aren't taught to shoot to kill, but rather to shoot to stop. If that meant killing a fleeing inmate, if that's what was necessary in order to protect people outside the facility, then so be it. "Shoot to stop 'em. Shoot to drop 'em," they would say. Turo knew this. And so, he knew he could not be seen climbing over the fence to freedom.

Or he would be stopped. Dropped.

Because the guards at federal prisons qualify with long guns marksmanship at fifty yards and the guards stationed in the towers were chosen because of their exemplary scores, climbing the fence wasn't a viable option.

That would have to be someone else's role.

He was going to drive out the back gate dressed as a civilian.

He decided he would offer the opportunity to escape by scaling the fence to Sidewinder. Get rid of one more racist, neo-Nazi pig, make the world that much better of a place.

CHAPTER 31

I misjudged how long it would take to grab coffee, then I ran into a snarl of traffic and didn't make it to the Pentagon until twenty minutes to eight.

Adira was already there at the south security checkpoint, waiting for me. She smiled. "Sleep okay?"

"Well enough," I said, opting not to bring up the gruesome skin-grafting nightmares. "You?"

"Like a bug in a rug. Thanks for pushing me on the time machine last night. I feel younger already."

"Glad I could help with that. Thanks for showing it to me."

"Any*time*. Get it?"

"Yeah."

She gazed at the parking lot. "Have you heard from Gunnar?"

I shook my head. "Not this morning, but he texted me last night that he'd meet us at eight."

It's not everyone who can get permission to bring a loaded weapon into the Pentagon, but Clarke could. And he could clear it for our team members to carry as well.

One of the perks of working for him.

I didn't own a gun myself, but Adira set her Springfield XD—which she liked because, being left-handed, she appreciated the ambidextrous mag release—on the conveyor belt at the checkpoint.

"Are you thinking what I'm thinking?" she said.

"Does it have to do with chocolate croissants?"

"How did you ever guess?"

We entered the world's biggest office building, representing only a tiny fraction of a percentage of the twenty-three thousand people who would be showing up for work here today.

Despite the early hour, the hallways were already bustling with Pentagon employees—both military and civilian, like me—hurrying on their way to get started at their cubicles or in their offices. That wasn't always the case at this time of day, but on a pleasant spring Friday like this, whenever possible, people did their best to finish up by noon so they could head out early for the weekend.

The Pentagon really is a city within a building, with a flower shop, a clothing store, a luggage store, a barbershop, fast food restaurants, and more. I'd seen the paperwork for how much background needed to be done in vetting the workers for those jobs and I sometimes wondered if it was even worth it. However, I had to admit that it *was* convenient having all those businesses here, and the newest shop, a pastry bakery started by two former Marines, really did have amazing chocolate croissants.

We had to pass it on our way to Colonel Clarke's office, so we swung inside.

A quick little chocolate-motivated detour.

Adira eyed the treats behind the glass case. "I'll take the most ginormousest and chocolatey-lookingest one. That one there." She pointed. "In the back."

The petite woman behind the counter confirmed that she had the correct pastry, then reverently tonged it out of the glass display, and offered me a raised eyebrow.

"I'll have the most ginormousest one that's left."

She looked at us curiously. "I don't think that's actually a word."

"It is now," Adira told her. "Every trend starts somewhere. And you were there when *ginormousest* entered the lexicon. Have a pastry and celebrate its birthday."

Carrying our croissants, we proceeded to Colonel Clarke's office. His receptionist informed us that he was on the phone but would be with us momentarily, which was just fine with us since it gave us the chance to make short work of those pastries.

As we waited for Clarke, I said to Adira, *"Joyless.* I think the answer is *joyless."*

"The answer to what?" She'd closed her eyes and was savoring the delight of biting into her croissant.

"The answer to the riddle you told me last night: the word that starts with what we desire most and ends with what we want to avoid becoming. We all desire to find joy and none of us want to be less than we are."

"Okay, that *is* a good guess," she admitted, somewhat reluctantly. "I'll give you that. However, it's not the answer I had in mind. Do you give up?"

"I'll get it. Don't tell me."

"Okay."

"Wait—*freefall*!" I said.

"Well, *free* is good, but *fall* doesn't quite work. Besides, that's two words—but you knew that, didn't you?"

"Maybe."

"Do you want me to tell you the answer?" She had an I-know-the-answer-to-a-riddle-that-you-don't gleam in her eye.

"No," I said. "Yes . . . Wait. No."

"No?"

"Yes. I mean, yes to no, but no to you telling me the answer."

The eavesdropping receptionist looked up briefly from her work and then back down again.

I couldn't tell if she approved of our banter or not, but she did look joyless.

Adira winked at me, and we finished off our croissants.

A few moments later, the office door swung open, and Colonel Oden Clarke shouldered through the doorway toward us.

At sixty-two, he was past the age of retirement in the military, but was still serving at the pleasure of the Secretary of Defense. He stood a strapping six foot three and could probably have wrestled most men half his age to the ground. He was a Scotsman with a Germanic deity's name, something I'd always meant to ask him about but had never gotten around to. With his heavy scruff it looked like he hadn't stepped quite close enough to his razor for the last week or so.

"Morning." He pumped my right arm and then Adira's left—honoring our dominant hands—with a brisk handshake. "And Gunnar?"

"He should be on his way," I said.

The colonel gave his watch a quick glance, then told his receptionist that we would be in the conference room and to let Gunnar in as soon as he arrived.

To get there, he first ushered us into his office. Once we were alone, he asked me, "What did you find out about Sienna? The DNA? Or are we still waiting for the results?"

"Still waiting. We should know sometime this afternoon."

"Okay."

Clarke approached arranging his office with the same assiduous precision as he approached his job—a place for everything and everything in its place. The desk was positioned at just the precise angle to allow him to observe the doors to the reception area and the adjacent conference room at the same time. That way no one would be able to approach him from any direction without him noticing.

His caution in this regard reminded me of Gunnar's choice to sit in the back of the airplane on our flight from Wisconsin. To a certain degree, the two of them were cut from the same cloth. Always assessing the situation for a threat. Always ready to respond.

Adira was too, come to think of it.

I'd better up my game.

"First things first," the colonel said to me. "TalynTek the other night. Just to confirm the report Gunnar filed: you didn't exchange fire with the security team?"

"Correct," I said. "I don't know if Gunnar did or not. I'm not sure."

Then, to Adira: "And you didn't discharge your weapon either?"

"No. Is there a problem?"

"Nothing that can't be sorted out. And you saw a couple there by the lake?"

"Yes. A man and a woman."

"Huh. Okay. Got it."

He led us into the conference room.

The video screen at the far end had been lowered, which might've been enough to explain why we were meeting in here instead of his office.

"I figured we might be in here for a while," the colonel said, "so I had some pastries and coffee brought in." Then, he added, "But I'm thinking we break at ten fifty for a visit downstairs."

That was his way of saying we'd be hitting the indoor shooting range. "I've got four lanes reserved from eleven to eleven thirty."

A coffee carafe and a set of mugs waited on the conference room's domineering table next to a tray containing an array of croissants from the bakery down the hall.

Adira and I shared a look.

"Have you tried these bad boys yet?" the colonel said. "They're amazing. I'm liking the chocolate ones the best."

"They sure look amazing," Adira said, wiping a few crumbs discreetly away from her chin. "Can't wait to give 'em a go."

I'd had enough coffee on my drive over here, but once Adira and the colonel had poured themselves a cup and she'd loaded hers with a handful of sugar packets, we each heaped some pastries onto our plates.

She got the ginormousest one once again.

Imagine that.

After we'd taken a seat, Clarke wasted no time in getting things rolling. "Here's what we know: Janice Daniels's partner in crime, Ivan Popovic, is in the States—or at least he was last night."

"Where'd the intel come from?" I asked.

"Someone traveling under a different identity flew inbound to JFK on an eight fifty-five from Paris. Facial rec at Passport Control didn't identify it at first, but that passenger—without his beard—the facial structure, it matches Popovic."

"How'd they catch that?" Adira asked.

"I have another team monitoring Passport Control. They red-flagged it for us."

"Impressive," she muttered.

"Yeah, we only identified it after he'd already left the airport, but it gives us a place to start. We're studying traffic cams and satellite footage, but so far, nothing. It was a British passport."

"Passport Control at JFK?" I found myself stating my thoughts aloud, noting what Adira and Clarke most assuredly already knew. "Fake British IDs of that caliber are tough to pull off. A counterfeit passport that well executed was probably created by a nation state—"

"Or at least with government assistance, yeah." Clarke nodded. "That's what I was thinking too."

"Huh."

He pulled up the video footage of the bearded man crossing through security. There wasn't anything extraordinary or atypical about his encounter with the Customs and Border Patrol officer. He basically just walked right through Passport Control after a brief, perfunctory nod.

"See anything unusual?" Clarke asked.

Adira shook her head.

"That officer, the one who cleared Popovic," I said, "what do we know about him? Have we looked into why he might not have caught this?"

"We did," Clarke said. "Nothing came up. He's twenty years on the job. A team supervisor. He's clear."

I studied the screen. "Play it again."

When he played the video this time, I asked him to pause it just after Popovic entered the checkpoint, then pointed out a woman in sunglasses who was standing on the far side of the checkpoint facing Popovic.

"Sunglasses?" I said. "Really? Inside the airport and at that time of night? Do we know who this is?"

"No. We'll have to look into it."

"Hit play again."

He did, and we watched as the woman turned from Popóvic just as he successfully cleared the checkpoint and started to walk in her direction. Then she strolled away, entered a crowd, and left the screen.

"It's not Janice Daniels," I said. "The stature's not right. Too tall."

"Hmm," Clarke said. "Interesting." He glugged down some coffee. "I gotta say: Popovic—he makes me think of a time back when I was maybe nine or ten. My older brother and I would go out and kill frogs in a stream that fed into the pond behind my house. We used our jackknives, sharpened sticks into spears, and then tested our skill by throwing them at the frogs."

"Why?" Adira asked.

"Thinking back, honestly, I can't come up with a good reason, apart from what you might just call the thrill of the hunt. Maybe it was a mixture of curiosity and challenge—to see if we could make those spears sharp enough and hit what we were aiming at—but I've come to believe that it was also to derive some sort of sadistic pleasure from the act of killing. That torturous nature of children on clear display."

"Really?" she said. "The torturous nature of *children*?"

He nodded grimly. "Torture is woven into the fabric of human nature. It's so ingrained in us, even from childhood, that we have to spend a lifetime trying to expunge it from ourselves. Kids incinerate ants with magnifying glasses. They pull the wings off bugs, just to see if the bugs can still fly. We prod, we insult, we push the buttons of others, we cut people down to watch them squirm, and then we secretly celebrate their failures. Schadenfreude is a real thing. Everyone has at least a little thread of sadism in them. We, as a race, are natural-born torturers."

"And lovers," Adira countered. "We're natural-born lovers too."

"Yes." He tapped a knowing finger against the air. "That's true. Both. We are *both*."

I believed he was onto something. "How do you make sense of that?" I said.

The colonel shook his head. "I don't know. I guess the goal of life isn't so much to make sense of it as it is to choose which side of your own nature you're going to give free rein to."

"That's what separates the good guys from the bad guys," Adira noted. "What separates us from them. We've made our choice—or at least what we're trying to pursue."

"That's right," he said. I wondered what his story might have to do with our search for Janice and Ivan, but before I could ask him, he continued, "You see, with Popovic, though, there is no struggle. Not anymore. There's no choice left. No love. He's made his decision. He works hand in glove with the Russian mafia, provides arms shipments to terrorists, and sells women and little girls into the sex trade. He's one cold, heartless . . . well, you can fill in the blank there. He's the one holding the pointed spear, aiming it right at the throat of innocent people everywhere, and we have to stop him."

As we were processing his sober assessment of Popovic, there was a firm knock on the door and the colonel called out, "Yes. Enter."

Gunnar appeared. "Sorry I'm late." He joined us and closed the door authoritatively behind him. "It hasn't been the best twelve hours of my life."

"What is it?" I asked. "What happened?"

"It started last night when I was having dinner at this pub with my sister. I step away to use the washroom and, on my way back, I see this creep hitting on her and she's making it *abundantly* clear that she doesn't want anything to do with him. But he doesn't stop and by the time I get there, he's placed his hand on her arm and she's trying to pull away. So, I stepped in."

"What'd you do?" I said, although, knowing Gunnar, I had a pretty good idea that things did not turn out well for the other guy.

"I handled it," he said simply. "I put an end to his inappropriate behavior."

"Did you get into a bar fight, Gunnar Bane?" Adira asked good-naturedly.

"It wasn't technically a fight. It was a punch. He didn't fight back after that, just scrambled to his feet and made for the door. So, I guess, in a sense, you could say I actually *stopped* a bar fight from happening. The pub owners should've probably been thanking me for that, rather than requesting, a bit flustered and from a safe distance, that I leave."

"Is your sister okay?" the colonel asked.

Gunnar nodded. "Yeah, she's good and I'm fine. But Maureen is missing. That's what I found out this morning. That's why I'm late. I was looking for her."

"Maureen?"

"He named his Smith & Wesson M&P nine mil 'Maureen,'" Adira told Clarke. "After an ex-girlfriend. She's his favorite gun."

"Ah. Gotcha." Clarke gave a quick nod, as if naming your favorite gun after a love interest was only to be expected. Then he turned to Gunnar. "When you say she's missing, did you misplace her?"

"No. I always carry, so I had her with me at the pub. Then, at home, I put her on my bedside end table where she always sleeps next to me. When I woke up this morning, she was gone. Of course I looked all over, thinking I might have misremembered where I left her, but she wasn't there anywhere in the house. Which means someone somehow broke into my home, came into my bedroom while I was asleep, stole my gun—and *only* my gun, my favorite one—and then left without waking me up. And, no, I hadn't had too much to drink at the bar. Also, I'm a light sleeper, and still, I didn't wake up." He sighed heavily. "I had to pull my SIG out of retirement today. Sinead."

"Another ex-girlfriend?" Clarke asked.

"Yeah. But now we're going way back to my early days. You're talking just out of college."

He'd lost another of his favorite guns, named Saundra, last month when it was destroyed after dropping more than two hundred feet from a tower and landing on a sidewalk. I wondered briefly how many girlfriends he might have had, and how many of them had the honor of having a gun named after them, but that's not what was foremost on my mind. Mostly, I was puzzled at how the intruder had been able to pull off the burglary without someone as wary and prepared as Gunnar waking up and stopping them.

"You don't think that it was the guy from the bar?" I said. "That he might have been involved in the burglary in some way?"

A question mark crossed Gunnar's face. "What makes you ask that?"

"Anomalies," I said. "It's what I look for when I'm doing my redactions, especially when I'm evaluating the connections between different programs or files. One anomaly is just life—things happen all the time that we don't expect and that don't seem to make sense. But two anomalies in the same night? The guy in the pub and then the missing gun? It speaks to something more going on."

"It could just be a coincidence," Clarke suggested.

"It could be," I admitted.

"But maybe it's not," Gunnar said reflectively. "That's something to consider. I'll see if any of my neighbors might've seen anything and check the video footage from the pub—they had two interior CCTV cameras and one exterior one."

He'd taken note of the camera locations. Of course he had. Why didn't that surprise me?

"Any idea why someone would take Maureen?" Adira asked. "Or why they might want to make a scene with you or your sister at the pub?"

"Nope. None whatsoever."

"Well," the colonel said, "I'm just glad you and your sister are alright. I was about to play some audio here for Travis and Adira. NSA intercepted a snippet of a conversation yesterday morning on a phone call from one of the encrypted numbers they've been monitoring."

Yes, some encryption programs were better than others. From files I'd redacted, I knew that NSA had a bead on most of the ones out there. It's a constant battle, but, at least for the moment, we were still one slight step ahead.

Gunnar snabbed a croissant and took a seat beside me as Clarke tapped his keyboard, bringing up an audio file with a visual equalizer that would track the audio levels on the screen.

And pressed Play.

CHAPTER 32

I watched the equalizer lines fluctuate as two different voices spoke in turn. Though the quality of the audio wasn't great, I could recognize the first voice as that of Popovic. The second was Janice Daniels:

"Are we ready for tomorrow night?"
"Yes. He'll be free by ten."
"And the device?"
"Out of play. Couldn't get it en route."
"Hmm. And Valestra?"
"I've got someone on it. I'll see you in DC."

And that was it.

"What do we know about this?" Gunnar asked Clarke. "Who's Valestra?"

"I don't think it's a *who*, I think it's a *what*," I said. "I'm guessing Valestra Pharmaceuticals, is that right, Colonel?"

"Yes. One of the largest pharmaceutical firms in the world. A four-hundred-*billion*-dollar company. And our analysts think that, yes, that's what they're referring to on the recording. There's been a lot of movement on their stocks this week and there's speculation about a big announcement coming on Monday."

"Who's Janice talking about?" I asked. "Who'll be free by ten?"

"We don't know."

Adira chimed in. "What does Popovic have to do with a pharmaceutical company?"

"Don't know that either," Clarke replied, "but that's what I want us to find out. Whatever it is, they're planning it for DC and they're planning to do it tonight."

"The device they refer to . . . ," I said. "The Project Symphony prototype?"

"That's our best guess at the moment. I've checked with Quantico and it's still there. Still being guarded."

The device was protected by perimeter security, an onsite sentry, and a vascular recognition scanner. I'd been cleared to access the prototype for when we used it up in Wisconsin, but that clearance would expire at the end of the weekend. All part of the security protocol. I honestly didn't know how someone would be able to breach all of those measures and acquire the device.

Clarke thought for a moment. "Gunnar, go ahead and take a look into what happened last night with you at the pub and with Maureen. I don't like the timing of those two events coinciding with the arrival of Popovic. A possible anomaly, like Travis was talking about. If someone is out there targeting members of our team or their family members, we need to know about it."

"Yes, sir."

He turned to Adira. "See if you can identify who that mystery woman is on the footage from the airport."

"Got it," she said.

"And Travis, find out what you can about Valestra and any connections between them, Janice, and Popovic. I'm going to focus on the timing, see what might be happening in DC tonight that could've brought Popovic crawling out of the woodwork, and also who they might be referring to as being free. We'll regroup at ten thirty, fill each other in, and then head downstairs for a little brain break."

"Sounds good," Gunnar said. "Give Sinead a chance to shine."

We split up to tackle our assignments.

—⁂—

LAGUARDIA AIRPORT
NEW YORK CITY, NEW YORK
10:02 A.M.

Dr. Maia Odongo stepped off the plane and entered the terminal.

Her connecting flight to Atlanta wouldn't be leaving until nearly two o'clock, which gave her some time to think, to evaluate her situation.

Everything that'd happened in the last month with Janice being accused of planning a domestic terror attack in Tennessee, and then going on the run after having her assets frozen, had been a huge shock to Maia. She'd trusted Janice, had spent the last five years working for her in Africa. She considered her a friend.

And now?

She didn't know what to think or who to trust.

She hadn't spoken with Janice since all of that occurred, but was hoping to see her this weekend. And as soon as she did, she was going to ask her if the allegations about her were true—and if not, why she hadn't turned herself in.

Maia wasn't sure if she was doing the right thing at all here, or if she'd been maybe doing the wrong thing for a long time.

It was deeply unsettling.

As she rolled her carry-on suitcase behind her, looking for a restaurant, she considered the circuitous route that had brought her here, to this moment, to this moral crossroads in her life.

Not long after she and her father had moved back to Uganda five years ago, he'd passed away quietly in the night. It'd been very peaceful and serene. He simply went to bed and didn't wake up in the morning.

A merciful way to go.

For a good and merciful man.

He'd been happy to be back in Uganda, and she had even arranged a guided safari of the Bwindi Impenetrable National Park for him. Amazingly, he'd seemed more alert and cognizant of his surroundings out in the bush than he had in the past few years back at home, sitting in that lonely living room in that small, isolated pool of impassive light leaking in through the window.

At first, she wasn't sure if she wanted to stay in the country and continue her research, but she soon realized that he would've wanted her to do so.

So, even while she was grieving, she'd found respite and comfort in the fact that the work she was doing with Janice's organization would relieve suffering and benefit people all over the world, just as her father would've liked to see.

Still, it hadn't been easy when Janice first told her about the new trials that she was planning to pursue.

At the time, the civil war in South Sudan had been at its height. No one knew the final tragic numbers for sure, but during the war, nearly two million people had been killed or starved and another five million were displaced. The Bidi Bidi Refugee Settlement—the largest refugee camp in the world at the time—had been established just over the border in Uganda to receive them.

That's where they moved the research.

That's when the compromises began.

How to describe the refugee settlement?

How to do it justice?

When it was originally designed, it was never meant to sustain hundreds of thousands of people, but with the sudden influx of displaced people, it ballooned to more than ten times its intended capacity. Everyone was living on top of each other in makeshift tents.

And everywhere you went, there were people waiting in line, always people queuing up—for food, for water, for medical care. The UN aid trucks didn't arrive on a regular basis because if they'd stuck to a specific schedule, it would've made it easier for rebels to ambush the convoys. Because of that, when the trucks did arrive, the lines formed quickly, and people took advantage of the moment, no matter what time of day or night that might be.

It was amazing the difference that only a few kilometers could make. The infrastructure of South Sudan was almost nonexistent—dirt roads, no running water, only generators for electricity. Squalor and despair everywhere. But in Uganda, European tourists would fly into Entebbe for holiday and stay in high-end hotels while visiting the lush shores of Lake Victoria.

Yes, South Sudan's civil war might officially be over now, but the suffering wasn't. The hatred and heartache weren't. The tension between the different ethnic groups wasn't. The hostilities hadn't ended. Though a few diplomats had signed a sheet of paper, the hearts of the people were not so easily ushered into peace. There were still factions that wanted only to exterminate each other.

The shade of your skin really could get you killed. Not simply mocked. Not rejected. Brutally slaughtered.

And here, even in the settlement, there was inequality.

Unlike the tents that the refugees lived in, the medical buildings were constructed of cinder block and protected from the sun with corrugated metal roofs. There were window openings, but they contained no glass, so there were flies everywhere in the operating rooms.

But you got used to it.

Or you didn't.

Because of the severe need, there was very little oversight from the UN over the NGOs that were providing medical services to the displaced people.

The clinics offered general medical care, but that's not what Maia was there to provide.

No. She'd been given a different role.

They had been at the settlement, walking toward the clinic, when Janice told her about Gelert the dog.

"Have you ever heard the old Welsh folktale of Gelert and Prince Llewelyn?" she'd asked.

"I don't believe so," Maia said.

"Once there was a prince named Llewelyn who owned a faithful hunting dog named Gelert. He was not only skilled in the ways of the hunt but was also a loyal and trustworthy companion who always obeyed when his master called. One morning, however, Prince Llewelyn called and called for Gelert to join him, but Gelert didn't come. Frustrated, the prince left to hunt alone, only to return later in the day with no game to show for it. When he approached his castle, he saw Gelert running toward him with blood covering his teeth and snout. Prince Llewelyn felt a terrifying chill as he surmised where the blood had come from. You see, the prince had a one-year-old son."

"Oh, no." Maia gasped, and only realized she'd said the words aloud when she heard herself whisper them.

"Yes," Janice said. "So the prince rushes to the nursery and finds the crib overturned and a bloody blanket and no sign of his son. Gelert comes bounding into the room. The prince turns toward him and, overcome by grief and horror, he immediately unsheathes his sword and . . ."

Even though she knew it was only a folktale, Maia felt herself drawn into the story. Her throat tightened. "Did he kill Gelert?"

"In some versions of the story the prince stays his hand, but yes, in most of them, the deed is done before he discovers the truth behind the source of the blood."

"Which is?"

"That Gelert had been protecting the prince's son."

Janice gestured toward the clinic, about eighty meters away. As they approached it, they passed a clutch of six barely clothed children playing with sticks in the dirt beneath the raging sun. A few crumpled plastic water bottles with brown-stained water lay strewn to the side. For calming the children's thirst later.

Janice went on. "The boy was under the crib and only when the prince threw open the shades did he see the dead wolf in the corner of the room—the wolf that Gelert had killed to save the boy."

Maia wasn't sure why Janice was telling her that story. "So, the point of the story is to avoid rash judgments?"

"Yes, that's one takeaway. But I think there's something more to the story: Gelert disobeyed his master and did what was better than obedience."

Maia anticipated what Janice was going to say. "Saving the child."

"Yes."

"But then he suffered the consequences. He was killed."

They passed a food queue that stretched back out of sight among the tents. It looked like at least eight hundred people were in line.

"Yes, he was," Janice said. "I believe there's a time when you have to choose to do what's right, even if you don't have approval. Even if it costs you everything. When people are dying and you have the cure, can you really look them in the eyes and say, 'Yes, I know you're suffering and I have the ability to save you, but I won't do so because someone somewhere hasn't signed a sheet of paper yet'? How many people have to die while we wait for some government functionary somewhere to check off a box or mail a form? How many lives are we willing to sacrifice to the god of bureaucracy?"

Having battled bureaucracy her entire career, Maia couldn't help but agree. Compassion must never be stifled by needlessly burdensome oversight. She knew that. She and Janice saw eye to eye on that.

"Our work here"—Janice indicated the clinic, just across the road—"has the potential to transform the lives of millions of people, reduce their suffering, give them new opportunities. Love requires that we do not wait any longer before we act."

"And you're saying that in this case it's better to ask for forgiveness than for permission?" Maia asked.

"I don't think we ever need to ask for forgiveness for doing the right thing," Janice replied. "We should never feel compelled to justify compassion or apologize for extending mercy to those in need."

Maia had a feeling she knew where Janice was going with this. "You're talking about moving forward with human trials. Before we have approval."

"Trials on mice and monkeys will only take us so far. And to finally get approval? Years. Decades maybe. Can we really afford to wait? I know it's just a folktale, but in the story, Gelert didn't need approval to save a life. If he had gone out in search of the prince, it would have been too late to save the child."

Maia knew that the implications of a breakthrough in the work they were doing were extraordinary. Those with access to the drug they were developing would have a distinct advantage in countless ways, further exacerbating the wealth disparity between the world's richest and poorest individuals and nations.

Unless . . .

Drugs of this nature should not be available only to those who could afford the astronomical price tag, but to anyone in need, regardless of their ability to pay.

Since the poor and underprivileged were so close to her heart, Maia wanted to do all she could to help them.

Some of the people in Janice's circles wanted to redistribute wealth, and Maia understood that urge. But what she wanted to do was redistribute *opportunity*. That was the truest, purest form of equity.

"What is it you have in mind?" she'd asked Janice.

"Follow me," Janice said. "It's in here."

And she led Maia to the back room of the clinic, the place where the children were taken for their vaccines.

That was where the procedures would occur.

And so, Maia had taken over the FGF17 research.

There are moments in your life when you do what you must for the greater good, and that's what Maia told herself she was doing, how she justified why she'd chosen the path she had.

Still, in her most honest moments, she had to admit that she might've very well become the type of person she would've given anything to protect the world from just a few short years earlier.

O God, her heart would whisper, *can you ever forgive someone like me?*

Now, here in the airport, she thought of Gelert and the prince's son and the wolf's bloodied body in the nursery.

And then there was Gelert's corpse as well, lying lifeless and cold beside the crying child.

Because there is always a cost to doing what's right.

And sometimes it costs you everything you have.

But it should not cost you everything you are.

Those were Maia's thoughts as she searched for a restaurant where she could sit and process things before boarding her plane for Atlanta, where she would meet with Janice's associate tonight to review the Nectyla research and evaluate how it would compare to the research she had done in Uganda, there in the back room of the clinic.

There, with the children.

CHAPTER 33

I'd spent the last couple of hours trying to find anything to tie Valestra Pharmaceuticals to the Pruninghooks Collective or to Janice Daniels or Popovic and his known associates, but so far had come up empty.

I wondered about the timing and Popovic's travels, if he'd ever visited Valestra's headquarters or their branches or offices around the world.

From the files of his that we'd seized, along with his travel logs, passenger manifests, and covert intel from one of our sources in the Russian mafia, our analysts had pieced together his known movements and travel routes over the last three years.

And, as I was examining it, I noticed that he'd visited Almaty, Kazakhstan, eight times in less than a year.

Which caught my eye.

There were no Valestra connections there, but Adira had also visited Almaty in the past and had promised to tell me why last month but had never gotten around to it. Never found quite the right time.

I hadn't wanted to bug her or pressure her, so I'd let it drop, but I was admittedly curious about it since, at one point, a Russian spy had told me that I needed to ask her about her time there. Somehow he knew about it. And for some reason, she had avoided the topic.

Odd.

Did Almaty have anything to do with this?

I felt a little like I was going behind Adira's back, but I looked into her travel records from Homeland while she was working for their Red Team testing airport security, and at first found nothing under her name, but then I decided to try her aliases and that's when I got a hit.

Meridian Vaughn had flown into Almaty the day before Popovic had last year, and flew out the day after.

What?

An anomaly? I doubted it.

A coincidence? Unlikely.

No, it was something more and I needed to find out what that was and what it meant.

I tried to hold back from making any assumptions, but it wasn't easy.

Popovic and Adira? Why would their paths have crossed in Almaty, Kazakhstan?

Take things one at a time. Study. Compare. Evaluate. Decide. Don't assume.

The first step was finding out why each of them was there, then I could see if the reasons had anything to do with each other. I started with Popovic and discovered that he'd invested in a joint venture with the Kazakh military to fund a dark matter research facility known by the nickname *"glubokaya shakhta,"* or "deep shaft." They'd constructed a shaft nearly a mile deep in a Cold War–era missile silo near Almaty.

Dark matter research?

I was no expert on particle physics, but I did know that dark matter was an area of acute interest in the field.

With a little digging, I soon learned that scientists believe that about 95% of the substance in the universe is actually dark matter or some form of dark energy. Even though they've never been able to directly interact with it, they're confident that it exists, because without it, there wouldn't be enough gravity in the universe to hold the clusters of stars and galaxies together.

If dark matter makes up that much of the universe, you'd think it wouldn't necessarily be that difficult to detect. However, that was not the case. It was proving to be annoyingly elusive.

But what did this have to do with Adira? I could understand why Popovic would be interested in funding research that might lead to a scientific breakthrough that could rewrite what we know about the universe before the West could. There could be money in that. Clout. Leverage. But why would Adira have been there?

I directed my attention to her Meridian Vaughn alias and found a Department of Energy memo that'd been heavily redacted, but that mentioned an address in Boston that was associated with that identity.

If you have a trained eye, and if you do this job long enough, you become attuned to the subtleties of understanding what has been redacted and what hasn't in files and memos. Over the years, I've gotten pretty good at guessing how much space different fonts allow for various characters and so on.

However, as good as I was at anticipating what redacted files might actually contain, I couldn't decipher what was being communicated in this memo.

The file concerned the DOE's Lawrence Livermore National Laboratory, which was part of their National Nuclear Security Administration. They studied alternate and emerging forms of energy and dabbled in a number of experimental areas to try to understand energy usage in order to help make the United States energy independent. They were responsible for the recent breakthroughs in quantum computing and in using lasers to produce fusion.

Could Almaty and the dark energy research have anything to do with that?

As it turned out, the NNSA was also helping to fund a research station at a remote location in Wyoming. It was a mine that stretched at least a mile down and was being used to try to identify . . . yep: dark matter.

Clearly, I needed to talk to Adira, but I wasn't sure how I could do that without making her think I was researching her, going behind her back, or not trusting her.

Why has she been so reticent to talk to you about this?

That was the question at the forefront of my mind as I glanced at the time and realized I was already five minutes late for our ten thirty regroup.

I decided it was something I needed to speak with her about in private rather than in front of the team. Unsure exactly when or how I could bring it up, I returned to the conference room adjacent to Clarke's office and met up with Gunnar, Adira, and the colonel, who were already there.

"What do we know?" Clarke said, then nodded toward Gunnar to go first.

CHAPTER 34

I couldn't come up with anything solid connecting the pub incident with Maureen being stolen," Gunnar said. "No evidence that the guy might've had anything to do with my missing gun. But I did discover that one of my neighbors has a doorbell camera. I had a chat with her and she gave me access to the footage. Turns out, it caught some movement—a figure, a woman walking toward my house. No way to see her face. On a whim, I matched her gait with the sunglasses lady at the airport."

"You're kidding," I said. "It was a match?"

"Yeah. It was the same woman."

"That was some whim," Adira exclaimed.

Clarke turned to her. "Do we know who she is?"

"No, but she appears on exterior surveillance cameras at the airport. Twenty minutes after passing through the checkpoint, Popovic gets into a car with her, and they drive off together. I tracked the license plates, but that was a dead end; they were stolen from another car a few weeks ago."

"What about satellite footage?" he asked. "DSCS?"

The Defense Satellite Communications System was run by the Space Force, an arm of the military that sounded more like something out of a sci-fi novel than real life.

However, the satellite array was not sci-fi, but very real.

Theoretically, it was able to view anywhere on earth at any time day or night, but in practice, many of our satellites were aging out. New synthetic aperture radar satellite technology was on the horizon and would be accurate enough to read the numbers off a credit card that was being held by anyone outside, anywhere on the planet, at any moment.

We weren't quite there yet though, and many of our defense satellites needed to be replaced and should have been retired years ago. There were inevitably gaps, inconsistencies, blips that were far more prevalent than we'd led our adversaries to believe.

"I checked," Adira said, "and, surprise, surprise, we don't have the footage at that time of day in that specific location."

The colonel looked at her quizzically. "Really?"

"I know, right? It's almost like someone knew we'd be looking for footage right in that place, right at that time and made sure it wouldn't be available to us."

The colonel looked my way. "Is it possible that Popovic or Daniels could have manipulated the footage, or even the satellites themselves?" I figured he directed the question to me because of the number of redactions I'd done on the DSCS over the last few years.

"It's possible," I said. "I wouldn't say it would be easy, but there are NSA initiatives out there that can affect the trajectory of the satellites and their image-capturing capabilities—ours or anyone else's. Given Janice's and Popovic's connections, I wouldn't put it past them to have obtained that technology."

He cursed, then asked me, "Did you find anything about Popovic?"

I didn't want to mention anything about dark matter and the research in Almaty yet, not until I'd had a chance to speak with Adira and find out what she knew.

"Nothing with Valestra," I said honestly, then added, "there are a few other things I'm looking into, but I'll need a little more time."

"Understood," Clarke said. "On my front, I've got nothing on the identity of who Daniels and Popovic might be referring to as being free. And as far as the events in DC tonight, you have the typical conventions, a few protests, a concert at the Kennedy Center, but nothing out of the ordinary. Because of the pharmaceutical angle, I looked into the FDA. Nothing tonight, but they are scheduled next week to review a Valestra request for clinical trials for some sort of new Alzheimer's drug. I'm not sure if it's related, but I'm also not sure that it's *not* related."

"Earlier you mentioned stock volatility with Valestra," I said. "Insider trading? Short selling futures? Could that be Popovic's game here?"

"Maybe." He debated that with a head tilt. "I don't know. There's money in that, sure, but I don't think money is really the issue here. Popovic is an opportunist, so money makes sense on that front, but Daniels is an ideologue. I'm not so sure about it being a motivator for her." He gave that some thought. "Still, it's worth a look. I'll get some data analysts on it." He consulted the time. "It's time to shoot. I'll meet the three of you downstairs in ten."

I grabbed the last croissant and followed Gunnar and Adira toward the elevator, wondering how to approach Adira with what I'd uncovered regarding her visit to Almaty, and if this was even a good time to do so at all.

Whether it's a good time or not, it's the right time. Learn what you can as promptly as possible to move forward on this.

Okay, I would.

As soon as we could talk in private.

CHAPTER 35

As Gunnar, Adira, and I headed toward the elevator to take us down to the shooting range, she said to him, "How's your book coming? Any new scenes you can read to us?"

"Unfortunately, not too much progress since the other night, but I am working on a section where the main love interests flirt," he said. "Hey, maybe you two can help me out with it?"

"How's that?"

He drew out his pocket-sized journal, which I hadn't even realized he'd brought with him. "Flirt for a bit and I'll take notes."

"Oh," I said, "I'm not really—"

"Sure," Adira said enthusiastically. "We're game. Aren't we, sweetie?"

"Um . . . I'm not really an expert on flirting. You're going to have to give me some guidance."

"Glad to."

We made it to the elevator bay and I swiped my badge to gain access to the sublevel where the range was located.

"Alright," Adira said as we waited for the doors to open. "When women flirt, we open our eyes more, look down slightly, and then look back up again. Very coy. Very alluring. And we sling one hand to our hip, thumb up, and turn one leg slightly toward the person we're flirting with."

She demonstrated.

"Nice," I said. The doors parted. We entered. "What about guys?"

"When men flirt," she said, "they sort of narrow their eyes a little, then offer a slight, corner-mouth smile, and square their jaw. Smoldering. Simmering. Try it. Narrow your eyes."

I did.

The doors shut and we began our descent.

"Not that much," she chided me. "You look like you're staring directly into the equatorial sun."

I opened them wider.

"And those would be Muppet eyes," Gunnar said, taking notes. "Not exactly conducive to flirting."

I narrowed them again.

Adira cringed. "Slitty eyes. You look like you might possibly be a lizard."

"Agreed." Gunnar jotted something down.

"Okay," I said, "this is harder than I thought."

We reached our floor and the elevator doors parted. The armory and the range lay at the end of the hall.

"Listen," Adira said as we left the elevator. "Try this: steamy eyes."

We paused outside the elevator long enough for them to observe my steamy eyes. I went all out.

"Those are stalker eyes." She winced. "Not steamy. You're scaring me."

"I haven't even squared my jaw or offered you my corner-mouth smile yet."

"Yeah, we may need to wait on those."

I sighed. "Maybe I'm just not cut out to flirt."

"Everyone's cut out to flirt, bro," Gunnar said. "It's ingrained in us. We're programmed for it. Reproduction and survival of the species. It's gotta happen."

"That's right," Adira agreed. "We just need to cure you of a lifetime of, well . . . not embracing your inner flirt. You need to own it."

"That might be a challenge," I said, "but I'm up for it. Anything to help an aspiring author reach new literary heights."

"Thanks." Gunnar pocketed his notebook.

But, honestly, as we proceeded down to the range, I was not primarily thinking of flirting.

I was thinking of Almaty.

And how Adira was going to react when I brought it up to her.

Clarke caught up with us in the slightly cramped classroom between the armory and the actual shooting range. The meeting room, which had seating for twelve people and a screen up front to show instructional videos, was designed to facilitate safety briefings and marksmanship review classes.

On my first visit down here a couple weeks ago, Adira had given me an in-depth orientation to shooting, and now Colonel Clarke decided to put me to the test: "Alright, Travis. Let's assume I don't know how to shoot, that I've never done it before. Talk to me. What do I need to know?"

"First," I said, "I'd go through gun safety: treat all weapons as if they're loaded, maintain muzzle integrity, aim only at what you want to destroy, keep your finger off the trigger until you're ready to shoot, know your target and be aware of what lies beyond it."

A brisk nod. "That's a good start. Then?"

"Once we're good with range safety, then marksmanship. There are six central aspects of it."

"Go on. Talk me through them."

"All six?"

"All six."

"Okay, first, stance. Keep the weight on the balls of your feet, knees slightly bent, nose over your toes. Show me."

I hadn't picked up a gun yet, so I handed the colonel one of the compressed rubber training pistols for him to demonstrate his stance to me.

Of course, all of this felt odd since he'd probably shot at ranges like this hundreds of times and this was only my second time, but I understood what he was doing: one of the best ways to remember is to teach, and one of the best ways to teach is to role-play.

He demonstrated an improper stance, bending too far forward, just to see if I would correct him.

"You're leaning into the gun," I said. "You're letting it dictate to you how you stand. Bring it up to where you want it. Remember, it's an extension of your will to end the confrontation. You're not bending yourself to serve it; you're using it to serve you."

"I like that." He nodded toward Adira, who was smiling. "You taught him that?"

"I did."

"Nice work."

"Thank you."

"Secondly," I said to the colonel, "we have grip. Both thumbs forward, with slightly more pressure on the gun from the support hand than the strong hand."

I watched as he held his gun, squeezing it improperly on purpose, and I instructed him to ease up on it. "Too much pressure in one direction or another will cause you to move your sights and consequently alter where the round will impact your target."

"Gotcha," he said.

I went on. "Third, gun presentation. This is how you draw, and it's in a straight line. No bowling, no fly-fishing."

"Meaning?"

"You're not going to make this easy for me, are you, Colonel?"

He shrugged and gave me a tiny slice of a smile. "Gotta give you a challenge."

"Bowling is when you sweep the gun up into position like you might swing a bowling ball forward. Fly-fishing is when you sling it down again like a fisherman might when you're getting it back into position."

He executed a perfect straight-line presentation.

"Good," I said, slightly relieved that he wasn't making me correct him again.

Then, I moved quickly through the three remaining aspects of marksmanship without pausing too much, so he wouldn't have a chance to test me. "Fourth, trigger control. The trigger goes in the middle of the pad of your trigger finger. You're going to bring the trigger straight back. Don't snap it, just pull it smoothly and evenly. Fifth, sight alignment. You're going to want the front sight aligned in the rear sight notch. The focus of your eye goes to the tip of the front sight. Sight picture is part of that—it's your aligned sights onto the target. And finally, last but not least, follow-through."

"Which is?"

"Settling your sights back onto the target after the shot breaks and recoil occurs so you'll be ready to take the next shot. Realign your arms. Transition your focus from the rear sight notch back to the front sight and you're ready to go."

"And with that," he said, "we *are* ready to go."

We went to the armory to pick up our weapons, or, in this case, I needed to pick up my weapon. Adira, Gunnar, and the colonel had all brought their guns with them.

The armorer had me sign for one, then told me, "Today you'll be shooting a gun that gun lovers love. It does what you ask it to do. It doesn't talk back. It doesn't argue. There's no second-guessing that there's going to be closure with this weapon. It gets the job done, right from the start."

"Okay," I said. "What is it?"

"The Glock 19."

"What? Really?" I couldn't hide my surprise. "A Glock? I thought it'd be some exotic gun or something."

"This gun is compact, concealable, and accurate like you wouldn't believe. At twenty-five yards, you'll hit what you're aiming at. There's a reason it sells as well as it does."

With that, he handed me the Glock I would be using and I made sure to physically and visually inspect it to make sure there were no rounds in the chamber. Then, he passed me a few boxes of ammo, we collected our "eyes" and "ears"—protective eyewear and hearing protectors—and entered the range.

I had an idea in mind for speaking privately with Adira. Now, just to see if it would work.

Each of the eight shooting lanes had a target waiting, hanging expectantly twenty-five yards away. There was just enough room in each station for the shooter as well as an instructor, if desired.

As we were ready to split up, I said to Adira, "Can you hang with me? That way you can help coach me, give me some pointers."

"Oh. Sure."

Also, then I can ask you about Almaty without doing so in front of Gunnar and the colonel.

Then Clarke and Gunnar went to their separate stations while Adira joined me in mine.

CHAPTER 36

Installing this shooting range last year was a bit of a challenge because the engineers needed to create an indoor range that had enough insulation around it to dampen the noise so it wouldn't disturb any nearby offices on this level, and also install a ventilation system strong enough to take care of the smoke from the burning gunpowder.

Without that ventilation, on this sublevel, the range would get cloudy, and the air would become raw to breathe. I wouldn't call the range an engineering marvel, but pulling something like that off in the Pentagon was at the very least an engineering *challenge*.

"Is something up?" Adira asked me. "You seem distracted."

"Couple things on my mind," I said a bit evasively, trying to figure out the best way to do this. I figured I needed a few more minutes to sort out what to say.

"Well, focus," she said amiably. "I want to see if your shooting has improved since last time."

The targets on the range were electronically controlled so we could move them forward or backward depending on how far away we wanted them to be. Hash marks on the floor and the walls indicated the distance in five-yard increments.

"I'm ready," I said.

She pressed a button on the panel in front of us and the electronic target in our lane zoomed toward us, coming to a floating stop just outside the booth we were standing in.

"Today we'll be shooting at silhouette targets that a friend of mine in Homeland designed. They're called Transtar IV Law Enforcement Targets. They were used at the main FLETC campus down in Georgia when I went through the program there, back in my Secret Service days."

Unlike many of the silhouette targets I'd seen before, this one showed an outline of a person down to, and including, the hips.

"Three guesses as to why this is a better target than most," she said. "And the first two don't count."

"Well," I said, "when you consider gunshot wound incapacitation, you're targeting one of three areas: mediastinum, brainstem, and lateral pelvis. This target has all three clearly delineated."

"Nicely done," she said. "Chest, head, and hip area. Tell me about the lateral pelvis."

"By targeting that region, you can stop the threat from bipedal movement. Also, there are lots of vascular elements running through your pelvis, so it's a good place to target if you're trying to stop an aggressor from advancing."

"With the goal being . . . ?"

"Stopping the threat." I was careful not to talk about killing a person. The goal is never to shoot to kill. Although, admittedly, it might in some cases be the product of the aggressor's choices. "Once he's no longer a threat, you don't need to shoot anymore. Until then, take the necessary action."

"Good."

"So, why don't more silhouette targets include all three areas of incapacitation?" I asked.

"That, Travis, is a good question."

We put our ear protection on.

Nearby, in the next station over, Clarke started firing and the sharp report of his weapon echoed across the range.

Gunnar followed suit.

The first time I was down here I'd obsessed a lot about my eyes, trying to figure out if I should close one, and which one that should be, and where exactly I should be looking when I aimed.

"There's something called eye dominance," Adira had told me. "But there's also something called field of vision. Your eyes are meant to work together. If you close one, you're fatiguing the open eye, changing your depth perception, and also closing off half of your peripheral vision."

"So don't close either of them?"

"Some people say that if you're shooting with your right hand, close your left eye. However, when you're shooting with a handgun, that's close-quarters work; you don't have time to close an eye. You raise your weapon and fire. Most police officers who discharge their weapons do so within nine feet."

I knew, from my redactions, that handgun qualification for correctional officers in federal prisons was just seven yards, but most military and law enforcement qualification went out to twenty-five yards, thus the distance here at the range. But she was right: nearly 90% of shootings in the field by law enforcement personnel occur from less than four yards away.

Adira nodded to me that she was ready.

I loaded the Glock, raised it in front of me, and looked through the rear sight while focusing on the front sight just as I'd explained earlier to the colonel.

Figuring that I had the best chance of hitting the silhouette's chest, I aimed at where I anticipated the lungs would be and pulled the trigger.

A flash.

And a jolt as the gun's recoil took me a bit by surprise—even though I knew it was coming and had thought I was prepared for it.

Though muffled by the hearing protectors, the shot's percussion was still definitely loud enough to notice.

I emptied the gun at the target and then Adira and I removed our ear protection so we could speak for a moment, and I pressed the button to bring the target in closer for inspection.

It zipped toward us along the relay track attached to the ceiling. I stopped it just a few yards away where we could study the holes to see how I'd done.

"Hmm . . . ," Adira said. "Your shots are a bit scattered."

That was an understatement. They were literally all over the target. Some rounds hadn't even hit it.

"The bullet will go where your sights are lined up," she said frankly. "The secret is just to aim where you want it to go."

"You make it sound so simple."

"It is simple. It's just not easy. Control the trigger more—keep your pull smooth. And tighten up your grip a little."

"Gotcha."

Okay, do it. Talk to her.

"Hey, um . . ."

She waited. "Yes?"

I heard the shooting in the lane beside us stop and wondered if Clarke would be able to hear me. "Never mind," I told Adira.

She looked at me curiously, and finally said, "You're being weird. What's up?"

"In a sec. Let me shoot for a bit, clear my head."

Over the next fifteen minutes or so I tried my best to pull the trigger back smoothly and to line up my sights as I'd been taught to do, and eventually, I started to group my shots in more tightly.

In between, she took a few turns, but for the most part, left the shooting to me.

We taped up the holes a few times with masking tape and replaced the target twice and now, finally, on the third one, I felt like I was getting the hang of it.

I took ten final shots and then, when I brought my target forward, found that I'd grouped six of the bullets in a space not much larger than my hand, right in the center of the target's chest.

I was a bit proud of the grouping and showed it to Adira, who nodded with satisfaction, then said, "This might seem paradoxical, but track with me. If your grouping is too small, you'll want to actually broaden it out to create different wound channels. We refer to it as 'tactical accuracy.' Remember, your goal is to create stress that would shut the threat's body down. With a grouping that's too tight, you're actually doing the bad guy a favor. To put it bluntly, you're not trying to win an Olympic medal for shooting accuracy out there; you're trying to stop a threat before they stop you."

Hmm. I'd never thought of it in those terms before. "So, effectual field accuracy is as much about shot placement as it is about grouping. Tight grouping can, in some cases, actually be a hindrance to the ultimate goal."

"Exactly," she said. "I noticed one more thing: you're holding your breath. Don't forget to breathe. In a kinetic situation, you're going to want to breathe, so do it now. Get used to it."

"Breathe. Right. Got it."

"I can't have you passing out in here while wielding a deadly weapon."

"Noted." Alright, like it or not, it was time. "So, listen . . ." I set down the Glock. "I need to talk with you about Almaty."

CHAPTER 37

S he looked at me quizzically. "Almaty?"

"In my research into Popovic's movements and the log of his travels I found that he visited Almaty eight times. His financials indicate that he funded a joint venture there with the Kazakh military."

"Okay."

"A dark matter research facility known as *glubokaya shakhta*. Deep shaft."

A pause. "Where are you going with this?"

"You also visited Almaty and, as it turns out, you two were there at the same time. The same day."

"You were investigating me?" she said coolly.

"No, no. It's not like that. I'm just looking for answers, and every stone I uncovered this morning just led to more questions. The Department of Energy paid for your trip? Why? I know they're involved in dark matter research here in the States. But why Kazakhstan? What's going on? What's all this about?"

She let out a deep sigh. "While I was with Homeland, they became concerned about the deep shaft initiative. I was sent—that is, Meridian Vaughn was sent—to, well . . . have a look around." A pause. "I didn't know Popovic was there. I swear it—until just now, when you told me."

"Why dark matter?"

"Not dark matter, exactly, but xenon."

"Xenon?"

"To search for dark matter, you use a giant titanium tank under maybe a mile or so of dirt and rock to block out cosmic rays. Then, you use liquid xenon to try to identify the dark matter passing through. Basically, charged particles are always hitting the surface of our planet and the researchers need to be that far underground to eliminate that 'noise' for the machines searching for dark matter moving through the universe."

"I'm still not sure I understand. What about the xenon?"

"To do all this you need a lot of xenon. I mean, a *lot* of it. That project of theirs uses fifteen tons of it—which is nearly thirty-eight percent of the world's annual yield."

"That *is* a lot of xenon."

"It's the most concentrated amount on the planet. Maybe even in the universe. Whoever controls the xenon controls the future of this type of research."

"Huh. And the Department of Energy?"

"Dark energy. Ties in with their interest in cold fusion. Unlocking the secrets to dark matter and dark energy could teach us more about the universe's origin, how gravity works, and even, perhaps, give us a better understanding of the time-space continuum."

Last year, I'd redacted some files concerning a DARPA initiative back in the 2010s that had explored the possibility of constructing a gravity ray based on capturing and utilizing dark energy. Suddenly, the concept didn't seem quite so silly and farfetched.

DARPA, the Pentagon's research branch, has been involved in some truly remarkable high-risk, high-reward R&D projects over the years, from plant-eating robots to lab-grown blood, mind-controlled prosthetics, nuclear bomb–propelled spaceships, gravity sensors that can see underground, submersible planes, and laser-guided bullets. It has even given us a few modern conveniences that we use every day, like, for instance, the Internet.

"Interesting." I processed what Adira had told me. "You mentioned to me once that your time in Almaty was memorable. What made it so interesting?"

"I had a shootout with some security forces there—now that you've told me about Popovic being present, I'm wondering if they were his. Probably, based on their tats, that's who they were."

Something didn't quite jibe.

"Did this have anything to do with Project Symphony?"

"No," she said. "But the prototype *could* be used to steal secrets or research from our site in Wyoming that might benefit what they're doing in *glubokaya shakhta*. Do you think that's what this is all about?"

"Beats me. We should contact the Department of Energy, though, tell them to beef up security at their sites until all of this settles down."

"Agreed."

"This explains why you and Popovic were in Almaty," I said, "but not why you were there at the same time."

"I don't have an answer for that." She thought about it. "Unless the person from Homeland who signed off on me going there knew more than I did."

"You mean, they knew Popovic would be there?"

"Maybe. Yes."

"Who signed off on it?"

"Nathan Lassiter," she said soberly. He'd been her mentor and had been murdered last month by the same operative who'd set fire to my house. Before Nathan was killed, he'd been compromised and had provided intel to Janice Daniels.

"Oh," I muttered. "Where does that leave us?"

"I'm not sure—but I have to say, I don't like it that you were researching me. I feel like you went behind my back. If we're going to work together—if we're going to be together in *any* meaningful way—we need to trust each other. Come to me first next time. Okay?"

I was a bit torn. I'd tried to talk with her about this in the past and that hadn't led anywhere. Besides, uncovering the truth—no matter what that might be—was my job.

And so is trusting your team members.

Your friends.

Or more than that—whoever Adira truly is to you.

Maybe there was still more to this that I needed to find out. But I didn't say that. "Yes," I replied to her at last. "I'll do that. I promise. I'll come to you first."

With thoughts of dark matter research and mile-deep shafts on my mind, I went with Adira to connect up with Gunnar and Clarke in the briefing room.

"How'd it go in there?" Gunnar asked me.

"Pretty good. I learned about shot placement, wound channels, and how important it is to breathe—oh, and to simply aim at what you want to hit. That's the key."

"That'll do it," he said.

We told them about the deep shaft initiative, then I suggested to the colonel that we reach out to DOE and give them a heads-up.

"Good call." A quick glance at the time. "We're closing in on lunchtime. We made some good progress this morning. Meet up again this afternoon?"

Gunnar and I shared a look.

I was supposed to meet my dad at two o'clock at Aurora's Coffeehouse. Gunnar was planning to be there as well. "Gunnar and I have an engagement at two," I told Clarke. "It should be short though, and then I'll be good for the rest of the day, as well as tonight if necessary. I can even make it a working lunch if you need me to."

"Not necessary," he told me. "All good."

"Listen," Gunnar said. "For lunch: you've heard of fish tacos—well, the place I have in mind, it's just down the street, just opened. They serve a killer lobster taco." He gestured toward all of us. "We should check it out."

"Lobster tacos?" Adira said. "Seriously?"

"Trust me. They're legit. Fast. Fresh. They really hit the spot."

"How fresh?" she asked, a little uneasily.

"The lobster tank is at the front of the restaurant. They give each of the lobsters a name. There are these little waterproof stickers pasted onto their pinchers. Last time I was there I had to choose between Ziggie, Wendy, and Beth."

"What?" Adira gasped. "Why would they do that? Why would they *name* them?"

Gunnar shrugged. "Makes it easier for you to point out which one you're choosing."

"Uh-uh." She shook her head. "I can't eat something that someone has taken the time to name. It makes me want to mourn her death rather than celebrate her delicious, mouth-watering goodness. I can't eat a lobster named Beth. No way."

Gunnar was quiet.

"Please tell me you didn't eat Beth," Adira said.

"I might've eaten Beth."

"Oh, Gunnar."

"Any vegetarian options at this lobster place?" Clarke asked.

Gunnar blinked. "Since when are you a vegetarian?"

A sigh. "My wife's trying to get me switched over to a plant-based diet. I'm hungry all the time, but at least I don't feel guilty about what I'm eating."

"How'd she convince you to do that?"

"Last week at dinner, I'm halfway through my T-bone—medium rare, just the way I like—and she says, 'Oden, you need to eat something green once in a while, and not just meals that used to have a face or a momma. Cows and pigs mourn their dead. Spinach does not. If someone might've chosen to pet or brush your meal while he was alive, or if he might've ended up being buried beneath a five-year-old girl's tears and prayers if he hadn't ended up on your plate, then don't eat him. Opt for something else.' I didn't know what to say to that. I started eating brussels sprouts and broccoli on the spot."

"Don't eat anything with a face or a momma," Gunnar muttered. "And a five-year-old's tears and prayers? And not eating something someone has named? Those might be the best arguments for vegetarianism I've ever heard."

"I know, right?" Clarke shook his head. "Then Katherine reminded me that we're the only mammals that drink the milk of other mammals. So . . .'"

"Wait," I said. "Are you sure that's true?"

"Well, at least we're the only ones who put it in our Cap'n Crunch and drink it that way."

"Can't argue with that," Adira said.

"So, lunch?" Gunnar inquired. "Is *anyone* in?"

Adira gave him an exaggerated eye roll. "I'll come, but I'm not going to eat Ziggie or Wendy." She looked at the colonel.

"I should probably make a few calls to DOE."

"What do you say, Travis?" Gunnar looked my way expectantly. "Lobster tacos?"

"I think I'll just grab something here in the food court," I said. "I was looking into Popovic's travel history earlier and still have some work to do on that front. But I'll plan to see you at Aurora's at two."

A brisk nod. "See you there."

We headed in our different directions for lunch. I swung by the food court, picked up a chicken fiesta wrap that was not named Beth, and elevatored down to my office in sublevel three—the level that didn't officially exist, but that I'd called home for the last fifteen years.

Before leaving for my two o'clock meeting with my dad, I wanted to see if xenon might be connected in any way to the Pruninghooks Collective, TalynTek, or Valestra Pharmaceuticals.

CHAPTER 38

ATLANTA, GEORGIA

12:39 P.M.

Søren's lunch meeting with Victor Dotson did not happen.

"I'm here to meet with Mr. Dotson," he told the security guard at the front desk of Valestra Pharmaceuticals' headquarters in downtown Atlanta. "I have a one o'clock with him."

She swallowed.

"What is it?" Søren asked.

"I'm not sure I'm supposed to say this, but he was taken to the hospital, not fifteen minutes ago."

"What happened?"

"I'm . . . How do you know him?"

"I was married to his daughter before she passed away," he told her truthfully. "I'm family."

The guard sighed lightly. "I heard that he collapsed in a meeting. They're saying a heart attack. I don't know, though. Not for sure."

"I see."

"I'm sorry. I hope he's okay."

Yes, Søren thought. *So do I.*

Once he was outside the building again, he phoned Jan at the number she'd given him and informed her about what'd happened. Suddenly, he had an unwelcome thought. "Was this you?" he asked her. "You and your people? Are you playing me?"

"No. It wasn't us."

"What do you want me to do? Should I go to the hospital and take care of things there?"

"No. Let me think about this. I'll call you back."

—m—

LAGUARDIA AIRPORT

NEW YORK CITY, NEW YORK

Maia had finished lunch and found her way to her departure gate.

She was watching a couple navigate their way through the airport with their daughter, who might've been eight or nine. And, as she saw that girl, it made her think of the back room of the clinic and she realized that she'd made a grave mistake, gotten in way over her head, and done terrible things in the name of compassion and of progress, things that could not be undone.

The children.

If only it hadn't been children.

Then, it might all be easier. Then, maybe she could've found a way to forgive herself.

But what if there was another way? What if she could do something about it? Make it right?

Yes. Tonight. Later tonight.

All of this.

All of it had been a mistake—if that was even the right word for it.

No, a stronger word was needed.

It was not a mistake. It was a perversion of all that she believed in. A perversion of love.

Ever since she'd agreed to do the procedures at the Bidi Bidi Refugee Settlement, she'd been struggling to convince herself that she was making choices that were aligned with what she believed in, with what was right.

And despite all of the medical advances she'd made, despite all of her logical-sounding justifications regarding her actions and her appeal to the greater good, she now found herself overwhelmed with regrets.

She knew she'd been rationalizing her choices. Of course she did. But once you've strayed as far as she had from your moral moorings, once you've done the things she had done, there really was no other choice than finding a way to justify your actions. How else could you live with yourself?

Honestly, there was only one place she could go, one thing she could do that would be a step toward making things right.

Turn yourself in. Become a whistleblower.

But then another thought, one that troubled her: *But that would mean turning in those you worked with as well.*

The consequences of doing that were staggering—devastated dreams, ruined careers, separated families, prison sentences—and the drug would likely never make it to the marketplace, meaning that her whole career would've been wasted and that millions of people around the world would still continue to suffer in troubling and completely unnecessary ways.

That was perhaps the most alarming consequence of all—the suffering she would be responsible for. The suffering that she could relieve by simply remaining quiet and moving forward as planned. By simply doing what she was told.

Is getting this off your chest really worth condemning so many people to this disease? Is that really the right thing to do? Just because your conscience has started to bother you? Just because you're finding it difficult to live with yourself?

No.

Perhaps not.

Certainly not.

Sometimes we keep secrets to protect interests greater than our own, and sometimes we have to carry the burden of our secrets as the price for extending compassion to others.

And that's what she needed to do.

Carry this burden.

While she was thinking of that, she received a call from Janice Daniels.

"Janice?" It'd been more than a month since she'd heard Janice's voice. All of their communication since then had been through encrypted email or text messages. "Is that you?"

"I know we haven't been able to speak recently," Janice said, "but I need you to change your plans. Don't fly to Atlanta. Fly to DC, instead. Today. This afternoon."

"Did you do those things?" Maia asked her. "What they're accusing you of down in Tennessee? Planning a dirty bomb attack last month?"

"It would be best to discuss all of this in person. And we can do that tonight. I'll have my people make the arrangements for your flight to Dulles. I'll see you when you get here."

—ɷ—

It wasn't long before Søren heard back from Jan.

"I know that I sent you to Atlanta to convince Victor to give us the files, but it appears that an act of God has gotten in the way. Change of plans. I want you to come to DC. Fly up here as promptly as you can, this afternoon if possible." She provided him with a credit card number to use for booking the flight and ended by saying, "I'll tell you more when I see you."

"And the video footage from the highway?" he said. "You promised it would never reach the authorities."

"I'm a person of my word. By this time tomorrow all the files I have regarding it will be destroyed, and you'll be done with me."

He evaluated that. "Why DC?"

"I've learned that the Nectyla files were already sent to the FDA."

"So, it's too late? Is that what you're saying?"

"There is another way. I'll explain it all when you get here."

CHAPTER 39

I didn't come up with anything in my research into Popovic's travel patterns and the xenon and its possible connection to Valestra Pharmaceuticals, TalynTek, or the Pruninghooks Collective.

I'd been distracted, but finally I looked at the clock and saw that it was already one fifty, so I left the Pentagon and made my way to Aurora's Bakery and Coffeehouse for the two o'clock meeting with my father.

Now, it was four minutes after two and I was standing outside the front door.

After twenty-eight years of no contact, I was going to see him again. I had no idea how the conversation was going to go, but I did know that it was a conversation I wasn't looking forward to having.

But for the sake of my mom, I needed to do it.

And I would.

For her. To keep her safe.

I didn't want to lose my cool, so I took a deep breath, trying to calm myself, trying to find a happy, centered place.

Yeah, that wasn't going to happen.

Opening the door, I stepped inside.

Aurora served gourmet coffee and baked goods throughout the day, but at lunchtime, her crew started dishing out specialty wood-fired pizzas.

Even though you might expect that pizza and beer would go together better than pizza and coffee, Aurora had found a way to make it work, and locals, especially, had taken to the place.

In the same way that some restaurants match up certain wine with certain entrees, she would recommend different specialty coffee drinks with different flavors of pizza, which I could now smell baking in the brick ovens behind the counter. Admittedly, the coffee-pizza combination was a little unusual, but she somehow pulled it off.

The place had an industrial vibe rather than the faux European one you might expect at an Italian restaurant or a high-end coffee shop. Carefully orchestrated lighting provided lots of dim corners for kids to hang out in, lounging on the couches that were pushed up against the walls.

Gunnar was already here, seated at a table beside the window. He had a to-go cup of coffee beside his journal.

When I walked past, he nodded to me ever so slightly to reassure me that he was ready for whatever I might need. I couldn't imagine that there was any danger being here, but I appreciated the gesture. I nodded back and he went back to jotting down some thoughts, presumably ideas for his novel.

I scanned the coffee shop, looking for anyone who matched the photo from my dad's prison release papers.

Nothing.

I checked the time: 2:06 p.m.

It could be that he was late.

Could be that he wasn't coming.

Then a thought struck me, a chilling and troubling thought: *He knows you're here at this time. He's been trying to meet up with Mom. What if he found out where she lives and went over there instead of coming here? What if . . .*

I drew out my cell and called her.

Let it ring.

It went to voicemail.

"Mom, if Terry shows up there, don't open the door for him," I said, trying not to sound too concerned or nervous. "Call me as soon as you can."

I switched my phone from vibrate to ring, and then texted her the same thing.

I was heading toward Gunnar to tell him about my suspicions when the restaurant's entrance door swung open.

And there stood a man slightly shorter than me, backlit by the day outside.

Maybe it was him, maybe not.

But as he entered, I saw for sure.

Yes, it was Terry. It was my father, with a graying ponytail and that distinctive angular face. The lines around his eyes made it look like he'd lived longer than his sixty-five years—which, having spent the last eighteen years in a state penitentiary, I supposed, in some ways, he had.

He saw me, smiled, and hastened toward me.

"Travis!"

I tensed.

"Terry," I said, opting for his given name. I hadn't called him "Dad" to his face in nearly thirty years and I didn't intend to start doing so today.

In an awkward gesture, he held out both arms, obviously hoping for a hug, but I simply shook his hand instead. I was surprised by how solid his grip was. He'd been working out. That much was obvious.

"Look at you," he said, sizing me up, as if I were twelve and had just gone through a growth spurt and not thirty-seven.

But of course, the last time he'd seen me was when I was only nine, back on the day he smacked me across the kitchen and then went on to break Mom's arm.

His eyes lingered on my scars, but I didn't want to start out the conversation explaining about the fire, so I didn't comment on the extended gaze. Eventually, he looked away toward the coffee bar.

"Can I get you a coffee?" he said.

"I'll get it."

He didn't press the issue, but joined me at the counter, where a sable-haired, lip-ringed barista jawed a glob of gum, curling it conspicuously around the stud in her tongue.

Terry's eyes were on the board behind the counter. "Wow, there's so many options." Then, he asked me, "What are you getting?"

"Just a large coffee. Black."

"Right. I'll go with that too."

I realized that, having just left prison, he probably didn't have much money, so I told the barista, "These will be together."

"No," he said. "I can—"

"It's okay."

"Well, thanks."

"A large is a *grande*," she corrected me irritably. "That's what you'd like? Two grandes?"

"Sure. Just black."

"Any flavors in there today?"

"Black," I said again. "Plain black."

She drummed her fingernails clackily against the counter. "Room for cream?"

"No. Black. And just the coffee."

"Would you like a slice of pizza to go with that?" She was clearly on upselling autopilot here. "We have our pesto-based Garden of Eatin' pizza on sale today."

"No," I said. "We just want two coffees. Nothing to go with them. Nothing to go in them. Just plain coffee. Large."

"Grande."

"Yes. In mugs. Please."

"Will that be for here or to go?"

Seriously? I thought.

"*Mugs* means *for here*," Terry cut in. "Not *to go*."

"Oooo. Kaaay." She turned to the coffee dispenser and poured us two cups as silence spread through the space between me and my father.

She mentioned the price, but I wasn't really listening. I simply swiped my credit card, and then, carrying our coffee mugs to a nearby table, we took a seat.

Terry gestured toward my face. "You were burned."

"Yes."

"Are you alright?"

"It was a year and a half ago. A house fire." I left out the parts about the arsonist, the woman's body on the stairs, and the DNA test we were still waiting to hear the results of. "The scars are healed. I'm fine."

"Well, praise God for that."

Hearing language like that from him rather than from my mother was jarring. It felt almost sacrilegious.

He lifted his coffee mug toward me as if he were offering a toast. "We have a lot of catching up to do."

"Actually," I said, "I think we can keep this relatively brief. I came here to tell you not to contact Mom again. Don't try to talk to her, text her, call her. Anything. Do you understand?"

"I get it, you're angry—and you have a right to be. Just let me say my piece, though. After all, we do have two fine grande cups of coffee here that you were kind enough to buy. Let's at least finish these together and then, if you want to be done with me, so be it."

My eyes were on my untouched coffee, which I suddenly regretted buying. "Okay." I took a gulp. "Say your piece."

"First, fill me in for a second. What are you doing these days? Are you married? Do I have any grandchildren?"

"No wife. No kids. I work for the government. I've been at a desk for the past fifteen years. I'm just a cog in the machine. Nothing exciting." It was mostly true.

I sipped some more coffee, maybe more than I would've typically had, but now there was a reason to drink it quickly.

"I've been in prison for a long time for something terrible that I did," he said. "Something I'm ashamed of."

"Louisiana State Penitentiary," I said. "Manslaughter."

A pause. "So, you know."

"Yes."

"I paid my debt to society. I did my time. I'm hoping you won't hold my past against me."

"In Louisiana, manslaughter in the first degree is defined as a homicide that would otherwise be considered murder, but the perpetrator was provoked," I said. "How were you provoked?"

"You've done your research."

"So, how?"

"It was a misunderstanding. It got out of hand."

That wasn't a very satisfactory explanation. I said nothing. Had some coffee. Waited for him to go on.

"I've changed, Travis. I'm not the man I used to be, the man I was back when you knew me."

"An abusive drunk?" I said. "A man who mocked and beat his wife and his little boy? A coward who skipped town rather than face the consequences of his actions? That man?"

His eyes narrowed enough for me to see the strain my words had placed on him. I couldn't tell if he was ashamed or if it was something other than shame lurking in there, looking for a way to escape.

I glanced toward Gunnar, who was watching us out of the corner of his eye.

"I deserve that," Terry said to me. "All of that. It's true. That is who I was. I'm sorry for it. I've repented of it. It's not who I am anymore. Really. That's all behind me. The drinking. The anger. The lashing out. I've given all that up. I don't drink anymore."

Really? You mean they don't serve cocktails in prison? I thought but didn't say it.

I went for some coffee instead.

"Jesus helped me turn my life around," he said.

Has he now? I thought.

"Good for you," I said.

"I'm here to tell you that I'm sorry for the way I treated you and your mother." He hadn't started his coffee. "I want you to convey that to her. I want her to know that I'll do whatever it takes to make things right."

"There's no making things right, Terry. The past is broken in ways you can't fix."

"Does she know Jesus?"

"She does."

"And you?"

"Listen to me: I don't trust you. Mom's broken bones are testimony enough to the type of man you are. If this conversion is real, if you've really changed in the ways you're claiming to have changed, then that's great. Congratulations. If it's not, you should be ashamed of yourself for using religion as an excuse to manipulate people."

My coffee was nearly half gone. I took another drink.

He swirled his around, didn't have any.

"I had no intention of killing that man," he said softly.

"What do you want, Terry? What is this all about? To make up for lost time? To get to the place where we can go fishing together on the weekends or watch the big game on TV and eat chicken wings together? We're never going to be buddies. What is it you want from me and my mother?"

"I just want to do what's right. I was hoping that we could mend some fences here today."

I finished off my coffee and set the mug down with finality. "Don't contact Mom again."

For a moment I saw a flicker of the man I knew—the cold, flinty eyes; the set jaw; the fists beginning to form. Yeah, there it was, and then he buried it again under the guise of the Repentant Sinner. He'd gotten good at pretending, but you can't hide who you are forever. His right hand was still tight with what I was sure was pent-up rage. I half expected him to say, "Or what?" but he didn't. He just nodded.

"Okay," he said at last.

My phone buzzed with an incoming call. I checked to see if it was Mom but the screen told me that it was the Lab at Quantico.

The DNA results. They're ready.

With a quiver of trepidation, I said, "I'm going to need to take this." I rose. "Give me a minute. I'll be right back."

CHAPTER 40

I felt uncomfortable taking a call from the Bureau here in public where someone might overhear something, so I slipped off to the restroom. When I found it empty, I locked the door behind me and tapped the screen to answer the call.

"This is Travis Brock."

"Sir, my name is Juneau Myers. I'm with the FBI Lab. I have the results of the DNA test you ordered."

A tug of anxiety. "Yes?"

"They're negative in regard to the samples you provided from the cemetery. Without going into all of the details, we can state with almost absolute certainty that whoever is buried in that grave is not Sienna Haven Brock."

The truth.

There it was.

I'd been deceived all this time.

Yes, I'd suspected this, but that hadn't prepared me to actually accept it, and I found myself reeling. "Do we know the woman's identity?"

"No. Nothing came up in CODIS. We can search genealogical DNA databases for mitochondrial DNA and Y-chromosome DNA for possible relatives, but for now she's a Jane Doe."

"Start by looking for anyone related to a woman named Lena Rhodes." I tried to remain objective, professional, detached. "She lived in DC, disappeared about eighteen months ago."

"Yes, sir."

"Thanks," I said softly, then ended the call.

And stared, dazed, at the phone's screen, searching it as if it might hold some answers, some guidance, some comfort. My hand was shaking. And so was something else, deep inside of me.

My dad wasn't the only one reentering my life. So was my "dead" wife.

As I was returning to our table, still deep in thought about the implications of what I'd just learned, I saw Gunnar standing beside my chair, speaking with my father. Anxiously, I hurried toward them. A broken coffee mug and a splattered mess of coffee spread across the floor beside the table. It was the mug my father hadn't even started, probably in his attempt to keep our conversation going.

Nothing left to drink now.

"Sorry about that, man," Gunnar said, pretending to simply be a clumsy bystander. "Total accident. Let me buy you a new drink. Unless you're done."

"No, thanks," I said. "We're good. We're done. We were just on our way out."

Gunnar lingered for a moment, then strode away, and I caught my dad watching him all the way to the door as he left the restaurant.

Still internally processing the call, I took a moment to inform the barista about the spilled coffee and broken mug and after a dramatic sigh, she sent for someone to clean it up.

When I returned to the table and took a seat, my dad said, "You're never going to forgive me, are you?"

"What difference would it make either way, Terry? You did what you did. Now, here we are."

He took a long look at the corner of the coffee shop before dialing his gaze back on me. "You really hate me, don't you?"

I hate what you did, I thought. *I don't know how to separate that from who you are.*

And I hate Sienna for putting me through this. Or I love her still. Or both.

I was still sorting through how to respond when he said, "We all make wrong choices sometimes, Travis, and I admit it, I've done some bad—some very bad—things. But I'm not a bad person."

When he said that, it was just too much. I couldn't hold back any longer.

"Really?" I said. "You're not a bad person? You're a drunk, Terry. A wife beater. You never loved your son, never told him that you loved him—not even once—but put him down every chance you got. You're a convicted felon. You killed a man. If you're not a bad person, then who is?"

His eye twitched. "You say I never told you that I loved you. Maybe I didn't. I don't know. Probably. I mean, you're probably right. I didn't love anyone back then but myself. I do now, though—I love you, Son."

And so, the ball was in my court. I knew what I was supposed to say—what we're all supposed to say when someone tells you that they love you. You're supposed to say, "I love you too." But I didn't say that. Instead, I said what I felt, what was honest to me in that moment: "I don't believe you."

"I can't fix the past," he said. "I can't redo what I did or undo the pain I caused you, but I can work to earn your trust again."

"No. You don't get to do that. You don't get to reinsert yourself into our lives."

One of the restaurant workers appeared with a mop to clean up the floor. As she started to work on the mess, my dad said to me, "I paid my debt to society."

"For what you did to that man in Louisiana, yes, but not for what you did to Mom. I'll tell you what: Turn yourself in for physically assaulting her. If you really are saved, if you really are a follower of Jesus, then prove it. Allow justice to be carried out. You attacked my mother and never paid the penalty for it. Instead, you fled. Go back to prison. Or aren't you quite that saved?"

Earlier, I'd looked up the statute of limitations for domestic violence of the nature he was guilty of and found that it'd run out, but I didn't tell him that. I wanted to see what he would say.

"Is that what it would take to convince you?" he said. "Turning myself in to the police? Is that what you want?"

"Don't contact Mom again," I said unequivocally. "Ever. And this is the last time we're going to talk to each other. Understand?"

His expression was impossible to read. "Alright."

I rose. "Alright."

And then I hastened out of the coffeehouse.

I left him sitting there.

It was time to move on.

To get on with my day.

To get on with my life.

Time to locate the woman who had, as far as I could tell, hired an arsonist to burn me alive.

My wife.

CHAPTER 41

From her seat at the outdoor cafe across the street, the dark-haired woman in sunglasses watched Travis Brock leave Aurora's Coffeehouse and head toward the next block, where Gunnar Bane was standing beside a food truck, waiting for him.

The afternoon sun caused a small bead of sweat to fall from her brow.

She'd orchestrated things from the beginning. Yes, she'd been the one behind the fire and, yes, when Travis survived it, she'd kept an eye on him from a distance over the last eighteen months.

Not every day. Nothing like that. But she had monitored him.

After all, he was her husband.

She'd even visited him at the hospital several times when he was asleep and recovering after his surgeries and skin grafts.

On that final visit, she'd stood there by his bed for a long moment, fingering the syringe containing the drug that would end his suffering while he slept, end it once and for all.

The machines monitoring him purred softly beside her. Outside the room, a man and a woman were speaking in hushed tones. The man chuckled as they walked down the hall, then their voices trailed off and they were gone.

And she and Travis were alone.

In the stillness.

In the quiet of the night.

She wanted to end all of this, wanted to close up this chapter in her life, wanted to do what her handler had been encouraging her to do for weeks.

And so.

She had gently untucked his feet from beneath the sheet.

The machines pulsed and murmured next to the bed.

She uncapped the syringe, then positioned the tip of the needle between two of the toes on his left foot, in a place no one would think to look for a needle mark.

He would pass away. It would be quiet, painless. And it would be over.

But then, something had stayed her hand: he stirred in his sleep and groaned slightly from the pain.

He might wake up. He might see you.

Yes, that was true, but that's not what caused her to hold back.

She'd heard that he went back into the house to look for her. He'd braved the fire to try to save her. His love for her was real. There was no other way to explain an act of courage like that.

Travis was no fool. He must have known that he might not make it out of the house alive. No, he wasn't irrational; he was in love. That's what led him to go back into the burning house.

And so, in that moment, there with the syringe in her hand, she had stopped.

He didn't deserve to die like that.

Not a man that faithful. Not a man that selfless.

She tucked the sheet over his feet again and left the hospital.

Yes, her original intent had been for him to die in the fire, but afterward she decided he could, perhaps, be more useful to her and her associates if he was alive, if he was working with them.

It'd taken some effort, but in the end, she'd convinced her associates to let him live, to bide their time and to go after him later, when the Project Symphony prototype was further along, which they'd actually tried and failed to do last month in Tennessee.

And now, with his knowledge of and access to the device, he was more useful alive than ever.

That small grimace of pain had saved his life.

According to her source at the FBI, he was going to be notified this afternoon—or perhaps already had been—that she was not the person in that grave with her name on the headstone.

She didn't know all that his team was tasked with doing. Her source hadn't been able to discover that—which in itself was informative. But she *did* know that he was working closely with two other people, Halprin and Bane, to search for Janice. And, most likely, Ivan. Up until now, she had enjoyed anonymity and the ability to move about freely. Now, that was about to change.

While following him last night, she'd seen him pushing Halprin on that swing at the park, then observed them kissing afterward.

Okay.

So.

What next?

The prototype. Everything revolved around getting the Project Symphony device.

Sienna Brock tipped her server, then, tucking a strand of hair behind her ear, rose and left the restaurant.

She knew there was a traffic camera on this street corner, so she ducked her head to the side as she crossed the street toward the SUV that Ivan Popovic had sent to pick her up and take her to the wharf for their meeting.

Although she'd partnered up with him to accomplish mutually beneficial goals and she understood his ideological perspective, the two of them were not *exactly* on the same page. She was not a communist. However, she *was* a true believer that capitalism was a scourge on society. In today's parlance, she was most closely aligned, philosophically, with democratic socialism.

After all, what is more important, the individual or the community? What matters more in the big scheme of things, the needs of the few or the needs of the many? Capitalism is based on greed, on self-promotion, on the individual, rather than on what's best for the community, the country, the planet. It's solipsistic and shortsighted and unsustainable.

But socialism was not.

She'd been recruited in college when she was studying abroad and found other like-minded individuals at the university that she was attending in Prague.

She didn't believe in the Christian God, but she did respect the early followers of Jesus. They didn't own anything, but instead, shared everything for the good of everyone in their community. She'd pointed that out last week to Janice Daniels, who'd profited lucratively from the benefits afforded to her from her privileged place in the capitalist economy of the West. "It's right there in Acts chapter four," she'd said.

"Yes," Janice had conceded. "But their wealth distribution was voluntary. It wasn't forced upon them. That's where you and I differ. There are still Christian communities where no one owns or earns anything, but it's a choice, made for the good of the group as a whole, not an obligation forced upon them by the ruling class. The elite, the privileged, should not impose their definition of equality on others."

"Our world is one of almost incomprehensible inequity and wealth disparity," Sienna had countered. "The top one percent of the world's richest individuals own nearly fifty percent of the world's wealth, while *half* of the world's population own less than two percent of the wealth."

Janice had been quiet.

After all, she was in the top 1% of that top 1%.

"How is that equitable?" Sienna had said, pressing the issue. "How is that fair?"

She knew that Janice had experienced a bit of an epiphany and had dedicated her life to philanthropy. The only problem was, her scheme with Valestra Pharmaceuticals and Project Symphony wasn't ambitious enough, wasn't taking things far enough.

Yes, Nectyla was powerful. Yes, with the findings of the Davita Group, it could truly alter the pharma landscape, but Janice wasn't envisioning all that Project Symphony could provide them with.

She'd taken the conversation with Janice one step further. "At what point does our responsibility to care for that bottom half of the world's population outweigh the needs of the few to live in extravagant, self-indulgent decadence?" she'd asked her. "How would you explain to a starving child *not* redistributing the wealth of billionaires when it could easily stave off her suffering and save her life, save the lives of everyone in her village, maybe even everyone in her country? Sometimes providing for the good of all requires you to sacrifice a few freedoms."

"But you're not talking about sacrificing a few freedoms," Janice had said. "You're talking about *taking* those freedoms from others."

"Not everyone is ready for the responsibilities that freedom allows."

"That's precisely the rationale behind fascism."

"The health of the community and the planet are always more important than an individual's desires. And that requires, at times, taking radical steps to address inequity in order to provide better lives for the poor and disen-franchised and disadvantaged."

Silence from Janice.

And Sienna had left it at that. Something for the capitalist to think about.

Now, she rounded the corner and saw her ride waiting for her just up ahead. She crossed the street and climbed into the SUV, then told the driver, "Hans, take me to the yacht. I need to speak with Ivan."

"Yes, ma'am."

This yacht wasn't registered to the Russian oligarch, but was owned by the CEO of TalynTek, a Big Tech firm with a headquarters just outside of Madison, Wisconsin, on a private island across the lake from a pristine nature reserve.

After she'd met Janice last month, Sienna had assisted her with designing a password for the company's root system files. Janice had insisted that she help them with that task before cutting ties to the organization. According to what she'd said, since it'd been her company, it was her legacy, and she wanted it protected.

So, Sienna had given her guidance on Federal Digital Database password construction and had, as an example, shown her one from her past, one that had special meaning to her: 4SF18O<3f22UzT!

Now, she thought of that as she rode to meet with Ivan Popovic so they could proceed with their plan of obtaining the Project Symphony prototype and more effectively combat capitalism around the globe, for the good of the many, for the betterment of all.

CHAPTER 42

On my way to meet up with Gunnar, I tried to make sense of the news that Sienna wasn't buried in that grave in St. Andrew's Cemetery. It needed to be sorted out in my head as well as in my heart.

Since it'd been eighteen months, there was, of course, no guarantee, but it meant that she might very well still be alive.

It also meant that an innocent woman, very possibly Lena Rhodes, had burned to death that night when my house went up in flames.

And finally, if Sienna was alive and had hired the arsonist, because of his connection to Janice Daniels and Ivan Popovic, it was very likely that my wife was working with the Pruninghooks Collective or the Russians who had come for me last month.

She'd been a translator for our intelligence community. Who knew how many secrets she might have passed along to our adversaries during the decade that she worked for our government?

It troubled me to the point of feeling physically ill to even think about it.

I had trusted Sienna, slept with her, loved her.

She had pursued me from the start, but it hadn't been love that brought us together.

You weren't her soulmate, I heard a voice inside of me say. *You were her mark.*

I texted Gunnar that I was on my way, but before I met up with him, I called Colonel Clarke. I felt that he needed to be the first to know about the DNA results.

He picked up on the second ring.

"Sir, I need to tell you about the DNA."

"I just heard from the Lab," he said.

"So you know it wasn't Sienna in the fire."

"Yes. That's what they said."

"If you want me to step away while there's an investigation, I will."

"What I want is you on your A game. I don't want this to be a distraction from what we're doing. If you let it get to you, it's going to throw you off, and we can't afford for that to happen. Understood?"

"Yes," I said. "Absolutely."

"For now, let's focus. We need to learn what Popovic and Daniels have planned for tonight here in DC."

"I've been thinking about it," I said, "and I believe there's an avenue we haven't explored far enough in-depth yet."

"What's that?"

"There's one person who had access to Daniels, met with her numerous times, worked with the arsonist, and has experience navigating around the dark web."

"You're talking about Cliff Richardson," Clarke said.

The former senator had sold his tech firm to Janice Daniels and had been involved in a foiled plot to expose the vulnerabilities of our supply chain in regard to national security. He was now in federal prison at a facility about an hour and a half from DC.

"Yes," I told the colonel. "He's at Culpeper. I'm wondering if maybe he can give us the answers we're looking for. Can you get us permission to speak with him? I can leave here in just a few minutes and probably be there by quarter after four."

"I think so. I'll talk to the warden." He paused. "Listen, I've been cooped up here all day. Why don't I drive? It'll give us a chance to process this news about Sienna. Also, you can review the files and transcripts from Richardson's interviews with the Bureau, see if there's anything in there that might relate to Sienna. It'll help prepare you to talk to him. Hell, you can scan those files and remember what's in them better than anyone else I know, probably better than anyone else in the country."

I wasn't sure he was right about that.

But he also might not've been wrong.

"Where are you now?" he asked me.

"Just down the street from Aurora's. I can be back at the Pentagon in ten minutes."

"Alright. That'll work. Let me make a few calls. I need to ask the SecDef something. You know where my car is? Where I always park?"

"Yes."

"I'll meet you there. If for some reason I can't get permission to talk to Richardson, I'll let you know, and we'll figure out another route forward."

After ending the call, I caught up with Gunnar and told him about the DNA findings, then wrapped up by saying, "It looks like Sienna betrayed me and wanted me dead."

"You're assuming she wasn't coerced into it or kidnapped or forced to cooperate with them in some way."

"I keep coming back to that password," I said. "It points to her."

A pause. "Were they able to identify the woman who was killed in the fire?"

"Not yet."

"How are you doing with all this?"

"Honestly," I said, "it feels like I was kicked in the gut."

"I can only imagine."

"The hardest part is the sense of betrayal: the realization that Sienna might very well be involved with all of this—TalynTek, Popovic, Daniels, maybe even last month's attempted terrorist attack in Knoxville."

"You think she was a spy."

"I think she had us all fooled." We directed our steps back toward the Pentagon's parking lot. "Clarke and I are heading to Culpeper to speak with Cliff Richardson and see if we can find out anything from him regarding what Daniels and Popovic might have planned for tonight. Also, we'll see if he knows anything about Sienna."

"Huh," Gunnar said. "That gives me an idea. Janice's bodyguard Turo Pärnänen is also being held over there. I had a little shootout with him down in Tennessee, as you might recall. I'm wondering if he might be able to give us anything. Because of his dealings with Janice, it's possible he has knowledge of Sienna's whereabouts. I'll tell you what, I'll drive separately and connect up with you two once we're at the prison."

"Perfect."

We called Clarke to get permission from the warden for Gunnar to join us, then walked in silence for a few moments. Finally, Gunnar said, "Listen, it's nothing personal, but I gotta ask: Did Sienna ever have access to your work? Did you ever speak with her about what you did? Did you ever bring anything home from the Pentagon?"

"She knew what I did in a general sense, but I never once brought work home. No papers. No files. Nothing. As far as I know, she didn't get anything from me."

"But she did work at times with CIA?"

"Yes," I said. "She did."

He shook his head and muttered something unintelligible.

"I need to ask you," I said, "what'd you tell my dad back there at Aurora's? I thought I saw you talking to him while I was on my way back from the bathroom."

"I told him that I knew who he was and what he was up to. I told him to do whatever you said and that I'd be watching him."

"You threatened him?"

"I forewarned him."

Forewarned is forearmed, I thought.

"Well," I said at last, "let's hope all that's over with now."

"Let's hope."

We made it to the parking lot and Gunnar peeled off to find his car while I located the colonel's Tesla. When I got there, I texted Adira about what was going on.

Almost immediately, those little floaty ghost dots appeared beside her name, fluctuated for a moment, but then drifted away and didn't return.

The colonel wasn't at his car yet, but I saw that he'd left the building and was on his way toward me. I took advantage of the moment to make one more call, this time to my mom, to fill her in about my conversation with the man who used to beat her and then bring her flowers and play the role of the penitent husband—until he went out drinking again and the whole tragic scenario repeated itself.

The man who had been forewarned.

And forearmed.

CHAPTER 43

I was able to meet with Terry, here this afternoon," I told my mom. "I spoke with him."

"How did that go?"

"As well as it could've," I said. "I think we understand each other better now."

"Did you tell him that I forgive him?"

A beat. "I didn't quite get around to that."

"Oh."

"But don't worry. He won't bother you again."

"I see."

Tell her about Sienna or not? I wasn't sure, and since I wasn't sure, I put it off for now.

Clarke arrived and I closed up by saying, "Mom, I have to go. We'll talk again tonight. I'll call you."

End call.

The colonel was carrying a briefcase and had changed into a freshly starched shirt and tie.

"You look sharp," I said.

"Thanks. I needed an excuse to wear this tie clip."

"Oh," I said, curious why that might be. "Okay."

He removed some manila folders from the briefcase and handed them to me, then positioned himself behind the wheel and we left for the prison.

ETA: 4:20 p.m.

While he drove, I pored over the Richardson files and interview transcripts, doing what I did best, committing facts to memory, looking for threads of meaning and connections other people have missed.

And this time, I was looking for information about the most intimate of betrayers, the woman who'd been my lover and was at the very least a liar, and quite possibly an enemy of the state.

—m—

Adira wasn't sure what to think.

Just a few minutes ago she'd received a text from Travis that Sienna hadn't died in the fire and might possibly still be alive.

She was working in the conference room adjacent to Clarke's office at the time and the colonel swung by to tell her that he, Travis, and Gunnar would be at the prison in Culpeper doing interviews for the rest of the day.

"Okay," she'd said. "I'm in the middle of a few things. I think I'll hang back and see what I can get done here."

"Sounds good."

Now, she stared at her phone.

She wasn't quite sure what to make of the fact that Sienna hadn't been killed. It meant, of course, that Travis might very well still be married—yes, to a murderous psychopath who was also very likely a foreign agent, that was true, but married nonetheless—and she'd never dated a married man before. It certainly threw a wrench into the state of their relationship, and it was something she needed a bit of time to evaluate.

She imagined how a conversation with him about it might go:

"Until we figure this all out," she would say, *"I think we need to press pause."*

"Because of Sienna? Because she might be alive?"

"She is your wife."

"And she's also a killer," he would say. *"She faked her death, hired someone to set my house on fire while I was asleep in bed, and had another woman killed in her place. I'd say our marriage is pretty much annulled by now. Don't you think?"*

Huh.

Maybe.

In the end, since the rest of her team was going to be working off-site, Adira decided to do so as well and finish up her research in her apartment.

She gathered her things and left for home.

—⁂—

4:09 P.M.

Søren arrived in Washington, DC, and parked his rental car in the lot of the hotel where he would be staying tonight.

He wasn't exactly sure what Jan would ask of him.

He had his suspicions that Victor Dotson's sudden hospitalization was no accident, and that the timing of it was no coincidence, but he had no proof of that and, if Jan and her people weren't responsible, as she was claiming, who was?

Could another group be involved? What else was really going on here?

Søren checked in, found his room, set his phone on the desk, and waited for Jan to call.

He was getting the impression that he was on a leash here, doing her bidding. And that revelation did not please him.

No. It did not please him one bit.

—⁂—

4:14 P.M.

Colonel Clarke exited off the highway toward the prison. It looked like we were about five minutes out.

For nearly an hour and a half, in between familiarizing myself with the Richardson interviews, I'd fielded questions from the colonel about Sienna, regarding what she might have known or had access to in her work.

We'd covered a lot of ground during the drive, and now I said, "Colonel, let's get a team looking for any evidence that she's alive. Facial rec at the airport. The woman in the sunglasses tilted them slightly at one point. Let's see if it was enough to show us her eyes."

"Interesting. A whim?"

"A growing suspicion that all of this is related in some way."

He put the call through using his car's Bluetooth.

Be.

Loved.

Betrayed.

When he hung up, I said, "TalynTek used that password of hers in their root system files. She left her digital fingerprint behind there. Let's find out if anyone at the company has had direct contact with her since the day of the fire. Whoever entered that password might know something."

"Good thought. I'll get someone on it as soon as we stop."

He turned onto the access road that led to Culpeper USP, guiding us past a stretch of forest nestled along the nearby hills where white oaks and scraggly pines were busy reclaiming a field bordering the facility.

My conversation with my dad was still on my mind. "Colonel," I said, "let me ask you about something. It doesn't have to do with TalynTek or Sienna. It's more of a personal question."

"Shoot."

"This afternoon I saw my dad again. I told you about him before, right?"

"He was abusive."

"Yes, well, he's also a felon. Manslaughter. Served eighteen years."

A pause. "I didn't know that."

"My mother wants to forgive him for what he did to her," I said. "For the abuse."

"It sounds like he doesn't deserve it."

"He doesn't. I'm trying to make sense of what forgiving him would even mean—that is, if I were to do it."

"Would it change anything in you if you did? Would anything be different?"

"I'm not sure." I hadn't thought of it from that perspective before. "Forgiveness, Colonel. If you don't mind me asking, what does it mean to you?"

"I gotta tell you, I'm no expert on it by any means." We pulled into the quarter-mile drive that led to the prison's parking lot. "But I'd start by looking at what it *isn't*: It isn't holding a grudge, nursing an old wound. It isn't denial about what was done or diminishing the wrong or the pain. It isn't vengeance or the desire for the other person to suffer."

"Okay, I'm tracking with you."

He continued, "I'd say that to forgive doesn't mean that you suddenly trust that person; it doesn't mean you're now reconciled with them; it doesn't mean that you excuse what they did. Mostly, I'd say it's about holding them accountable, but not holding the act against them."

"How do you do that?"

"Beats the hell out of me. I just try my best. I don't know any other way forward, toward any sort of resolution."

"You're not giving yourself enough credit," I told him. "I'd say you *are* somewhat of an expert on forgiveness."

"Maybe at explaining it, but not at extending it. I'm sure Katherine would tell you that. I've been with the same woman for over three decades—just hit our thirty-one-year anniversary the other day. If you're going to be with someone that long, you have to learn to forgive—and be forgiven. Goes with the territory."

While I was thinking about that, he parked in the lot just outside the prison's gate.

We exited the car, he called in to get a team to interview the IT workers at TalynTek, then we walked toward the security checkpoint.

The razor wire–topped fence stretched out menacingly in both directions before us.

"Alright," he said. "Here we are."

"Yes," I said. "Let's find out what the former senator knows about my wife."

CHAPTER 44

B y the time Colonel Clarke and I made our way through security and filled out the requisite paperwork for the warden, it was almost quarter to five.

We learned that Gunnar wasn't here yet, but was still en route. Maybe he'd stopped off somewhere on the way. I figured we could touch base with him later, when we were done.

"What's going through your mind right now?" Clarke asked me as we walked down the corridor toward the interview room we would be using for our discussion with Cliff Richardson.

"Honestly," I said, "those DNA results, and what it might mean if Sienna really is alive, really was compromised, really is a traitor."

"Let's hope Richardson can give us an answer to that question."

We came to Interview Room 1B, where a slender correctional officer with a thick ponytail was waiting for us with a clipboard. The colonel signed off on it, she unlocked the door, and as she walked away, Clarke said, "You ever been in a prison before?"

"No, sir."

"Well, at least today you'll be able to walk back out those doors you just came through. Think about what it'd be like knowing that you were entering this place and would never leave it, not ever again."

"I can't even begin to imagine that."

We entered the windowless, airless room. It appeared pretty much like I expected it would: blank walls painted a bland yellow, a sturdy steel table centered in the room with two stiff-backed chairs pulled up to it. That was it as far as furniture. The ceiling's recessed fluorescent lights hid behind neglected cracked and dirty plastic shields, dotted with dead flies.

Just four empty walls. I would've thought one might be a two-way mirror. I was also a bit surprised that there were no surveillance cameras tucked up near the ceiling in the corners of the room. But then again, considering that this was where lawyers spoke with prisoners protected by attorney-client privilege, the lack of surveillance was understandable. Actually, for what we were planning with Richardson, it played to our advantage to be in a room without CCTV cameras.

The room smelled of old cigarette smoke, probably permeated into the paint from back in the days when smoking in here would've been allowed.

Since there were only two chairs, I gestured toward the closest one for the colonel to have a seat, but he declined. "You've met Richardson before," he said. "You should be the one doing the talking. Go on."

"What are you going to do?"

"Surreptitiously fade back into my surroundings, over here by the far wall."

I doubted that. "Gotcha."

"First thing, though—help me with this table." He slid the chairs aside. "I want to move it into the corner. It's always best to do interviews in a corner, with the table pushed up to the wall."

"Intimidation?"

"Makes the interviewee more apt to confess, but in this case maybe it'll make him more apt to cooperate."

I remembered that Clarke had studied social psychology, and here was an example of how to put that expertise into practice, how to let the degree pay off.

However, as it turned out, none of that mattered, since we immediately found that the table had been bolted securely to the floor.

Chairs back in place, I took a seat while the colonel studied the room, turning in a slow circle, perhaps looking for any hidden listening or recording devices.

"Was Richardson in the hospital the last time you saw him?" he asked me.

"Yes. In downtown Knoxville, recovering from being poisoned."

"By the same guy who burned down your house."

"That's right."

A head shake. "That guy got around."

"Yes, he did."

"You sure you're ready for this?"

"I am."

Someone rapped once on the door and then, before either of us could respond, it edged open and a looming, goateed correctional officer appeared, followed by Cliff Richardson.

Even though he'd only been here for a few weeks, it was evident that prison life had not been kind to him.

Weary lines traced across his sleep-deprived face and converged in around his bloodshot eyes. The left eye was severely blackened and swollen, probably from meeting someone's fist or the service end of a blunt instrument of some type. He was in his early fifties, but wearing his prison blues, and looking as beaten up as he was, he could've easily passed for someone a decade older who'd already served a ten-year sentence rather than just a month-long pre-trial detention.

Earlier this spring, this man had been a presidential hopeful; now he was a prisoner facing an almost certain decades-long sentence.

How quickly things can change.

The former senator's hands were cuffed in front of him, secured to a chain that encircled his waist. His ankles were also shackled, allowing him just enough freedom of movement to shuffle into the room.

Another guard, this one compact and muscular, brought up the rear. He let his gaze shift from me to Clarke and then back to me, perhaps trying to discern which of us was in charge. Finally, he settled on me, perhaps because I was seated in preparation for the interview and had the briefcase with me.

"The warden told us you didn't want us to stay." His voice was flat, and I couldn't quite tell if he was offering that as a question or not.

"I'm a lawyer," I said truthfully. "We need to speak with Mr. Richardson in private."

At that, both guards shifted their attention to Clarke.

"I'm working with my colleague on this case," the colonel said prudently.

They exchanged a glance, then the bigger guy shrugged and led Cliff to the chair, where he sat down, rather deftly, actually, considering how he was hobbled.

"You sure you're good?" the shorter correctional officer asked me.

"We're good," I answered him.

And with that, the two guards disappeared, closing the door definitively behind them.

Alright, I thought. *Here we go.*

"Hello, Cliff," I said, "I'm hoping you can help us answer a few questions."

CHAPTER 45

He studied my face. "You're Travis Brock, right? From the Pentagon. We spoke in Tennessee."

"Yes. You were in the ICU. It was touch and go there for a bit. I'm glad to see you've recovered."

He let his gaze wander over to meet Clarke's. "And you are?"

"Oden Clarke." The colonel held up a small notepad. "Don't mind me. I'm just here to observe."

"Uh-huh."

"Your eye . . ." I gestured toward Richardson's bruised face. "Are you okay?"

He raised his hands, palms up, as high as the chain allowed. "As good as can be expected, given the circumstances."

"What happened?"

"A slight disagreement with someone who didn't share my politics. My new friend was definitely not a fellow Democrat." He smiled wryly. At least he hadn't lost his sense of humor.

"Alright." I decided on a direct approach. "We're here because we need your help finding Janice Daniels. She has something planned for DC tonight with a co-conspirator. We want to figure out what it is and stop it."

"I honestly don't know what I can do for you on that front. I've been cooperating with the FBI. I've told them everything I know."

"I've read the transcripts." I placed the briefcase on the table. "So, it's time to learn something new."

He looked at me inquiringly. "I'm not sure I understand."

I unlocked the briefcase and drew out the laptop while Clarke pulled out his cell phone and scrolled across the screen and then tapped it to create a secure Wi-Fi hotspot.

Richardson leaned forward, eyeing us curiously. "They let you bring a cell phone in here? And a laptop?"

"We said 'please,'" Clarke ad-libbed. "Turns out it was the magic word."

"I . . ." Richardson seemed to be trying to sort out how seriously to take us. "In any case, I'm afraid my online privileges don't permit me to access anything other than my JPay email account."

"Consider those limits lifted," I said. "You sold your tech company to Janice and met with her at least half a dozen times over the years. Plus, you worked with the man she took care of as a teenager. Her foster son."

"That man was . . . Well, let me say, yes, I did know her, and I did work with him, but he tried to kill me. I wasn't aware of anything Daniels had planned there in Tennessee," he said solemnly. "I swear it."

I wasn't sure if that was true or not, but it did match up with what he'd told the FBI. "Your background in Big Tech and your relationship with Daniels. That's what brings us here. Plus, you know your way around the dark web."

A slight pause. "I've been there on occasion."

"I have to ask, did Janice or Joshua ever mention someone named Sienna?"

"No." He shook his head. "Not that I know of."

"What about a password containing the word *beloved*, or the numbers four, eighteen, twenty-two?" I wrote down the actual password, 4SF18O<3f22UzT!, on a sheet of paper and slid it to him. "Does that mean anything to you?"

He studied it carefully. "Uh-uh."

"Nothing with TalynTek?"

"No." He looked back and forth from me to Clarke. "Listen, as I said, I already spoke with the FBI about all of this."

"The FBI is carrying on their own investigation," I said. "This would be a . . . well, one parallel to theirs."

"You're with the Pentagon," he observed once again. No upward inflection. It wasn't really a question.

"Yes."

"And which arm of the Department of Defense is it that you work with again?" he pressed me. "Exactly?"

I glanced at Clarke, who remained silent, leaving it up to me to answer.

We're with the one that's not on the books, I thought. *The one that works in the dark. The one that isn't hindered by endless paperwork and buried in mountains of red tape. The one that gets things done.*

I said to Richardson, "We're with the one that can bring a laptop and a phone here, inside a federal penitentiary."

Clarke took off his tie clip. "How about we get you out of those cuffs?" Without waiting for an answer, he approached Richardson and expertly picked the handcuffs with the clasp of his tie clip, freeing his wrists. "I'm guessing it'd be rather tough for you to type with your hands cuffed like that."

Richardson sat there, dumbstruck, rubbing his wrists one at a time to help with the blood flow. "Who *are* you people?"

"We're the good guys," I said. "As I mentioned earlier, taking into account your background with Daniels, your hacking skills, and your experience with the dark web, you're uniquely equipped to help us, and if you do, we can help you."

"How can you help me?"

"We can get you transferred to a minimum-security facility," I said. "We'll let the DOJ know you're cooperating with us—which will help tremendously when it comes to your trial. And we can also get you a supervised visit once a week to your mom's nursing home. You assist us, you'll see her again. You choose not to, all of that goes away."

He evaluated my offer. "Can I have that in writing?"

I opened the briefcase and produced the document Clarke had prepared earlier, outlining what I'd said.

Richardson perused the form.

I was anxious to get started but all of this was part of the process. I knew that; still, it didn't make me any less impatient.

"The Secretary of Defense signed off on this?" Richardson said.

"As my colleague said," Clarke told him, "we're the good guys."

Using the pen that I offered him, Richardson scribbled his name on the bottom of the form with a stylized, practiced flourish that he'd likely developed during his tenure in the Senate.

I filed the agreement in the briefcase.

"Alright," he said. "What exactly are we looking for?"

"Anything regarding plans that Daniels might have this week to meet with a man named Ivan Popovic or with this woman Sienna. We're looking particularly for anything tonight in DC." I didn't mention Project Symphony.

It wasn't something he should know about, and we had no clearance to speak with him about it.

"We get the news in here," he said, "so I've read about what Popovic and Janice were trying to do, their scheme of manipulating the country's natural gas supply. What about this Sienna lady? What's her role?"

"We're not sure," I told him. "There's evidence that Popovic is here in the region. We believe that if we find him, it'll lead us to Daniels."

"Or vice versa."

"Yes."

Richardson tapped his chin thoughtfully. "It's possible that this could take a while. How much time do I have?"

"As long as we need," I said. "We'll have dinner brought in."

"And breakfast, if necessary," Clarke added.

Richardson looked at us dubiously. "I think we're limited to an hour in here."

I laid another sheet of paper on the table in front of him.

He scanned it. "Huh. You two really *do* get results."

I entered the computer's password, then spun the keyboard to face him.

"Okay," he said. "You have a VPN?"

"Yes. And this laptop comes with a few NSA enhancements. If anyone manages to somehow do a reverse–IP address lookup, this IP address will take them to a pig farm in Venezuela, and download a Trojan onto their device that will upload their media files and all of their contacts to a secure NSA server if they try to download any illegal videos or porn."

"Nice." He stared at the laptop. "I should mention that no one on the dark web uses their real name."

"What's your username?" I asked.

"I've had a couple of them over the years." A pause. "I think tonight we'll go with AnarchyTurtle24."

I avoided asking the obvious question: were there really already twenty-three other AnarchyTurtles?

"It's been a while since I've used that identity," Richardson said, "but it carries some clout, and it should still have enough cred to get us into the sites where we need to be." He placed his fingers on the keyboard, but didn't type anything. Instead, he said, "Before I do this, I have two questions for you. First, certainly you have people who know at least as much about the dark web as I do. Cybersecurity teams. Hell, whole agencies dedicated to this type of thing. Why come to me?"

"Because you worked with Janice's foster son and they didn't," I said. "He died committed to her cause. Go through the process you did when you met him. See if there are any threads connecting him to Ivan Popovic or Sienna Brock."

Only after I'd said her full name aloud did I realize how this might come across.

"Wait," he said. "Brock? Isn't that your last name?"

"We have a history together," I said vaguely.

"I see." He gazed at me as if he were waiting for me to go on and give a more detailed explanation. When I didn't, he said, "Second question: If I do this, if I visit some of these sites, we're going to be opening a can of worms. You never know what might crawl out. Are you ready for that?"

"We're ready," I said. "Open up the can."

CHAPTER 46

As Gunnar walked with the correctional officer down the corridor through Cell Block D, the other prisoners eyed him, probably trying to discern if he was a new guard, a lawyer, or a cop—the three most likely possibilities, since he wasn't dressed in prison blues.

The lanky, dreary-faced guard, whose name badge read simply *Haley*, kept his eyes trained straight ahead.

They say it takes more muscles to frown than to smile, Gunnar thought. *So, it's pretty clear this guy's face likes a good workout.*

"Are you sure about this?" Haley asked him.

"I'm sure. People are more forthcoming when there isn't an audience," Gunnar told him. "Also, I've found over the years that folks are more apt to be open when they're on their home turf, in their natural environment."

"Well," Haley said, "in this case, at this time of day, that's gonna be the laundry room. He should be finishing up in there in the next fifteen minutes or so. Dinner's at six."

"That'll work."

They came to the door, and Haley unpocketed a keycard for the lock but didn't swipe it quite yet. "Just so you know," he said, "word is, your friend in there killed another inmate yesterday. The vic was a real nasty piece of work: molested his twelve-year-old stepdaughter and then doused her with lighter fluid and set her on fire. So, I wouldn't say that solving the mystery of his death is at the tippy-top of our priority list, but we did question Pärnänen about it. He was right there next to the guy when it happened."

"Let me guess: he didn't see anything."

"Yeah." Haley swiped the card. "The medical examiner is still trying to figure out how the killer was able to jam the rolled-up magazine that far down the guy's throat. She had to cut him open from the sternum up to remove it."

A pause. "Okay."

"It was Pärnänen's magazine." Haley swung the door open. "Just so you know."

The scent of dryer lint and the overly sharp, tangy smell of lemon-scented laundry detergent met them.

Inside the room, four inmates were either sorting clothes or removing them from the industrial-sized dryers lining the walls.

One of the dryers was still churning, and must have had a loose screw somewhere because it rattled rhythmically, annoyingly, with each spin.

Haley indicated which inmate was Turo Pärnänen, but Gunnar already recognized him from their encounter last month in Knoxville. The six-foot-six behemoth was a human wrecking ball.

The three other men briefly sized Gunnar up, then silently went back to their work. Turo didn't bother to look their way.

Gunnar gestured toward the other inmates and said to Haley, "I'll need you to take those three gentlemen back to their cells."

"You sure?"

"Lock the door on your way out. Give us five minutes."

Haley shrugged. "Suit yourself." Then he muttered, just loud enough for Gunnar to hear, "It's your funeral."

Though the three inmates grumbled about it, they dutifully left, then Haley closed the door behind him, and Gunnar heard a solid metallic click as the reinforced door sealed him in the room with Janice Daniels's former bodyguard, who'd now paused folding laundry on the table in the center of the room, surrounded by front-loading dryers and washing machines, and was staring at Gunnar.

The annoyingly noisy dryer tumbled.

Rattled.

Gunnar strode toward it, opened the door to stop the cycle and the noise, and let it hang open.

Slowly, the spinning stopped, and the damp clothes dropped wearily to the bottom of the dryer.

"Wet clothes," Turo said. "Someone's not gonna be too happy about that."

"Dealing with adversity builds character," Gunnar told him helpfully.

"Besides, a little peace and quiet makes it so much easier to carry on a conversation."

Near Turo, a wooden mop handle slanted up out of a bucket that was filled nearly to the brim with filthy water. For some reason Turo's eyes went to it. Gunnar took note.

"And what exactly are we talking about?" Turo asked.

"Do you recognize me?"

"Yes. From Tennessee. You shot at me."

"Shot *back* at you," Gunnar corrected him gently. "Maybe if you had better aim I wouldn't be here."

"I could say the same thing."

"Touché."

Turo cocked his head at him. "What are you doing here, Mr. Bane?"

"I never told you my name."

"Huh. I wonder how I picked it up, then."

Gunnar approached him and paged through a sports magazine someone had left nearby. "I hear you were nearby when someone was killed yesterday. That must have been very traumatic."

"It's prison. It's a violent place. People die in here all the time." Turo sauntered over to the mop and bucket. "What do you want from me? Why are you here?"

Gunnar set the magazine down and watched Turo closely. That mop handle, broken in half, could become a formidable weapon, and would put him at a distinct disadvantage, especially since he was basically out one arm, still nursing that sore left shoulder's shrapnel wound. Still recovering.

Okay, observe. Respond as necessary. Quell any threats. Do whatever it takes.

Four meters separated them.

A jumbo bottle of liquid detergent sat nearby on one of the counters. It was within Gunnar's reach. Its cap was off.

"I want to talk to you about Janice Daniels," Gunnar said.

"You already know that I'm not gonna tell you anything, so why bother asking?"

"Why would you go to the mat for her? It won't benefit your case. But if you tell us where she is, what she has planned with Valestra and with Popovic, you might find some leniency with the judge."

Turo grasped the mop handle with one massive hand, wrapping his meaty fingers firmly around it, the muscles in his python-like arm tightening. "I have no idea what you're talking about."

"Of course not. Do you know a woman named Sienna Brock?"

"I don't believe I've made her acquaintance. By the way . . ." Turo offered him a glimmer of a smile. "How's Maureen?"

Gunnar narrowed his gaze. "What did you say?"

"Maureen. You should keep a better eye on her."

Gunnar wasn't sure if he was referring to his missing gun or to the woman by the same name, the woman he'd asked to marry him fifteen years ago. But either way, it was definitely something Turo should not have known anything about.

Gunnar picked up the laundry detergent bottle and strode toward him until he was less than two meters away. Yes, Turo had a height advantage—close to eight inches, in fact. And, yes, there was a weight difference—Turo probably had him by eighty pounds. But Gunnar wasn't intimidated. He was actually kinda jacked and ready for a fight.

"Why did you ask me about Maureen?"

"Just trying to be neighborly." Turo worked his jaw back and forth. "Come another step closer and let's see what you're made of."

"I'm made of fire and dreams." Gunnar took the step. "Tell me who broke into my house, who—"

And that's when Turo made his move.

Without a word, he swiftly drew the mop out of the bucket and snapped it in half like it was a mere twig. He dropped the shorter piece, but expertly stabbed the sharp, splintered end of the other one at Gunnar's stomach.

But Gunnar had anticipated this—not by much, but by just enough.

He spun to the side, kicked the mop's bucket over onto the tile floor beneath Turo's feet, then tossed a long slather of laundry soap across the pool of water, taking Turo's footing away from him. While the man wasn't going to just fall over, it was also unlikely that he'd be able to maneuver very well in the soapy mess.

Gunnar splashed on more detergent, then tossed the bottle to the side and lowered himself into a ready position. "You wanna dance?" he said. "Let's dance."

The door clicked.

Opened.

But it wasn't Haley who was standing there holding the keycard.

It was a convict with two tattoo sleeves.

And only one eye.

CHAPTER 47

Turo wondered what'd brought Sidewinder here and how he'd gotten a keycard, but then again, someone like Sidewinder could probably get just about anything he wanted in here.

"Who are you?" Bane asked the gang leader. "Where's Haley?"

"He's otherwise occupied at the moment." Sidewinder studied the scene, taking it all in: the man in civilian clothes facing off with Turo, who held a snapped-off wooden mop handle in his hands, a soapy pool of water underfoot. "What's going on in here?"

"Two on one?" Bane said, seemingly unfazed. "Is that how this works? Alright, bring it on."

"Easy there, cowboy," Sidewinder said. "I just needed a little sit-down with Turo here."

"Wait your turn." Then Bane faced Turo again. "What's happening in DC tonight?"

"Fireworks," Turo said cryptically.

Haley abruptly appeared behind Sidewinder and called to Bane, "Sorry I wasn't here. You okay? Everything alright?"

"All good. We're just having a friendly little chat, aren't we, boys?"

Turo shook the water off one of his soggy shoes. "I've got nothing more to say to you, except this: the next time I see you, I'm going to kill you."

"Good luck with that. I'll be looking forward to the reunion."

~∞~

Gunnar decided that he wasn't going to get anything more from Turo at this point, and besides, now he had a more pressing matter to address: contacting the woman he'd named his Smith & Wesson M&P after and making sure she was alright.

He approached the door, the tattooed inmate stepped aside, and Gunnar joined Haley outside the laundry room.

"Let's go," Gunnar said to him. "I need my phone."

Haley locked the two inmates in the laundry room.

"Who was that?" Gunnar asked. "The guy with the tats?"

"They call him Sidewinder. Leads a neo-Nazi gang. Not exactly a leading candidate for citizen of the year."

"They pals?"

"Hardly. The guy who was killed yesterday was pretty tight with Sidewinder."

"Huh. Good to know," Gunnar said reflectively. "And you're just going to leave them in the room together?"

"They'll be fine until I can get you to the checkpoint. If they're not, they're not. One less scumbag the taxpayers would need to foot the bill for. Or if we're lucky, two. You learn anything in there?"

"Yes," Gunnar said. "Not what I'd expected, but more than I'd antici-pated. How far to the checkpoint?"

"Just across the yard. Three minutes, max."

—᚜—

In the laundry room, Turo waited for Sidewinder to say something.

Finally, the gang leader cleared his throat slightly. "I saw you speaking with Pablo earlier," he said. "You two seem to have really hit it off."

Turo stepped out of the puddle of soapy, slimy water, being careful not to slip and fall on the slick floor. "What can I say? I'm an easy guy to get along with."

Sidewinder stood about fifteen feet away and didn't seem to pose much of a threat, but still, Turo didn't want to be careless, so he didn't set down the broken-off piece of mop handle.

"You've got something in the works with him," Sidewinder said coolly.

With Bane poking around, Turo decided it was time to call an audible and move up the timeline. "I'm getting out of here," he told Sidewinder. "Tonight. Right after dinner."

"Uh-huh."

"Listen to me: I can get you out too."

"That so?"

A nod. "Yeah. It is."

"And how am I supposed to get over the concertina wire on the top of the two security fences surrounding this place?"

Turo unpocketed the palm-sized blade that'd been in the gutted rat's carcass and handed it to him.

"What's this for?"

"That's for removing the cushion from the weight bench in the rec yard. Slice it off from the bench and take it with you."

"Why would I want to take the cushion from a weight bench anywhere?"

"To place over the razor wire on the fence when you crawl over it. People usually make the mistake of underestimating how dangerous that concertina wire is, how lethal it can be. It's designed with one purpose in mind—to shred human flesh. Too often, overly enthusiastic escapees try to pad it with bedsheets or blankets or an old set of clothes and end up inevitably regretting it. There's no way a threadbare bedsheet will take care of razor wire."

"But that leather cushion from the bench," Sidewinder said, tracking with him, "the padding, that's thick enough."

"Yes."

"What made you think of that?"

"Bedtime stories from my old man."

Turo expected Sidewinder to be pleased with the idea and with the opportunity to escape, but the gang leader simply scoffed and set the knife on the table next to a neatly folded set of blues. "You think I want out of here?" he said. "Why would I want that? It's safer for me in here than it is out there. With what I've done, with who I am, I'd be dead by day's end from some heathen out there who doesn't see eye to eye with my . . . ideology. I can run things in here just as well as I ever could on the outside. And in here, the feds pay for my food, my bed, my meds, *and* my protection. It's a sweet deal. Doesn't get much better than that."

"But you'd be free," Turo countered. He really wanted someone to try scaling the fence right after he drove away in order to create a distraction. Someone to get shot and dropped. Stopped for good. "You could do as you please."

"I do as I please now."

"But you could flee the country. Live anywhere you want to."

"I'd rather be calling the shots than living on the run. And I don't flee.

From anyone. Ever." Sidewinder slid the blade to him. "I came in here to talk to you about Pablo."

Turo accepted the knife. "What about him?"

"I don't think you're gonna get out," Sidewinder said, "but if you *do* make it, don't do anything to him or his family. He's a good man and that counts for something. They're hard to find, especially in here."

"Alright," Turo said.

"I mean it. He respects people. Give me your word."

"You have my word."

"Say it."

"I won't harm Pablo or his family. Listen to me, if you won't go, choose someone else who wants to be free, and we'll get him out tonight. There'll be a distraction at seven seventeen. The transformer will blow. Tell him to go then."

"Seven seventeen?"

"Yes."

The door clicked open. Turo pocketed the blade. He thought it would probably be the guard from earlier at the door but was pleased to see that it was Pablo instead who stood there.

"Time for dinner," Pablo told them.

"Hello, Pablo," Sidewinder said.

"Asher."

After a pause, Sidewinder turned and left.

"Asher?" Turo said to Pablo. "That his name?"

"Yes."

"How'd you know that?"

"I asked him what he prefers to be called. A courteous guy, once you get to know him."

"Uh-huh."

Turo tossed the broken mop handle shaft into the corner, then left the laundry room with Pablo.

"I have the clothes for you," Pablo told him, keeping his voice low. "They're in the custodial closet near the pantry in the kitchen."

"I'll get them later."

As Turo walked, he checked the phone he'd gotten from the rat's body to confirm that Rollan had done his part with Pablo's wife and daughters.

"Hang on," Pablo said. "What is that? You have a phone?"

"That's what they call 'em, yeah. And I know: I can get three years added to my sentence for having this in my possession, but—"

"You need to give me that."

"I don't think you're going to want to see what's on here, Pablo. But you need to. I want you to be thinking clearly, processing what's happening." Without another word, Turo handed the cell to him. Pablo gasped when he looked at the screen—a video feed of his wife and two daughters tied up in their basement rec room, trembling in fear.

"No." His voice was a strangled whisper. "What have you done?"

"They're in good hands."

"Is this live? Is this happening right now?"

"Yes. I trust the person who's with them, but he's not a very patient man. Given enough time he might want to start playing games with them, games that I'm anticipating you wouldn't want him to be playing with your wife or your young daughters."

"You are one sick son of a—"

"Careful, now. Focus, Pablo. I need you to listen attentively because I'm only going to say this once and the future of your family depends on you doing exactly what I'm about to tell you. Do you understand?"

"Why me? Why my family?"

"Because you have access to the two things I need."

"And what are those?"

"The kitchen and the transformer."

"What are you asking me to do?"

"At seven o'clock when the food delivery truck comes through, I need you to help supervise the removal of the dry goods. When I show up, dismiss the other prisoners who are helping. I'll take things from there."

"How are you going to get through the electronic locks from your cell?"

"Let me worry about that. And the transformer—can you get it to blow?"

"I'm not sure. I could overload the power supply—but that'll only give you maybe ten or fifteen seconds before the generators kick in."

"That'll work." Turo offered Pablo the wad of hundred-dollar bills from the rat. "That's five thousand dollars. There'll be twice as much in an envelope in the mailbox at your house once I'm free."

"And my family?"

"They'll be freed as soon as I'm out. If anything happens to me tonight, though, something happens to them. You understand what I'm saying, don't you?"

Pablo studied the blood-flecked bills, but didn't take any. "Do I want to ask how you got these in here or whose blood that is?"

"Probably not."

"Keep your money. I don't want it. Any of it. I just want to be done with you."

"Alright. Let's go so I can get some chow. It all happens after dinner. I'm hungry and I've got a long night ahead of me."

—⁂—

As soon as Gunnar had his phone from the security checkpoint, he made the call to Maureen Osgood.

The only number he had for her was more than a decade old, so he realized it might not still be good, but he tried it anyway.

The call went immediately to voicemail, but there was no name given, just an electronically generated voice that repeated the number he'd called and told him to leave a message.

"Maureen, it's Gunnar. If this is you, I need you to call me. I wouldn't reach out if it wasn't important. Okay. So, give me a shout as soon as you get this." He left his cell number.

Awkward, but necessary.

Based on what Turo had said, Gunnar realized he really did need to confirm that she was safe—and that couldn't wait. He had some off-the-books channels he could use, but they weren't 100% reliable. Clarke would have the resources at his disposal to find her, no matter where she might be.

He asked Haley, "Do you know where Cliff Richardson is being interviewed?"

"Sure. Interview Room 1B. He's with those two guys from the Pentagon."

"Take me there. Let's go."

CHAPTER 48

The text that Adira Halprin received shocked her, but also intrigued her and zeroed her attention in to a laser-tight focus: **Six thirty tonight. The Metro Museum of Modern Art. Tell no one. Come alone. I'll know if you don't—JD**

The text came from an unknown number, and it disappeared within seconds of her reading it. Gone. Vanished into the thin air of cyberspace from some sort of time-release data deterioration file.

It was almost as if her phone's camera had registered her eyes moving across the screen, reading the message, and then deleted it as soon as she'd done so. She knew that NSA had the capability to pull off something like that, but she seriously doubted that this message had come from any NSA employees, or NSA-ers, as they liked to call themselves.

Besides, why would anyone from NSA warn her to come to a meeting alone and sign it with just their initials?

No.

She had a pretty good idea who this was from.

Her old "friend" Janice Daniels.

Six thirty, huh?

That gave her less than thirty minutes.

Yes, maybe enough time to organize a TAC team to be present, but she was worried that if she even tried to, Janice would somehow find out and wouldn't show up. And that wasn't something Adira was about to chance happening.

She'd only been to the museum once, so she didn't know its layout very well, but it was a public place so she didn't necessarily feel like there was any threat to her and, if Janice really did show up, it could give her an opportunity to apprehend her, or at least notify museum security of the domestic terrorist's presence.

On the other hand, the text had said not to tell anyone.

Okay.

Fair enough.

Despite how well Adira knew that she *should* contact her team, she had the sense that, if she did, Janice would somehow discover that she'd done so.

Maybe it's a test.

Hmm.

The museum wasn't far. Maybe a fifteen-minute drive.

There was a parking garage nearby. It was after work hours now, so it was likely she'd be able to snag a parking spot, but in DC that was never guaranteed.

So, leave now, get there as soon as possible, be prepared for the unexpected, and play things by ear.

Adira snatched up her keys and took off.

Yeah.

Buckle up.

Things were about to get interesting.

CHAPTER 49

As promised, Clarke and I had dinner brought into the interview room for Cliff Richardson.

Prisons are infamous for their cuisine, and when we smelled the mystery meat and saw it laid out there on the tray in all its greasy grandeur on a soggy bed of pee-colored mashed potatoes, the colonel and I opted to wait until later to grab a bite. He was on a vegetarian diet anyway. I wasn't sure if any five-year-old would've petted or named that gray slab of meat while it was alive, but I could think of plenty of names for it now.

Richardson had been tooling around the dark web for over an hour and had found exactly zero references to Sienna or her passcode. While that might've been a dead end, it wasn't the only avenue we were exploring. When AnarchyTurtle24 logged in to the site where he'd first met up with the arsonist, we learned that one of the organizations that the man's foster mother, Janice Daniels, had founded was mentioned where it should not have appeared.

"Do you know anything about the Davita Group?" Richardson asked me.

Adira had mentioned that name to me, but I had no idea why the name would show up here, on this website. "It's a nonprofit NGO that does humanitarian work and provides medical care in refugee settlements," I said. Earlier, I'd been planning to look into it more, but hadn't had a chance to do so yet. "Janice headed it up until she went on the run. As far as I know, they're still operating. No red flags."

On this site, people were bidding for information regarding when shipments of aid would arrive from the United Nations to a burgeoning refugee settlement in Uganda, located along the border with South Sudan.

It didn't take long to figure out that rebel groups were currently the top bidders for the intel. Knowing those arrival times and locations would allow them to hijack the shipments, steal the food and medical supplies, and then sell them on the black market, or the gray market, as it's called in Africa, at up to a hundred times what they were worth.

"What do you want me to do?" Richardson asked. "They've already started the auction."

"Bid," Colonel Clarke said.

"They'll want payment in cryptocurrency."

"That can be arranged. I want to know who's behind this, leaking this information. Popovic, you think?"

"That's unclear."

"Alright, bid up to fifty thousand dollars. Let's—"

A knock at the door interrupted him.

All of us turned to see who it was, and when Gunnar appeared with a correctional officer beside him, Colonel Clarke gestured for him to join us, but Gunnar said, "Colonel, can I talk with you for a sec?"

"Sure."

Clarke joined him in the hall, closing the door behind him.

"He's a colonel?" Richardson said to me questioningly. "What branch of the military?"

"Army," I said. "Make the bid."

While AnarchyTurtle24 entered the auction, I asked him, "Do you have any idea how a password that Sienna Brock came up with might've ended up being used in your old company TalynTek's files?"

"I can't see how it could be possible. Unless she was working with someone from there, from the inside."

Two minutes passed as Richardson monitored the auction and bid on the intel. Finally, he announced, "Alright. We got it. We won. Tell the colonel that he needs to cough up forty-five thousand dollars' worth of crypto."

I wasn't sure how this information was going to help us, but it might lead to a better understanding of how this leak had occurred and help facilitate a more secure supply line for getting food and medicine to people who really needed it. So, in that case, it'd be worthwhile, but it seemed of little use to us right now in finding Janice Daniels or Sienna.

I was on my way to the door to get Clarke when it opened and he appeared. "I need my phone for a minute," he said. I let him know about the auction. He hesitated for a moment, then gave Richardson the access he needed for the funds transfer.

After retrieving his phone, the colonel ushered me into the hall, leaving the door open so we could keep an eye on Richardson. Clarke nodded toward Gunnar. "It looks like Turo and his people know about Gunnar's past relationship with a certain woman, Maureen Osgood. I'm sending some police officers to make sure she's alright. Is there anyone you have that you'd like us to look in on?"

"Just my mom."

"We'll have a car swing over to watch her place."

"Why all the concern?"

"I'll tell you while the colonel makes the calls," Gunnar said.

Clarke stepped away and Gunnar summarized his conversation with Turo and how the man had said that he needed to keep a better eye on Maureen and that there would be fireworks tonight. Afterward, I filled Gunnar in on what Richardson had been doing. When I mentioned the bidding and the hijacking of humanitarian aid, he said, "That's got Popovic's name written all over it."

"That's what the colonel was thinking too."

Clarke finished up on the phone, then rejoined us. "I want you two back in DC. I'll conclude Richardson's interview." He gestured toward Gunnar. "You good to give Travis a ride?"

"No problem."

"Perfect." Clarke gave a brisk nod. "We'll reassess and regroup in the morning."

I left the briefcase and laptop with the colonel, then assured Richardson that I would follow up regarding our agreement and what we'd offered him.

He hadn't touched his meal.

Smart man.

"Stop them," he said to me as I was on my way out the door. "Whatever it is they have in mind, it won't be good."

As Gunnar and I left him alone with Clarke, I found myself wondering once more if the former senator knew more about what was going on here than he was letting on. If that was the case, I assured myself that if anyone could get him to talk, it would be Colonel Clarke.

—ɷ—

Adira found a parking spot on the lower level of an underground garage less than two blocks from the Metro Museum of Modern Art. She made sure a round was chambered in her Springfield XD, and then headed to her meeting with the mystery person who'd texted her.

—ɷ—

I wasn't sure there was a delicate way to ask Gunnar this, so as we were approaching his car, I just went ahead and said, "Can I ask what the deal is with Maureen?"

"The gun or the woman?"

"If you named your gun after her, she must have been pretty special to you."

"We were engaged." He tapped his key fob and unlocked the car. "Back in another life."

"Oh." I wasn't sure if I should ask him to elaborate, but decided that since he'd shared that much and it might involve this woman's safety, I would give it a shot. "What happened?" I asked. "I'm not trying to pry or—"

"No, it's fine." We climbed into his Lincoln and Gunnar fired up the engine. "My best friend is what happened," he said. "He happened to seduce Maureen. She happened to fall for it. And then they happened to end up in bed together. And that happened to put an end to our wedding plans."

"Oh, man. I'm sorry."

"It's water under the bridge."

I believed him, but I also believed that there was more to the story. After all, he'd named one of his favorite guns after her and, as far as I'd been able to tell while getting to know him over the last month, he wasn't the type of guy to dwell on the tragedies or mishaps of the past, but rather to focus on the possibilities of the future.

Or, maybe, he was just better than I was at forgiving people.

As we drove toward the access road, he said, "I actually haven't spoken to either of them in years. Turo was probably just referring to my gun getting stolen. But better safe than sorry. Right?"

"Right."

If Maureen Osgood's dalliance really was water under the bridge, that would explain why Gunnar named his gun after her. But still, why continue to let yourself be daily reminded of a betrayal like that? Of the pain she caused you? Why, unless you still had feelings for her? Then, it just might make sense.

That's what I thought, but I didn't bring any of that up.

It wasn't the time and, truthfully, it wasn't really any of my business.

We were leaving the prison's property when we got word from Clarke that his people had located Maureen and her teenage son. Apparently, she'd gotten a divorce five years ago and her ex-husband—Gunnar's ex-best friend—was no longer in the picture. I put the colonel on speakerphone and he informed us that Maureen and Liam had been taken into protective custody until all this could calm down a bit and we could confirm that they weren't in any danger.

"Also, we checked on your mom, Travis," Clarke added. "She's fine. Metro sent an officer to watch her place."

"Thanks."

End call.

Earlier, Gunnar had mentioned that Turo said there would be fireworks tonight.

Now, as we drove toward DC, I thought of that, and wondered what exactly Janice's incarcerated bodyguard might have been referring to.

CHAPTER 50

Adira entered the museum.
Alert. Wary.

She had twelve minutes.

Although some art museums might close at five, she'd checked, and this one was open until nine on Friday nights—she guessed in an attempt to entice people to swing by after work.

The last text she'd received just a few minutes ago had told her to wait on the bench that was nearest to the window on the first floor. As it turned out, that wasn't difficult to find since, as far as Adira could see, there was only one window on that entire level, about forty feet from the bench.

A museum guard stood sentry near an emergency exit door not far from the window, and for a moment Adira wondered if he was a plant. Would Janice really have chosen a spot to meet where there was a guard that close? Unlikely.

He wasn't armed, which didn't surprise her. Still, something felt off.

Although not packed with visitors, the museum was far from empty, and Adira didn't like the idea that any of these people might get in the way or might get hurt if things spun off sideways.

Some of the patrons were moving from painting to painting thoughtfully, as if they were trying to decipher all the meaning that the artist was trying to convey. Others walked by the artwork with hardly a glance, clearly in a hurry and disinterested, perhaps just to check *Visit the Metro Museum of Modern Art* off a to-do list.

Before taking a seat on the bench, Adira quickly walked the upper levels to see if there was anything suspicious or anyone she might recognize. Finding nothing out of the ordinary and no sign of Janice, she returned to the first floor.

The security guard was gone.

The room was large—fifty by sixty feet.

Six people were in there with Adira: two were perusing the pictures, four were mindlessly staring at their phones, scrolling through the day's feeds rather than looking at any of the artwork.

Modern art versus social media?

No contest there.

The painting that hung on the wall facing the bench was a giant painting of blue.

That was it.

Blue.

A six-foot-by-six-foot blue canvas.

Oh, except for two spots of crimson on it, near the upper right-hand corner.

Art?

Adira studied it, then read the plaque beside it:

Wound
by Willow Granai
Acrylic on linen
Museum purchase, 2023

Willow Granai is a gender-nonconforming artist who uses minimalist forms and colors to create powerful, expressive pieces that explore the paradoxes of the human condition. In *Wound*, they use an immersive shade of blue to evoke a relationship to the centrality of water both on our planet and in our bodies. The red gashes represent the harm we do to the natural world when we don't give ourselves over to it to care for it, and to the subsequent wounds we cause to ourselves and to humanity as a whole when we fail to live in harmony with the fragile biosphere that supports all life.

Wound is as much a meditation on our place in the universe as it is an exploration of our deeper selves and a desire for an expansion of understanding inspired by the power of colors to evoke emotion and inspire restorative action.

Wow.

How about that.

Adira had recently read that in 2022 someone discovered that Piet Mondrian's painting *New York City* had been hanging upside down in a museum for more than seventy-five years, and no one had noticed. Oopsie. In the end, the museum owners decided to leave it upside down to honor its "heritage."

If you can't even tell if a painting is upside down or not, how can you call it art?

No, Adira did not get the modern "art" world at all.

She checked her phone.

Messages: none.

Time: 6:27 p.m.

Three minutes.

She wondered if she should have contacted law enforcement after all, or at least told her team what was going on. However, she'd been explicitly warned not to do so, and she didn't want to take any chances that Janice would find out that she'd notified anyone and bail on the meet. The billionaire fugitive seemed to have ears everywhere and to always be one step ahead.

Well, Adira thought. *That's one thing that's about to change.*

—✺—

As Gunnar drove us toward DC, I recalled that I'd promised to check in on my mom. Even though I would've ideally liked to speak with her in person about the DNA findings, I didn't want to wait any longer and have her somehow hear the news from someone else, so I tapped my screen and put the call through. "Mom, listen, I need to tell you something."

"There was a police officer here earlier. Is everything alright?"

"Yes. That's just a precaution. That's not actually why I called, though."

"Is it about your father?"

"No, it's . . . By the way, are you doing alright with all of that? He hasn't contacted you again, has he?"

"No. He hasn't. So, why *did* you call?"

"It has to do with Sienna, actually. I don't know a good way to say this, but she didn't die in the fire. It was someone else."

"What do you mean? You saw her on the steps."

"I saw *someone* on the steps. I assumed it was her, but it turns out that it wasn't." *Tell her or not? Yeah. Go ahead.* "And there's some indication that Sienna might've been the one who hired the arsonist."

A pause. "I don't understand."

"Yeah, it's a little hard to wrap your mind around, but it looks like she wasn't the person we thought she was. Not at all."

A longer pause this time. "How do you know this? How do you know any of this?"

I didn't like the idea of telling her that we'd disinterred the body that she'd seen lowered into the ground, but I sensed that it was time for honesty and openness both. "We did a DNA test," I said, "on the woman that we buried at Saint Andrew's. The test confirmed that it wasn't Sienna."

"Travis . . . I . . ." My mom's voice tapered off into silence as she let all of that sink in. "Who was she?"

"We don't know for sure. We're looking into it."

"No," she clarified. "I mean, who was Sienna?"

"I don't know, Mom. I really don't."

"Do you know where she is now?"

"No. I know this is a lot to process, especially with what's going on with Terry, but I felt like I needed to let you know about her. I'm busy tonight, but maybe we can talk tomorrow. I'll call you."

We said our goodbyes and I-love-yous.

I still hadn't heard from Adira since letting her know that Sienna wasn't the victim in the fire, so, as Gunnar hopped onto I-95, the highway that would take us past Marine Corps Base Quantico and on to DC, I texted her to see how she was doing, and waited to hear back.

CHAPTER 51

6:29 P.M.

Adira was scrolling past Travis's text to see if there were any more messages from the unknown sender when she felt a slur of air stir beside her as someone took a seat next to her on the bench.

"Don't make a move," the woman said softly, and Adira recognized the voice right away: Janice Daniels, the woman they'd been searching for all this time.

Do it, Adira thought. *Take her down. Cuff her. Get this over with. You can deal with the consequences of it all later.*

Her pulse raced as she mentally rehearsed how it would go down, but before she could do anything, Janice said, "Look outside, Adira."

Adira turned to her right, and glanced out the window.

Outside, next to a fountain, a woman who was pushing a stroller had paused and was gesturing enthusiastically toward her child about the water.

The window was about twelve or thirteen yards away. The emergency exit door waited beside it. The guard had not returned.

"Her name is Esmé Dupont," Janice said. "Her son turns two next month. I have an associate out there who has a gun aimed at Esmé's head. If you try anything, that boy grows up without a mother. We have four minutes before I need to text her to leave Esmé and her son alone. If I don't send the text, she'll take the shot. So, this gives us a chance to speak to each other one-on-one, and then let Esmé and her son go home and enjoy a wonderful life together, never even knowing how much of their future rested in a stranger's hands."

Adira processed that.

From earlier, she knew that the museum's window was mirrored on the outside. So, from where she was seated on this side of the glass, there was really no good way to signal to or warn Esmé.

Although Adira didn't see the shooter, based on all that she knew about Janice, she trusted that the billionaire was not lying to her. She had no choice but to believe that the threat was real.

There was no good option here, except for taking advantage of the next four minutes and finding out all she could about what Janice had in mind.

Only two other people were in the room with them now, and they were too far away to hear them if they spoke in hushed tones, which Janice did. "You don't want to be responsible for Esmé's death, do you?" she said. "Her son would have to grow up without a mother and you would know that you were the one responsible for his suffering."

Adira faced her. "Why is it always kids, Janice? Why do you always go after them, target them, threaten them? What kind of a person are you? You claim to be religious, to be a Christian, and yet you can't seem to get enough of directing violence and orchestrating tragedy against the most innocent and defenseless people of all. How do you justify that?"

Rather than answer any of Adira's questions, Janice just looked past her out the window. "Did you ever wonder why there are so few windows in art museums?" She pointed with her chin. "That one right over there, that's the only one you're going to find in this whole building, as a matter of fact. Why would that be, do you think?"

"Janice, I'm not interested in the number of—"

"We have three and a half minutes. Humor me."

Adira felt her jaw tighten. "Something to do with the sunlight damaging the paintings, I'm guessing."

Even as she spoke, she was trying to figure out a way to let Esmé know that she was in danger, but nothing actionable came to mind. Adira knew full well what Janice was capable of and was afraid that if she did anything to warn Esmé, Janice's associate would kill her.

"I believe it's something more profound than faded canvas," Janice said.

"What is it, then?"

"The competition. The artificial world cannot hold a candle to the natural one. A piece of canvas can't compete with the sky. Even in our wildest dreams we can't capture the wonder of the sea or the vastness of the desert or the majesty of the mountains on a piece of fabric. Beauty, Adira. We are drawn to it. We cannot turn from it for long and retain our humanity."

Adira noticed that Janice had placed a museum gift shop bag between them on the bench. She wondered if it might contain a weapon, but whether it did or not, it gave her an idea.

She just needed to wait for the right moment . . .

"What do you want from me?" Adira asked her.

"Let us be. Call off your team. There are too many innocent people, just like Esmé and her son out there, who are going to get hurt if you don't, and too many people who're going to suffer if we're not able to proceed."

"With Valestra."

Janice looked at her curiously. "How did you—?"

"What is it you have planned? And Popovic—why's he here in DC?"

"Walk away, Adira."

"You know I can't do that. Last month you had my friend killed. Not to mention all the others who've suffered already because of your crimes. I can't drop it. I won't. You should have known that before you even set up this meeting."

"I'm not the villain here, Adira."

"Said every movie villain. Ever."

"The two of us—we're really not all that different."

"Wow. I think you've been watching too many spy films. We're *very* different, Janice. Polar opposites, in fact. I would do anything to save innocent lives and stop your agenda; you would take as many innocent lives as necessary to advance your agenda."

When Janice said nothing, Adira decided to try a different approach, one that she'd prepared for while she'd waited for Janice to show up. "God hates those who love violence," she said. "It's a thing. That's in the Bible you like to quote so much. I looked it up after you texted me earlier. Psalm 11:5: 'Those who love violence, he hates with a passion.' You want to plan evil, you want to shed innocent blood, well, that's on you. God doesn't just hate the evil you have planned; he hates you for planning it."

"I don't love violence. I accept it. I reluctantly turn to it when absolutely necessary in order to accomplish what both God and I *do* love—peace."

"Peace. Really? You just claim that to justify your bloodshed."

Janice glanced at the screen of her phone and Adira followed her gaze, noticing the timer was at two minutes.

"In a perfect world, we would all be pacifists," Janice said. "But it's not a perfect world. I've wanted to abandon the idea of violence in all situations, but over the years I've learned that it's easier to be a pacifist from the sidelines. It's hard to stand by and do nothing when people are suffering right in front of you."

"I know a good place for you to contemplate all of that. It's called a prison cell."

"Have you ever heard of Dietrich Bonhoeffer?"

"I want to talk about Popovic."

"I know."

Adira hated to be manipulated in this way, but figured she needed to keep the conversation going.

She was by no means an expert on the famous German theologian, but she'd read a little about him over the years. "He was a pastor back during World War II," she said somewhat impatiently. "Orchestrated an attempt to assassinate Hitler. Obviously, that failed. He ended up being arrested, imprisoned, and eventually killed. What does that have to do with anything?"

"Before all of that," Janice said, "he was a pacifist. There's a story that one day his sister said to him, 'If there's a madman driving out of control on a busy street running people over, is it not the pastor's duty to do more than bury the victims and console the survivors? Shouldn't he also stop the driver?'"

Adira wasn't familiar enough with Bonhoeffer's life to know if Janice's little anecdote was true or not, but she gave her the benefit of the doubt. "Who's the madman here, today? What are you trying to tell me?"

"We're not at war with you Adira."

"Then who? Who's the enemy? Who are you fighting?"

"Extinction. Suffering. What we have in mind, what we're trying to do, will offer millions of people more hope and a better opportunity to live more successful, meaningful lives."

They had to be close to the four minutes by now and Adira had the sense that Janice was about to wrap up. She needed to find a way to either keep her talking or take her down.

"Call off your shooter," she said. "Leave Esmé and her son alone. I want to hear more about your plan, what you have in mind to help all those people."

Janice glanced at the timer on her phone and then looked back up at Adira. "Here's what's going to happen," she said. "I'm going to stand up and walk out of here. Only when I'm in the clear will Esmé and her son be safe. Don't attempt to follow me."

"I can't let you go," Adira said unequivocally. "You know that, don't you? I have a duty to protect our national security. If one woman dies and we're able to stop you from killing thousands more, then that's a risk I'm willing to take."

Okay, yes, it was a bluff.

Well, *sort of* a bluff.

It was true *to an extent*, but she was still hoping to find a way to both save Esmé and stop what Janice had planned.

"Janice, turn yourself in. It's—"

"You're not seeing the big picture, Adira." The timer was down to twenty seconds. "I'm sorry we couldn't come to an understanding here today."

Adira still had her phone on her lap. She'd started the voice recorder when she was sitting alone, before Janice had joined her. Now, as surreptitiously as possible, she tapped the send icon to share the audio file with her team, and maybe that's what did it. Maybe Janice noticed her thumb move across the screen, but whatever it was, Janice looked at her sadly but with fiery, unflinching resolve.

"If you leave now, you just might have enough time to save her." She tapped the screen of her own phone. "Goodbye, Adira."

A deep chill. "No, Janice—"

Even through the reinforced glass of the window, Adira heard the report of the gunshot outside.

A cloud of red mist burst from Esmé's right thigh, and she dropped heavily to the sidewalk beside her son's stroller.

CHAPTER 52

It'd happened.

It had.

All in a breath. All in an instant.

Adira swung her hand toward the shopping bag that Janice had set beside her, then rose and bolted toward the emergency exit door, threw it open, and darted outside.

From behind her, the siren from the open emergency door blared into the day. Ahead of her, terrified bystanders screamed and scattered from the scene.

By the time Adira made it to Esmé's side, the shooter, wherever it might have been, was nowhere in sight.

A stringy-haired teenage guy wearing skinny jeans stood nearby, filming Esmé on his cell phone. "Call 911!" Adira shouted to him, then rested a gentle hand on the woman's shoulder. "I'm going to help you."

Esmé was holding her leg and keening in pain.

Adira knelt and assessed the extent of her injuries, all within a matter of seconds: The bullet had entered Esmé's thigh, but there was no evidence of an exit wound, so that meant the round had fragmented in her leg. Maybe a hollow-point bullet. They're designed to break apart in the target, not to sail through it and cause collateral damage to someone else behind it. They expand and deform and transfer kinetic energy into the tissue, creating a severe wound tract. So, in this case, it could mean catastrophic damage, especially if the round had damaged her femoral artery, which the spurting blood indicated was probably the case.

You need to stop the bleeding now if this woman is even going to have a chance.

Adira laid Esmé's hand firmly against the wound. "Put pressure on it," she said urgently. "Lots of pressure. I know it hurts, but we have to."

Esmé's purse had dropped onto the ground beside her stroller. Adira emptied it out onto the sidewalk and found a hairbrush that would do the trick.

She tore the strap off the purse and quickly secured it around the hairbrush to make a windlass so she could tighten the makeshift tourniquet she was putting together. Then, she wrapped the strap around Esmé's leg above the GSW and tied it off. After cinching the strap with the hairbrush, she was able to twist it, like a screw, to snug up the tourniquet.

It wasn't perfect, but it was all she had to work with and it was going to have to do.

But they needed to get her to a hospital ASAP.

She saw that the guy was still filming them and hadn't called 911. She repeated herself in a tone that he could not misinterpret, then added, "Do it. Now!"

"Please." Esmé squeezed Adira's hand weakly. "My son. Is he okay?"

Adira had been so focused on helping Esmé that she'd forgotten about the boy, who she now realized was crying loudly in the stroller beside her.

She showed Esmé how to hold the brush in place, then stood and studied the child, feeling all around him for any blood or evidence of injury. "He's okay," she assured her. "He's—"

"Let me hold him."

"I'm not sure that's—"

"Please. I need to." Esmé's voice was faltering. "If I'm going to die, I want to hug him one last time."

Adira almost said, *"You're not going to die,"* but held back. It was a promise she wasn't prepared to make, not with the extent of blood loss Esmé had experienced.

Adira gently picked up the child and then knelt beside Esmé and tucked him up into her arms.

The guy on the phone was nodding to Adira, indicating that he'd gotten through to emergency services.

"Help is coming," she told Esmé.

However, the blood was refusing to stop surging from Esmé's leg. Adira warned her that this was going to hurt, then turned the windlass to tighten the tourniquet in order to quell the bleeding.

Esmé cried out in pain, and Adira was afraid she might lose consciousness. "Stay with me, Esmé. I'm here. Help's on the way. Hang in there."

Then, as Esmé held her son in her bloodied hands, trying to calm him, Adira said it, the words you should never say in a situation like this: "It's going to be okay. You're going to be alright."

―∽―

Just moments ago, I'd received an audio file from Adira and when I listened to it, my blood ran cold.

Gunnar was driving, so I played it loud enough for him to hear. When it finished up, he cursed under his breath.

On the audio, Janice and Adira were speaking in hushed tones. Janice mentioned a museum and by pinging Adira's car I found out it was currently at a garage not far from the Metro Museum of Modern Art. I phoned dispatch to get some officers over there and learned that there'd already been an EMS dispatch call and that an ambulance and two patrol cars were en route.

I tried calling Adira back, but she didn't pick up.

―∽―

Most people don't know that food deliveries are made to prisons in the hour after dinner while the majority of inmates are back in their cells but there are still some workers in the kitchen who are there cleaning up and doing the dishes and are therefore available to assist with unloading the boxes from the delivery truck.

Most people don't know that.

But Turo did.

So now, the Langmore Food Distribution Services semi drove through the security checkpoint at the Culpeper United States Penitentiary, backed up to the loading bay, and the driver and the inmates from the kitchen began unloading the food shipment for the week, while the correctional officer on duty, Pablo Serra, supervised their work.

And, after ten minutes, Turo Pärnänen arrived to help.

―∽―

Maia Odongo's flight landed in DC.

She sent a text to the number Janice had provided her with, and almost immediately got a response from the man who was supposed to be picking her up: **I'll meet you outside baggage claim. I'm driving a red Taurus. Text me when you have your bags.**

CHAPTER 53

The EMTs arrived, placed Esmé on a gurney, and hustled her onto the ambulance. When Adira asked about her son, a responding Metro officer who had a small child of her own showed Adira how to collapse the stroller into a car seat—which was very clever and something she immediately wished she would have thought of—then left with the boy to drive him to the hospital to be with his mother.

As they took off, Adira escaped from the scene and returned to the museum.

Just before she'd run outside, when she'd passed her hand over Janice's bag, she'd dropped something into it. Something that was going to help her team track the billionaire.

Her cell phone.

However, Janice must have noticed, because when Adira got to the bench, there was her phone, sitting right where Janice had been, a manila envelope beside it.

Adira's name was printed elegantly on the front of the envelope.

For a moment, she thought of fingerprints and DNA and of not contaminating whatever might be inside, but then realized that the urgency of the situation dictated that she find out what it contained, now, while Janice was still somewhere in the area.

Trying her best not to damage the envelope too much so the lab techs could study it afterward, Adira opened it and removed the single sheet of paper and the photograph that Janice had left behind for her.

The photo was a close-up of twenty-one hash marks scratched into a wall. It looked like they'd been scraped into it with some sort of sharp object, and when Adira studied the bottom of the picture, she saw a tooth lying there.

A chill.

Someone had used a tooth to scratch twenty-one hash marks onto that wall.

Days.

Those are days.

Could those really be days?

Walk away, the note read. **Or there will be more lines drawn on the wall.**

Confinement? Prison? Kidnapping?

Did this mean that someone else would be taken or maybe someone would not be freed? If—

Wait. If Popovic was involved, it could very well mean human trafficking. If so, it seemed more like a threat he would make than Janice would.

It struck Adira that the two of them must be working even more closely together than she and her team had initially thought.

Walk away?

No. That wasn't an option. Quitting was something she was not very good at or very experienced with.

She hurried to the museum's security suite and studied the CCTV footage of the facility, but even then, it wasn't clear how Janice had slipped away. There just "happened" to be a hiccup in the video right before the shooting occurred, and then, when the footage returned again, Janice was gone.

Another video footage glitch.

Huh. Imagine that.

High-end signal jammers and camera scramblers weren't cheap, and even though her team had done their best to seize or freeze Janice's assets, she'd probably been able to squirrel away plenty of money. That, along with her association with Popovic, would undoubtedly provide her with the resources to afford the best jammers money could buy.

Adira called Travis to update him.

She whipped through her explanation, but he already knew about some of it from the audio file she'd sent.

"Janice left me a note," she told him quickly. "And a photo."

She snapped a picture of the hash marks and sent it to him.

"You think they're days?" he said, coming to the same conclusion she had.

"I do."

"Any sense of where or when this picture might've been taken?"

"No," she said. "Where are you, by the way?"

"On our way back from the prison. About an hour out from the Pentagon. Gunnar's with me. Are you okay?"

"Yeah, but I'm pretty pissed that Janice got away."

"We'll get her. I'm just glad you're alright. And Esmé and her son?"

"I haven't heard since the ambulance arrived."

"Okay. Hang in there. I'll see you when we get to DC."

After the call, the Metro police wanted Adira to give her statement and, even though she was anxious to get away from the museum, she met with them to relive it all once again. And then they left to fill out their paperwork, to file their reports, and head home.

Life goes on.

Or it doesn't.

Adira phoned the hospital and, when she identified herself as Esmé's sister, she learned that Esmé was recovering and her son was safe.

Well, good. So, maybe things weren't turning out so badly tonight, after all.

—␣—

Here's what happened at the prison.

Here's how it all went down.

Pablo excused the other prisoners from helping unload the boxes of food and Turo cornered the driver in the kitchen.

Down went the Langmore Food Distribution Services driver.

Out came the duct tape.

Pablo helped him drag the unconscious man into the dry goods storage pantry, where Turo changed into the civilian clothes Pablo had brought for him and donned the cap that the driver had been wearing.

Then, he said to Pablo, "Here's the deal. You helped me escape and they'll find out about it. You'll end up spending the next five to ten years in here, serving time in the very place where you were a guard. You can imagine how well that'll go over. Or, I can kill you now and you can be remembered as a hero who died trying to stop a hardened criminal who was trying to escape. What's the legacy you want to leave in the minds of your wife and two daughters? That of a vile convict, or a valiant hero? What'll it be? It's your choice."

"How could you even—?"

"Choose now or I'll choose for you."

"What about the transformer? About overriding the system?"

"Changed my mind."

Pablo studied the blade that Turo was holding. "Cut my arm. Make it look like I tried to stop you."

With that, Pablo held out his arm, but Turo didn't slice him there. Instead, he leaned forward and stabbed him violently three times in the gut. "It'll be more realistic this way," he said, as Pablo collapsed. "Trust me."

He tossed Pablo's radio out of reach across the kitchen, then left him crumpled on the floor, gasping for breath, bleeding out. If he did manage to make it to the radio, he deserved to survive.

Turo gave it fifty-fifty odds.

Sidewinder had warned him not to harm Pablo, but currently, the one-eyed racist was locked up safe and snug in his cell and wasn't going anywhere. This was between him and Pablo, not him and Sidewinder.

After wiping off the knife, Turo drove the truck toward the guard at the prison's exit, who flagged him to stop.

He'd anticipated that the officer would inspect the truck for any prisoners hoping to sneak out—that was only to be expected. So, he rolled to a stop, handed over the paperwork, and then said, "Do you need to check the back?"

"I don't know, do I?" the officer said somewhat curtly.

"I mean—"

"Step out of the vehicle, please."

Turo obeyed, palming the blade.

The guard led him to the back of the truck and watched carefully as he opened the doors.

He inspected the back and found it empty. "Alright," he told Turo, with a flippant wave of his hand. "You're good to go."

"Thank you."

But as Turo was climbing into the cab again, the officer called to him from behind. "Hang on a sec."

Turo tensed and faced him, wondering if he was going to ask for an ID. "Yes?"

Instead, the man just had him sign a clipboarded delivery confirmation form. "You be safe out there."

"Always."

And with that, Turo drove five miles into the countryside, sticking to back roads, then ditched the truck and swapped vehicles with the nondescript sedan that Rollan had left for him earlier. From there, he would head to Curtis Bay in South Baltimore to join Janice and Ivan.

But first, he needed to meet Rollan in DC to pick up Maureen.

—m—

In the cabin of the yacht docked in the Potomac, Sienna Brock evaluated where things were at.

Janice and Ivan were there with her, seated facing each other at the table, an open laptop between them.

"Adira didn't listen," Janice informed them. "I don't think she's going to stop. I don't think any of them will."

"And you left her the photo?" Sienna asked.

"Yes. But I'm not sure that'll be enough."

"I've been thinking about it." Sienna rapped the table with her knuckle. "I think I know how we can get the prototype without a lot of carnage or bloodshed—or even without attracting undue attention. And I think we can do it tonight."

"How's that?" Ivan inquired in his thick Russian accent, his tone cool and serpentine. Late sixties. A singularly emotionless stare. Eyes that never seemed to blink or let you off the hook.

"We simply ask my husband to deliver it to us."

Ivan squared his gaze at her, obviously trying to discern if she was being serious or not. "And why would he do that?"

"Well, we could just ask nicely, but I think a little incentive might not hurt."

This time it was Janice who asked the question. "What kind of incentive do you have in mind?"

"Saving something that he cares about," Sienna said. "Something that breathes and bleeds: Adira Halprin." Then she nodded toward Ivan. "Have your people pick her up. Don't kill her. Just bring her in. Do that and we can make a trade."

"For the prototype."

"Yes."

He evaluated that. "And if your husband doesn't comply?"

"We tell him that you'll sell her. She's in her midthirties—not as young as most of your clients are inclined to appreciate, but she still has some years of use in her. A former Secret Service agent and Homeland operative? Surely you can think of someone who would be more than happy to provide a new home for her? Someone with her pedigree?"

A pause. "I know a buyer—a certain businessman in London who has . . . particular tastes. He's been asking for a natural blonde with no eyes and no hands. A very specific request."

"Well, there you go. That can be arranged easily enough."

A nod. "Yes. It can."

Janice blanched. Swallowed.

Huh, Sienna thought. *She would be willing to kill children, but she's uneasy with this? What is wrong with her?*

"If Travis is reluctant," Sienna said to them, "we can get started on her—if necessary, if he needs additional convincing—just to confirm to him that we're serious. I'll be glad to oversee the procedure myself. But I think that when we make Travis aware of the future she has waiting for her, he'll comply."

"And you think this will work?" Ivan said.

"Travis has a weakness for women he favors—it clouds his thinking. I know him. He'll cooperate. He went back into a burning house for me. The least he'll do is deliver a little device to us in exchange for Ms. Halprin."

Janice shook her head. "I can't go along with this. You're taking this too far."

Sienna was losing her patience and beginning to doubt that the idealistic billionaire had the resolve within her to see this through to the end. "Janice, you're not thinking big enough with your drug distribution scheme. With the Project Symphony prototype we can steal any secret from any computer on the planet. Consider the possibilities, the opportunities it affords us. Ivan's people can reverse-engineer it, replicate it. We can create as many devices as we like. That's the priority here. We have to be willing to go the distance to see that come to fruition. All of us do. And that might mean making some unpleasant choices."

—⁓—

What have you done?

Janice Daniels looked across the table at the two people she'd aligned herself with—Sienna, the traitor; Ivan, the smuggler. Not the kind of people you wanted to be in bed with.

She should have known earlier that this was a mistake.

Well, it was time to remove the blinders and see things as they really were, and to make the bold choices that she knew she needed to make but hadn't been ready to until now.

The two of them had been a means to an end for her, but now she was ready to be rid of them.

"I only want that device for one thing," she said to them. "That's why I'm working with you, and when that's done, I'm done. With this. With you. Both of you."

Neither Sienna nor Ivan said anything. Ivan simply studied her dispassionately, as if she were a piece of meat he was considering purchasing.

Or maybe throwing to the dogs.

Janice doubted that he would traffic her. At sixty-three years old, she wasn't a prime member of his clients' typical demographic. However, she couldn't be sure. After all, there were probably people out there with "particular tastes," as Ivan had put it, who would be interested in buying someone like her, despite—or maybe because of—her age.

Janice knew that it was not easy to walk away from someone like Ivan. And so, in that moment, she decided that she wouldn't walk away from him until he wouldn't be able to follow her. Ever.

Turo would be here soon enough. She trusted him. He would take care of Ivan and, if necessary, Sienna.

But if not Turo, then someone else could finish the job.

"Excuse me," she said to Ivan and Sienna. "I need to use the washroom."

Once she was out of sight, she sent a text to her wild card, the one that only Rollan knew about: Søren Beck, the architect from South Carolina.

Did you pick Dr. Odongo up at the airport? she asked.

The reply: **Yes. She's at dinner. I'm at the hotel.**

Janice wrote, **Keep your phone on. I may need you tonight. I'll call you soon.**

As she went to rejoin them at the table, Janice heard Ivan speaking to Sienna: "Can we find Ms. Halprin? Do we know where she is?"

Janice entered the cabin in time to see Sienna consult the laptop screen. "If she's with her phone, she's still at the museum. Her car is nearby, though, in a parking garage."

Ivan called for two of his men: Hans, a former KSK German special forces soldier, and a hulking Croatian mercenary named Keb. "Find her," Ivan said. "Bring her in. We do this tonight. We do it now."

CHAPTER 54

7:34 P.M.

Gunnar took an exit off I-95 so we could grab a quick bite to eat.

———※———

Dr. Maia Odongo was finishing dinner at a restaurant just down the street from the hotel. She fumbled with her credit card, paid the bill, and then searched out the exit.

She had so many things to sort out. The plan was for her to review the Nectyla research, but she wasn't even certain how that was going to happen, now that she was here in DC and not Atlanta.

As she crossed the street, she was distracted thinking of regrets and of forgiveness and redemption and—

A honking car swerved to the side, barely missing her.

Gathering herself, Maia scrambled to the curb and realized that she was clutching the brooch she was wearing, the one that held all her secrets, the one that she was ready, if necessary, to hand over to the authorities.

A whispered prayer found its way to her lips to the Creator of the heavens and the earth and the very star she was named after: *Forgive me. Please forgive me for what happened to the children.*

———※———

Just a few minutes earlier, Søren Beck had gotten word from Jan. She'd given him his assignment for tonight, which amounted to yet another decisive detour off the road he'd thought his life was on.

He felt like he was in a car, skidding along an icy road that led to the edge of a cliff. He wanted to steer his way out of the skid or jump out and roll to safety before it was too late, but he didn't know how to do either at the moment, or what it would even look like if he could.

A car skidding.

A cliff he could not avoid.

Choices he never imagined he would be making.

This last week it was as if he were becoming someone else, someone he did not recognize.

Or, maybe, he was emerging from his shell, his safe little carefully constructed, middle-class, daily grind, life-on-the-treadmill shell, and becoming who he was always destined to be all along.

Are we more than the sum of our past choices? Do they define us, or are we free to chart a new course despite the decisions and mistakes we've already made?

Jan had told him that he was just the right person for the job she had in mind, a job that was now sending him skidding across the ice. Toward the precipice.

Maybe she was right.

—m—

Adira finished speaking with the police and left the museum for the underground parking garage where she'd left her Mazda earlier.

As she descended the steps, she was thinking of Esmé and her little boy and she vowed to herself that she would not let Janice and the shooter get away with what they'd done to that innocent woman.

She headed through the aged garage toward her car, past the smears of oil and dark skid marks that marred the gray concrete floor. In places, the dripping overhead pipes had left dirty mineral deposit stains beneath them. The ceiling, held up by massive cement columns, was interspersed with a network of ventilation ducts, sound baffles, and arrows pointing toward more parking or toward the garage's exit. Stark, unconcerned overhead lights illuminated the strict rows of parked cars. Every so often, an orange cone appeared beside a reserved parking space.

Adira had her keys out and was nearly to her car when she saw the man approaching her from the other side of the garage.

But she realized a moment too late that there were two men instead of one.

CHAPTER 55

Adira knew what to do.

She just needed to do it, to put her training into practice.

She'd taught self-defense classes to other women—if you're ever attacked, especially by someone with a size disparity in their favor, you take the situation seriously. You GREET the person with resolve: GRoin, Eyes, Ears, Throat. Kick him in the groin as hard as you can, gouge his eyes, punch or yank on his ears, strike him in the throat with the edge of your hand.

And never, ever allow him to get you into his vehicle.

"If someone comes for you," she would tell her students, "don't let him get you into a car. Fight him off. He's going to come at you with handcuffs, with rope, with duct tape. Don't let him get started. Fight him off. GREET him with a frenzy of pain. Once he has control over you, once he gets you helpless, you're his to do with as he pleases. No matter how he tries to assure you that he means no harm, no matter what he promises to give you if you cooperate, no matter what he threatens to do to you if you don't comply, do not get into that car. Kick, scream, scratch, punch. Do whatever it takes to make him rethink his decision to come after you and do you harm."

"But what if he *does* get us into a car?" someone would inevitably ask.

"Spit on the floor, smear blood on the door, pee on the seat. Leave your DNA behind however you can. That's your lifeline when the cops come looking."

And so.

Now.

When she saw the man stalking toward her, all of those thoughts came back to her, informed her. Prepared her.

She clicked her key to unlock her Mazda.

He was about twenty feet away and striding quickly in her direction.

Out of instinct, she palmed the keys, with her apartment key protruding between her fingers, and faced him.

"Excuse me, ma'am. I'm sorry to bother you," he said with a touch of a German accent. "I locked myself out of my car. Can I use your phone to call my wife?"

He was less than ten feet away.

He looked down at her hand, saw the key sticking out of her tight fist, and smiled faintly.

And his smug little smirk gave it all away.

She knew he was coming for her.

In a breath, he'd closed the space between them and was lunging at her.

As he did, as he distracted her, she caught just the slightest glimpse of movement from her left. Someone had been hiding on the other side of her car.

When the first guy tried to grab her, she swung the key decisively across his face, going for his eyes. He cried out and threw his hands up to his face.

Yeah, she'd hit her mark.

One down.

She turned to face the second man, but he planted a solid side kick into her gut just as she was discarding her keys and going for her gun.

Wheezing and trying to catch her breath, she tried to gather herself, but the first assailant rushed her and threw his arms around her, taking her by surprise.

So, not blinded after all.

Crap.

He tackled her savagely and she slammed hard onto the concrete, the back of her head thudding against it, dizzying her vision.

She could tell he was wearing body armor, so she tucked the muzzle of her Springfield up beneath his armpit where the plates wouldn't protect him, and then it was all instinct as she fired and fired and fired until he went limp and was no longer a threat.

But as she was shoving him aside and struggling to get to her feet, the second man kicked her viciously in the side of the head.

She was already disoriented, and the impact was enough to send her torquing around and dropping back to the ground.

Everything went all wavery—a blur of time and space and movement as the parking garage took wings and flew in a circle around her.

She struggled to orient herself and target him with her weapon, but there were two of him. How were there two of him? She managed to get one shot off, but at the wrong man, and then he was on her, twisting her wrist fiercely backward and wresting the gun from her hand.

Oh, no, no, no.

And then he was grabbing her and flipping her over onto her stomach.

And holding her down with brutish strength.

And wrenching her arms back.

Stop him, Adira. You have to—

She tried to roll and fight him off, but then he was kneeling on her back, still grasping her arms securely. He was too strong. Too big.

He fastened plastic cuffs around her wrists.

Zipped them tight.

Then tighter.

Once he had her restrained, he stuffed a gag into her mouth and, seemingly with no effort at all, lifted her onto his shoulder, carried her toward a nearby sedan, and dumped her into the trunk.

She twisted in the confined space and tried her best to kick him, but he slammed the lid, catching her ankle harshly in the process. He shoved her foot back in, then immediately closed the trunk before she could roll out, sealing her inside.

And then it was all darkness, and she knew that spitting or peeing on the carpet was not going to be enough to save her.

Not this time.

Not enough at all.

―⁂―

Sienna was on the deck of the yacht with Ivan and Janice, watching the day slip away into early twilight, when Keb called to update them.

She put her phone on speaker. "How'd it go?" she asked him. "Do you have her?"

"She's a feisty one. Sadly, Hans won't be joining us for dinner."

"Ever?" Ivan said.

"I'm afraid not. I took care of the body. There are going to be some happy fish at the bottom of the Potomac tonight. But you need to be careful with her. I don't think she'll be very cooperative with what you have in mind."

She'll be more cooperative, hands down, when we're done with her, Sienna thought, considering the irony of the phrase *hands down* for someone who'd had both of her hands amputated, but she didn't say that. Instead, she asked him, "When can you be here?"

"I'm close. Ten minutes, tops."

End call.

She turned to Janice. "As soon as he gets here, call Brock and inform him we have her but that we'll exchange her for the device. Tell him what's going to happen to her if he doesn't cooperate."

"I'm not—"

"Do it," Ivan ordered her. "Make the call."

—⁂—

Janice took a deep breath and accepted the encrypted phone from Sienna.

The minutes dragged by, taking forever, until finally Keb joined them at the wharf.

Once they had their captive aboard, she put the call through to the man who knew more secrets about the United States government than anyone, and had the access and contacts to get the Project Symphony device to them, tonight.

And waited while it rang.

OWEIRP
OFII
POEI
ERPF
OPFI
IIAJWE
;LKMERO
OMW'GFP
V;NAVPO
PIGUHER
VG;GANNE;
ANRV;OOAN
VPOAEWIJVGG
RV;AKJERVPO
IREJB
IJ

AW;
OWEIRPO
OFIIJAS;OOJ
POEIFJAPWOIE
ERPFJR3POIAP
OPFIJAWEPEOO
IIAJWEPEOFIJA
;LKMEROFIFIJ
OMW'GFPOOAWG
V;NAVPOAWEEHFA
PIGUHERE;FNSE
OOKBJPO
IOAUERH
C;OAJVPOJJ
NFDEIOJOIJA
IUUHVHNAOIU
HERVUNEV;OZ
JVPOOEARJHV
POOEARJHU
ORI
AW;OFIJAW
OWEIRPOWIURT
OFIIJAS;OOJ
POEIFJAPWOI
ERPFJR3POIAP
OPFIJAWEPEOO
IIAJWEPEOFI
;LKMERO
OMW'GF
V;NAVPOAWEEHFA;
PIGUHERF;FNSE
OOKBJPOKBJ
IOAUERHRF
C;OAJVPOJJHS
NFDEIOJOI
IUUHVHNAOIUS
HERVUNEV;OZ
JVPOOEAR
RV;AKJERVPOAIJ
IREJBEOIJVPO
IJERGBOOAIJ
ERVBEOAWIEJG
POOEARJHVVOA
ORIIHQWPOIFFH
AW;OFIJAW;OFIJAWAE
OWEIRPOW
OFI
PO
R
P
IA
OPFIJAWEPOOIP
;AWEREOFIJAWE

PART IV

Soon to Die

A corpse on the pier.
Cold steel against her throat.
Dark currents.
The wild card.

CHAPTER 56

Gunnar and I were at a fast food joint when I got the call.
We'd ordered some cheeseburgers and fries and I had slipped down the hall to the restroom and was finishing washing my hands when my cell rang.

The screen told me it was from an unknown number and, even though I wouldn't typically respond to those, with everything that was going on with this case, I went ahead and picked up.

"Hello, Travis."

I knew that voice. "Janice."

"I need you to listen carefully. We have Adira, and the people who took her are very serious individuals, not to be trifled with. They will sell her and she will spend the rest of her life servicing men who'll pay her handlers handsomely for the opportunity to do as they wish to someone who used to be a Secret Service agent."

I felt a choking surge of rage and fear. "What've you done?"

"She's safe. She's here. She's with me." And then she spoke to someone else. "Remove the gag."

As soon as she said that, I heard Adira's voice. "I'm on a yacht. DC. At least three men. Tactical rifles. Ivan's here. I—"

"Enough," a rough male voice shouted. Then I heard muffled cries as whoever was with her presumably stuffed the gag back into her mouth.

My mind was spinning and I needed to lean my hand against the sink to maintain my balance.

A yacht. DC. You need to move. Find her!

"This isn't you, Janice," I said. "It's—"

"This is the only offer you're going to get. The wheels are set in motion. This is your chance to save her. Now. Tonight."

Last month, a Russian assassin had nearly killed Adira, but she'd managed to take him out. However, I had the sense that this time, if there were at least three men, things would be different. The "serious individuals" Janice was working with would likely be quite attentive with someone who had Adira's background and skill set.

And, as men who worked for a human smuggler, they would be used to doing whatever was necessary to guarantee that their captives did not get away.

I thought of Adira's time machine and our pinky promise that I would come for her if she were ever kidnapped. A promise made less than twenty-four hours ago.

I leveled my voice, trying to maintain the impression of composure. "What do you want?"

"The Project Symphony prototype. According to our intel, it's at Marine Corps Base Quantico. They use vascular recognition and you're one of the only people who can get to it and get it off that base."

How? How did she know that?

They must have an inside person at Quantico or someone close to our team.

"That's not going to be possible," I told her.

"Where are you?"

A beat while I debated what to say. I went with honesty. "About thirty minutes from there. From Quantico."

"You need to find a way to do this, Travis. They're going to amputate Adira's hands, gouge out her eyes, and then sell her."

Fire rose within me. "I'm—"

"We'll contact you," she cut me off, "with a time and location to make the exchange."

Stall. Keep her talking.

But that didn't happen. Before I could reply, the line went dead.

Immediately, I contacted NSA to have them trace the call, but even the record of it had already disappeared from my phone.

Then, I reached the US Coast Guard Station Washington, identified myself, and said, "Look for a yacht in the area, anything unusual. Any boat that shouldn't be where it is. At least three armed men are aboard." I gave them my authorization code from the Pentagon and hoped that it would be enough, since I didn't want to bring this to Colonel Clarke's attention quite yet.

He would never approve of an exchange of this type, and I was actually thinking about going through with it.

I did a locate on Adira's phone—nothing.

And on her car—still at that parking garage near the museum.

I hurried out of the washroom and found Gunnar collecting our food at the restaurant's register.

"We need to go," I said stiffly.

Back in his car, I told him about the call from Janice, quoting it word for word as closely as I could remember—which was probably pretty close.

When I finished, he cursed under his breath. "Well," he said, "we can't give them the device. You know that, right?"

"They're going to cut off her hands and blind her, Gunnar. They're going to traffic her. Imagine what else they'll do to her if we don't stop them."

"And imagine what they could do with the prototype if we went through with the exchange, what kind of havoc they could cause, what kind of information they could obtain: passwords, root files, encryption keys, classified documents. They could upload ransomware or viruses to any of our most secure networks."

"I know," I said. "I know, I know. But—"

"There is no *but*. Adira knew what she was getting into when she signed up for this. We all did."

"She didn't sign up for this, for what they're going to do. No one did. No one would. You're not thinking straight. If we don't—"

"No. I *am* thinking straight. You're not," he said. "You care about her. I get that, but this is a matter of national security. We can't let that device end up in the wrong hands, no matter what. You've spent your whole career making sure our secrets remain safe. That all comes to a head tonight."

"This is—"

"No." He pounded the steering wheel. "There's no option here but to double down the security on the prototype there at the base, buy as much time as we can, and find another way to locate Adira."

As I was considering how to reply, NSA called back and notified me that they couldn't track the unknown number. "It's no good," the analyst told me.

"They might be using Spectre. It's a program we developed here. No one on the outside should even know about it. Who are you dealing with?"

That really was the question.

I ended the call.

I needed to think.

Throwing open the door, I stepped outside, closed my eyes, and tried to process everything.

We were parked on the edge of the lot next to a reeking dumpster and the smell made it hard to focus.

In frustration, I kicked the car's front tire.

I was evaluating different options and scenarios—all grim, all unacceptable—when Gunnar joined me and I said, "I told Janice we were thirty minutes from Quantico. If there's some way they're tracking us, they'll know if we don't comply, and that much alone might get Adira killed."

"Yeah," he muttered. "Or worse."

"We need to head that direction, even if it's just to stall for half an hour. Maybe we can come up with some way to locate her by then. In the meantime, let's get a team to study satellite footage of the wharfs in the area. Adira said they were on a yacht. Maybe there's an image of them boarding it or they drew undue attention to themselves."

He considered that for a moment. "Go through Clarke?"

"Not yet. Other channels."

"Why?"

"I don't want to implicate him. If this goes south, he doesn't deserve to lose his job. That's not right by me."

"Fair enough. We stall for now. You have thirty minutes to convince me to make this exchange." Then he added, "And that's not going to happen."

—◊◊◊—

Adira was back in the trunk again, her wrists raw from rubbing against the plastic cuffs, her left ankle throbbing from when the second assailant had slammed the trunk lid on it.

At least they hadn't gagged her this time.

They'd blindfolded her earlier until they got to the deck of the yacht and made the call to Travis. She'd tried to take in what she could and feed him intel, but she hadn't had much time without the blindfold, and she doubted she'd given him enough.

And now it wouldn't matter. They were rolling. On the move.

She railed at herself for not stopping both of her attackers in the parking garage when she had the chance, but now that dog had barked. It was time to make a new play.

She didn't know everything that was going on, but she knew enough: they were trying to get Travis to exchange the Project Symphony prototype for her safety. Well, there was no way he would go for that.

But maybe he will. Maybe his feelings for you are strong enough to muddy up his judgment.

The more she thought about it, the more she realized it could go either way.

But she could not let an exchange happen.

Either she needed to get free, or she needed to eliminate herself from the equation.

If she was dead, Janice and Popovic would have no bargaining chip. It'd give Travis and Gunnar the upper hand.

Although, that wouldn't really be the ideal situation for you.

No.

Not exactly.

As it turned out, she had no easy way of taking care of things in that regard. No poison. No suicide pill. No cyanide hidden in a tooth.

Screw it.

She was going to get out of this.

She struggled to find a more comfortable position, but the confines of the trunk gave her very little space to move and having her arms restrained behind her made it even tougher.

She would've liked to get her arms in front of her, but the way she was situated, she wasn't able to get her hands down past her ankles. She felt like she was flexible enough to do it, but just couldn't quite make it happen with the trunk the size that it was.

Normally, she wore shoes with a type of parachute cord for laces. The cord could then be used to saw through plastic cuffs, but today that hadn't been the case.

Of course not. That would've been too convenient.

Those shoes were at home.

Assets in a trunk: maybe a set of tools with wire cutters? A first aid kit with scissors in it? Anything sharp, really.

Maybe.

It was pitch black, so she wasn't able to see what was around her.

Find something. Get free.

The best she could manage with her hands bound behind her, she started the search for anything that might nudge the dial in her direction.

CHAPTER 57

Over that last twenty-five minutes during the drive toward Quantico, I'd sent Metro PD to Adira's apartment, just to check, just to be sure. Nothing.

Her credit cards hadn't been used.

She was off the grid.

The last location we had for her was the museum, near where her car was still parked. A pool of blood on the concrete next to it was not a good sign, but forensics quickly established that it was not hers.

We were trying to get access to the garage's CCTV footage, but they were holding out for a warrant, which I wasn't sure we could obtain without notifying Clarke of what'd happened.

We approached the exit that led to the base's delivery entrance. It was the closest one to Building 141, the place where the prototype was being stored and tested, and would save us time, instead of requiring us to go to the main entrance up by Triangle.

Four miles.

"Alright," I said to Gunnar. "Hear me out. This whole thing might actually play in our favor."

"How's that?"

"This is an opportunity. It'll get us close to Janice and Ivan. We can't let this pass without taking action. Look, Janice met with Adira at the museum, tried to warn her off. Now this. For whatever reason, right now they feel cornered. They're desperate."

"We can't hand over the prototype, Travis. We can't jeopardize national security for one person's life."

"I know . . . but . . ." I wasn't sure if he knew the story or not. For the moment I assumed he did not. "In the Second World War, after England deciphered Germany's Enigma machine, they had to send some ships out into battle, but because they'd decoded the communiqué, they knew that it was a trap, that their ships would be destroyed and their sailors lost. However, if they rerouted the ships, the Germans would realize their cipher had been cracked. So, England sent those sailors out into the ambush, knowing they wouldn't be coming home, because they realized it was the only way to win the war. Sometimes you have to sacrifice your pawns to win the game. And sometimes you have to sacrifice your queen."

"Adira."

"No, the prototype."

"We can't do that."

"Okay. But we can make them *think* we will. I know the Project Symphony team has been working on a way to make it trackable, to find it anywhere on the planet. Do you know if they ever completed that?"

"No, I haven't heard."

A pause as I contemplated things. "I think we need to show up for the exchange."

"With what? We have to assume they know what they're looking for. They'll never go for a fake."

"No. I'll bring the real thing, but I think there's a way to do both—to save Adira and to protect the prototype."

He didn't reply right away. "Go on," he said at last.

"Here's what I have in mind: it has to do with a deepfake audio, a drug lord, and a sniper rifle."

CHAPTER 58

I told him what I was thinking about the deepfake audio we would need, the radio transmitter, the Wi-Fi spoofing, and the type of rifle I had in mind.

"And you know all of this from your redactions?" He sounded somehow both doubtful and impressed.

"I'm not on this team because of my tactical experience or close-quarters combat skills. It's amazing what I've read. Secrets are where I live. That's home for me."

"Just don't let anyone else in through the door who doesn't need to be there," he said, somewhat reprovingly. "With the deepfake audio—you have the samples you need? I mean, that's not easy to pull off."

"Two months ago, Clarke and I were testing a program. We recorded enough audio for the app. I think we should be good. I can access it through my Federal Digital Database account."

"Huh," he said. "And you think we can actually make this work?"

"I can take care of most of it, but can you get the rifle?"

"Not that one exactly, but one that'll do the trick. I know someone who can hook us up." He thought for a moment. "If we're talking about an exchange, that means they're going to want to meet us in an isolated location and they'll likely try to double-cross us and keep Adira as well as the device. And they're going to want you dead. Wait—you mentioned something earlier about a drug lord?"

I smiled. "I was just getting to that. There's a car that was impounded by the DEA a few months ago from a Mexican drug smuggler. It'll be perfect for what we need."

"Why's that?"

"No VIN. Bulletproof glass. Two secret compartments in the trunk."

"Is one of them big enough for me?"

"No. But it's big enough for a couple of guns. Big guns. Plus, the car has the capability to self-destruct, with a detonator on the key fob."

"We can blow it up whenever we need to?"

"That's right."

"That'll work. And it's in DC?"

"In Springfield, at the impound over near DEA headquarters."

"Let me guess: another redaction?"

"A recent one. Yeah."

"I could get used to this noetic memory of yours. And you can get it for us?"

"Clarke can. Let me give him a call."

"Are you sure you want to ask him?"

My phone rang.

"I'll be circumspect."

When I picked up, I found out it was Janice. "Do you have it?" she asked.

"We're almost to the exit," I said truthfully.

"Curtis Bay. Ten thirty. I'll text you the exact location. No tricks, no gimmicks, no games, or you'll never see Adira again."

End call.

"It's Curtis Bay," I told Gunnar. I checked the time. "We have just under two hours."

I wasn't too familiar with that area of South Baltimore, apart from the fact that it lay across the Patapsco River from Dundalk. By pulling up satellite images of the neighborhood, I was immediately able to tell that it was an industrial district. In fact, the Coast Guard Yard, a shipyard dedicated to building and maintaining their fleet, was located nearby.

An interesting place for Popovic to choose.

It appeared that Curtis Bay was also home to an international automobile import company, served as a fuel depot with a collection of towering oil terminals, contained a commerce train transfer area, and bordered a nearby waste treatment facility. Dozens of old warehouses lay scattered on and around the docks. Plenty of places to hide and to disappear.

Or to make someone disappear.

Is that their hub for human trafficking? Is that why they chose it?

It was just over seventy miles away.

I called the colonel about the car. I didn't want to tell him the specifics of what was going on, but instead asked him to trust me. "Bring it back without a scratch," he told me.

"Will do."

As I hung up, Gunnar said, "We have a location and a time. What about HRT? Go in with tactical assets in our favor?"

The FBI's Hostage Rescue Team was certainly a possibility, but I didn't want to chance it. "It's a big area, Gunnar. Without exact coordinates we'd be lost, and Ivan's people could easily be alerted to a bigger presence. These people are good at hiding and if they suspect for even one moment that we have a TAC team there, they'll be in the wind and we'll lose our best chance at locating them. They'll be gone—and if they get Adira out of the country, you know we'll never see her again."

"Just checking off the boxes. Agreed: a team would draw more attention and show our hand for sure. I'm no marksman, but with the right rifle and scope, I should be good up to *maybe* three hundred yards."

"That oughta work. I'll get them to show their hand, to reveal her location; then you take it from there."

He didn't reply right away. "Yeah," he said at last. "I'll samepage that."

"Did you just turn *same page* into a verb?"

"I might have."

"I like it."

"Let's hope it catches on."

We exited the highway and headed under the overpass toward the base.

—⁂—

On his way from the prison to convene with Janice, Turo met up with Rollan at a deserted strip mall in south DC.

"Thanks for getting that rat over the fence," Turo told him as he joined him in his Jeep. "It had everything in it that I needed."

"You're welcome. You ready for tonight?"

"I think so. The assignment with Pablo's family. Nice work."

"Thanks."

"Did you kill the wife and girls?"

"No. Pablo?"

"When I left him, he was bleeding out."

"Huh," Rollan said disinterestedly. "Oh yeah! I've got something for you.

Sienna was kind enough to pick it up last night." Rollan produced Gunnar Bane's nine-millimeter Smith & Wesson M&P and handed it over.

"Maureen." Turo cradled the gun in his hands. "It's a pleasure to make your acquaintance."

"Janice told me she has a special job for you tonight."

"Oh, yeah? What's that?"

Rollan fired up the engine. "I'll tell you on the way. But I should say, I think you're going to be a bit surprised to hear what she wants you to do."

CHAPTER 59

Most people who've heard of Quantico know it as the location of the FBI Academy.

They may not even be aware that the Academy is located on a much larger tract of land owned by the Marines. In fact, the Bureau's campus is less than 550 acres out of the more than 55,000 acres that make up the Marine base. Less than 1% of the property, yet that's what Quantico is most known for.

Not a bad job of hiding by the Marines.

With our Pentagon creds, getting through the initial security checkpoint wasn't too much of a hassle, but I knew that the building we were heading toward might be a different story.

The drive to Building 141 took us ten minutes.

As we wound through the wooded landscape toward the secluded facility, Gunnar asked me, "You good?"

"I'm good."

When he parked, I made sure I had the correct app open on my phone and confirmed that he would be ready in case I needed him, then I exited the car and approached the front of the long, angular building that currently housed the prototype. It stretched back nearly a hundred yards into the surrounding forest.

As I entered, I had my ID ready, but the Marine waiting beside the metal detector recognized me. "Good evening, Mr. Brock." He appeared a little puzzled, probably because of the time. "It's good to see you."

"You too. I need to pick up the prototype for an op."

Even though Corey knew me, he went through the process of confirming my identity and studying my creds.

"Do you have your paperwork?" he asked me. "The authorization forms?"

"No. Not with me. It was a last-minute decision. I have the access number, though, and Colonel Clarke's phone number. You can call him and verify everything."

Corey evaluated that. For a moment I thought he might just let me through without making the call.

Finally, he said, "So, what's that number, then?"

Doing his job. That was a good thing.

I gave it to him.

It was Colonel Clarke's actual mobile number—I couldn't chance giving Corey a non-legit one that he couldn't substantiate, but with the NSA app I had on my cell, we should be alright, as long as my phone was within two meters of his.

I edged in a little closer to his desk just for good measure.

He tapped in the number that my phone would intercept and transfer to a line Gunnar was using. The AI deepfake audio program we were using would have fooled even Clarke's wife.

Well, maybe not her. But just about anyone else.

Gunnar answered as Clarke, and within less than a minute Corey was saying, "Yes, sir . . ." and "I know, sir . . ." and "Sorry, sir."

As he hung up, he dry-swallowed, obviously not comfortable with how the conversation had gone.

I set my phone in the tray on the conveyor belt, passed through the metal detector, and then met up with him on the other side. No problem with the nanobots in my system. Huh. Maybe they weren't going to be an issue with metal detectors anymore.

Corey directed me down the hallway toward the VPR scanner outside the room that housed the Project Symphony prototype.

Vascular pattern recognition, or vein pattern authentication as it's sometimes called, was a biometric way to verify a person's identity by reading the vascular patterns in their hands using near-infrared light.

Unlike fingerprints—which can be lifted with clear tape and spoofed with something as commonplace as gummy candy—or retinal scans—which certain contact lenses can fool—vascular recognition was a different beast altogether and was proving quite difficult to fool, since blood has to be pumping through the veins of the person being verified. In other words, you can't just cut off someone's hand and lay it on the scanner. The person needed to actually be there, and be alive.

Because VPR was so tough to fool, its use was becoming more popular among certain branches of the military.

I waited while the near-infrared light shone through my hand and the machine verified that it really was me, and then the door's lock clicked.

Corey led the way as we entered.

We crossed through a long corridor that was lined with hundreds of models of computers, phones, printers, mobile devices, wearable tech, and smart appliances—each one of which would be manually tested for intrusion susceptibility to the Project Symphony device. If we couldn't hack into the vast and ever-widening Internet of Things, what good would it really be?

The prototype we'd used in Wisconsin the other night was version 11.9, but the one in the glass case before me was V12.0, which I'd heard they were working on, and which added more distance to its capabilities and included tech to pass through glass or walls and sense any electromagnetic emanations from inside the room.

I carefully picked it up and placed it in the black faraday duffel bag that was lying nearby and was designed to protect the prototype.

"Can that thing really hack into any computer?" Corey asked me curiously.

It can do more than that, I thought, but didn't say it. "I'm afraid I'm not authorized to discuss its capabilities. I'm sure you understand."

"Yes, sir," he said dutifully, but I could hear a trace of disappointment in his voice.

Then I zipped up the duffel bag and returned to the car.

Once inside, Gunnar gripped the steering wheel, but didn't start the engine. "Are you sure we're doing the right thing?" he said at last.

"No," I said, "but I don't see another way for us to both find the people who took Adira and also get her back alive. We're doing the only thing that might end up *accomplishing* what's right."

He was quiet and I had the sense that, even though he might not want to admit it, he agreed with me.

Then we left to pick up the car and the rifle and a tracking device from Gunnar's place that we could put on the prototype, just in case. With traffic and getting what we needed in the city, making it to Curtis Bay in time might be bit, but we were in this now up to our necks.

I just hoped we wouldn't drown.

CHAPTER 60

Adira cursed aloud.

She'd found nothing in the trunk that she could use. As far as she could tell it was empty apart from her and a discarded plastic water bottle.

She struggled to get her hands positioned to remove the bobby pin that she was wearing on the back of her belt and kept with her at all times in case she needed to pick a set of handcuffs. It's much tougher to get out of plastic cuffs, actually, but in this case, with the way the cuffs were secured, the bobby pin proved to be useless.

Additionally, these were thick and secure. She wasn't going to be able to snap them.

Some trunks have a seat release mechanism so you can flop down the rear seats from the back.

It took some effort, but she was able to position herself in a way that she could search for it with her hands.

—◊◊◊—

Søren got word from Jan. "I need you to help me with a small project. Tonight, you're my wild card."

Put your feelings aside, Søren thought. *You're hers until tomorrow, and then you're free.*

"What is it you need?" he asked.

—◊◊◊—

Since leaving the Marine base, Gunnar and I had picked up the drug dealer's car from the DEA lot and borrowed a sniper rifle and a scope—a 7x35

Precision Day Optic with night vision capabilities from one of Gunnar's friends.

"That's a very specific model," I'd said to them.

"It's the one for the job," his buddy replied. Then, he told us in no uncertain terms that he didn't want to know what we were using the rifle and scope for. He handed over the ammo. "Just don't do anything stupid," he said, "that you end up getting caught for."

"Roger that," Gunnar said.

As we stepped outside, I pointed out to Gunnar that the model of sniper rifle he was now carrying was still being beta tested. "How did your buddy get an Mk22 Mod 2? I didn't know they'd released them yet."

"They haven't," he said. "Welcome to my world."

On our way to the car, we heard from Clarke that Turo had escaped. I put the colonel on speakerphone. "Drove right out the gate," he told us, "in a food delivery truck."

"He must've had help," Gunnar noted. "Someone from the inside."

"There was a guard found stabbed," Clarke said. "Pretty serious, but it looks like he's going to pull through: Pablo Serra. The delivery driver, he's alright as well. Turns out Turo's people had someone go to Pablo's house, tie up his wife and daughters, and threaten to kill them if he didn't comply. Thank God they didn't go through with it. People will do almost anything when the ones they love are endangered."

I said nothing.

After the call, in the car, Gunnar said, "I wonder what Sidewinder thinks of Turo getting out."

"Who?"

"Fellow prisoner. A bit of bad blood between them, from what I understand. Based on the guy's tats, I'd say he's the one calling the shots in there. But Turo's not the kind of guy to like being told what to do. Hmm . . ." He reflected on that. "Something to keep in mind."

A text from Janice gave us the latitude and longitude coordinates for the exchange.

I confirmed that it was in Curtis Bay and saw that it was at Pier 3, right near the shore beside an old warehouse that'd been built to extend out onto the dock.

I took the wheel as we left to meet up with them, twenty-five minutes away.

CHAPTER 61

CURTIS BAY
PIER 3
10:24 P.M.

Janice knew it was time.

Turo hadn't arrived yet, but she expected him shortly. Still, she had another way to take care of what she had planned. She texted Turo where she would be in case he came while she was gone—at least then he would know.

Then, while Sienna waited beside the SUV, keeping an eye out for her husband, Janice invited Ivan to the backside of the warehouse that straddled the dock. "I have something I need to tell you," she said. "Something important."

Oleg, one of Ivan's men, tagged along, almost as if it were an afterthought.

The night had folded in around them, dark and deep. Metal mesh fences lined the road and a tangle of overhead wires and phone lines hung precariously close to the building from the leaning telephone poles nearby. A crane rose out of the night in the shipyard three-quarters of a mile away, a few caution lights on it, blinking red to warn off low-flying aircraft or helicopters that might be entering or leaving the Coast Guard's shipyard.

In the distance, maybe half a mile away, Dundalk's lights glimmered on the other side of the Patapsco River.

A jungle of shipping containers, piles of wooden pallets, and long-abandoned warehouses and industrial buildings languished all around them.

Once the three of them were alone, Ivan asked Janice impatiently, "What is it? What do you want?"

Yes, this was far enough. They were out of sight of the others.

"I've been thinking a lot lately," Janice said.

"About?"

"The future."

He studied her face in the muted light. "And?"

"I want to give you the chance to repent."

"What are you talking about?"

"It's time to make your peace."

"Oleg," Ivan said coolly. "Shoot her in the stomach. I want to see her bleed out."

But Oleg did not shoot Janice Daniels; instead, he turned his gun on his boss, Ivan Popovic.

"What are you doing?" Ivan's words seared the air.

Oleg sneered. "She pays better than you do." He leveled his gun at Ivan's forehead. "On your knees."

Ivan erupted, spewing out a string of Russian expletives. "You are a dead woman, Daniels. My people will find you."

"Kneel, Ivan," she said. "And pray, if you wish. This is your last opportunity to find redemption."

But instead of kneeling, Ivan Popovic just paced directly toward Oleg until he was right in front of him, and the gun's barrel was pressed up against the front of his chest.

Oleg swallowed, obviously conflicted. Obviously scared.

"Are you going to pull the trigger?" Ivan asked him coldly.

"Shoot him," Janice exclaimed. "Do it!"

But Oleg hesitated and that was his last mistake.

—⁓—

Ivan was lightning quick as he went for the gun with one hand and Oleg's throat with the other. He delivered a brutal upward strike with the edge of his hand against Oleg's windpipe.

As Oleg gasped and clutched at his throat, Ivan grabbed his wrist, wrenched the gun away, and spun to kill Janice, but she'd already escaped back into the night.

Ivan faced Oleg, this man who had turned traitor on him, and fired one shot. The bullet traveled straight through the hand he was holding against his throat, through his neck, and burst out the other side as he dropped, dead, to the ground.

Then, Ivan shot him again, in anger, this time in the face, just for betraying him.

Then he studied the area.

If the gunshots had alerted anyone else on the pier, they didn't seem to take notice of them. They probably thought he and Oleg had dispatched the billionaire.

All was quiet except for the rhythmic sound of the waves lapping against the wooden pilings supporting the dock. The distant murmur of city traffic laid down the background track for the night.

A dog somewhere began to bark.

Ivan stepped forward warily and, gun ready, pivoted around the side of a nearby shipping container, leveling the weapon in front of him.

No one.

"Oh, Janice," he called. "Where are you?"

The warehouse door lay six meters away.

She must have slipped in there.

He started toward it.

Life and death had always been a mystery to Ivan Popovic. How could it be that one moment you're alive and dreaming and hoping and planning for the future, and then, suddenly, like Oleg, you're nothing but a graying skin-bag of bones and blood and cooling meat? All your thoughts, every lesson you ever learned, every memory you ever procured, every goal you ever had—all gone, as if they had never even existed.

How could it be?

And yet, it was.

The one thing we are all good at, all adept at, is dying.

Ivan had seen it happen, oh, so many times.

And then, afterward, it does not take long at all for every ripple your life has caused to disappear and become quiet and still in the sea of time.

He opened the warehouse door and took a moment to allow his eyes to adjust to the vacant, dark space stretching before him.

The high, grimy windows on what would've been a second story held back most of the transient light from outside, but enough of it crept in for him to make out the shapes of the looming machines and the conveyor belts stretching back into the belly of the deep, shadowy building.

"I'm coming for you, Janice."

Yes, we are, each of us, experts at the very thing we strive the hardest to avoid. With no practice or expertise or experience whatsoever, all of us are able to die with very little effort at all.

A breath.

Life is but a breath.

And death is always just a heartbeat away.

His mother used to tell him that everyone experiences three deaths. The first death is when your spirit leaves your body. The second death is when you're buried. The third death comes when someone speaks your name for the last and final time.

Ivan had taken lives, yes, of course. And he had watched many others die. In his line of work, death went with the territory, so to speak. And many of those who had departed this life in his presence had experienced all three deaths.

But to what end? What did any of it matter?

For more than a decade he had made it a habit to read the obituaries every weekend.

The people who were listed had been alive and then they were dying and now they were dead. One. Two. Three. And gone.

Dead.

Forever departed.

The fate of everyone. The destiny of us all.

You get one paragraph and then the world moves on.

Ivan studied the shadows, but his cataract-weakened eyes were struggling to become accustomed to the darkness.

Still, he edged forward into the warehouse.

Most people navigate through their days by filling their time with distractions and diversions so they can *hopefully* perpetuate their desperate denial of their impending and imminent death—oh-so-frantically filling the space between the moments with something, anything, to help them *not* think about the fact that this next moment, this very one, might be their last.

Ivan did not believe in God. He did not believe in some sort of final justice or reckoning for our decisions here on earth. He believed that there were choices and consequences, and that was all. There was no universal right or wrong. Morality was simply a social construct that was subjective and malleable and a slave to the times and cultures it inhabited.

He did, however, believe in context.

Yes.

Right or wrong?

Well, it all depended.

Kill one person, and you're a murderer, destined to be despised.

Wipe out a civilization, and you're a conqueror whom millions will revere.

Context. Yes. It was all about context.

Some people get ahead because of their choices, and some people get dead because of them.

And tonight, he planned to be one of the former and not one of the latter.

But it was not to be.

Not tonight.

No, his eyes had not adjusted enough.

His response was not quick enough.

As he heard the shuffle of heavy feet nearby him in the dark, Ivan took his final breath.

Felt his final heartbeat.

Had his final thought.

No. Destiny does not favor the brave. It favors no one, but deftly swallows us all. And tonight, with two shots to the chest and one to the head, it swallowed Ivan Popovic.

And so, this man, the one who laughed with and lounged with and drank martinis with world leaders, who kidnapped and then sold little children to insatiable pedophiles, who armed suicide bombers so they could blow themselves up in mosques where their neighbors were worshipping, who traded blood for money and read obituaries every weekend and did not believe in a deity up above, died effortlessly and quietly and much sooner than he expected in a dark, lonely warehouse on Curtis Bay.

And entered the eternity he did not believe in, to meet the Judge he was not prepared to face.

—⁂—

With the toe of his boot, Turo nudged the body of the man he had just shot three times with Maureen.

Yep. Dead for sure.

He phoned Janice. "It's done."

"He's dead?"

"Quite."

"Alright. Get to the pier. I think I see a car approaching."

"Brock?"

"I'm not sure."

"I'm on my way."

And then, Turo left behind the body of Ivan Popovic, which was now nothing but a graying skin-bag of bones and blood and cooling meat.

Left it there to rot.

CHAPTER 62

Adira managed to find the trunk release.

Managed to kick the seat down.

Managed to scoot forward into the backseat of the car.

Only to find that two men were ready for her. Only to find that they were waiting and, after punching her hard in the jaw, one of them said, "It's time you learn to behave, little girl."

He tugged her forcibly from the car, but when she got her footing, she threw herself forward, headbutting him brutally in the face. He hollered out in pain, clutching at the smashed mess of cartilage that used to be his nose.

She'd hoped that it might kill him, that the angle might've been right to send the cartilage skewering up into his brain. That didn't happen, but at least she'd broken his nose. He would remember this night every time he looked in the mirror for the rest of his life.

And if she had anything to say about it, his life was not going to be a long one.

The other man shoved her against the car and locked some sort of steel collar around her neck, then roughly dragged her toward a waiting SUV while she writhed, trying to pull free, and while his partner cursed and fought to suppress the flow of blood gushing from his face.

—m—

I was driving now, with Gunnar beside me. We were both wearing the body armor that he'd insisted on us collecting from his place before we left DC.

Mine was a little tight, but I was glad to have it and hoped I wouldn't need it. He'd also grabbed a fixed-blade tactical knife and sheath.

The tracker was in place on the prototype. We were good to go.

We rounded a bend near the shore, which lay a quarter mile ahead of us, and came to a street sign that indicated we were at an intersection where, somehow, Northbridge Avenue met up with Northbridge Avenue.

Gunnar consulted his phone. "We're close. Take a right up ahead."

A network of deep cracks infested the potholed road and I needed to slow down as we rumbled toward the river. At the edge of my headlights' reach, a tenacious snag of underbrush tried, but failed, to hide a ramshackle mobile home that someone must have ditched here years ago.

Between us and the Patapsco River lay a nightmare of neglected parking lots, derelict warehouses, and boarded-up factories. A maze of rusted security fences led everywhere and nowhere. Every so often, a streetlight appeared, but there seemed to be no rhyme or reason to where they were or which ones were operating.

We passed half a dozen transport trucks loaded with new cars shipped in from overseas. A water treatment plant hunched nearby, and eight cylindrical oil terminals rose around us, blank against the night.

"That'll work." Gunnar pointed to one of them. "It looks like that's line of sight to the pier. From up there, I should be able to get a clear shot."

I stopped and he surreptitiously exited the car, retrieved the Mk22 from the backseat, and slung the strap over his shoulder. Then, he agilely scrambled over a pile of cement blocks that'd been randomly dumped beside the road, and merged into the darkness on his way to the ladder leading up to the top of the nearest oil storage tower.

As I drove toward Pier 3, I tried to process everything, but found it hard to think in a straight line.

Eventually, as I approached the water, I saw a black SUV waiting a hundred feet in front of me, parked about twenty feet from a warehouse that squatted out onto the landing. A man holding a tactical rifle stood beside the SUV, and when I rolled toward him, he directed the rifle at me.

I stopped.

Let the car idle.

He motioned for me to drive closer, and I warily nosed the car forward.

As I did, two other men emerged. One of them was Turo Pärnänen, Janice Daniels's fugitive bodyguard. The other was a man I didn't recognize, and from here I couldn't tell for sure, but it looked like he had a cruelly bloodied and broken nose that probably should have been bandaged up but wasn't. It gave him a fixed sneer that seemed right at home on his face.

A shadow cast because of a dead streetlight near the dock fell across the SUV, cloaking it in the night.

I wanted to keep some space between us, so I rolled to a stop about fifty feet away from the three men.

Parked.

In my earpiece, I asked Gunnar, "Do you think it might be a trap?"

"There's no *might* about it, brother. Go in with both eyes open."

"You in position?"

"I am. I can see you. I'm at a hundred eighty yards."

Knowing that he was eyeing me through his buddy's scope was a bit unsettling, but if he could see me, then, when the time came, he would be able to see his targets as well.

"Do you have a bead on that guy with the rifle?" I asked him.

"Yes. But if I take him out, they'll drive off and it's over. Make sure she's safe and then I'll take the shot."

I took a deep breath and eased my door open.

"Engine off," the man with the gun called to me before I could even climb out of the car. He was stocky, but not as tall as Turo. "Then bring the keys with you."

I killed the engine, and then, holding my hands up so he could see that I wasn't armed, I edged out of the car, and nudged the door shut with my leg.

The reek of gasoline from boat motors sullied the air, but the stench of dead fish almost managed to edge it out.

"I'm unarmed," I said.

He scoffed lightly. "Well, I'm sure you can understand my reticence to believe you."

He signaled to the man with the broken nose, who lumbered toward me. I held my arms out to the sides as he patted me down and found nothing. He nodded to the guy who was calling the shots, then waited near me for further instructions.

So far, only that one man had spoken; now he said, "Where's the prototype?"

"It's close," I told him. "Let me see her first."

"Do you have it with you?"

"I told you, it's close. Bring her out."

He called out to the man who'd frisked me, "Check his car."

I realized that it wasn't going to do me any good to argue or repeat myself, so I said nothing, but waited while he drew a handgun from a shoulder holster, and then cautiously approached the car. Aiming the gun directly in front of him, he flung the driver's door open, then studied the inside of the sedan and confirmed that there was no one else there and nothing inside.

"The trunk too," his boss said.

He went to the trunk and, when he found it locked, called to me to open it.

I had the key fob with me. If I slid the cover to the side and depressed the hidden interior button, the Mexican drug lord's car would explode. If I pressed the button on the outside of the fob instead, the trunk would open. Simple as that.

Carefully, purposely, I tapped the correct release button to unlock the trunk.

The guy popped the lid and studied the trunk's interior. "Nothing here," he shouted to his associate, then slammed it shut once again.

"Where is it?" the man with the automatic rifle demanded.

"Bring her out first," I said. "Let me see her."

He glanced at Turo, who nodded slightly, making the call.

Evidently, Turo was the one who was ultimately in charge here. Good to know.

While keeping me in his sights, the gunman directed his broken-nosed minion to join him back beside the SUV. "Show him," he said, and the sneering man opened the rear passenger door of their vehicle, reached in, and yanked Adira out.

Her hands were drawn back behind her. A cloth gag was tied around her mouth so she couldn't speak, but she shook her head urgently at me and I took it to mean that she didn't want me to do this.

She's telling you she'd rather spend the rest of her life being trafficked than let the prototype fall into the wrong hands.

No, this is—

"Alright," the gunman said impatiently. "Now tell me where it is."

"It's in the trunk," I replied.

"Keb checked in there."

"Keb didn't check carefully enough."

He glared at the man who was apparently named Keb while I backed up and approached the trunk.

"Slowly." Turo spoke for the first time. "Don't try to be a hero here."

I clicked the trunk's key fob button, then slowly lifted the lid as I whispered into my earpiece to Gunnar, "Take the shot."

"No good. They can still get her back into their car. Show them the device. When she steps forward—as soon as she starts walking toward you— I'll end this."

My heart whomped inside of me like it didn't belong in someone my size, like it was too large for my chest and was prepared to burst as a way of punishing me for trapping it where it didn't want to be.

I reached into the trunk and released the hidden lever that opened the first secret compartment, down near the far-right corner, where the black duffel bag containing the prototype waited. The other compartment held an M4, courtesy of Gunnar's personal arsenal, ready in case I might need it later.

I went ahead and eased the rifle out, then laid it in the trunk beside the spare tire so I could easily get to it if that's how things played out.

I lifted the duffel bag slowly, then eased the trunk closed, but not so far that it latched, and rounded the car.

"How do we do this?" I asked.

"Bring it to me," the man with the rifle commanded. "I'll tell you when to stop, then I want you to set it down, open the bag, and remove the device. Once I see it, we let her go. Not before."

Adira was shaking her head more urgently now and I wanted to reassure her that things were going to be okay, that we had this in hand, but I truthfully couldn't promise that she would be okay.

I couldn't promise anything.

I opted to remain quiet instead.

She tried to speak again but the gag swallowed her words.

Something was around her neck. I couldn't quite make out what it was. Some sort of thick metal collar?

A chill gripped me as I remembered reading about Brian Wells. Back in 2003, he robbed a bank and was then killed when a collar bomb that was locked around his neck detonated during his apprehension. In the ensuing years, the DOD had experimented with possible prototypes of similar devices for prisoner swaps, but had abandoned the research, calling it "too barbaric for modern warfare."

My pulse raced and I wished there was some way to calm my shredded nerves.

I took four steps toward him. We were maybe thirty feet apart.

"That's far enough," the gunman yelled.

I carefully set down the duffel bag, unzipped it, and reached inside.

CHAPTER 63

E asy now." He targeted me carefully with his rifle. "No sudden moves."
I removed the device and held it up by its slender handle for him to see.

"How do I know that's really what we came here for?"

"How do I know you're not just going to shoot me right now and take both the prototype and Adira? Trust. This is the real deal."

He worked his jaw back and forth and I was surprised that this scenario hadn't occurred to him earlier. How were they planning to test things to make sure I'd brought the actual Project Symphony prototype?

Who knows? Who cares? Just get her away from them so Gunnar can do what he came here to do.

"There are explosives inside the device," I said, taking a play out of Janice's playbook from back at the museum. "Your people will be able to remove them easily enough later, but there's a timer that's already been started. Four minutes. It'll destroy this thing unless I make a phone call and pause the timer—and I'm not going to do that until Adira's with me and we're at a safe distance. You decide: do you go back to Ivan and Janice with nothing, or do you trust me, make the exchange, and we all walk away from here with what we want?"

It wasn't true.

I wished it was, but I hadn't thought of it earlier and right now I needed to come up with something that would convince them to turn Adira over. The only thing inside the device was the tiny, almost invisible transmitter hidden in the handle that would allow us to track it, as long as we were within half a mile. I had no doubt that they would eventually discover and disable it, but I was hoping that it'd be there long enough to get Adira to safety and for Baltimore SWAT to respond.

Gunnar and I both had an app on our phones that could track it.

But first I needed to get her away from those three men.

"Send her to me." I was still holding the prototype. "Do it."

The gunman didn't look happy, but he indicated for Adira to proceed toward me. After two steps, however, Turo grabbed her shoulder to stop her, then called to me, "You see this thing around her neck? It's an explosive collar. You're familiar with those, aren't you? I'm guessing you are. And so, you know there's a timer on there. It's set for thirty seconds. When it reaches zero, it'll go boom and you'll be mopping this fine lady up from the road and taking her home in a bucket. Give me the device or I'm going to start the timer."

"Take it off her."

"There's a release mechanism on there," he went on, ignoring me. "You're not going to get it off her without the combination, and I'm only going to give that to you once I have the prototype."

Maybe he was bluffing.

Maybe.

Maybe not.

You were bluffing, so—

"You better hurry," he said, "or I'm gonna start that timer and—"

"Okay!" I set the device down and stepped back. "Okay."

"Farther."

I backed away, nearly to my car.

Turo let go of her shoulder and Adira started toward me again.

She'd made it about ten feet when the guy with the rifle tilted his head toward his shoulder, obviously listening to a transmission coming through his radio.

Something was up.

Come on, Adira, just a little further. Just—

The man's eyes widened. "There's a shooter!"

"Run!" I shouted to Adira.

I sprinted toward her to get in the way in case they took a shot. I had that body armor on; if I could get to her, I could shield her.

Get her back to the drug runner's car with the bulletproof windows. Just get—

She paused, leapt, and drew her knees up to her chest while swinging her cuffed hands beneath them in order to get her hands in front of her.

Nicely done.

The gunman leveled his rifle at me, but as he did, his head jerked back and he collapsed in a heavy heap. There was a nearly simultaneous sound of a gunshot.

That report was too quick.

There should've been a longer lag. Gunnar said he was a hundred eighty yards away.

As Adira ran toward me, Turo tapped his phone, and even from where I stood, I could see a red operational light on the collar blink on.

He'd started it.

She had thirty seconds to live.

I had thirty seconds to save her.

CHAPTER 64

Adira could feel a slight vibration against her throat as the timer ticked off each second.

She grabbed the collar and tried to tug it off, but it was secure.

No, no, no.

She yanked out the gag. "Get back!" she yelled to Travis, as shots rang out behind her. "And get the prototype!" She angled away from him so he wouldn't be close to her when it blew, but instead of grabbing the device, he ran toward her. "No, Travis!" she hollered.

It had to be less than twenty seconds by now.

And ticking down.

Every second.

Another pulse.

Against her throat.

She needed to put some space between her and Travis.

But then, an idea—and she whipped around, ran to the device, and snatched it up. They wanted it, well, if this collar blew and she was holding it, they weren't going to get it.

"No!" Travis yelled. He was quickly approaching and less than twenty feet away. "Drop it!"

She flagged her hand to warn him off and he stopped where he was. "What's the combination?" she shouted to Turo.

He said nothing, but all at once, Janice Daniels's voice called out from the shadows: "1612!"

Adira fumbled at the keypad on the collar, but since she couldn't see it, she couldn't tell where the numbers were.

Another vibration.

Another second.

"Travis." The word caught in her throat. She set down the prototype and pulled at the collar. "I need you!"

He was already on his way.

—m—

By the time I got to her, the readout on the collar's timer was down to thirteen seconds.

I tapped in the sequence: 1-6-1-2.

Eleven seconds.

The collar clicked open but continued its countdown.

The prototype was right there, right at my feet.

Wait.

Yes.

"Go on," I said to her urgently as I locked the collar around the handle of the device. "Get to the car. Bulletproof windows!"

Eight.

I joined her on the way to the sedan as the seconds ticked down.

But when I glanced back, I saw that Turo had raced toward the prototype. He grabbed it and tore off toward a shipping container that separated us from the tangle of underbrush flanking the river. Then he disappeared behind the container.

Less than three seconds later, an explosion rocked the night.

I didn't know if it'd killed him, if the blast had destroyed the prototype, or if he'd somehow managed to remove the collar and discard it in time.

No way to tell.

A spray of gunfire kept Adira and me from getting to the car, and we had to dive for shelter behind a stack of pallets near a van-sized mound of concrete with a dozen bars of rusted rebar bristling up from it. A nest of giant steel thorns.

Careful to avoid the rebar, we crouched there as the man with the broken nose took shots at us with his handgun.

"Gunnar," I said. "Take him out!"

No reply.

"What have you done?" Adira admonished me. "They got the prototype!"

"It blew."

"Maybe not!"

Someone fired up the SUV and sped toward us.

"We need to stop them," she said. "Do you have a gun?"

"No. Something better." I unpocketed the key fob and slid the cover aside to expose the detonation button. "Cover your ears."

As the SUV approached the car, I pressed the button and a mushroom of fire engulfed the sedan, torquing it violently into the air. The shockwave slammed into us and knocked us both backward.

As the burning car landed, it did so on its side at an unfortunate angle, tottered clumsily, and then rolled onto its roof in the path of the SUV. The driver frantically veered away from the explosion and smashed into the side of the warehouse.

More flames.

A gush of gasoline emptied from the van's punctured tank, poured into a crack in the pavement, and snaked toward us.

The driver leapt out, but inadvertently stepped into the gasoline as it ignited, and his clothes burst into flames. Screaming, he waved his arms erratically, stumbling forward, until a shot from the shadows ended his misery and his body dropped into the lake of burning fuel and the hungry flames had their way with him.

Status: The driver was dead. The gunman with the rifle was dead. Turo and the device? Impossible to say.

That left Janice and the guy with the broken nose.

At least those two, if not more.

To get away from the raging flames, Adira and I tried to escape toward the underbrush fifteen feet away, but gunfire kept us pinned down beside the skewers of rusted rebar.

"Are you okay?" I asked her urgently.

She held up her cuffed wrists. "Do you have a knife?"

"No, I—"

Through the earpiece, I heard Gunnar grunting, obviously scuffling with someone. I trusted that he could take care of himself, but we needed to get Adira free and confirm that the prototype really had been destroyed.

A few strangled gasps and then the earpiece went silent.

"Gunnar?" No reply.

"Gunnar!"

Nothing.

The remaining shooter was about twenty feet away, illuminated by the two blazing vehicles, the runnel of burning gas, and the incinerated body of the SUV's driver. The light of the flames flicked and whorled hellishly across the guy's bloodied face. "Come out, come out, wherever you are!" he shouted, taunting us.

A knife came pirouetting across the ground and skidded to a stop about a yard from my foot.

Expecting that somehow Gunnar had been the one to fling it toward me, I looked up, but he wasn't the person crouching twenty feet away in the underbrush.

Janice Daniels was.

I had no idea why she was helping us, but at the moment I wasn't about to question it. She was assisting us, and that was good enough for me.

Quickly, I cut through the plastic cuffs to free Adira's wrists.

"You seriously don't have a gun?" she said with clear exasperation.

I studied the car I'd driven here, now fully ablaze. Gunnar's M4 was still in the trunk. "Not anymore."

Police sirens pierced the night. With a Coast Guard facility so close by, and with all of the gunfire and explosions, I wasn't surprised by the response time.

Good. That means—

"All I want is the prototype," Janice called. "This is much bigger than any of us. I'm just trying to help people, to save lives, not take them. You have to understand that."

Adira ignored her. "Stay here," she said to me as she took the knife. "I'm going after the device."

Then, she bolted toward the shipping container Turo had vanished behind. I couldn't track the prototype until I had a phone with that DOD app, and my cell was in the burning car.

When I looked back toward the place where Janice had been hiding, I realized she was no longer there. A faint shift in the shadows indicated that she was on her way to the warehouse.

The man with the broken nose stalked toward me and leered down at me, his teeth gleaming. I raised my hands slowly, trying to think of a way to stop him, to get the upper hand, to somehow—but then, before he could kill me, a shot rang out and he collapsed forward, plunging heavily onto the rebar spikes jutting out of the ominous heap of concrete beside me.

One of spikes lanced his shoulder; the other impaled him gruesomely through his abdomen.

Looking away from the grim sight, I assessed things.

Whoever had taken that shot couldn't have had better timing.

"Gunnar?" I called into my earpiece. "Are you there?"

Still nothing.

You can't let Janice escape.

The dead guy in front of me wouldn't be needing his handgun anymore. I grabbed it.

And, as Adira went in search of Turo and the prototype, I took off toward the warehouse to stop Janice Daniels from getting away.

CHAPTER 65

I opened the warehouse door.

Stepped inside.

Behind me, the gunfire had subsided and in here, the thick silence was disturbed only by the claw-soft scurrying of rodents somewhere out of sight and the sound of water lapping up against the pilings supporting the floorboards.

No sign of Janice.

The dark expanse of the building reminded me of a time in the not-so-distant past when a Russian spy had threatened to torture me in an abandoned warehouse not so different from this one, down in Tennessee.

Not the ideal memory to be considering at the moment.

"Janice?"

I saw no one, but up ahead of me, maybe thirty feet away, a figure lay prone on the floor. Apprehensively, I edged toward it, wishing I had something with me to help me see better—a flashlight, mobile phone, anything.

"Is that you, Janice?"

The person didn't respond.

The dank, stifling air seemed to press in against me from all sides.

I crept closer and finally, when I was about ten feet away, I was able to identify that it was Ivan Popovic lying there, motionless, shot dead.

Well, at least that was one problem solved.

Continuing my search for the billionaire, I circumnavigated past a series of conveyor belts and through a jumble of bulky, rusted chains hanging randomly from the ceiling, the floorboards spongy and uncertain underfoot.

Water dripping from high above or maybe spraying up from the river below must have weakened the boards over the years, and I was worried that they might give way at any moment and send me plummeting into the river.

The farther I moved in through the faltering light, the louder the sound of water slapping against the pilings that held up the pier became.

Louder? Why louder?

That's when I noticed it—just in time and only five feet in front of me: a fifteen-by-fifteen-foot jagged gap of missing boards yawning open, swallowing what little light there was. The water below swirled and surged like it was infested with a swarm of dark eels curling around the pilings.

And then, footsteps.

Ahead of me, maybe thirty or forty feet away, on the other side of the gap.

I readied the gun. "Janice?"

Someone emerged from the shadows and stood before me in the subdued light. I raised my gun partway up, finger off the trigger. I couldn't tell if it was Janice or not, but for now I assumed it was. "Don't move, Janice."

"I'm sorry," the person said, "Janice isn't here." I recognized that voice. Of course I did.

It was the voice of my wife.

"Sienna?"

Saying her name, hearing her voice, identifying her here in the dark brought it all back. The fire. The sting of grief. The suffocating desire for justice. And now, the tight twist of anger stemming from her betrayal of my trust, my heart.

She faked her death. She's been working with Janice. With Popovic.

She was your lover.

She is a stranger.

A traitor.

"It's been a minute, Travis." She stepped forward to where I could see her and then continued all the way to the other side of the saw-edged gap separating us. "I didn't expect that we would meet again. Not like this."

Unsure what else to do, I leveled the gun at her.

Don't aim at anything you don't want to destroy.

I hesitated, lowered it again, but not all the way.

"What are you going to do with that gun?" she asked me. "Are you really going to shoot me?"

I reviewed the marksmanship lesson from this morning, the three areas to aim at to cause incapacitation: mediastinum, brainstem, and lateral pelvis.

Chest. Head. Hips. Shoot until the threat is no longer a threat. Disperse the shots to create more decisive wound channels for incapacitation.

"Hold your hands out to the sides," I said.

"You're not going to pull that trigger. I'm unarmed. Would you really shoot an unarmed woman? Would you really shoot your wife?"

"I'm seriously considering it." I brought the gun back up into position. "Now, let me see your hands."

I couldn't tell if she had a weapon, so it was tough to assess how much of a threat she posed.

I whipped through the three reasons to justify the use of deadly force: opportunity, intent, and ability to inflict bodily injury or death. You need all three.

Was Sienna a threat? Did she have the opportunity, intent, and ability to take me down?

Opportunity: Yes.

Intent: I believed so.

But she might be unarmed. If she is, she's no threat. She might not have the ability to harm you.

You can't know that. You can't assume that.

Yes! You have to assume it.

That's when I realized that I'd already made a mistake.

I recalled that intent might be clear from the circumstances, or it might be implied or communicated through a person's actions or words. You shouldn't really say, "Show me your hands," because the person might just do that and shoot you in the head. Instead, you should say, "Turn around. Get on your knees. Hands on your head." And if the aggressor doesn't comply, she has intent. It was that easy. And I'd forgotten it in the heat of the moment.

I tried it now: "Turn around. Get on your knees. Hands on your head."

Sienna didn't move.

Intent: there it was.

Surely, she had the motivation to kill me—after all, she'd paid to have me burned to death.

But was she armed?

I aimed at her feet, ready to raise the gun to her chest if I needed to.

Be.

Loved.

Betrayed.

With the police on their way, maybe all I needed to do was stall. "When did they turn you?" I said. "Or were you a traitor from the start?"

"Why do you think I initiated things with you? I pursued you, Travis."

"All this time."

"Yes."

Her mark. You were her mark.

I honestly didn't know what to do. Because of the missing floorboards between us, I couldn't get to her, and if she decided to bolt into the darkness toward the far side of the warehouse, I wasn't about to shoot her in the back.

Besides, if someone's running away from you, they're no longer a threat. You only shoot to stop a threat.

She still hadn't made a move. Instead, she just stood there stock-still as the sirens pulsed closer toward us. "I knew you would come for Adira," Sienna said. "After all, you went back into the house for me."

"You were going to traffic her," I said tightly. "Cut off her hands. Blind her."

"I was watching you out there, Travis, with the exchange. You've changed. Risen to the occasion. You're not the man you used to be. I like the new you."

"I'm not here to talk about me. The woman who died in the fire—was it Lena Rhodes?"

"She was drawing undue attention to my work. It needed to be handled. I handled it."

"Your 'work'? You mean betraying your country?"

She didn't disagree.

I couldn't believe I had ever trusted this woman. Ever loved her.

But I had.

In some ways, I still did.

"And it was you, wasn't it?" I said. "Stealing Maureen? Meeting Popovic at the airport? Have you been working with him this whole time?"

"I could've killed you, Travis, after the fire when you were at the hospital. I visited you, you know, after your surgeries, while you were asleep. I could've ended your suffering."

"Why didn't you? What stopped you?"

"The night of the fire, you went back into our house while it was burning. Why?"

"Because I loved you," I said, "and I thought I could save you."

"That's why I didn't kill you. Because anyone who has loved that deeply deserves a chance to find love again."

I was at a loss for words. It was all too much. "Why, Sienna? Why would you do this? Any of this?"

"Capitalism is overrated, Travis. It's fueled by greed and will inevitably collapse under the weight of humanity's collective selfishness—but I'm not here to convince you of what I believe or why I believe it. The masses need leaders. I'm just here to give them what they need."

"We need leaders," I said. "Not despots."

"Semantics."

I searched for leverage. Anything. "Ivan is dead," I said.

"No, he's not."

"Yes." I eyed down the barrel and thought of shot placement and wound channels and incapacitation. "He is. His body is behind me, here in the warehouse."

Since she was working with him, I wasn't sure how that news would affect her, what she might do.

"I would have pulled that trigger already," she said to me.

"I know."

Stop the threat.

Shoot to stop the threat.

But from there she isn't a threat, unless—

The sirens grew louder. The patrol cars couldn't be more than a block or two away. "It's over," I told her. "Make it easier on yourself. Turn yourself in."

All at once, she reached for her waist, a cross-body draw.

She's going for a gun!

Aiming for her pelvis, I took the shot. I didn't want to kill her, just needed to stop her.

I couldn't tell where I hit her, but she did jerk to the side.

I expected her to collapse or to whirl around and retreat into the darkness, but she didn't do either of those things. Instead, she leapt forward and vanished into the inky black water roiling between us.

—⌇⌇—

The person with the prototype watched as six police cruisers came racing onto the scene.

The destroyed SUV and blown-up sedan were still ablaze and were heaving black smoke into the night. With the bodies strewn around, the shoreline looked like a war zone.

The woman behind all of this couldn't get taken in. If she did get arrested and interviewed, she might talk, might share more than she should. No, that couldn't be allowed to happen. So, as a police officer exited his patrol car about thirty yards away, the necessary steps became clear.

The observer crouched as the officer stalked his way, and then, once the two of them were alone in the shadows, acted in the decisive manner that the moment required.

CHAPTER 66

G un lowered and ready, I studied the water.

Ten feet below me, dark currents slithered and slurred around the moss-covered pilings supporting the pier.

I waited. Watched.

Sienna didn't surface.

"Did you get all that?" I called into my radio. "There's a hole in the pier here. Sienna jumped into it."

Gunnar didn't reply.

Though the current wasn't particularly swift, I wouldn't have wanted to be caught in it. But there was no guarantee that Sienna was dead. The last thing I wanted to do was underestimate her again.

Shouting police officers and a fanning array of flashlight beams burst through the door at the far end of the warehouse. I knew this was going to take some explaining and I didn't want to get shot, so I dropped the gun, got on my knees, and interlaced my fingers behind my head.

While one of the officers cuffed me, another called for his team to clear the building. I tried to tell them that they needed to search the water for Sienna—a wanted spy—and search the waterfront for Turo—an escaped prisoner—and search the underbrush for Janice—a domestic terrorist—but they weren't too interested in any of that at the moment. They were more interested in shuttling me to one of their cars.

We'd just left the warehouse when the officer beside me got word from his commanding officer that I was not a threat, that I was not the person they were looking for.

As he was uncuffing me, Adira's voice came through his radio. "I need to talk to him."

Another voice, male, authoritative: "Let her do it."

Someone in charge.

"I have Janice Daniels," Adira told me. "You okay?"

"Yeah. I shot at Sienna, but she got away. Do you have the device?"

"No."

"Ivan's dead as well," I said. "Where are you?"

"About fifty yards south of the warehouse, right beside the river. There are three officers here. You can't miss us."

"Are you safe? Are you alright?"

"I'm good."

I still hadn't heard from Gunnar. "Are you there, Gunnar?" I asked urgently into my earpiece.

Nothing.

After notifying the officer beside me that we needed to find another member of our team, he radioed it in and then escorted me south, toward where Adira had said she was.

As it turned out, we met up with her and Janice on their way back to the police cars that were now parked near the warehouse.

Adira had restrained Janice by tying her wrists behind her back with her belt.

"What do we know?" Adira asked me.

"Turo's in the wind. But at least Ivan's dead."

"And we've got a couple of bonus dead bad guys over there by the burning cars," she noted.

"Yes, we do."

"So that's a plus."

"Well . . ."

"But we don't have the prototype."

"No," I said with disappointment. "Could you tell if it was destroyed in the explosion?"

"I could not. Can we track it?"

"I need a phone with the DOD app on it. If the device didn't blow and it's still in the area, we should be good. My phone's in the car."

"The one that exploded."

"Yes."

She shook her head in frustration. "And Gunnar?"

"I haven't heard from him since the shooting began. The cops are looking for him."

An uneasy moment passed between us as I processed all of that—especially the fact that I still hadn't gotten an update from Gunnar. And the last time I had heard from him, it'd sounded like he was in a fight.

As we led Janice toward one of the waiting police cruisers, I said to her, "Why did you help us? You could've let Adira die. You didn't need to tell us the collar's combination or give me that knife."

"It wasn't meant to go down like this," she said imperatively. "This is bigger than any of us and what we have in mind—it's the path of compassion, not of oppression."

I wasn't certain if she believed that or not, but for now I didn't question her assertions. "The men by the burning cars," I said, "did they work for you?"

"One of them did. Rollan—he had the rifle. The other men were Ivan's."

"Where would Sienna go?" I asked her. "I shot at her. I think I hit her."

Janice shook her head. "I don't know."

"What about the prototype?" Adira asked. "Where would Turo take it if it's still intact?"

Janice was quiet.

"Janice," Adira said, "at the museum you told me you weren't at war with us, that you weren't the villain here. Now's your chance to prove it. Tell us what we need to know and let's put an end to this."

Janice eyed a nearby officer who was lumbering in our direction, then said to us, "I'll tell you everything you need to know, tomorrow, at the police station."

"Tell us now," Adira said urgently, but Janice remained quiet.

It wasn't ideal, but her promise to tell us more was something. Despite all the pain and suffering that Janice had caused, I did believe she was a person of her word, so I figured a meeting tomorrow was at least a *step* in the right direction.

The officer cuffed her, gave Adira back her belt, and then began to lead Janice toward his cruiser.

"Hang on," I said to him. "This has to do with a counterterrorism investigation. Should we wait for the FBI?"

"They're not here and I'm not gonna sit around waiting for them." He did not sound happy. "We'll hand her off at the station. If they even bother to show up there."

While Adira walked with them to the patrol car, still trying to get Janice to talk, I looked around and tried to take everything in.

A surreal, fire-enshrouded, corpse-laden landscape surrounded me. The smell of gasoline, melting plastic, and burned flesh filled the air.

While I'd been speaking with Adira, a fire truck had arrived and the fire-fighters were battling to suppress the burning vehicles, trying to make sure the entire warehouse and adjoining pier didn't go up in flames.

Earlier, Turo had told Gunnar that there would be fireworks tonight. I was pretty sure this wasn't quite what he had anticipated, but the man had not been wrong.

Flames.

Death.

Devastation.

It made me think of the arson fire once again, the night that I thought I'd lost Sienna.

In a way, that fire was tied to this one. A series of tragic, blood-soaked dominoes stretching back eighteen months, all tipped over by my wife.

When I asked an officer nearby if we knew anything about Gunnar, she relayed the question to her commanding officer and he radioed back that Gunnar had been picked up by the paramedics, no word on his condition.

There were two ambulances on-site—one that had its lights on and was pulling out; the other stood stationary, with the back doors open. Empty inside.

I sprinted to the ambulance that was already en route and banged on the back door. After a few seconds, the driver stopped and an EMT opened it up. "We need to leave," she told me impatiently.

"Is he with you? Gunnar Bane?"

"Yes, but—"

"Is he going to be okay?"

"We need to—"

"It's alright," Gunnar cut in. His voice sounded thin and strained. "Let him in. I need to talk to him."

With an exasperated look on her face, the EMT moved aside, giving me just enough space to climb in next to Gunnar. "What happened?" I asked him. "Are you alright?"

He wavered his hand back and forth. "Been better. The guy I was fighting, he jabbed me with a needle. Injected me with something. I'm kinda woozy. Tore my earpiece out too. Also, he somehow knew that my left shoulder was bothering me. Wrenched my arm to the side, managed to dislocate it. But this nice paramedic here was kind enough to get it back into its socket." He nodded to her. "Thank you by the way."

"You're welcome," she said.

"Her name is Ruthie," he informed me helpfully.

"We need to go," Ruthie emphasized to me.

"In a sec," I said to her, then I turned to Gunnar again. "That was a good shot. Earlier. That headshot. The guy with the rifle."

"That wasn't me."

"What are you talking about?"

"Someone beat me to it."

"Another shooter? Someone who turned on his team? Killed one of his own men?"

"Looks like it."

"Huh." I processed that. "What about the guy who attacked you?"

Gunnar patted the sheath of his combat knife. "He won't be bothering us anymore."

The paramedic cleared her throat emphatically, and I said to Gunnar, "Do you have your phone? I need to try tracking the prototype."

"It's gone?"

"Might've blown up. I'm not sure."

He cringed as he dug his cell out of his pocket, then unlocked the screen and handed it over.

"Adira?" he asked.

"She's safe. She's fine." I placed a hand on his good shoulder. "Be okay."

"I will."

Then, he was overcome by whatever drug he'd been injected with, and he closed his eyes and became still. Ruthie bent over him.

I exited the ambulance, her partner closed the door, and they took off for the hospital.

I was left with that lingering image of Gunnar lying there, his eyes closed, his breathing ragged, as the ambulance's departing siren wailed through the night and its fading lights cascaded overhead, dissevering the darkness and the smoke-infested shadows hovering above me.

As I was opening the app on his phone, Adira caught up with me, informed me that the officer had left with Janice, and then said, "Was it true what you said earlier, that there was an explosive ordnance in the prototype?"

"No," I said, scrolling. "That was a bluff."

"But there is a way to track it?"

I typed in my password. "Working on it."

It only took a moment for the app to ping a location.

"That doesn't make any sense," Adira said, staring at the phone's screen. "It's in the middle of the river."

"No." I pointed toward the water. "It's in the middle of a yacht."

CHAPTER 67

11:37 P.M.
13 HOURS LEFT

The Coast Guard had already made it to the yacht when Adira and I caught a ride on one of their skiffs to see if the prototype was aboard.

She asked the Coast Guard officer we met on the deck for an update and he told us that they hadn't found anyone aboard when they arrived.

"Do you mind if we have a look around?" she said.

He gave us the once over. "Are you law enforcement?"

"I'm the person they were going to sell into the sex trade," she said. "They were going to cut off my hands." She held them up to show him the red marks still encircling her wrists from the plastic cuffs. "We won't touch anything," she informed him, "so the crime techs will be able to get whatever they need. We just want to see if there's anything here that might lead us to the people who took me."

"We work for the Pentagon," I added. "This is a matter of national security."

But his eyes were still on Adira's wrists, and he seemed to give more merit to her plight than to my explanation. "They were going to cut off your hands?"

"Yes," Adira said. "And blind me."

"Have at it."

As we examined the yacht, we found no evidence of the prototype, although its handle with the tracker had been torn off and was in the cabin, indicating that someone had brought the device onboard—or wanted us to think they had.

In the hold, we came across a reinforced room that brought us pause.

A large tray of cat litter sat in the corner. A chain with an ankle shackle was bolted to the hull beside the litter box. Bottles of water waited near a ratty cot. And there, on the wall above the mattress, were the twenty-one hash marks that'd appeared on the photograph Janice had given to Adira at the museum.

"That was almost you in here," I said soberly.

"Yeah," Adira agreed. "But it was already somebody else."

I was quiet. I didn't know what to say to that, and I couldn't even imagine what it was like for her to be here now, to see those marks and speculate on what might have been her fate.

A crime scene unit arrived to process the yacht and, since that wasn't our job and we would've just gotten in the way, we left in the skiff again, to head back to shore.

We were about halfway there when a military helicopter pivoted on the edge of the air and landed in an overgrown field near the warehouse where everything had gone down.

As we were leaving the boat, Colonel Clarke departed the chopper, gave the area a quick once-over, then locked his eyes on us, and hastened our way.

He listened carefully as we filled him in. I thought he might start by reprimanding me for taking the Project Symphony prototype in the first place and then, even worse, losing it, but he didn't. Instead, he just asked about Gunnar and took time to confirm that Adira truly was alright after her ordeal.

"I am," she assured him. "I'm good."

"Sir," I said to him. "Bringing the prototype here was my call all the way. Whatever disciplinary action you need to take—take it against me and me alone. Not Gunnar."

A pause. "I'm going to need to process all of this," he said at last, in a tone that was impossible to read. "We'll talk more about it in the morning."

In nearly every spy movie I'd ever seen, this would've been the moment when I was rebuked, disavowed, fired, or arrested. The trope was out there. I wasn't sure what to make of his response—if I should be thankful for it or if it should give me pause, if something else might be at play.

He indicated the smoldering remains of the drug smuggler's sedan. "Is that the car you were going to return without a scratch?"

"Yeah," I muttered. "That's the one."

"I heard you shot Sienna."

"Well, I shot *at* her. I think I hit her; I'm just not certain. She disappeared into the river. I never saw her come up."

"How was that?" he asked me. "Firing a gun at her?"

"Honestly? Not as upsetting as I thought it might be."

"That's good to hear."

I looked at him curiously. "Why's that?"

"In this business, you need to be able to make the tough calls, and shooting the person you love? That's as tough as it gets."

Adira looked away, toward the skyline, and I wondered if she was troubled that he'd indicated that I loved Sienna.

He asked if there were any phones or IDs on those who'd been caught or killed, but I told him we'd heard the cops saying that they didn't have anything, any way of immediately identifying the dead.

"Too bad," he muttered.

"Yeah," I said.

After surveying the scene one more time, he cleared us with the responding officers to go home as soon as we'd given our statements. They wanted to take us in for questioning and weren't too happy about us leaving, but when he informed them in no uncertain terms that this incident involved issues of national security and wasn't simply a local law enforcement matter, they finally gave in. Maybe it was the call he put through to the Secretary of Defense and the resultant call from the SecDef to their police chief.

Yeah, that might've had something to do with their abrupt change of mind.

Finally, when Clarke left us alone, Adira shook her head, and said to me, "You know, when I was with Janice earlier, she mentioned that it was Sienna's idea to sell me as a sex slave."

Sienna hadn't admitted that outright to me, but it fit.

I didn't know what to say.

Adira went on. "Your wife is one heartless . . . the word I'm thinking of rhymes with *witch* and doesn't *just* refer to a female dog."

"She's not at all the woman I thought she was," I admitted.

"I have a few other adjectives to describe her too," Adira added. "In case you're curious."

"I'll bet you do."

"When the dust settles on all this, you need to get a divorce."

Maryland State Police set up roadblocks sealing off a ten-block radius, local law enforcement scoured Curtis Bay and the surrounding neighborhoods, and the Coast Guard searched the water, but there was no sign of Sienna or Turo or the unknown shooter. Or the prototype.

The cruiser with Janice in it had left nearly forty-five minutes ago. Now, Adira and I were about to call for a rideshare driver to take us back to DC. However, before we could, one of the officers—the woman who'd radioed her commanding officer to ask about Gunnar—heard what'd happened to Adira and offered to give us a ride, which we readily agreed to.

The two of us climbed into the back of her car and, as we were leaving, she said, "Seriously, who *are* you people?"

It was the same question Cliff Richardson had asked me earlier at the prison. I gave her the same reply I'd given to him. "We're the good guys." At this point, it seemed like that conversation with Richardson had happened a week ago instead of just earlier in the evening.

Adira had been right last night when we were at the swing set near her apartment: there certainly are moments that seem to last forever, and others that pass by in the blink of an eye.

Time travels forward, I thought, *our memories travel backward, and never at the speed or in the way we expect.*

As we drove, I took Adira's hand, and we were silent as the city lights flashed past us in the night.

"Where do you want me to drop you off?" the officer asked us.

"Stay with me tonight," Adira said to me softly. "I just want you to be near me."

"Yeah," I said. "Okay."

"Head to Pentagon City," Adira told her, then gave her the address.

And then, we rode in silence, hand in hand.

—◊◊—

FORTY MINUTES EARLIER

"Are you okay?" the man who was driving the police cruiser asked the cuffed woman who was now seated behind him.

"I am," Janice Daniels replied.

"I have what you were looking for. It's up here with me."

"How did you get it? The last I saw, Turo had it."

"Ah, so that's his name. He was a bit reluctant to give it up, but I convinced him."

"Is he dead?"

"No. He'll recover."

"You felt the need to take it from him."

"I didn't know how loyal he was to you."

A pause. "And the officer whose car this is?"

"He's alive too. He's in the trunk. Wasn't too happy when I took his clothes, but when I gave him the option of removing them himself or me removing them from his corpse, he made the more prudent choice."

Janice nodded. "Good. You turned out to be quite the asset. I'll make all of this worth your time."

"Yes."

"Thank you, Søren."

"You're welcome, Jan."

—⚉—

NOW

At Adira's apartment, we spent a few minutes dictating our preliminary reports of what'd happened there at Curtis Bay, but we were both exhausted and wrapped it up as quickly as we could.

I grabbed a blanket to crash on the couch, but Adira joined me. "Just hold me," she said.

So I did.

She nestled up beside me, I put my arm around her, and it wasn't long before her soft, rhythmic breathing told me that she was asleep.

Sleep, however, eluded me. Everything that'd happened was on my mind—from the encounter with Sienna to the fact that I'd allowed a domestic terrorist group to get possession of one of the most valuable devices our military had ever developed.

Protecting our nation's secrets was supposed to be my specialty, and now I'd managed to clear the way for those secrets to be shared indiscriminately, with the whole world.

—m—

Maia took a long, deep breath and walked to the front entrance of the FBI's headquarters in Washington, DC.

Despite what it would mean for her, despite her misgivings and fears, despite the fact that her research might never reach the marketplace, she felt like—for the first time in years—she was doing what was right and not rationalizing her choices by claiming that the ends would one day justify the means. Instead, she was looking at what was directly in front of her. What was right. Right now.

And always.

Yes, it was the middle of the night, but after hearing in the news about the explosions and gunfight attributed to Janice's group in Maryland, she'd made her decision, and she was afraid that if she waited until morning she might lose her nerve.

Of course, the headquarters' doors were locked. No surprise there.

An austere FBI Police officer sat stationed at the front desk just beyond the glass, and when she tapped the intercom and asked to come in, he replied into his mic with an irritated edge to his voice, "It's past office hours, ma'am, in case you hadn't noticed."

"Yes," she said. "But I think your supervisors are going to want to hear what I have to say."

```
JAWIUFIJAWEUFIJAWAEL
POWEIRPOUHTPDPTDPDSIT
POFIIJ
WPOEI
JERPFJ
EOPFI
OIIAJWE
VILKMERO
AOMWIGFP
VVINAVPO
FPIGUHER
EVGIGANNE
OANRVIOOAN
IVPOAEWIJVGG
ERVIAKJERVPO
OIREJBIO
AIJER
JF

EP
JAWI
POWEIRPOW
POFIIJASIOOJ
WPOEIFJAPWOIL
JERPFJR3POIAPL
EOPFIJAWEPEOOI
OIIAJWEPEOFIJ
VILKMEROFIFIU
AOMWIGFPOOAWGF
VVINAVPOAWEEHFA
FPIGUHERF
BOOKBIPO
OIOAUERHF
HCIOAJVPOJI
UNFDIIOJOIJAB
AIUUHVHNAOIUS
UHERVUNEVIOZI
WJVPOOEARJHVV
VPOOEARJHWI
EPORII
JAWIOFIJAWI
POWEIRPOWIUR
POFIIJASIOOJ
WPOEIFJAPWOIL
JERPFJR3POIAPL
EOPFIJAWEPEOOI
OIIAJWEPEOFI
VILKMERO
AOMWIGFI
VVINAVPOAWEEHFA
FPIGUHERFIFNSI
BOOKBIPOKBIAPOI
OIOAUERHRFL
HCIOAJVPOJJHSI
UNFDIIOJOIIARIL
AIUUHVHNAOIUSH
UHERVUNEVIOZIII
WJVPOOEAR
ERVIAKJERVPOAIJI
OIREJBIOIJVPOI
AIJERGBOOAIJEI
JERVBIOAWIEJGII
VPOOEARJHVVOAI
EPORIIHQWPOIFFL
JAWIOFIJAWIOFIJAWAEI
POWEIRPOUHTPDPDSI
POFII
WPOE
JER
EOPI
OIIA
EOPFIJAWEPEOOIUPP
OIIAJWEPEOFIJAWI
```

PART V

Follow Me Down

Two secrets deep.
The tents where the children cry.
A foot wedged in the doorway.
The worms crawl out.

CHAPTER 68

5 HOURS LEFT

I made Adira breakfast.

Nothing special, just some over-easy eggs and two slices of toast with jam. I found some orange juice in the fridge and whipped it slightly in her blender to make it frothy, the way she liked it, then brought it all to her in the living room on a tray.

"Thank you," she said sleepily, stirring on the couch.

I handed her a bottle of Tabasco sauce. "Ta-da."

"You thought of everything, my dear."

"Tried to."

"What about you?"

"Already ate. Cereal."

"Tooty Fruity Curlydoos?"

"You know me all too well. Thankfully, you had some on hand."

"You never know when there's gonna be a zombie apocalypse and you're going to need some staples to make it through, and there's nothing more staply than Curlydoos. Gotta be prepared." She sat up, rubbed the sleep out of her eyes, then dolloped a generous glob of supplemental jam onto her toast. "Any news on Gunnar? You still have his phone, right?"

"Yes. I contacted the hospital. He's stable, but unconscious. They're monitoring him closely. They still haven't been able to figure out what he was injected with."

She was quiet for a moment. "Okay."

"No word from any hospitals in the area about someone fitting Sienna's description coming in with a gunshot wound. So, maybe I missed her after all."

"Or she dug the bullet out with a needle-nose pliers, then cauterized the wound with a blowtorch and sewed herself up with fishing line in some seedy part of town, like they do in the movies."

"A blowtorch?"

"I'm just saying. Oh, by the way, I don't think I ever told you last night—thanks for coming to my rescue. Even though I had everything in hand."

"You did, huh?"

"I was about to take them all out when you showed up. But your heart was in the right place. It was very action hero-ish of you."

"I had to. I made you a pinky promise, remember? Out by your time machine."

"Ah. Yes."

I indicated her laptop on the table. "I used your computer to log in to my account—I hope you don't mind."

"No worries." She took a juicy, jammy bite of toast. "What'd you learn?"

"Nothing about Turo or the device, but I did find out something regarding Janice Daniels: she never showed up at the police station last night."

She paused in midbite. "What?"

"The man we saw her leave with wasn't a Baltimore Police officer after all. His identity is still unknown. They found the cruiser in a vacant parking lot in South Baltimore. The officer that the car was assigned to was in the trunk—the imposter had taken his uniform. He's alright, but obviously his body cam is gone too, so there's no video of what happened. Do you remember the guy's face?"

"Only vaguely," she admitted. "It was dark. I was honestly pretty distracted. You?"

"Good enough to pick him out of a lineup."

She sipped at her orange juice. "You think he was the shooter? The one who killed that guy holding the tactical rifle and then shot the burning man? Maybe even the one who offed Ivan?"

"Maybe. Two more things. I checked up on Esmé, from the museum. She's doing okay, thanks to you and that tourniquet you MacGyvered for her. So that's a bit of welcome news."

"I'm super glad to hear that. And number two?"

"There was apparently someone filming you when you helped her."

"Oh, no."

"Oh, yes."

"That teenage kid," she muttered.

"You've gone viral." I retrieved her laptop. "Kind of like last month when you helped that little boy in the parking garage in Tennessee. The Internet loves you."

"Do I even want to see this?"

"Probably not." I pulled up the video that was making the rounds. "It's aptly titled: 'Hot Blonde Saves Lady With Purse Tourniquet.'"

Adira sighed and rubbed her head as she watched the footage.

Trying to keep the mood light, I said, "I can't argue with the 'hot blonde' part."

"That's kind of you to say."

When the video was over, she groaned. "I seriously wish he hadn't posted that. Visibility makes it all that much tougher for me to do my job."

"You can always take on one of your identities."

"Temporarily, I suppose. Long-term, not gonna happen."

She took the hot sauce to task on her eggs, then tore into them like she hadn't eaten in a week.

"As far as last night," I said, "at least Popovic is out of the picture."

"I'm not going to lie," she muttered. "I'm glad about that. I don't think there are going to be too many people mourning his death."

"You're probably right." Then I bridged to the other topic I'd wanted to bring up. "Remember when Clarke told us the story about killing frogs when he was a boy?"

"Spearing them." She nodded. "Yes."

"I think both of you made good points—we, as a species, are capable of astonishing acts of kindness and sacrifice, and also capable of carrying out unspeakable horrors against each other."

"Case in point: Popovic."

"Yes," I said. "We have torturous desires and we have holy ambitions. Both. We are as much drawn to the light as we are lured by the darkness. Both. Always both."

She studied my face. "You've been thinking about this a lot."

I shrugged. "I've just been wondering about the enigma: humans are the only animals we know of who feel regret, because we're the only ones who go against our better natures and act in ways that we know we *should* regret."

"We know what's right," she said thoughtfully, "but we don't always do it—don't even always *want* to do it. And sometimes we *do* want to do the right thing, but still do the opposite thing anyway, despite ourselves."

"Yes. There you go."

She finished off her orange juice and attacked the rest of her hot sauce–saturated eggs.

"War," I said. "Do you think it's a necessary evil?"

"Wow. That's a big question. And a pretty big non sequitur." She swallowed some of her eggs as she considered her answer. "I don't think I'd say war is a *necessary* evil, but I think that, given human nature, it's an inevitable one. I think we need to always be prepared for war and also—always—strive, at all costs, to avoid it. Both, somehow, at the same time."

"'*Si vis pacem, para bellum,*'" I mumbled, quoting the Latin axiom.

She looked at me quizzically.

"Oh, sorry," I said. "From Vegetius's writings back in the fourth century. It means, 'If you want peace, prepare for war.'"

"Do you agree with that? Does preparing for war simply acknowledge that the world is the way it is, or does it make it the way we don't want it to be?"

"I guess I'd say that preparing for war is a way of being honest about human nature," I told her, "and pursuing peace is a way of striving to overcome it."

"But this isn't really about war, is it?" she observed. "Or even Popovic or human nature? All of these questions? What's going on? What's on your mind?"

I was quiet for a moment. "I'm trying to understand why my mom would forgive my dad after what he did to her."

"Torturous desires. Holy ambitions. Regret. All that."

"Yes."

She forked her eggs around her plate for a moment. "I don't suppose I ever told you this, but I once found a French proverb in a fortune cookie at a Thai restaurant. It said, 'To understand is to forgive.'"

I considered that. "Interesting. So, the importance of empathy."

"That's the idea, but I'm not one to base my philosophy of life on a French proverb in a made-in-America Chinese fortune cookie from a Thai restaurant." She eyed me. "Know what I mean?"

"You don't believe that to understand is to forgive?"

"You can understand all you want, but you still need to hold the person accountable for what they did. To forgive is something entirely different than to understand."

"I can't just pretend that what happened didn't happen, that he isn't the kind of person he is."

"See, and I don't think forgiveness is about pretending. I think it's the opposite, actually. It's about brutal honesty. But also love."

"How's that?"

"If you seek *revenge*," she said, "you're being honest about the action but not loving toward the person. On the other hand, if you just *excuse* their behavior, you might be showing them love, but you're not being honest about the pain they caused—and that's just as bad. Denial has no place in forgiveness."

Huh. Colonel Clarke had noted that to me as well yesterday afternoon on the drive to the prison.

"I don't know," I said to Adira. "Maybe I like the fact that I have something I can hold against my dad. Maybe I don't want to give that up."

"Fair enough. That's your choice. Just don't forget that holding onto resentment only harms you; it doesn't punish the other guy. Unforgiveness is a cage you build around yourself. What about Sienna, though?"

"What about her?"

"I mean, she did way worse to you than your dad ever did. She hired a guy to burn you alive."

"True," I acknowledged. Adira's observation about unforgiveness being a cage you build around yourself wouldn't leave me alone.

"So," she asked, "do you forgive your wife?"

"I don't even know what that would look like. What it would mean."

Adira ate for a moment while I considered all that we'd been talking about: the paradox of human nature, the dichotomy of our desires, forgiving those who don't deserve it. Peace. War. Love. Honesty. Excuses. Cages. Any way you cut it, it was a lot to process. Finally, I said, "I think it's maybe *heartache*."

"Heartache?"

"Your riddle. The word that starts with what we desire most and ends with what we want to avoid becoming." I thought more about it. "But, no, that's not quite it, is it?"

"Not quite. You're on the right track, though."

"*Pain free*—no, wait. That's like the exact *opposite* of the answer."

"Plus, it's two words. Keep thinking about it. You'll get it."

I grabbed some coffee, and as she was using the remaining scraps of toast to mop up the rest of her eggs, a notification came up simultaneously on her laptop and on Gunnar's phone: Colonel Clarke requesting a video call.

Here we go, I thought. *Time to face the music for losing the prototype.*

On the laptop, I mouse-hovered over the Accept icon for a long moment before finally clicking it.

After a hasty confirmation that we were both doing alright this morning, the colonel said, "I got a call from the Bureau. There's a woman who showed up last night at FBI headquarters. A whistleblower—apparently. She claims to know Janice Daniels and what she has planned. She might even have information about where Janice is or might go. She knew your name, Travis. She asked for you. She's at a safehouse up in Chevy Chase. Her name is Dr. Maia Odongo. I want you two there to talk to her."

"I've never heard of her before," I said, bewildered. "Why would she ask for me?"

"I was hoping you might be able to answer that."

"No clue." Something else was on my mind and I felt like I needed to bring it up. "What about the device, sir? The fact that I lost it?"

"There'll be plenty of time to be pissed at you later about that, once we have it back in hand. In the meantime, let's find it and return it to Quantico. We've got every three-letter agency in the government on high alert in case Janice's people try to use it against them. How soon can you be downstairs?"

"Downstairs? I mean, we don't have a car here, but—"

"I sent one. It's at the curb. And the driver has new phones for both of you."

"Gotcha," I said.

"And Travis?"

"Yeah."

"Try not to blow this one up."

—∞—

Janice Daniels studied the printed map of DC laid out before her on the hotel room desk. The Project Symphony prototype sat beside it.

Søren was with her. She hadn't seen Turo since last night. And Sienna? She wasn't even sure if she was alive or dead—which, truthfully, bothered her a bit. She didn't really want her to show up out of the blue and ruin this morning's plans.

Or take revenge on her for Ivan's death.

No, there was no love lost between the two of them. A couple of weeks ago, in fact, she'd leaked Sienna's special little password to TalynTek's IT supervisor. She'd hoped that it would be enough of a bread crumb to alert Adira and her team that Sienna was still alive so they could maybe get her out of the way.

That'd occurred alright, but not in the way she'd anticipated.

In any case, what'd transpired had transpired. It was time to move on.

Now, this morning, three main things were on Janice's mind.

First, what had happened to Maia? According to Søren, she'd left the hotel last night and still hadn't come back. Also, she wasn't returning her messages, which Janice found disconcerting.

Second, where was Turo? He hadn't shown up at their prearranged meeting place.

And third, would April Lane really get them close enough to the FDA's headquarters to exfiltrate the files with the Project Symphony device?

When Victor Dotson, the CFO at Valestra, had been taken to the hospital yesterday, her strategy for getting the files directly from him had been thwarted. She still wasn't sure if his hospitalization was random or someone's fault. The timing made her suspicious.

In either case, that'd been plan A. The prototype was plan B. Her contingency.

And here was what she wanted to do: obtain the files for Nectyla so they could be combined with Dr. Odongo's research. She would then post the compositions to the drugs, patent-free, online, for anyone in the world to access, to benefit everyone, regardless of their income level or ability to pay.

It would mean millions of people could live better lives. Also, it would save billions, maybe even trillions of dollars on healthcare worldwide over the next twenty years alone. That money could then be better spent on universal health provisions or on supplying food and pure water to isolated villages in developing countries.

Using that money, governments could also invest in novel solutions for protecting the environment, fight the devastating effects of global climate change, and find cures for diseases that ravage the health of so many of the poor, so many of the disadvantaged and the disillusioned. Together, we could take substantive strides toward a better, greener, more equitable future for our planet, for us all.

No, the research in Uganda had not been legal and that would taint it in the eyes of the scientific community, but when has what's legal been synonymous with what's right? What's legal in one time and place isn't necessarily legal in another, but what's *right* is always right, now and forever and wherever you go. Morality extends beyond borders and beyond the age in which we live, and compassion should never be curtailed by legislation that only prolongs the suffering of the poor and pads the pockets of the rich.

A physician would never wait until a patient is dead before administering a vaccine to them. This new drug regimen would be the vaccine for battling poverty, suffering, inequality.

The time to wait was over. The time to act had come.

The Nectyla files had been transferred to the FDA for possible approval, so she was going to use the prototype to obtain the data directly from their servers.

"What else do you need from me this morning?" Søren asked her.

"Can you drive me to April Lane? I think that'll be close enough to the FDA's White Oak campus up there in Silver Spring." Janice tapped the spot on the map in front of her. "I need you to get me into an apartment here, just off Lockwood Drive."

CHAPTER 69

Our driver didn't have much information about the woman we were on our way to interview, but I read the files Colonel Clarke had sent along, then handed the laptop to Adira as I considered how best to approach this.

The potential whistleblower, Dr. Maia Odongo, was a Ugandan neuroscientist who worked with the same nonprofit organization that Cliff Richardson had stumbled across last night on the dark web and Adira had identified earlier: the Davita Group. According to what we knew, they did medical research and provided humanitarian aid to refugees in war-torn countries. For five years, Dr. Odongo had led a team that oversaw medical care to children—vaccines mostly—but was also battling malaria outbreaks at the Bidi Bidi Refugee Settlement in Uganda.

But all of it seemed a bit off. Could this be related to the supply chain information we'd bid on during the dark web auction? If the Davita Group did medical work with vaccines, could it possibly have something to do with that pharmaceutical firm, Valestra Pharmaceuticals—maybe vaccines that they produced? If Dr. Odongo was a neuroscientist, why was she administering vaccines to children? Maybe to check the neurological effects? Finally, if she worked with Janice, would she perhaps know Sienna and her whereabouts?

Taking all of that into consideration, since Janice was free at the moment, it made sense why Dr. Odongo was afraid and had gone to FBI.

I was just glad she was at a safehouse.

The driver notified us that Clarke had instructed him to leave us the car since ours were both out of commission at the moment—Adira's was still in the parking garage and mine was at the Pentagon, but the keys for both of them had been lost in the mayhem last night.

"Perf," Adira told him. "That'll work."

He parked in front of a nondescript split-level home that lay about fifty feet back from the road, gave us each a phone, then left on foot for the Metro to head back to the Pentagon.

I looked around the high-end residential neighborhood. Nothing suspicious or unusual about it.

"According to what Clarke sent," Adira said, "Dr. Odongo was clear that she doesn't want us to record anything when we interview her—not yet at least. I think you should go in alone to start with. She asked for you, anyway, and plus you won't need a notebook. You'll be able to remember what she says, right?"

"Depending on how long we talk, yes, but I'm not a machine, Adira."

"I know, I know. I'm just trying to figure out the best route forward here."

"I think I'll be good."

She studied the houses lining the street.

"What is it?" I asked.

"Nothing . . . I don't know. A gut feeling? It's just a nice, quiet neighborhood, but . . . I'm wondering if it's maybe *too* quiet. I'll tell you what, I'm going to have a look around. I'll join you in a minute."

While Adira went to spy out the neighborhood, I approached the front door, unpocketed my creds, and gave the door two quick, firm raps.

A beefy man with a buzz cut cracked the door open, studied my ID, and then gestured for me to come in. Once I was inside, he promptly locked the door behind me.

"My associate will be here shortly," I informed him.

He said nothing, just nodded toward a doorway just beyond the living room, where a frizzy-haired fortysomething woman stood watching us with hawkish intensity.

From what I knew, Dr. Odongo was Ugandan, and this woman was white. "Dr. Odongo?" I asked.

"No. I'm Emily Benton. Agent Benton," she said. "Follow me. The doctor's in here."

We found Dr. Odongo in the next room, sitting at a table cluttered with smudged paper plates and crumpled napkins that were strewn beside a half-finished pepperoni pizza still languishing in its grease-stained delivery box.

Cold pizza.

The breakfast of champions.

And, based on when Dr. Odongo had gotten here—close to two in the morning—that would've been one late delivery. Or a very early one, depending on how you looked at it.

The shades had been drawn across all the windows, no doubt for security purposes.

"Dr. Odongo," I said, "I'm Travis Brock. I work at the Pentagon."

"This needs to be in private. And call me Maia."

When Agent Benton hovered, I assured her we would be fine. I said to Maia good-naturedly, "You're not going to attack me, are you?"

"Certainly not."

"Well," the agent said to her at last, "let me grab your tea for you. It should just about be ready by now. I'll bring it in, then leave you two to talk."

"Thank you," Maia said.

Benton still seemed uncertain, but finally left us alone.

"I understand you might have some information for us?" I said to Maia. "Something regarding Janice Daniels? Perhaps her location or what she's planning?"

"Janice's son mentioned you, Mr. Brock—well, her foster son."

"Joshua."

"Yes. He visited us when I was working at the Bidi Bidi Refugee Settlement. That's why I asked for you."

The questions kept coming: *Why would he mention me? Why would that even come up?*

Regardless, he had, and now that actually might help us.

I wasn't sure if I should bring it up, but Maia needed to know what kind of person Joshua was. "A woman hired him to burn down my house while I was in it. An innocent person died."

She gasped. "I had no idea. Your scars?"

"Yes." I nodded. "That's how I got them."

Agent Benton returned with a cup of steeping tea balanced on a delicate saucer and offered it to Maia.

"Thank you."

Benton turned to me. "I should have asked, would you like some too?"

"Oh, I'm a coffee guy, not tea. But thanks."

She lingered for a moment, then, at last, trooped off.

Once we were alone again and the door was closed, I asked Maia, "Did Janice ever mention something called Project Symphony?"

"I don't think so."

"What about a woman named Sienna Brock? She's . . . a relative of mine. Did you ever meet her or hear that name?"

A head shake. "No." Then she said, "To give context to what I'm going to tell you, let me start by asking: what do you know about Alzheimer's?"

"I'm no expert, but . . . memory loss, cognitive decline, confusion. From what I've read, a buildup of plaques or proteins in the brain is often present in those who suffer from it."

"Beta-amyloids. Yes. And also, neurofibrillary tangles."

Valestra Pharmaceuticals came to mind again. I waited to see if she would mention it.

She dipped the tea bag up and down a couple of times, then removed it and laid it on one of the paper plates. "Are you aware of how long it takes to get a drug to market?"

"No, but it's quite a process, from what I understand."

"It is. Getting a drug approved is incredibly rare. In fact, only one out of every ten thousand or so compounds studied with the intention of developing a new drug actually makes it through FDA approval—from lead generation to target identification to validation to preclinical trials, and then clinical trials and—hopefully—final approval . . . The process might take as long as fifteen years. And all that time, people are suffering who might be helped; people are dying who might be saved."

Her intense tone made it clear how deeply this affected her. She sipped some tea, then continued. "Imagine a world where there is no dementia and where everyone's IQ is twelve to fifteen points higher. All from an attention-enhancing drug that allows people to focus better, think more clearly, reason more keenly."

"Some sort of nootropic?" From my redactions, I knew that nootropics had been used for years with fighter pilots and soldiers who needed to stay awake and alert for extended periods of time.

"Something far beyond that," Maia said. "Something that can help the general population, and also forestall dementia and actually reverse the effects of Alzheimer's."

"That sounds extraordinary."

"It is." She looked around the room nervously.

"You're safe here," I assured her. "Tell me what you're thinking. What's going on?"

She was quiet for a long time. "Nectyla. The files for the composition of it. That's what we need. To combine it with what I've been researching for the last five years. Increasing the FGF17 found in cerebrospinal fluid . . ."

"All of this is about a drug?"

She had a little more tea. "Once it's complete, it'll be a drug everyone will want, but only the rich can afford. A drug like that could be worth hundreds of billions of dollars to the company that manufactures it."

"So, money, then?"

She shook her head. "No . . . that's . . . We need them both—my research and theirs." Her words became soft and precious: "I should never have gone back. Never have agreed . . ."

When her voice trailed off and her gaze went unfocused, I looked at her questioningly. "Are you alright?"

"I'm just feeling a little queasy all of a sudden." As she set down the teacup, her hand trembled and the cup toppled to the floor, where it shattered, sending steaming tea splattering across the floorboards.

"Maia?"

"I'm sorry. I . . ." She closed her eyes and swallowed hard.

Fearing the worst, I ran to get help, calling for the two agents stationed here, but there was no reply. "Hello?"

A quick look around.

The house was empty.

Oh, no, no, no.

Unpocketing my cell, I rushed back to Maia's side and called Adira. Maia really did not look well. "Get in here, now," I told Adira. "I need you. Something's wrong."

Maia blinked and swayed slightly to the side. "I think I need to lie down."

I was helping her out of the chair when she collapsed and I barely managed to catch her and lower her to the floor. Her breathing was becoming more labored.

"Maia, relax."

She quivered and fumbled to unhook a brooch from her blouse. "It's in the pictures." Her voice was fading.

"What is? What pictures?"

"The children . . . On April . . . Lay . . . No. Janice . . . she'll—"

As I was cradling her head with one hand, Maia began to convulse. The brooch fell out of her hand and scudded across the floor beside her.

Then her eyes rolled back, and a thick, viscid foam burbled from her mouth, and before she could say anything more, she stopped seizing, and her body went limp in my arms.

—⟡—

The last thing Dr. Maia Odongo saw was a sky full of luminous stars shimmering in the vast and distant heavens, shining through the infinite darkness where they'd been glistening for countless millennia, ever since the dawn of time.

You were named after a star, she thought. *Just like your sister. Your dad did that. As a gift. Because he loved you.*

And as she lay there dying, the last thing Maia did was ask God for forgiveness for what she'd done to the children there, in Uganda. There, in the land where she'd been born. The land so close to her heart.

And then, Star Girl breathed her last breath.

And her regrets were swept away.

At last and forevermore.

—⟡—

I called 911, then started chest compressions, but I was pretty sure it was too late.

I heard the front door bang open and when I shouted for help, it was Adira who showed up, not the team that'd been here when I arrived.

"Find the agents who were here." I kept up the compressions. "Don't let them get away!"

It took her only a fraction of a second to process everything and bolt outside again.

I was still doing chest compressions on Maia ten minutes later when the paramedics arrived, but my worst fears were confirmed when they slowly rolled her out of the house with a somber white sheet pulled up over her head like a cerement.

I called Clarke and told him what'd happened. "Who were those two agents?" I was devastated, infuriated. "By all indications, they were responsible for this. How could the Bureau let this happen?"

"I'll find out."

"Gunnar was drugged with something last night too. We need to get someone over there to the hospital to keep watch. Someone you trust."

"On it. Did you get anything actionable from Dr. Odongo?"

"I'm still trying to piece it all together. She spoke about treating Alzheimer's, raising IQs, and FDA approval. She mentioned her regrets and a drug—Nectyla. And children. Something with children. That's about as far as she got. I'll follow up on what I can."

"Okay. Keep me informed on what you find out."

"Yes, sir."

As soon as he was off the line, I phoned Gunnar's hospital room, expecting to reach a message mailbox. Instead, he answered, his voice weary. "Bane here."

I gave him the rundown of what'd happened, where we were at, and the news about Maia's death.

After processing that for a moment, he asked solemnly, "How are you doing? You okay?"

"I should be asking you the same thing."

"I'm fine. I didn't just have a woman die in my arms."

I was quiet.

"Grieve for her later," he said. "Right now, focus. Figure out what she was trying to tell you."

"I will."

"And from last night—Turo's still missing?"

"As far as I know, yes," I said. "Also, Janice and the man who impersonated the cop—and maybe Sienna. If she's alive."

"And the prototype?"

"Still gone."

"We have our hands full."

"Yes, we do."

"Listen," he said, "I want you to make it known that I'm here, at the hospital. Let it leak to the press."

"Why?"

"Yesterday when I spoke with Turo Pärnänen in prison, he vowed to kill me the next time he saw me. I want to give him the opportunity."

"Bait," I said.

"Yeah. It's time to go fishing."

After the call, I texted Clarke to send out a press release as Gunnar had requested, briefly delineating the reason why.

Then, as I waited for Adira to return to the house, I thought of what Leon, the vault man, had said to me on Thursday in the cemetery, and I prayed that, if Maia was shedding any tears in the afterlife, they were being wiped away, even now, by a loving hand.

Adira returned, shaking her head. "I looked all over. The only thing I noticed was that a blue van down the block was missing. I didn't write down all the license plates earlier. I should have."

"You had no reason to," I said. "We'll find them."

She said nothing, but I sensed that she was berating herself, as if this had all been her fault.

"DNA." I pointed to the used napkin by the pizza box. "Let's get the crime scene techs on it."

"Good call."

While she was speaking with the responding officers about possible DNA evidence, I heard from Clarke—apparently the two "agents" who'd been here when I arrived had relieved the previous team just five minutes earlier. "They verified their creds. It all checked out. Looked authentic."

"But it wasn't."

"No," he said grimly. "Any idea who they were?"

"I'm guessing they're working for Janice, taking care of loose ends. The woman said her name was Emily Benton."

"I'll look into it." He closed up by telling me the press release was out there. "If Turo is watching the news," he said, "he's going to find out where Gunnar is."

Once I was off the phone with the colonel and Adira was back in the room, I took one last look around and noticed Maia's brooch on the floor near the table.

I picked it up.

"What do you have?" Adira asked.

"Maia's brooch." I showed it to her. "She was holding it when she died. I got the sense that she was trying to tell me something." I studied it. It looked like a standard decorative brooch, nothing special about it.

"Let me see it," Adira said.

I handed it over and she scrutinized it. "This isn't just a brooch."

"What do you mean?"

"You gotta know that for women, jewelry and little hidden compartments go hand in hand. Check this out." She carefully readjusted it with her fingertips, and sure enough, the top swiveled to the side, revealing a small, discreet chamber.

Just the right size for the SIM card it contained.

I told Adira, "Right before Maia died, she said, 'It's in the pictures.'"

"What was she referring to?"

"I don't know, but she was clinging to that brooch when she said it. We need to find out what's on that card."

Adira took out the phone our driver had given her earlier. I anticipated that she was planning to insert the SIM. "Hang on," I said.

"You don't trust these phones?"

"I don't know if I trust that driver. I don't know who to trust."

"Alright." She thought for a moment. "We need a secure way to see what's on this SIM."

"Back at the Pentagon?"

"NSA's closer," she said. "You good with that?"

"Let's go."

If I was right, whatever was on this card was important enough for Maia to risk her life for, and threatening enough to someone else to kill for.

It was time to find out exactly what that was.

—ɷ—

Gunnar phoned the prison to arrange for a chat with Sidewinder. It took some doing, but finally the warden agreed to allow Asher to call him back in half an hour.

Asher. So that was his name.

Gunnar thought that the tattooed, one-eyed inmate seemed like the sort of man who had connections both on the inside and on the outside of the prison walls.

Yeah. When you're fishing, you don't just need bait.

You need a hook.

CHAPTER 70

9:37 A.M.

3 HOURS LEFT

Adira took the wheel as we drove toward NSA's campus, and I spent the trip searching online for the drug Maia had mentioned—Nectyla.

I tried every variation of the spelling I could think of but came up empty.

Huh.

"What do you make of that?" I asked Adira.

"You told me that Maia said something about the FDA approval process; maybe it's a drug that's in development and isn't on the market yet."

"That would explain it."

She exited toward the Fort Meade entrance, there on Canine Road, and pulled in line at the security checkpoint. "Those two agents in the house," she said to me. "What did they look like?"

"The guy was about my height, but stockier. He had a buzz cut. The woman looked to be about five six or so and had sort of wild, frizzy hair and a very penetrating gaze. Both white."

"Hmm."

"What are you thinking?"

"It's just that, the other night in Wisconsin, remember when I saw that couple down by the lake?"

"Oh, you're kidding me," I said.

"I don't know. I mean, obviously, I couldn't say for sure since I never saw the two people at the house, but the way you describe them—Mr. Buzzcut and Ms. Frizzyhead—it certainly sounds like it could be the same couple."

"So, with TalynTek, the Davita Group, Valestra—it's all tied together." I wasn't exactly sure how, but if these were the same two people, it certainly seemed like that was the case.

But who was directing them?

Was it really Janice, or was someone else pulling their strings?

Once we'd cleared security, we made our way to the digital forensics department. I knew a specialist there and figured it would be the best place to start. She worked in OPS1, one of the Big 4 buildings on the Fort Meade campus that was open 24/7—that along with the headquarters, Ops 2A, and Ops 2B.

As we crossed through the corridor toward Najah Bouazizi's cubicle, I asked Adira, "Why would Janice's people kill Maia?"

"Maybe it wasn't her people."

"Then whose?"

"I don't know," she admitted. "But from here on out, we need to keep an open mind. They might've been working for anyone."

—ᴍᴍ—

Turo Pärnänen was angry.

Angry that he'd lost the Project Symphony device.

Angry that the man who'd attacked him last night at Curtis Bay was able to get it from him.

And angry at Gunnar Bane for managing to take out his associate when they were fighting at the oil terminal last night, despite getting injected with that drug cocktail.

Turo had been keeping tabs on the news ever since waking up at six, so when he learned that Bane had been taken to Metro Medical Center he knew right away what he needed to do.

Taking Maureen with him so that he could kill the former soldier with his own weapon, Turo left for the hospital in the car that he'd stolen late last night.

A thirty-five-minute drive.

And then, closure.

—∞—

Najah was glad to help us, but mentioned that she had a ten thirty meeting, which didn't give us much time.

I introduced her to Adira, then Najah found a secure, air-gapped computer and inserted the SIM.

Though the files were encrypted, it didn't take her long to hash the password and bring up seven photos of what appeared to be life in a refugee camp.

Crowded makeshift shelters. Deprivation. Neglect. Malnutrition. And yet, amazingly, smiles on the faces of the children. Maia had mentioned the Bidi Bidi Refugee Settlement, so I assumed that's what we were looking at. It was mostly women and children and I suspected that was probably because so many of the men would've been killed in the hostilities.

Adira and I studied the pictures carefully, looking for anyone we might recognize, but found nothing. "Run facial rec on these," Adira said to Najah. "Find out if there's anyone the DOD or Interpol might be looking for. Known associates of Janice Daniels and Ivan Popovic. Terrorist watchlists."

"Gotcha."

While Najah did the search, I had an idea.

If we needed to find out more about Alzheimer's research and memory-enhancing drugs, there was one person I knew of who might be able to help us out.

When I was a boy, a researcher named Dr. Farling had studied my fMRIs and given me countless cognitive tests. She'd been thoughtful and helpful, and now I wondered—if she was still around—if she might be able to help me better understand the enhanced nootropics Maia had told me about.

Adira saw me looking up her number and I told her what I was thinking.

"Hey, give it a shot," she said. "Can't hurt."

I found a number for a Dr. Judith Farling in Orlando and decided that, since we had a shared history together, I'd try a video call request first and see if she accepted it. Even though my new phone was encrypted, I changed a setting to allow my name to come up on her screen, hoping that seeing it would be enough to get her to pick up, even though it would still be from an unknown number.

And, as it turned out, it was.

She had to be in her mideighties now, but I recognized her right away. Not so much by the shape of her face as by the sparkle in her eyes.

"Dr. Farling?" I said. "It's Travis Brock. We met a long time ago when I was a young boy."

"Yes, yes. Travis." She smiled faintly. "I remember you. Of course. Are you still purposely answering questions on tests incorrectly so no one will notice how much you can actually remember?"

"Ah, you were on to me. Well, no. Not so much. Not lately."

She propped the phone against something on the table in front of her so she wouldn't need to hold it. "You've caught me in the middle of knitting a sweater for my great-granddaughter." She held it up to show me the colorful reindeer design. "I figured I needed to get started now if I was going to finish it in time for Christmas."

"It looks nice," I said. "I'm sorry to bother you. I won't take up much of your time. I'm working for the government these days and I have a question that I thought you might be able to help us with. It has to do with a neuroscientist . . . I wondered if your paths might've ever crossed. Her name is Dr. Maia Odongo."

I didn't mention Maia's death. The news hadn't been released to the public yet and this wasn't the time to bring it up to Dr. Farling. There was no reason to.

"Dr. Odongo . . . ," she said reflectively. "Maia Odongo . . . Yes . . . I *do* know the name, but I don't believe we've ever met."

"She worked for an NGO in Uganda called the Davita Group. She might have also been involved in studying a drug named Nectyla—but I can't seem to find anything about it online."

"If it's in the pipeline, that wouldn't be surprising. Pharmaceutical firms are quite protective of their proprietary information."

"That's what my associate was thinking as well," I said. "This might also have to do with Valestra Pharmaceuticals. I'm hoping to find out what Nectyla does and how it might help treat Alzheimer's." I had another thought and added, "And if it might be used in some way to treat children."

"Yes, yes . . . Huh. Let me do some checking. Can I call you back at this number?"

"Sure. As soon as you can, if possible."

"Of course."

End call.

—⚉—

The phone beside Gunnar's hospital bed rang. He picked up. "Bane here."

"This is Asher."

"Sidewinder."

"Yes, that's right."

Gunnar explained that he had unfinished business with Turo Pärnänen. "Do you have any way of locating him?"

"No, but if you do manage to find him, I have some unfinished business of my own with him. He vowed not to harm a guard here, then stabbed him. Nearly killed him. I respect that guard. Not Turo. Not so much."

"Well, he made a vow to me too—that he was going to kill me—and I think he meant it."

"Huh." Asher gave Gunnar a number. "That's my private line, shall we say. Where are you?"

"Metro Medical Center in DC."

"I'll send two men. Text me if he shows up. If Turo comes for you, my associates will take care of everything."

—⚉—

While Søren drove, Janice studied the apartments just off Lockwood Drive where it ran along the outer perimeter of the FDA's 130-acre campus in Silver Spring, Maryland.

Stout fencing and tight security measures precluded them from getting any closer.

Along here, the FDA property was mostly wooded, but just off Lockwood, on April Lane, there were a few openings in the forest that provided line of sight to the FDA building she would need to target, the one that housed their servers.

"Let's pull in here," she said.

Søren parked.

She pointed to the top floor of the Birch Terrace Apartments building nearest the campus that had a window facing the correct direction. There really was only one choice. "I'm going to need to get into that unit."

"What if there's someone in there?"

"I'll leave that up to you to handle as you see fit. You came through last night. I'm trusting you can take care of things this morning." She cranked open the car's door. "Let's go."

—w—

"Nothing on facial rec," Najah informed us.

Hmm.

Why were these photos so important to Maia?

"There are lots of ways to hide or encrypt text messages within digitized images," I said, thinking aloud.

"Steganography," Najah said. "Sure, of course. Let me tool around for a bit, see if I can find anything."

"Also," Adira added, "I don't know if this is possible, but see if there are any audio files embedded in there somehow as well."

"Absolutely."

Adira and I stepped away to let Najah work.

"So, this drug," Adira said, "Maia told you it would help raise people's IQ, reverse Alzheimer's?"

"Yes."

"And that only the rich could afford it?"

"That's what she said. It would involve combining her research with Valestra's work on Nectyla."

"Remind me again how that's such a bad thing? If it's true that millions of people can benefit from what Janice and her people are doing, shouldn't we be *helping* them instead of trying to stop them? I mean, are you sure we're the good guys in this scenario?"

"If sharing proprietary intel really is what they have in mind, we can't have people stealing from the rich and giving to the poor."

"Governments do it all the time," she countered.

"Really?"

"It's called collecting taxes."

"Adira, this isn't a joke."

"I'm not joking."

"Look, this isn't a Robin Hood story. This is real life. If Nectyla really can provide all those benefits, I'm sure it must've cost millions to develop— maybe more. If that money isn't recouped, it'd undermine the whole R&D process in the search for other medications."

"That sounds like something a Big Pharma rep would say."

"Adira—"

"I mean, just so I'm clear: We have to stop a group of pacifists from helping millions of suffering people worldwide live healthier, more productive and fulfilling lives?"

"I don't think it's quite that simple."

"Can't an argument be made that Janice and her people are doing something worthwhile?"

"We can't have terrorist groups doing whatever it is they have planned here while indiscriminately breaking dozens of federal and international laws, no matter how honorable their motives might appear to be at first glance."

"I know what you're going to say next."

"Really?" I said. "What's that?"

"That it would set a precedent and encourage other bad actors to try the same thing to get what they want, just like ransomware does." Her voice was tight. Steely. "I know all that already. All I'm saying is, I can see where they're coming from."

My phone rang and I glanced at the screen.

Dr. Farling's number.

"We can debate the morality of all this later," I said to Adira. "For now, let's just focus on getting the prototype back."

As soon as I answered the video call, Dr. Farling dove right in. "I might have something for you, Travis."

"I'm listening."

"As you may know, as we age, many of us experience cognitive decline. Neuroscientists aren't exactly sure *why* that occurs, but we are aware of some of the factors that accompany it."

For a moment, Dr. Farling appeared deep in thought. Then she reached down and held up the skein of yarn she was using to knit the reindeer sweater. "See this yarn? How it's all balled up nicely? No snarls or snags? That's a healthy brain. The older we get, however, the more frayed and jumbled things can become." With that, she showed me a knotted mess of yarn she must have discarded earlier.

"Neurofibrillary tangles," I said, recalling what Maia had told me.

"Very good." She nodded. "Some Alzheimer's research focuses on trying to stop those from occurring; other research looks for ways to untangle them. Maia was involved in both areas of study, presented on them, even wrote papers on them, then, very abruptly, left her research behind about five years ago."

"What about FGF17?" I said. "She referred to that as well. And cerebrospinal fluid."

"Yes, there's been some work in that area—of taking the spinal fluid from younger rats and injecting it into older ones, but there haven't been any human trials involving that process, at least not that I'm aware of."

"And Nectyla? Anything there?"

"I made a few calls. Valestra Pharmaceuticals is working on it. Very hush-hush. I'm sorry if I haven't been much help."

"Oh, on the contrary. You were very helpful. Thank you."

We said our goodbyes and, as I ended the call, I saw Najah smiling. "Tell me you have something," I said.

"I have something." She tapped her space bar, and a flood of words scrolled across the screen.

"What are we looking at?"

"Luganda. It's the *lingua franca* of Uganda. This text appears to be mostly scientific findings, so it might take a bit of work to get an accurate translation, but we have people who can do it. It'll take longer than I have, though. I need to go. I'll download it to your phones and have someone on my team start on the translation. Walk you to the door?"

I wished we had more time here, but knew we needed to respect her schedule.

After a quick check to confirm that there was no spyware on our phones and that it would be safe to send us the files, Najah escorted us down the hallway.

As she did, I tried to piece together what we'd learned so far.

Spinal fluid.

Nectyla.

Valestra.

The Davita Group . . .

Hmm . . . Maybe we were in a Robin Hood story after all.

Once Adira and I were back outside the building, I said, "I think Janice is going to use the Project Symphony prototype to steal secrets from the Valestra Pharmaceuticals database on this new drug, Nectyla, that they're trying to get approval for."

"Based on?"

"What Maia and Dr. Farling said. Also, remember when Clarke told us yesterday that the FDA was going to review a Valestra drug this week? I think Janice might be trying to get out ahead of that."

"Which explains their sudden urgency yesterday."

"Maybe. Yes."

"We should contact Valestra," she said. "Let 'em know there's a good chance they might be the target of an act of corporate espionage."

"I think their main office is in Atlanta," I told her. "I'll reach out to law enforcement there to have them search nearby for Janice and Sienna. To use Project Symphony—"

"They'll need line of sight to the server's room," Adira said, finishing my thought for me. "So they'd need to be somewhere close by."

"Exactly."

On the way to the car, she looked up Valestra's head of global security and I phoned the Atlanta Police Department.

—〰—

Providentially, there was no one at home in the top floor apartment that Janice needed, so it'd gone rather smoothly with Søren picking the lock and obtaining access to the unit.

"You're full of surprises," Janice said as he finished up.

He led her inside. "How long will it take you to get that device up and running?"

"I'm not sure," she said honestly. "Give me half an hour."

CHAPTER 71

2 HOURS LEFT

Turo paid for the flowers at the hospital's gift shop and took the elevator up to Bane's room on the sixth floor.

He half expected there to be police officers guarding the door and was prepared to deal with them if that were the case, but no one was seated in front of 6204, so he eased the door open and quietly entered the room.

Bane lay there, asleep.

Or pretending to be asleep.

Turo closed the door softly.

Firing a round through a pillow with another one wrapped around the muzzle would muffle the sound of the gunshot plenty. It would be enough.

Before moving any closer to him, Turo made sure they were alone in the room. No one in the bathroom. No one in the closet or under the bed. Then, he stood close and stared down at the former Ranger.

"You're not asleep." He kept his voice low and hushed. Hardly a whisper. "Are you?"

—∞—

Gunnar opened his eyes. "I thought you might swing by."

Earlier, he'd asked to borrow the phone of the officer that Clarke had sent to watch the door before asking him to leave.

Now, Gunnar waited with his finger poised against the screen of the phone beneath the bedsheets, ready to send the text to Asher. Once it went through, things would happen quickly—but he didn't want to be premature.

Hang on. Timing matters.

"Are those flowers for me?" he said to Turo in a friendly manner.

Turo set down the bouquet, revealing that he was holding Maureen. "Both of these things are."

"Ah, so that's where she went." Gunnar nodded toward the gun. "Now, Turo, I need to tell you something."

"Let me guess: you still have that knife you used last night to kill my associate."

Gunnar was quiet.

Turo leveled Maureen at his face. "Let's see it."

Gunnar produced the knife from where he'd hidden it beneath his leg. He laid it on the table beside the bed.

Turo moved it out of his reach. "You have anything else squirreled away under there?"

Gunnar held up the phone. "Just this."

"What are you going to do?" A slight smile. "Call 911?"

"That's not the number I had in mind."

For whatever reason, Turo let him keep the phone. Gunnar thought it was maybe arrogance.

"It was you last night at the pier," Turo said. "You shot Rollan."

"I didn't shoot anyone at the pier. There was someone else there. Did you know I'm writing a book? A romance novel."

"Is that so?"

"Yes. And when you're writing a story, you always want to find that moment when everything pivots, when the unexpected meets the inevitable."

"A twist."

"Something like that."

"What's the big twist waiting for me here, today?" Turo scrutinized the room suspiciously. "I turn myself in and you promise not to kill me?"

"Not quite. This is the point in the story where I offer you a choice."

"Really? I thought it was the place where I shoot you in the head."

Gunnar tapped the phone's screen. "They're on their way up here, now. Two minutes. That's not a long lifespan."

"Who?" Turo snatched the phone away from him. "Who's on their way up here?"

The screen showed a timer, counting down to zero.

"Asher's friends. Turns out, he's not too happy with you for stabbing that guard. I have a feeling he's going to want to watch remotely on his own little private line when his men get started on you. They say that when you sow the wind, you reap the whirlwind. Well, today your whirlwind looks like a pair of pissed-off white supremacists, and you're about to reap the worst that they have to offer."

Turo tossed the phone aside and it landed in the chair, screen up. "You're bluffing."

"Maybe. Here's what we're looking at: There's a SWAT team on this floor awaiting my signal and two of Asher's men are coming for you. You walk out that door and you're going to be making some new friends, one way or the other."

"Yeah? Then what's this choice you were going to give me?"

"It's four options, really—face SWAT, face Asher's men, or work with me."

"That's three options."

"You could always turn that gun on yourself and save us all a lot of paperwork."

Turo eyed the window.

"Six stories up?" Gunnar said. "That's a long drop with a very abrupt coda waiting at the other end. Why do you think I asked them to transfer me to the top floor?"

Turo approached the window and peered outside, studying the parking lot. "I don't see any SWAT vehicles."

"Of course not. The officers wouldn't be very good at their job if you did." Gunnar caught sight of the phone's screen. "Time is ticking. What are you going to do—become a source for us, face the ire of Asher's men, or let SWAT take you back to prison? It's your decision. I won't tell you what to do. But I *will* tell you what *I* would do."

"Oh, really?" Turo faced him squarely. "And what's that?"

"I'd avoid prison, and I'd choose to stay alive long enough to make another choice tomorrow, whatever that might turn out to be. One day at a time sounds a lot more inviting to me than no time at all, and that's what we're closing in on here pretty quickly. This is sort of a choose-your-own-ending kind of thing."

Turo said nothing.

"You're a survivor, Turo. I like that about you, so here's a way for you to survive—work for us. You can give us Janice Daniels and Sienna Brock. Locate them for us and we can provide a new identity for you."

"Witness protection?"

"But first you have to help us find them."

A knock at the door.

"Time's up, Turo."

And with that, Turo Pärnänen made his decision.

—〰—

After leaving Najah, I'd driven Adira down the road from NSA, we'd grabbed a quick sandwich, and were now parked near the restaurant's drive-through, finishing up lunch, talking about where things were at.

"I believe there's more to all of this than meets the eye," I said to her.

Adira stared at me.

"What?"

"You need a new writer, Doctor Obvious. That line—it's been around forever. It's a bit of a cliché."

"I see. What about, 'There's an ending waiting for us that you would never expect.'"

She rolled her eyes.

"'This isn't over until it's over'? Or, wait: 'I could tell you what I do for a living, but then I'd have to kill you'? Or maybe, 'I've got a bad feeling about—'"

"Oh, please stop."

"I'll have to see if Gunnar can help me with my material."

"Good luck with that."

My phone chimed. An unknown number.

I was getting used to that by now.

I picked up. "Hello?"

"It's Gunnar."

Well, speak of the devil.

"They're going after the FDA," he said urgently. "Janice is planning to exfiltrate files regarding a new drug and then post them online, patent-free."

Robin Hood.

Yes.

"How do you know this?" I asked Gunnar.

"Turo told me. He's actually being quite helpful at the moment."

"Did he give you any specifics? Say where Janice is?"

"She'll be somewhere near the White Oak campus. That's all he knows. Or at least, that's all he's saying. For now."

"And Sienna?"

"No word. He says he thinks she's dead."

—⁂—

"There," Janice said to Søren as she finished setting up the device. "I think we're good to go."

"Two days ago," he said, "you promised that you would keep the details regarding what happened on Highway 17 secret. I want you to destroy the evidence that you might have. I think it's time you make that call."

"Agreed." She took out her cell. "Give me just one moment."

—⁂—

"The FDA?" Adira gasped when I was off the phone with Gunnar and had filled her in on what he'd said. "Where do we start? That campus is huge. It's gotta be over a hundred acres."

"Turo told him that Janice will be *near* it," I specified, "not *on* it."

"Still, we need to contact them and have them shut down their servers. Even if they're air gapped, even if they're in Faraday cages, they're not safe."

"Yes," I said. "Definitely call them."

"And do we go looking for Janice?" She had her phone out.

"We do." I started the engine. "Silver Spring's not far."

While Adira was reaching out to the FDA, the translation of the embedded text on Maia's SIM came back from Najah's translator friend at NSA.

I let the car idle as I studied the phone.

The document began with specifics on refugees and casualties of the South Sudanese Civil War.

I was no expert on the conflict, but I knew a little about it from a friend of mine who had worked at the State Department during the war's peak.

His office had issued informal warnings to American citizens not to travel to South Sudan. It wasn't stated officially in their press releases, but according to Greg, they gave US citizens a thirty-six-hour life expectancy from the time their plane landed in the country.

As he had put it to me at the time, "That's not thirty-six hours from the time you get kidnapped, that's your life expectancy from the time the airplane's wheels touch down. And we will not come for you in South Sudan. Don't expect military intervention. Don't go to that country unless you've put your affairs in order, prepared your last will and testament, and realize that you will almost certainly not return."

His words had brought me pause, but based on what I knew about the turmoil in the country, I had no doubt that he was telling me the truth. Thankfully, I hadn't been planning a visit. "What about journalists and medical personnel or aid workers?" I'd asked.

"The warring factions in that country aren't very discriminating about who they slaughter or rape based on that person's job title," he'd told me.

Very violent. Very volatile.

Here in Maia's translated files were references to the FGF17 found in cerebrospinal fluid, the enzyme HDAC-2, and nested in the middle of it all was a DOD budgetary routing number that I'd seen before, about five years ago.

Huh.

It was all here: names, dates, patient records.

Taking into consideration the pictures and the text, I processed what we were looking at.

The FDA campus? What's nearby? Where would Janice go?

Maia had mentioned children to me, and then said, "On April." I'd thought at the time that she was maybe referring to a girl or to something happening on a date during that month of the year, but now I wondered if it was something else.

She'd said, "On April. Lay. No."

Or maybe, she'd really said, "On April Lane. Oh."

Oh, yeah. That fit.

She was trying to tell you where Janice will be.

From living in DC all these years, I knew that April Lane was just off Lockwood Drive, which skirted along the FDA's campus.

That's it. That's where Janice was going to be.

Pulling out of the parking lot, I took off for the network of apartment complexes that lined Lockwood Drive.

—⚬—

"It's done," Janice told Søren. "Your past will remain our little secret. The only other person who knew about it, our mutual acquaintance Rollan, is dead."

"Yes."

"Are you the one who shot him at the pier last night?"

"I am."

A slight pause. "Are you going to kill me now?"

"Not now," Søren said. And with that, he walked out the door, leaving her alone on the balcony to exfiltrate the data from the FDA server.

—⁂—

As I drove, Adira contacted local law enforcement, but they weren't nearly as convinced about Janice Daniels being nearby as we were. However, they did agree to send a car to the neighborhood "to have a look around."

As she ended the call, Adira smacked the console in front of her in frustration. "Do we know what kind of car Janice might be using?"

"No," I said. "But she'll need line of sight to the building that houses the servers. Either through or over the woods. That narrows it down. Do we know if they shut down their servers?"

"They told me they can't just power them down without the danger of corrupting or damaging open files. They're on it, but it's a process. It's gonna take time."

Which was not what I wanted to hear.

—⁂—

Janice directed the prototype at the server's building.

The operational light flashed on.

Now, it was only a matter of time and the files would be hers, and then they would be the entire world's.

—⁂—

Terry Brock knew better than to start drinking again, let alone to do so this early in the day, but he was still reeling from his rather disastrous conversation yesterday with his son, and still processing the idea that he might never see him or Isa again.

Yes, he knew that, but now, when he found himself at a pub ordering fish-and-chips for lunch, and the server asked him what he wanted to drink, and he saw all the beer on tap and all the whiskey bottles lined up so patiently and invitingly behind the bar . . . when all of those factors came together, he thought about how well a nice Irish whiskey would go with the fish-and-chips he was about to enjoy.

One drink should be alright.

One wouldn't hurt.

"Tullamore D.E.W. Original," he said to her.

"Good choice." She flicked him a smile. "I'll get that right out for ya."

CHAPTER 72

11:37 A.M.

1 HOUR LEFT

We found April Lane.

Found an apartment complex bordering the forest—Birch Terrace Apartments.

Found a unit that faced the FDA campus.

As I swung into a parking space, I saw a man walking toward a car on the other side of the lot, just beyond a grassy divide near a parked ambulance.

A man I recognized.

"That's him," I told Adira. "The guy from last night, the one who impersonated the Baltimore Police officer and then freed Janice."

He climbed into a silver sedan.

She threw her door open. "He'll know where she is."

Before I could respond, she was already tearing across the grass. I was a few steps behind her, but he was too far away and already driving off and there was no way we were going to catch him. And then, he was gone.

Adira flicked out her phone as we returned to our car. "I got the model, the make, and the plates."

Me too, I thought.

"Nice," I said.

While Adira called the police to have the patrol car that they'd assigned to the area pull him over, I studied the forest, considered the heights of the trees, the distance to the FDA's buildings, and all that we knew of Janice's plan. The woods were thick here.

"She'll need to be above the tree line . . . ," I muttered, "have line of sight . . . I don't know for sure, but if she's here, I'd say it's gotta be the top floor." I pointed. "Up there, maybe?"

A balcony door in one of the eighth-floor units appeared to be open. From here, I couldn't see inside, so I couldn't be sure, but it was a place to start.

Adira rounded the car and flipped open the glove box, but found it empty. "Do you have a weapon?" she asked me. "A gun? Knife? Anything?"

"No. You?"

"Popovic's thugs got my Springfield when they took me last night. But we need something . . . Wait. Take off your shoes."

"My shoes?"

"We need your socks. Mine are too thin. Men's socks work better." She scanned the ground and muttered, "No rocks . . . Okay. Your phone. I'll need that too."

I slipped off my shoes. "Ah." I realized what she was thinking. "A lock in a sock. A prison weapon."

"Yep—although in prison they usually use a padlock, batteries, or a pocket Bible soaked in water. But these'll do just fine." We each dropped our phone into a sock and then she twirled her improvised weapon around, testing it. "You see anyone coming at you," she said, "you swing your phone at their face as hard as you can and as many times as necessary. You'd be amazed at how quickly they'll comply."

After I had my shoes back on, we found a set of exterior steps leading up to the apartment's eighth floor.

"Alright," Adira said. "Let's do this."

—m—

Terry Brock was not quite drunk when he received the notification that there was a message waiting for him on his Krazle account.

He opened the app and let it load.

—m—

As we raced up the stairs, Adira said, "Just so you know, if your wife is here, we're going to have a little chat. I have a few things to say to her about suggesting that they sell me as a sex slave."

"I'm sure you do."

—⚏—

Terry read the Krazle message and was both floored and thrilled by what it said.

It was from Isa.

He paid for his meal, called for a rideshare driver, downed the rest of his whiskey, and left the pub for her townhouse.

—⚏—

We reached the apartment and I rapped on the door. "Janice?" I called. "Are you in there?"

A voice cried out, "Stop!" It was maybe Janice, maybe not, but whoever the woman was, she was in distress.

I tried the door. Locked.

"Kick it in," Adira said to me urgently. "You're bigger. Focus on punching your foot *through* the door, not *at* it. Connect hard with your heel right beside the doorknob. Do it."

I went for it. The first time was no good, but on my second attempt, the lock mechanism splintered apart and the door flew open.

Fifteen feet away from us, Janice was seated in a chair. Sienna stood behind her, holding a pistol to her head. "Hello, everyone," my wife said. "Come on in. Welcome to the party."

As we entered, I took in the apartment.

A hallway led off to the left; a living room lay on the right. Twenty feet beyond the women, the balcony door stood open. The prototype sat on its deck table. The FDA's wooded property stretched out beyond it. From here, I couldn't tell if the device was active at the moment, if it was downloading data or not. Maybe we were too late.

"How did you know I'd be here?" Janice asked Sienna.

"You don't think I would let you go roaming all over the city with that phone of yours without a way to track you, do you?" she said. "I swear, Janice, your propensity to underestimate people will be your downfall."

Sienna eyed our socks weighed down with those cell phones.

Honestly, I felt a little silly holding mine, considering the fact that she had a gun.

"Really?" she said incredulously. "A slock? Is that the best you can do?"

"Travis shot you last night," Adira said to her. "Were you hit?"

"Grazed."

"So you didn't have to dig out a bullet with a needle-nose pliers in a sketch part of town?"

"A needle-nose pliers?" Sienna looked at her curiously. "What?"

"It's a thing . . . in the movies . . . Never mind. Are you in pain?"

"It's manageable."

"Too bad."

"Ha," Sienna said. "Put down the socks and whatever's in them. Do it."

When we hesitated, she shot my phone and it burst apart next to my leg, startling me.

Clarke had told me not to blow this one up.

I had a feeling this was probably close enough to count.

"Go on," Sienna told Adira. "Or I'll do some more target practice on his kneecaps."

Adira bent as if she were going to comply, but instead, she swung her phone and launched it across the room toward Sienna, releasing the slock just as the cell phone reached its peak momentum, sending it flying with fierce speed straight at her face.

It wasn't a perfect sling, but it was close enough to make Sienna duck, which gave Janice a chance to leap out of the chair and run toward the prototype, but Sienna was only distracted for a moment and, as Janice scurried toward the balcony, Sienna aimed and fired.

The bullet ripped into Janice's left hip, sending her to the floor, crying out in pain.

While Sienna was distracted, Adira raced toward her to stop her and I sprinted toward Janice, who waved me on to the balcony. I was powering down the prototype when Sienna called out behind me. "I'll take that."

I faced her.

Time seemed to pause, to catch its breath.

Sienna was maybe twenty-five feet away. Janice lay between us, just inside the apartment, a slow seep of blood pooling beside her onto the floor, her eyes clenched shut in pain. Adira was momentarily out of view—Sienna must have shoved her to the side, into the hallway.

I thought of wound channels and how, just last night, Sienna had told me that she would've taken the shot at me if she'd been the one with the gun.

She's going to kill you.

Holding the prototype to the side, I made a decision.

I flung it backward, tossing it off the balcony and into the forest. I wasn't sure if it would survive the fall, but I needed to get it away from Sienna and that was the first thing that came to mind.

She cursed at me and leveled the gun at my face, but before she could fire, Adira swept in and tackled her, sending the gun skittering across the floor, out of everyone's reach.

Adira and Sienna wrestled for a moment, then, in a breath, they were both on their feet, facing off with each other.

Janice groaned weakly. I'd already watched one woman die today. I didn't want this to be death number two.

I knelt beside her. My phone was in pieces; Adira's was across the room. So, using Janice's cell, I called 911. I quickly summarized what was going on and the nature of Janice's injury. "There's already an ambulance close by, here in the apartment complex's parking lot," I said, and then gave her the address. "We need it. And police," I added. "Send lots of police."

I balled up the sock that'd held my phone and, after warning Janice that it was going to hurt, I held it firmly against the gunshot wound to quell the bleeding.

Janice cringed.

I could feel the spine of her pelvis above the wound. A couple inches higher and the bullet would've fractured her pelvis and there probably wouldn't have been anything I could have done to stop her from bleeding out internally. As it was, she might have a chance.

I heard Adira in the living room, where their fight had taken them: "You were going to cut off my hands. Gouge out my eyes."

And Sienna: "It's not too late. I'm going to knock you out, and when you wake up again, you're going to *wish* you were dead."

Janice spoke to me, her voice weak: "Do you know what we did?"

"It was the spinal fluid, wasn't it?" I said. "Maia was taking it from children and giving the FGF17 to adults, there at the refugee settlement, where no one would bother her with oversight."

She nodded.

"You paid their caregivers to give you access? Food? Money? Medical care? And then . . ." I was afraid of the answer, but I had to ask. "What happens to the children?"

"Mostly they were fine. But . . ."

"But?"

Janice was quiet at first, but finally said, "It was fatal in only two percent of the cases. Infections mostly. Paralysis was more common."

I swallowed. "And how many children were involved?"

"In five years, two thousand four hundred."

Forty-eight children. They murdered forty-eight refugee children and paralyzed even more.

I was stunned. Horrified.

I could hear scuffling from the fight in the other room but couldn't see what was happening.

Janice coughed and shuddered in pain. "But think of how much suffering we'll be able to alleviate, how many breakthroughs we'll . . ."

And then she went quiet.

"Are you with me?" I said, shaking her slightly.

A nod.

How could someone with such noble goals become so lost?

Her breathing remained steady.

"Relax," I told her. "Hang in there. Help is coming."

"Get the prototype!" Adira shouted to me. "What if that fake cop comes back? Secure it. I'll take care of Sienna."

"You good?" I asked Janice.

"Go."

I ran to the steps and then flew down them two at a time to get to the device.

—⁂—

Adira assessed her situation.

Travis's psycho wife was just two short strides away.

"Oh, you're going to take care of me?" Sienna said. "Well, here I am. Come and get me."

Adira felt adrenaline coursing through her, sharpening her focus. Fight or flight?

Fight.

Oh, yeah.

"Were you ever trained in close-quarters combat?" she asked Sienna. "I want things to be fair."

"Krav Maga." Sienna lowered herself into a ready stance. "Before I met Travis."

Adira was familiar with Krav Maga. The Israeli-developed system emphasized winning over form, real-life situations rather than competitions, and situational awareness in lieu of carefully choreographed routines.

"Krav Maga . . . Huh. Not a bad choice," Adira acknowledged.

Sienna came at her.

In a fight, when possible, you want to use your feet, your elbows, and your knees instead of just your fists. The bones in the hands break too easily. Case in point: one crooked pinky finger, but—

She blocked Sienna's side kick with her forearm and repositioned herself to be the aggressor, sending a flurry of kicks at Sienna, who expertly blocked or evaded each one.

Yeah. She was good.

But not careful.

When Sienna came in too close, Adira rewarded her impulsiveness with an elbow to the face and a knee to the stomach. The elbow caught her above her left eye and split the skin open, sending a spray of blood droplets splatting across the room.

Sienna gasped and spun to kick Adira's leg out, connecting solidly and causing Adira to lose her balance. Sienna capitalized on the moment and punched her twice, viciously, in the face, knocking her backward onto a glass end table, which collapsed and shattered beneath her weight.

Adira scrambled away from the broken glass toward her slock.

A cut just above your eye bleeds a lot. It's annoying, but it's not necessarily that serious, so, despite the amount of blood now smearing Sienna's face, Adira was watchful not to let down her guard.

Grabbing a pillow cover off the couch to protect her hand, Sienna snatched up one of the larger glass shards and vectored toward Adira.

An ambulance siren screamed to a stop outside the building.

Adira gripped the slock.

Sienna was almost to her.

Force equals mass times acceleration.

Yeah, sometimes physics is your friend.

She swung the cell phone as hard as she could at Sienna's face.

Mass.

Impact.

Plus speed.

Equals.

Pain.

Sienna's head snapped back, whipping her around and corkscrewing her backward to the floor.

—⁓—

It took me longer than I expected to locate the prototype. Once I had it, I raced to our car and locked it inside. "Eighth floor," I called to the paramedics who were exiting their ambulance. "Cops?"

"On their way," one of them replied.

Without missing a beat, I headed for the steps to help Adira.

—⁓—

With blood splotching her face and shirt, Sienna leapt to her feet and lunged at Adira, swiping the glass toward her abdomen. Adira backed up, out of the apartment, and toward the steps.

She thought she could hold onto her balance, but then in one final moment, as Sienna thrust the glass shard at her throat, she stumbled backward and felt herself teetering off the top step.

—⁓—

Adira tumbled toward me and crumpled with a thud onto the seventh-floor landing. I rushed to her side. "Are you okay?"

She was stunned, but nodded. "Yeah."

"Sienna?"

"C'mon." She shook off the fall and we ascended the steps.

But there was no sign of Sienna, either on the walkway or back inside the apartment.

While Adira went searching for her on the next level down, I knelt beside Janice and put pressure on her gunshot wound, then called the paramedics over when they reached our floor.

During the swirl of activity in the next few minutes, Adira returned with no word on Sienna, the police arrived and took over the hunt for her, and the EMTs hustled Janice to the hospital.

As I processed everything, I thought of the man we'd seen driving away earlier and felt a stir of uneasiness. Yesterday, we'd been concerned that someone might go after Maureen or my mother. What if he did? What if he was targeting her?

I still had Janice's cell. I phoned my mom.

No answer.

Texted her. Nothing.

I called dispatch and learned that the police officer who'd been sent to watch her place yesterday had been reassigned.

She was alone.

The Krazle account I'd set up to message my dad yesterday was still active and I knew that Mom checked her Krazle messages regularly, so I logged in and found an unread message that she'd sent to me about twenty minutes ago:

I haven't been able to reach your phone, so I thought I'd try this.
I'm just letting you know that I invited your father over. I know
you spoke with him yesterday, but I felt like I needed to meet with
him myself. I'll call you later and let you know how it goes. Talk
soon. I love you.

I left an urgent message on her voicemail and on Krazle: "Don't let him into your place, Mom. Wait for me. We'll sort all this out as soon as I get there."

I told Adira about her Krazle message.

"Go," she told me. "Hurry. She needs you."

We ran down to the car, I gave her the prototype so she could shepherd it to a nearby police cruiser until it could be transferred back to the Marine base, and then I tore out of the parking lot toward my mom's townhouse.

CHAPTER 73

Terry Brock climbed out of the rideshare car and shambled up the steps toward the front door of Isa's townhouse.

It'd been more than eighteen years since he'd had a drop of alcohol. Back then, he'd learned to function well—at least well enough to get by—while he was tipsy. But now, after so many years away from the bottle, he didn't feel as in control of himself as he used to, as he should, even though he'd only had three shots. Or so.

He just wanted to see Isa. Just this once. He just wanted to talk to her. Maybe he could apologize and make things right.

Feeling wobbly, he braced himself with a hand against the porch railing, then stared at the door for a long, reflective moment. He tried to play out what he would say: *"It's been a long time . . ." "I'm here to say I'm sorry . . ." "I missed you. I need you . . ." "Jesus loves you and wants you to forgive me . . ."*

Terry couldn't decide where to start, and finally he figured he would just play it by ear, say what seemed natural and most appropriate.

He rang the doorbell and heard the muffled sound of the chime ringing inside the townhouse.

Then, the sound of footsteps approaching the door.

And then, Isa opened it.

—m—

Isa Brock stared at Terry, the man she had loved, the man she had married, the man who had violently assaulted her and her son all those years ago. She'd invited him here today to forgive him for the wrongs he had done to her. Her faith, her beliefs, her trust that it was the right thing to do compelled her, but now she saw the unsteady way he stood, smelled the alcohol on his breath.

"Have you been drinking, Terry?"

"I just—"

And that's when she started to close the door. "No. Not if you've been drinking. You need to leave."

But he jammed his foot into the doorway. "It was just a couple sips of whiskey to go with my lunch." But there was a slur in his words. "I promise."

"Move your foot." A tremor. "Now."

But he was stronger, so even though she pushed fiercely on the door and tried to force it shut, he was able to pry it open.

Which he did.

And he was able to shove her backward.

Which he did.

"Please, Isa," he said. "Don't shout. I'm not here to hurt you."

She pulled out her phone. "I'm going to call the police. Stay away from me."

She backed up, but he stalked toward her, assuring her that he meant no harm, promising her that he had changed.

And then, she whipped around and rushed toward the bathroom, where she could lock herself safely away from him, but she didn't make it. He was on her and he was able to get the phone from her, and then he was roughly spinning her around to face him and she had to decide, in that moment, what to do.

—m—

12:37 P.M.

BLOOD ON THE KNIFE

I screeched to a stop in front of my mom's townhouse and rushed to the door.

Silence from inside.

I didn't have my key to her place with me, so I kicked the door open.

And burst inside.

And saw my father lying on the floor of the living room, my mother standing over him, holding a bloody kitchen knife in her hand.

Oh, no, no, no.

"Mom," I said urgently. "Put down the knife."

Her eyes were wide with fear, her hands trembling. "He came at me." Her voice quivered.

"Okay. Step away from him."

Terry was moving, breathing, but his shirt was soaked with blood.

"Terry?" I said. "Are you okay?"

He groaned.

"He wanted to hurt me again," my mom stammered. "He wouldn't stop."

"Alright. You need to give me the knife, Mom."

She backed away from him, from me, toward the kitchen. "I didn't mean to do it. I was scared. I thought . . ."

Twenty-eight years ago, she'd held a knife up to him to protect herself but didn't use it. Now, today, she had.

I approached her slowly, hands out and open to remain as nonthreatening as I could, just to calm things down, to deescalate them. "Mom. Please. It's over. Give me the knife."

She was nodding and shaking as I closed the space between us. Finally, I grasped the trembling blade carefully, and waited for her to release her grip.

At last, she did.

Once I had the knife, I went to my dad's side. "Terry," I said, "where are you hurt?"

He was muttering something about Jesus. I couldn't tell if he was praying or cursing.

From what I could tell, the blade had sliced across his right shoulder, leaving a long angular gash that extended across his chest to his other arm. The wound looked pretty deep but there wasn't any sign of arterial bleeding. It didn't appear that she'd hit any vital organs.

"Did you call the police yet?" I asked my mom.

"No. He smashed my phone."

I had the knife, and this man who had attacked my mother was lying at my feet.

He might've killed her just like he killed that man in Louisiana.

She was terrified. He tried to harm her.

And now, I had the knife.

Now, I could harm him.

So many thoughts.

In that moment, holding that knife dripping with my father's blood, I thought of what Colonel Clarke and Adira had told me about forgiveness. The colonel had said that it's about holding people accountable while not holding the act against them. Adira had said that denial and excuses and revenge have nothing to do with forgiving someone.

She'd also told me that unforgiveness is a cage, and now I decided that I wasn't going to let someone else keep me locked inside it.

Not Terry.

Not Sienna.

Not anyone.

It's a dark place to visit.

And a deadly place to live.

I gazed at the knife.

Then down at my dad.

"Are you alright, Travis?" Mom said to me. Her voice held a trace of fear.

No, I thought.

"Yes," I said.

She had been right too: Scripture tells us to forgive and to show mercy, even as we've received it ourselves. To love as we've been loved. No denial. No grudges. No revenge.

Si vis pacem, para bellum, I thought. "If you want peace, prepare for war." *Not just in the world, but in your heart, as well.*

The war will come. In a sense, it's always here. And so is the choice that goes with it.

Forgiveness isn't about retribution. It's not about punishing others, but about freeing yourself.

The choice.

I looked at my father for an anxious, brutal moment that lasted longer than it should have and then, using Janice's cell, I phoned dispatch. They were probably getting tired of hearing from me by now. After hanging up, I strode to the kitchen, placed the knife on the counter, found a hand towel, and returned to my dad's side.

"I don't hate you anymore," I told him, and then I knelt beside him and I pressed a gentle dressing against his wounds, and he did not pull away.

It wasn't the end of the journey, but it was the first step along the way.

CHAPTER 74

EIGHT HOURS LATER

I t's twilight and Adira and I are at the park.

She's on her time machine. She could be swinging higher than she is, but she's taking it easy, letting me push her instead.

"*Lovesick,*" I say to her. "That's the answer to your riddle about the word that starts with what we desire most and ends with what we want to avoid becoming. Am I right?"

"That's it!" she exclaims. "That's the answer! It means you're so in love that you can't think straight."

"Yes." I give her a push.

"Do you ever feel that way?"

"It's been known to happen," I admit.

"With Sienna?"

"Once upon a time." Another push. "Not anymore."

"I should hope not."

"It's been quite a while since I've been lovesick," I say.

"There's a cure for that, you know."

"Yes. I do."

Another push.

"She's still your wife," Adira reminds me. "And she's still out there, somewhere."

"I know."

"So, where does that leave *us*?"

"I'm not sure," I say honestly.

"Well, I'll be here for you when you're ready to find out."

So much has happened in the last few days.

So much to keep track of and sort out.

When the police found out that Terry had attacked my mom and that she'd only been defending herself when he was injured, they let her go, but started an investigation. It might lead to Terry going back to prison. I'm not sure what to think about that, but I'm cheering for the justice system to prevail.

So, he's recovering, and Mom is going to be okay. She remains committed to forgiving him, even if they never reconcile. Those two things are not the same. Colonel Clarke had told me that, and he was right. I understand that now.

Gunnar is out of the hospital. Janice is in it, and it's touch and go. The gunshot wound in her hip was pretty serious. The unidentified police officer impersonator was never found and is still at large.

Turo's in witness protection and is sharing intel with the Department of Justice. We'll see where that leads.

Dental records confirmed that Lena Rhodes is the woman buried in Sienna's plot, and arrangements are being made for her to receive a proper burial of her own.

Based on the information on Maia's SIM card, the Davita Group will be investigated, and I doubt they'll be doing any more research on refugees anytime soon. Thankfully, we'd made it in time to April Lane and Janice wasn't able to exfiltrate the files from the FDA servers. So, at least for now, the Nectyla research is secure. At the right time and in the right way it'll be available to benefit those who need it. And that's enough for now.

The two white supremacists who were waiting for Turo at the hospital were questioned by the SWAT team Gunnar had called in, and it turned out they both had outstanding warrants—imagine that—so they're in lockup.

The prototype was damaged when I tossed it off the eighth-story balcony. So there is that. The research team expects to have another version of it operational soon. I'm just glad the cost of repairs isn't coming out of my paycheck.

The DNA from the napkins at the safehouse is being tested at the FBI Lab, so hopefully that'll lead us to the identities of Maia's killers.

Oh, and I've got another new phone. We'll see how long this one lasts.

As I'm processing everything and reviewing the last four days, I realize I'm still pushing Adira, but now, she swings forward, then leans back and does one of her graceful backflips—which is evidently her preferred way of leaving her time machine. I would've probably landed on my face.

"How did it work?" She joins me on my side of the swing set. "I mean, I understand some of it: the families in the refugee settlements were in desperate need of medical care, so they'd be willing subjects—especially if they got paid with extra rations of food or water. And I guess, since they're living so close together, there's easy follow-up. Plus, where else can you administer a drug to thousands of people and monitor them with little to no regulatory oversight? People probably die and disappear all the time in refugee settlements. I'm guessing no one asks a lot of questions. But . . ."

"But?"

"What about a control group?" she says. "What about a double-blind study? How can researchers monitor any of that in a refugee camp? There's too much chaos; there are too many factors beyond your control."

"Those are good points," I acknowledge, "but if you're not doing things by the books anyway, why worry about following protocol?"

That makes me think of the DOD routing number in the hidden text on the SIM card.

And there's something about it that I don't like.

It was five years ago.

That's when Maia moved to Uganda.

That's when all this started.

If what I'm thinking is correct, this is an issue I need to speak with Colonel Clarke about, and it's not something I can really discuss with him over the phone; I need to do so in person.

There's a secret within a secret here, buried further down than I'd guessed.

Two secrets deep.

Yes, better to talk to him sooner rather than later.

As soon as possible.

"I need to go, Adira," I say. "I need to speak to Colonel Clarke."

She looks at me curiously. "Now?"

"I'm sorry. I know it's kind of abrupt, but it's not something that I think can wait."

"Did I do something? Is it me?"

"No." I hold her hand tenderly. "It's not you. It's something else. Something from far away."

In my car, before I leave, I log in to my account and verify what I suspected.

Verify it by what I don't find: evidence.

—*m*—

Gunnar was at home, fleshing out a scene for his novel when he heard a knock at the door.

He answered it and found a woman standing there with a teenage boy. It took him a moment to recognize her—after all, it'd been fifteen years.

"Maureen?" She was still fit, obviously still active. She'd dyed her hair red and there were a few more lines around her eyes, but she was the same woman he'd proposed to all those years ago.

"Hello, Gunnar."

"Are you alright?"

"They took us into protective custody," she said.

"Yes. There was . . . well . . . cause for concern, but that's resolved now."

She was quiet. "There's someone I'd like you to meet."

"Okay." Gunnar's gaze went to the teenage boy standing beside her. He was a bit gangly, as if he'd just gone through a growth spurt and his weight hadn't yet caught up with his height. He looked maybe fourteen or fifteen.

"Gunnar, this is Liam, my son."

Gunnar reached out to shake the boy's hand. "Hello, Liam. It's good to meet you."

The boy held out a tentative hand of his own. "Hi. It's good to meet you too. Dad."

Dad?

—*m*—

Colonel Clarke invites me into his house with a questioning look on his face. "What is it?" he asks once we're inside. "Did something happen?"

"It might have. I have a question to ask you and it didn't feel right waiting until tomorrow."

"Or asking me over the phone?"

"Yes."

A pause. "Katherine hasn't been feeling well. She's in bed. I don't want to wake her up. Let's step into my office."

He leads me down the hallway to his home office.

Once we're alone and the door is closed, I come right out and say it: "Colonel, was the Pentagon providing financial or logistical support to the Davita Group to do illegal human trials of a memory-enhancing drug in South Sudan for the last five years?"

A pause. "Why would you ask that?"

"A routing number on Maia's SIM card. Were funds released to pay the caregivers of the children?"

"You found evidence of this? A paper trail?"

"No," I say, somewhat reluctantly. "No trail. No files. No one signed off on anything. No records whatsoever."

"Gut instinct?" he asks.

"Educated guess."

He eyes me carefully. "I see. And now Dr. Odongo is dead."

"Yes. And Janice is in critical condition. I don't think we can count on getting any answers from her."

"And," he says, "there aren't too many people who could authorize something like what you're suggesting, and do so without leaving any sort of a paper trail behind."

"No, sir. There aren't."

"But I'm one of them—is that it? Is that why you're here?"

"What do you know about this, Colonel?"

He's quiet for a long moment, then says, "I know that I receive orders and I follow them. That's the way it works."

I step out on a limb. "Who are you protecting?"

"All of us," he says softly.

"I don't understand."

Clarke rounds his desk, stares at the dark window before him. Since the light in here is on, it's impossible to see outside, but I have the sense that he's not searching for something out there, but inside of himself. "If what you're saying is true," he tells me, "this is how the reasoning behind it would go: we would have a distinct, tactical, and measurable advantage over our adversaries if we had smarter soldiers."

"So, we were involved?"

"You and I, we're in the business of protecting this country. Secrets can save—"

"And secrets can kill," I say impatiently. "I know, Colonel. But they were children. Dozens of them died. Even more were paralyzed."

"It sounds like you have a suspicion, but no evidence; like you have an accusation, but no proof."

I'm not sure if it's the man I know so well speaking, or his job.

"Did you send two people to murder Dr. Maia Odongo?" I ask.

"No. But . . . there is a chance I might know who did." I wait, but he doesn't specify who it might be. Instead, he says, "I'm taking steps to find out what happened there. What *really* happened."

I'm not sure what to say.

"Listen to me, Travis. You could shake the tree here, see what falls out of it. You could make these accusations publicly, but that would hurt our strategic interests, undermine national security, and potentially hinder our efforts to assist in other humanitarian crises around the globe. There are many other refugees out there that we can help—but only if we're trusted to do so. You have to make a choice, and it's an important one: Ask yourself, 'What matters more, accountability or national security?' This goes to the heart of all you do as a redactor."

"Yes," I say. "It does."

—⁂—

Colonel Oden Clarke watched as Travis drove away. He wasn't sure if his friend was going to pursue this any further or not.

He picked up his phone, the secure line, and made the call.

"I was never told about this," he said to the person on the other end. "From what I understood—"

"There are many things you haven't been told, Colonel," the voice said, cutting him off. "This concerns protocols that have been put in place."

"No. You don't get to hide behind protocols and procedures this time," Colonel Clarke countered with resolve. "This is about children. It's about doing what's right."

"What's right isn't our concern," the person replied. "Doing what's best for this country is. Don't you agree, Colonel?"

He hung up.

And so, it looked like Colonel Clarke had a decision of his own to make.

—ɯ—

Søren was back in South Carolina.

The lake before him would swallow his car, would devour all the evidence that remained of the recent hit-and-run.

He placed the car in neutral and got out.

Ten days ago, he had not known a murderer's guilt. He had not realized what he was capable of. *Truly* capable of. And now? Well, now, he'd found that collaborating with the Grim Reaper was not as distasteful as he would have expected.

Søren pushed the car forward, down the embankment, and watched as it rolled toward the water, picking up speed as it did.

Sometimes good people do bad things and sometimes people are just plain bad. Søren hoped that he was one of the former and not the latter. But he wasn't sure. Not anymore.

The car slurped into the lake and began to sink.

An architect.

That's all you are.

No. He was much more than that.

As he watched the car go under, he wondered where this new revelation would take him and where these new interests, these new desires, would lead.

Would it be a trial to ward off who he was becoming?

Or would it be like coming home to who he truly was?

Time would tell.

The water eased up and slid across the roof of the car. A series of bubbles burst on the lake's surface, and then the water was calm as the ripples faded and disappeared.

And the car was gone.

And the night was still.

But the soul of Søren Beck was not still.

It was stirred up in ways that both frightened him and thrilled him.

New possibilities. New avenues.

New priorities.

Yes, time would tell who he was.

After all, it is very good at scratching away at the crust of pretense and letting what lies beneath our masks come to the surface.

Whether that be a light shining in the darkness.

Or darkness, edging up, like a knife, into the light.

—∞—

As I arrive home I am thinking of the secrets we keep and the interests we must protect.

I am thinking of accountability and national security, of children who have died on the altar of Progress, and refugees who can be helped in the future. I am thinking of the wars we fight in our world and in our hearts. And I am thinking of denial and second chances and the cages of unforgiveness that are strewn across the landscape of my past.

That place is a dominion of darkness and death and of self-imposed chains.

Yes, it is my choice—and also my only hope—to leave that fatal domain.

And I am thinking of what I told Gunnar yesterday: that secrets are where I live.

They are my home.

It is my job to keep them safe.

So, for now, I will hold tonight's secret close and I will not let it find legs. After all, Colonel Clarke was right: it goes to the heart of all I do as a redactor.

I'm getting ready for bed when my phone chimes.

The return number is the Culpeper United States Penitentiary.

I answer: "This is Travis Brock."

"It's Cliff Richardson, from the prison."

"Cliff? What is it? Has something happened?"

"Remember yesterday when I said that if we went probing around the dark web we'd be opening up a can of worms?"

"Yes," I reply. "And that some might crawl out."

"Well, I think they have."

We're ready, I think. *Bring 'em on.*

"Okay," I say. "Tell me what you know."

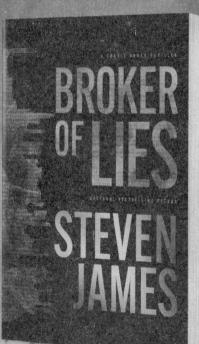

DON'T MISS THE FIRST THRILLING TRAVIS BROCK NOVEL

IN STORES AND ONLINE NOW

JOIN THE CONVERSATION AT

CP1826

Acknowledgments

Thanks to Jan, Karen, Sarah, and John. Thanks to my wife, who put up with so many months of long writing days; to my friends, who encouraged me along the way; to the scientists and specialists who redirected and corrected me; to my office manager, who brainstormed with me and proofread for me; and to the many faithful readers who've walked with and encouraged me all these years—thank you from the bottom of my heart. This book is better because of you, and I am blessed that you are a part of my life and my writing journey.

Steven James is a critically acclaimed author of nineteen novels and numerous nonfiction books that have sold more than 1 million copies. His books have won or been shortlisted for dozens of national and international awards. In addition, his stories and articles have appeared in more than eighty different publications, including *The New York Times*. He is also a popular keynote speaker and professional storyteller with a master's degree in storytelling. Since 1996 he has appeared more than two thousand times at events spanning the globe, presenting his stories and teaching the principles of storytelling to writers, speakers, teachers, and leaders. When he's not writing or speaking, he hosts the weekly podcast *The Story Blender*, on which he interviews some of the world's leading writers and storytellers. In 2020 he was inducted into the Christy Hall of Fame for excellence in fiction writing. *Publishers Weekly* has called him "[a] master storyteller at the peak of his game."

TYNDALE HOUSE PUBLISHERS IS CRAZY4FICTION!

Become part of the Crazy4Fiction community and find fiction that entertains and inspires. Get exclusive content, free resources, and more!

JOIN IN ON THE FUN!

 crazy4fiction.com

 Crazy4Fiction

 crazy4fiction

 tyndale_crazy4fiction

 Sign up for our newsletter

FOR GREAT DEALS ON TYNDALE PRODUCTS, GO TO TYNDALE.COM/FICTION

CP0021